A
N E W
Y O R K
S E C R E T

BOOKS BY ELLA CAREY

Beyond the Horizon
Paris Time Capsule
The House by the Lake
From a Paris Balcony
Secret Shores
The Things We Don't Say

A
NEW
YORK
SECRET

ELLA CAREY

bookouture

Published by Bookouture in 2021

An imprint of Storyfire Ltd.
Carmelite House
50 Victoria Embankment
London EC4Y 0DZ

www.bookouture.com

ISBN: 978-1-80019-215-7
eBook ISBN: 978-1-80019-214-0

For my daughter, Sophie

"The greatest dishes are very simple." Auguste Escoffier

"After a good dinner, one can forgive anybody, even one's relations." Oscar Wilde

Author's note

All characters appearing in this work are fictitious. Any resemblance to real persons, living or dead, is purely coincidental.

Part One

Chapter One

Lily

New York, Fall, 1942

Lily Rose put on her red felt hat, reached for her matching coat and gloves and dashed out of her Gramercy Park home. She hopped into her little American Bantam, resting her head for one precious second on the steering wheel. Thank goodness for the treasured automobile. Fact was, it could always get her out of here.

Her mother Victoria's shrieks ricocheted around the private, gated New York square, flooding the peaceful morning air, and Lily's father Jacob's entreaties filtered out behind.

Lily fired up the engine on her darling blue-and-white car with its pink leather trim and scooted away up Third Avenue, before turning into the parking lot closest to her beloved Valentino's, the restaurant where she was thankful every day for her job as sous-chef.

Lily slipped out of the Bantam, closed her gleaming car door with a satisfying click, adjusted her smart red hat, and strode out to East 63rd Street, her head full of recipes and her senses pricking with anticipation of all the wonderful and elaborate dishes she'd help conjure up at Valentino's today.

She rushed along Park Avenue from the parking lot, the city's beaux arts apartment buildings dazzling in the morning sun. Lily clipped her way across the red carpets that ran underneath the bright canopies that led to the grand lobbies of glamorous homes, elderly doormen standing about in their white gloves and smart uniforms, hands folded behind their straight backs. She only stopped to catch her breath once she stopped outside the impressive entrance of Valentino's.

Flanked by its pair of intricate streetlamps, their yellow globes ghostly in the misty morning, Valentino's art deco bold wooden bar gleamed proud in front of its grand fan-shaped mirror inside. The geometric paneling that lined the walls provided a sumptuous backdrop for intimate leather banquettes under the romantic lights that threw a warm glow into the beautiful interior.

Lily strode around to the tradesman's door, garnering some interested attention from the older men who'd not been drafted and who populated the streets of Manhattan these days.

As Lily had worked her way up the *brigade de cuisine* from lowly vegetable chef to sous-chef, she'd recognized so many names among the clientele who ran in her family's circles that she'd learned not to be fazed anymore. She'd cooked for debutante balls for girls she'd grown up with, decorated wedding cakes for young women whom she'd shared notes with in class at her Upper East Side school, and she'd slaved in the sizzling hot kitchen while her mother's friends held ladies' luncheons in the private rooms, gossiping with their chairs pulled close on the soft woolen carpets, tables decorated with glorious white lilies, all overlooked by masterpieces of modern art collected by the restaurant's owner, Giorgio Conti.

But Lily knew her mom, Victoria, held not a whit of appreciation for any of Valentino's cultural allure. All Victoria wanted was for Lily to marry the wealthiest bachelor in New York. It was Victoria's long-held dream, and having a daughter who preferred cooking in the basement kitchen of Valentino's to attending her social rounds was a source of constant conflict at home, and something Lily fought to escape.

Lily tapped her gloved hand on the discreet black staff door. One of the busboys let her in.

"Morning, Miss Rose!" The young man stood proud in his freshly ironed uniform.

"Hello, there." Lily freed herself of her hat and shook out her long black hair, her deep blue eyes meeting the tall busboy's head-on, her height being so close to his five foot nine.

He saluted her, his gold buttons catching the light. "I'm not saluting for no reason, you know."

She paused while taking off her gloves. Her laughter died.

Excitement lit up the busboy's face. "I've been drafted. I'm joining the Marines."

A cold wave passed through her. "How did Giorgio take the news?" The owner of Valentino's, Giorgio Conti, adored every one of his staff. Lily suspected he wept every time one of them left for the war.

"He placed a hand on my shoulder, took in a deep breath and told me that I had a job when I came home."

"Oh, my dear. How long 'til you leave?" She searched his face. It felt mighty strange wishing him safe harbors from here, with the comforting scent of Valentino's signature caramel cakes and pistachio cream pies drifting up from the kitchens below.

"I leave in three days."

Lily reached out a hand to his arm.

"Chop chop!"

Lily jumped.

Valentino's head waiter, Sidney, bustled out of the restaurant and looked down his nose at Lily and the mere busboy she was passing the time with in the corridor. Sidney held a white napkin over his arm and his gray hair was slicked back and oiled. A red rosebud peeped from his buttonhole, and his forehead creased with concern. "Down to the basement, where you belong, Lily. What are you doing lingering about up here?"

"Oh, Sidney, you know that there's no place I'd rather be than in the kitchen," Lily said. "As you see, I'm running down there right this minute."

Sidney shot her a level gaze and disappeared.

The busboy grimaced. "I'm gettin' back to work before he busts his chops. Good to see you, Lily." He swiped his hand in another salute.

Lily went downstairs to the basement, passing through the cool wine room. Precious aged bottles lined the walls, and rich Turkish carpets underfoot softened her footsteps in the hushed, vaulted space.

In the women's staff restroom, Lily tucked her hair into her scarf, tying it around her head and placing her chef's hat on top before changing out of her smart, red-fitted suit. She slipped into her black cook's skirt and white buttoned top and pushed open the swinging wooden doors to the kitchen, already abuzz with the line cooks who were set to start chopping carrots and slicing onions, carving up raw meat and preparing chicken for the restaurant's individually baked Parisienne pot pies.

Lily adjusted her eyes to the dim, basement lighting. "Good morning, everyone. According to my calculations last night, we have over four hundred covers today."

Jimmy, Valentino's fish cook, rushed to her side. He frowned, his graying eyebrows knitting tight, his chef's outfit still immaculate on his slim frame, even though he'd spent the early hours filleting fish. "The salmon's not up to scratch, Chef. Come and have a look, will you?"

Lily followed Jimmy to his station. She opened the hatch to the icebox and reached inside to feel the salmon. It did not spring to her touch. "It will have to be replaced," she said, pulling her hands out and wiping them on the wet cloth Jimmy held out for her. "I'll get straight on the telephone to the suppliers to tell them they need to send another batch."

Lily moved to the bottom of the line, ignoring the raised eyebrows from some of the older men, cooks who'd been working here since Valentino's opened.

Giorgio Conti had begun with a grand splash back in the 1920s, quickly establishing his Park Avenue location as one of New York's most popular restaurants with the most glamorous of clientele. He was aided by his head waiter, Sidney, who knew everyone worth talking about in New York and enticed them back to dine here again and again.

Valentino's had been a runaway success for twenty years, surviving the Depression and now marching headlong into the war. Lily had applied the moment she heard there was a job. Line chef, kitchen hand, she would have worked for free.

She'd walked past Valentino's on her way home from school every day, gazing through the plate-glass windows in her school uniform, long legs reflected in the glass, dark hair tied back in a ponytail, blue eyes staring through the window, satchel hanging by her side. She always wished she could transform into a graceful butterfly and slip inside into the golden art deco surrounds. The impeccable, handsome waiters carrying plates of delectable food aloft, setting tempting dishes down in front of beautifully dressed customers at tables with white tablecloths, champagne in ice buckets, soft lamps casting a warm glow and lending the restaurant a magical feel—it was through these very windows that Lily had realized cooking was not only the nurturing, wonderful hobby that she'd long loved to indulge in, but an art form, and something that could genuinely make folks happy.

And now she was lucky enough to be a part of Valentino's, she would not give up the opportunity for the world.

Slipping into her role overseeing the kitchen and holding responsibility for inventories and quality of supplies, Lily started her daily inspection of produce at the bottom of the line of cooks with the pantry chef. Towards the top of the line she could see the grill chef, Leo, leaning his large hands on the stainless-steel kitchen bench with its heavy iron burners and long warming pans spreading the length of the kitchen under rows of huge copper pots hanging from the ceiling. The sounds of cooks rushing about, slicing, chopping, sliding food into pans and steam hissing from the stovetops rang through the sweltering air.

Leo's expression darkened and his eyes narrowed at Lily's approach.

Lily ran her expert eye over Leo's neatly arranged preparations, the porterhouse steaks all ready to hit the pans in hot butter, the filets looking moist and tender before they were pre-sliced and served with a perfectly rosy interior, and the sirloins pink. She was more than aware that Leo had been taking care of the meat at Valentino for over twenty years, and he made it abundantly clear that he saw no reason to work his way any further up the *brigade de cuisine* as so many other cooks did.

"Good morning, Leo. Nothing to complain about in terms of the deliveries from the markets today?" Lily asked.

"I know how to prepare my produce well enough for a sous-chef, Miss Rose. Have been doing so since well before you were born." He grunted and turned back to his station.

"I am glad things are up to scratch." Lily ran a second check over his produce and was about to move up the line when her fellow sous-chef, Martina, appeared by her side.

Martina folded her arms across her five-foot frame, her dark eyes flashing under her chef's hat. "Lily, Giorgio wants to see us. You, me and Tom. Now."

"Well, is that so, Martina," Lily said. "Do you happen to know why?"

Martina shrugged and Tom Morelli looked up from his *chef de cuisine* station at the top of the line.

"Tom." Martina's tone softened when she spoke to him. Only one ranking below their adored head chef, Marco, who was away at the war, Tom was responsible for most of the actual cooking at Valentino's.

Lily gazed about the kitchen. Everything looked to be running as normal, but she felt Marco's absence keenly. She knew the other chefs did too—she'd seen several of them march up to Marco's office with a question, only to remember their head chef was gone on a troopship to who knew where. His office was dark, his chef's hat hanging forlorn on the back of the door.

Without a full-time, dedicated leader for the kitchen, the line cooks were improvising, and yet it was impossible to imagine anyone other than their beloved Marco in charge. Marco had taught Lily everything she knew and had fast-tracked her promotion, moving her up every station until she'd made sous-chef in record time. She owed him her career.

Tom Morelli pulled off his own apron and strolled across the kitchen floor, his body lean and muscled in the blue jeans only he got away with wearing. He rolled up his white chef's shirtsleeves and lounged by Lily, his green eyes crinkling, his dark hair hidden under his tall chef's hat. His cooking was to die for, and he melted the hearts of all the staff.

"Afternoon, Lily," Tom said, flicking her a grin.

"*Morning*, Tom." She hid her smile at his joke. They both knew she'd been here until past eleven o'clock last night, and because she'd been rostered on for dinner service, she didn't need to be here as early as some.

At the same time, she pushed aside the thought that Tom's soft Italian accent was something any girl would like to have whispered in her ear. Tom Morelli was utterly out of bounds for her. If she caught the slightest whiff of an attraction between Lily and one of her workmates here at Valentino's, Lily's powerful mother would have her out of here on her ear. No, her mom had far grander plans for Lily's future than some cook.

Tom waited for her to go ahead of him. "Let's see what Giorgio wants."

Lily was certain he must have some glamorous girlfriend. Probably had half his neighborhood in love with him as well, if his status at Valentino's was anything to go by. She frowned and tried to concentrate.

Giorgio Conti stood outside his office, waiting to usher them all inside.

"My dear ones…" he said, his lyrical Italian accent more pronounced than Tom Morelli's.

Lily started at the sight of Giorgio's pinched features. His usually immaculate, oiled gray hair was disheveled, and telltale dark circles shadowed the skin under his eyes. As the owner of Valentino's, he'd not only been interviewing prospective head chefs, he'd been doing the departed head chef Marco's job for weeks. Clearly it was taking a toll. Valentino's was Giorgio's passion, and he lived and breathed it. Everyone knew he cared for it as if it was his child. He would not hire anyone for the vital position of head chef without complete confidence in their ability to handle the demanding role.

"Tom, Lily, Martina," he said, rolling his r's and drawing out his consonants. "Please. Come in and sit down, my dears."

Lily sank down onto an upholstered chair.

Giorgio rested his hands square on the neat stack of creamy notepaper that he used for his little notes of correspondence. His expression clouded. "I… There is no easy way to say this. We have had shocking news. Brace yourselves."

Bile churned in Lily's stomach.

Giorgio's eyes were downcast. "Marco is dead. Our head chef is gone."

Lily drew a hand to her mouth. Beside her, Martina gasped and Tom gripped the sides of his chair.

"Marco was killed during the Allied landings in North Africa," Giorgio said, his head bowed. "I read only a few days ago that the operation was a success overall, but there was artillery fire from the German-supported Vichy troops in the area against our forces on landing, north of Casablanca. Overall, the Allies won, you see, and I had just begun to relax about it when his mother called this morning. Our dearest Marco has been confirmed as one of the dead."

Lily blanched. "Not Marco," she whispered, her voice quivering in the silent, heavy room. "I'm sorry, my mind is going to pieces…"

Alongside every other New Yorker, Lily felt frightened of the war. The Nazis had labeled the city "Target Number One," and every morning Lily read the dire warnings in newspapers that the Germans could send bombers into American skies or shell the coastline from U-boats. But even though four hundred thousand New Yorkers were serving as air-raid wardens, and anti-aircraft guns ringed the city, she hadn't experienced personal loss until now.

Tom loosened his collar and leaned forward in his seat, his head over his knees, and Martina brought a hand to her mouth and choked back tears.

Giorgio slowly lifted his head. He stared at Lily, and she looked helplessly right back at him, bringing a shaky hand to her forehead.

"Excuse me, a moment," Giorgio said, his voice high-pitched. He placed his head in his hands and wept.

For the first time since the neon signs in Times Square had gone dark, for the first time since Mayor La Guardia had warned of terror from the skies, calamity had arrived on the doorstep of Valentino's seemingly safe world.

Lily swallowed the lump that had formed in her throat. It seemed incomprehensible that their respected, admired and universally liked Marco would never be coming back, that she'd never see the tall man in his early thirties, with his tortoiseshell glasses steaming up from the heat, warm smile never far from his face and his dark curls seeping out from underneath his chef's hat.

He was, simply, always there, if not in the kitchen alongside them, he'd be in his office, thumbing through the considerable body of recipes he'd created throughout his years devoted to cooking for Giorgio, pen stuck behind an ear, leading them all, teaching them with the utmost patience how to perfect the recipes Giorgio adored. Staying after hours with them, no matter he had to be back before dawn to go to the markets, encouraging each and every one of his team to do their absolute best, to work to the highest standards, and all this done in such a kindly way.

It was a terrible loss for Valentino's, for the New York restaurant industry. Like so many others in this awful war, this was a man whose life was done before he'd even reached middle age. Lily bowed her head, and silently, hands shaking, she let her own tears fall freely down her cheeks.

Chapter Two

Twenty minutes later, after Sidney had delivered four strong espressos to Giorgio's office, Lily slumped back in her chair, her eyes sore and breath still hitching. Tom Morelli tipped back his head and drained his espresso in one gulp, and Martina only stared at her coffee cup.

"Unfortunately, I need to face the fact that I have not been able to find a suitable new head chef, my dears. Not one man that I've interviewed shares Marco's talent for cooking, nor his dedication to his career," Giorgio said. He shook his head and ran his hand over his chin. "He knew everything there was to know about the restaurant."

Lily shook her head in disbelief.

"It would be naïve of us not to be prepared for the fact that Tom may be drafted as well," Giorgio continued. "Otherwise, I would have trained him by now."

We can't lose Tom as well as Marco. Please no. Lily risked a glance at the handsome man by her side. He stared, white-faced, at Giorgio.

Martina stirred in her seat.

"We are facing great upheaval," Giorgio said. "Even greater than we saw in the last war. I have had no choice but to place women as chefs, my dears. Unheard of before Pearl Harbor." Giorgio tried to smile.

Lily's heart began to race. She avoided looking at Martina.

Giorgio dropped his voice. "But Marco's tragic death has forced my hand again. I have decided, from hereon, that we will train you both, Martina and Lily, to take over the role of head chef, should Tom be drafted. But I will carefully observe both of you, and, shortly, we will decide who will become head chef. Training will commence immediately."

Lily didn't know what happened first, Martina's cry of indignation or her own triumphant shout. Lily turned to see her co-sous-chef's lips turn into a sneering curl. Ever since she'd started working here, she'd never been able to break through Martina's cold veneer. Whenever Lily tried to be friendly, Martina would cut Lily's attempts at conversation off.

Now Martina pushed her chair back so hard that it scraped against the polished wooden floor. "Everyone knows that Lily will leave us at the end of the war. It is only a matter of time before she is married to some wealthy society type—one of your customers will no doubt whisk her off her feet and build her a country house in Connecticut before you can say whipped cream!"

Lily sat, poleaxed. That was absolutely unfair. She lifted her chin. As much as she did not want to enter into personal discussions in front of Giorgio, she would have to defend herself against such an ill-deserved attack. "I am as dedicated to my career as any man. More so. And I have no intention of marrying. Who on earth would I marry?" Lily felt her cheeks reddening. *Her mother had an idea...*

Giorgio had spared the inevitable questions about engagement plans and children at her interview for the job, but gossip abounded in the kitchens and she was well aware that some of the other staff only thought of her as a society girl doing her bit for the war. *But how dare Martina talk about it in front of Giorgio!*

"It is for many reasons that I wish to consider Lily as well," Marco said, his eyes roaming from Martina to Lily and back.

Next to her, Tom's eyes narrowed in concentration.

Lily's heart beat in her mouth. Head chef. *Executive chef,* at Valentino's. In the face of the tragic, awful destruction of war, she suddenly felt guilty that she might just catch her dream to be able to create her own recipes for one of Manhattan's most famous restaurants. She should be thinking of Marco, not her career. But the chance to nurture a whole team of cooks, and to work with some of the best suppliers in New York, head chef at Valentino's? There would be nothing more rewarding for any cook.

However, Martina was of Italian heritage and cooked Giorgio's beloved homeland cuisine like a dream.

"My apologies to you, Tom," Giorgio added. "For discussing your departure before it's been planned. And, of course, I hope you do not leave us."

"Not at all," Tom said, but still, he turned to Lily and sent her a concerned frown.

She shook her head ever so slightly back. She had no idea that Martina's animosity toward her ran so deep.

Giorgio sighed. "I'm only sorry necessity has forced me to raise this in the same breath as losing Marco. But we cannot go any longer without a proper head chef."

Martina rolled up her sleeves. "Of course not, Giorgio. Although I cannot understand why a chef who has been here only half as long as I could seriously be considered for the role when I could do you proud."

Giorgio folded his hands on his desk. "Martina, Lily not only has true passion for her cooking, she is in the unique position of understanding our restaurant clientele. She can effortlessly cross the boundaries between the kitchen, management and our guests, and that is very valuable to me."

The look that Martina gave Lily could have withered one of her cast-iron skillets.

"Lily and Tom, tomorrow morning at three o'clock sharp you will come out to the markets with me."

In spite of the anger fuming from Martina next to her, Lily could not contain her mixed emotions as she followed Tom and Martina out of Giorgio's office door. Her heart wanted to split in two over the tragedy of losing Marco, while her mind would not stop conjuring up recipes that would prove how determined she was to win the head chef position.

She'd cook her heart out for Marco, and if she must take over his job in tragic circumstances, at least she'd do his memory proud.

After luncheon service was done and the kitchen staff had gone for their break, having been told of Marco's death, heads bowed at Giorgio's devastating news, Lily moved toward Marco's old office, stepping tentatively inside the quiet space for a moment. She folded her arms against the shiver that ran through her as she went inside.

His chef's hat still sat on top of a shelf of recipe books and a stack of his neatly handwritten produce orders lay on his desk. It was as if he'd gone up to see Giorgio and would be back any minute now. Lily dug for a handkerchief in her skirt pocket and blew her nose.

On the bottom shelf, below all Marco's cookbooks, a whole row of his leather-bound recipes sat just as he'd left them. The last one unfinished. He'd never finish it now.

"Lily."

Lily lifted her head slowly.

Tom Morelli's eyes lingered on hers, holding a question of their own. Several times during service, she'd seen him sending glances her way.

He rested a hand against the door frame. "You okay?"

She nodded. Her fingers pulled at her apron ties and got stuck.

"Okay if I help you with those knots?" He smiled at her, his lips curving upward in a charming, boyish way.

Lily closed her eyes a moment. Finally, she turned around and felt him deftly loosening the apron strings, achingly aware of his close proximity. Once he was done, she swiveled back to face him again. She had to pull herself together. It was the emotion of losing Marco that was hitting her so hard, causing her to feel Tom's presence with a keenness that she knew ran deeper than it should. She, Tom, Marco—they'd worked together so often. Marco and Tom had been close friends, and Lily was certain Tom must be devastated at the loss. "Thank you," she whispered.

Tom handed the apron back to her. "You take the reins," he whispered softly. "Don't let Martina get to you. You and I both know that Marco thought you were worthy of… every opportunity you've earned. He once told me he thought there were unlimited possibilities for you."

The quiet room seemed to whisper around them. She glanced up at Tom, her words coming out softly. "Do you think he suffered, Tom?"

Tom slumped against the door. "I hate to think of what he went through." A wave of emotion passed across his face, and then he dropped his voice. "I do know he'd want you to give this opportunity everything you've got."

"Well," Lily said, "I don't believe anyone else on staff thinks like you do about me, Tom, but that's mighty kind." Certain that Tom would understand, she blurted out her worries. "I worry that Giorgio wants to train me because my family have connections that might be useful to him. You know how savvy he and Sidney can be when it comes to getting the right people to dine at Valentino's."

Tom raised a brow. "You worked your way up the stations in record time. You're a fabulous cook. And, for the record, I think you'd make a terrific head chef. Giorgio might be a businessman, and Sidney… well, don't worry about him, but Giorgio does have an eye for good staff." A shadow passed across Tom's face. "Pity we're going to lose most of them. That's what's draining Giorgio now."

Lily nodded. She *had* to believe in herself if she were going to fight for this dream. "You know, I hate to think of… yet more people leaving." *Especially you.* She frowned at Marco's recipe books. "I think the pivotal challenge will be the need for recipes that are compatible with rationing." She rushed out the words. "I'd love to work out some wartime recipe ideas."

"And I'd love to work them out with you," he said, flashing a wide grin. "If I have to eat K-rations, I'll be especially grateful that you helped save dried beef just for me and the thousands of other men fighting. And if and when I'm drafted, I'll look back and remember how much fun we had."

"And I'll promise to prepare you a beef Wellington after the war so delicious that it will make you forget any bad K-ration memories. Valentino's will always be here when you come home, Tom. She's not going anywhere."

"A beauty who creates mouthwatering dishes and gives folks the chance to at least imagine they are still carrying out their normal lives." His expression softened in the hushed space. Lily wasn't sure if they were talking about Valentino's anymore.

She smiled at him, sighing at the warmth in his eyes. "Here am I, rambling on about head chef when you're facing the possibility of going to war. The challenges I face bear no comparison to it." She looked down.

"No, Lily…" His voice was soft as he lifted her chin. "Either you or Martina will become the country's first female head chef in a place the caliber of Valentino's. This war won't be won unless people back here keep the home front strong." He searched her face. "You have family at Valentino's, you know."

"Thank you," she whispered, eyes locked with his, heart hammering in a way that she knew would send her mom into a fit worthy of her own Broadway debut. "It means so very much." *More than you know.*

"So… how will you get up here at three o'clock in the morning? Ride a bike? Hitchhike up Third Avenue?" He cracked a dazzling smile.

"Oh, you are a nut!"

"Would you like to catch the train with me? You've mentioned that you live in Gramercy Park."

"Well now, there's a plan." The idea of catching the train with Tom seemed far more of an adventure than driving in the middle of the night on her own. She had nearly used up her ration of gas this week.

And as for breaking the boundaries that she'd set up around the lovely man standing opposite her, whom she knew, should she have free reign, she could fall for any day of the week, why, they were only traveling to work together. What could be wrong about that? It was as if he'd offered to carry her books home for her, or some such kind thing.

No big deal…

He tossed his chef's hat from one hand to the other. "I get nervous in the subway late at night. I could do with some company."

She let out a laugh. "Oh, don't you worry about that. I'll protect you."

"Good," he said. "I was a *little* bit worried you'd say no if I asked." He pressed his thumb and forefinger into a pinch.

Lily swiped at him with her apron string, and he dodged her.

"Sleep well," Tom said, his eyes crinkling. "I'll see you at two-thirty on the corner of Park Avenue and Gramercy Park?"

"It's a deal. I don't know whether I'll bother going to bed!"

He raised a brow, and she sent him a grin. She walked into the ladies' restroom at the end of her shift for the day and caught a glance at her reflection in the mirror. But, despite the terrible tragedy that had hit them all today, her face was flushed and her blue eyes sparkled more than they had in months. She stared at herself sternly, but she couldn't help it. She was grinning like a fool.

Chapter Three

Lily

After she'd checked out of Valentino's for the day, Lily zipped down Park Avenue, anger now nipping at her insides over Marco's senseless death. She weaved like a whizz through the achingly slow traffic before turning off toward Greenwich Village and the retreat of her beloved gram's house. She barreled too fast, on past Washington Square Park, breezing through the surrounding narrow streets with their old New York townhouses and underground comedy clubs and Italian delis and fresh produce stands and grocer's stores.

Lily careered to a standstill outside the three-story, red-brick building on Bank Street that was home to her grandmother, Josie. She yanked the keys out of the ignition and slipped up Josie's front steps. Josie's maid was at the door before Lily had time to reach for the brass doorknocker.

"Miss Lily." Emmeline held out her hand for Lily's coat and hat.

Lily shook out her hair from its workaday bun and pressed her fingers into the palm of the maid's hand. "Dearest Emmeline. Is my darling Josie at home? I'm in awful need of a heart-to-heart with my gram."

"Oh, I'm sorry, miss, she's gone down Bleecker Street, but I'm expectin' her back real soon. That is, 'really', not 'real'." Emmeline blushed, her peaches-and-cream complexion turning a becoming pink to the roots of her fine blond hair. She looked up at Lily from her tiny stature.

"Oh, don't worry about things so bothersome as grammar." Lily waved aside Emmeline's attempts to smooth over her Brooklyn accent. "You speak just fine. If I can't speak to Josie, then I must go downstairs and cook. My mind is in a whirl."

"Of course, miss." Emmeline spoke as if it was the most normal thing in the world for Lily to arrive in the late afternoon only to make a beeline for her grandmother's kitchen.

Lily trotted downstairs to her gram's basement, pulling an apron from a drawer in the old wooden dresser. She reached for utensils, sighing with relief at the sight of Josie's welcoming kitchen, the golden afternoon sun shining down on the scrubbed wooden table, Josie's reading glasses resting atop a pile of recipe books next to a ceramic pitcher filled with flowers. The enormous old English oven warmed the room and a pot of fresh coffee sat brewing deliciously on the hob.

Josie had made the kitchen the heart of her home, with a pretty view of her flowering pots in the alcove through the window, along with tubs filled with creamy roses, under-planted with miniature daisies and ivy trailing along the wall. At Lily's parents' house, every meal was taken in the formal dining room with its carmine-painted walls. The family even had breakfast under the gaze of portraits that Victoria had bought of unknown strangers because it was the thing to do.

Emmeline stood beside Lily, her steady presence a balm to Lily's troubled mind. "Would you like some help, Miss Lily?"

"Oh, thank you, Emmy dear, but only if you have time," Lily said.

Emmeline nodded, smiling at Lily. "You know how I love to cook with you."

"Wonderful. I need some shortening, honey, flour, baking soda and a dash of salt, along with a beaten egg, orange juice and grated orange rind. I'm going to gather them all up now."

Lily tied the apron over her red skirt and her white blouse and started mixing shortening and honey into a satiny swirl. Next to her,

Emmy sifted flour, baking powder and salt into a blue-and-white striped ceramic bowl. Josie's kitchen was filled with the sound of wooden spoons clicking against the sides of bowls, and Emmy started humming a lilting tune. Lily took the dry ingredients from the maid, adding the flour mixture to her creamed honey mixture, while Emmy beat the eggs.

"Emmy, the Contis would give you a job at Valentino's any day of the week if my gram could spare you," Lily said. "But Josie would die a million deaths without you here."

"I'm hardly qualified to work in a famous restaurant like you." Emmy handed over the perfectly blended eggs.

Neither am I, thought Lily. *But Marco made me see differently.* As she worked, she could see his face and felt a pang of sadness.

Lily folded the eggs into the mixture, while Emmy grated orange rind and measured out juice. Once everything was done, Lily placed the creamy batter into the refrigerator and closed the door with a snap.

"Now," she said, "while that sits for half an hour, I am going to pour us both a cup of coffee."

Five minutes later, Lily was seated at the kitchen table with Josie's white cat, Cosmo, twirling around her legs. Golden-brown leaves floated from the old trees outside the tall basement windows. When she heard Josie's footsteps coming down the stairs, Lily clasped her hands together and rose to greet her gram.

"Lily?" Josie's thick gray hair was swept back from her beautiful face, her striking blue eyes running over Lily. She pulled off her favorite, ancient, navy-blue cape, and adjusted the sleeves of her low-waisted velvet dress, edged with silk ribbons and dating from about 1923. "Oh, you look piqued, dear. I hope there are no disasters?"

Lily stood up and gathered her grandmother into a hug, breathing in the familiar scent of eau de cologne, her head resting on Josie's soft shoulder a moment. "Dearest Gram, I have such news that I hardly know where to begin."

The front doorbell pealed and Emmeline dashed off to answer it.

The sound of Lily's mother's voice resonated through the house from the front entrance. Cosmo scurried off. "In the *kitchen,* Emmeline? I should have guessed!"

Josie raised a brow and went upstairs to greet her daughter-in-law.

A few moments later, Lily sagged at the sight of her mother appearing in the kitchen doorway, her black fitted costume decorated with a white rose pinned to her breast, her dark hair waved just so. Over her shoulder, she held a cream cashmere shawl and her long, shapely legs were encased in Macy's finest silk stockings. She'd stockpiled them at the merest hint of war.

Thinking of their argument this morning and seeking a distraction, Lily made for the fridge. "My orange cookies must be put in the oven this minute."

"Lily! I came down here expressly."

Josie came back from greeting Victoria, appearing at the other entrance to the kitchen. The servants' entrance. She'd made her way safely down the back stairs. Lily swiped a glance at her beloved grandmother from under her eyelashes and hid her smile.

She collected her bowl of creamy dough from the refrigerator. "Perfection."

"How my only daughter became obsessed with kitchens is beyond me." Victoria's Katharine Hepburn accent rang through the tall ceilinged room.

One would wonder at it, given you never set foot in any rooms except the parlor, your bedroom and the dining room.

Victoria addressed Lily from the doorway, her nose crinkled. "I'm not going to discuss your future in the basement. Come upstairs at once."

Lily pulled out a rolling pin, rolled up her sleeves and leaned over the kitchen table to smooth out her dough.

"I will not be high-hatted by my own daughter."

"These cookies need to be prepared." Lily reached for a cookie cutter and began pressing the round metal into the soft dough. "They are for Josie's afternoon tea."

"Oh, for pity's sakes!" Victoria threw her hands up in the air. "Both of you. All this fuss about Nathaniel Carter. He is so fond of Lily, *and* he is the most suitable bachelor in New York."

Lily rolled her dough furiously. *The most suitable boy in New York for whom, Mother? You?*

Victoria lowered her voice and addressed Josie. "Dear Jacob wants to retire from the millinery business after the war, and with a perfect stroke of ingenuity, he's managed to see to his succession planning to boot."

"I don't follow, Victoria." Josie came to stand by Lily and folded her arms. Lily passed her a piece of dough to try.

"Tell Gram the rest of it, Mother," Lily said. "Go on."

"Lily can't inherit her father's business, of course she can't. She'll be busy with a family of her own when that time comes around."

Lily gasped. Her mother could be tactless, but the casual way she mentioned inheritance and the death of Lily's father, Josie's only son, was astounding. Lily reddened with embarrassment at her mother's tasteless words.

"But Lily can produce a son who will inherit," Victoria continued. "And if my daughter's son is a member of the Carter family, then what a wonderful future the Roses will have."

Josie pressed her lips into a fine line. "You forget that not every woman can produce a son, Victoria."

Lily's eyes widened. She concentrated again on her rolling pin for a moment, and heaved out a long sigh.

There was a silence.

Lily risked a glance at her mother and saw two red blotches appear on her cheeks.

"I remind you, Josie, that your late husband, my father-in-law, worked for fifty years to build the family millinery business up from the ground. But if Lily insists on making a fool of herself carrying on under the stairs in that dashed restaurant, she risks losing Nathaniel's interest, and the family business as well."

At the ugly look on Victoria's face, Lily had a flash of an unhappy memory that took her back almost twenty years. Lily's chest still sometimes ached at the way Victoria had intervened with her childhood friends, especially a little girl called Ettie, whom Lily had adored at grade school, only to have her mother forbid the friendship the moment she discovered Ettie lived in the Lower East Side. Victoria told the young, then impressionable Lily that nice young ladies didn't go below Fourteenth Street.

Lily, bewildered, had trusted her formidable mother unquestionably, believed Victoria when she'd told Lily that only bad folks lived down there.

She had long felt ashamed about the way she had watched sadly, her heart contracting, as her bewildered friend coped with Victoria's decree that Lily no longer play with her. Ettie's dad had worked in a hotel near Gramercy and he'd brought Ettie up to the local grade school with him every morning on the train, cap swinging in his hand, waiting cheerfully outside the gates for Lily to run into her friend's arms. Ettie had always brought special homemade gifts into school for Lily, a paper doll, a selection of homemade biscuits lovingly wrapped in waxed paper, with so much to tell her, even after only one night apart.

And to see her, standing motionless, her face crumpling when Victoria would whisk Lily home without allowing her to as much as say goodbye.

Lily knew now that her mother had broken young Ettie's heart. And she'd let her do so.

Finally, when Lily's downcast moods had driven Victoria to distraction, she'd moved Lily to private school. Lily, swallowing the lumps in her throat, had complied, not understanding, but still thinking, *wishing,* perhaps that her mother must be right, that the way she was upending Lily's world had to be for good reason. She'd long tried to believe in her mom.

Until, finally, Lily had watched with a slow, horrible revulsion at the way her new friends relentlessly snubbed and bullied the school's very few representatives of those categories who did not meet their definition of what a girl should be, whether they were employed as staff, from a different class, handicapped, from another religion, background, or ethnicity.

And now, the United States was in the middle of a war against a country whose government were, staggeringly, treating those very people in the most reprehensible way.

And yet, Victoria forged ahead.

"A girl like you should be attending her debutante balls, not sweltering in that basement like some common workhorse," Victoria said with disdain, jolting Lily back to the present. "Just the other day, one of my society friends questioned me about you. Why have I let my daughter become a servant when all the other girls are getting their beauty sleep and folding bandages for our men at war?"

Josie spoke quietly. "Giorgio Conti is an excellent man. He would never view Lily as a servant."

"Giorgio Conti is a luminary in the restaurant industry," Lily added.

Victoria threw her hands in the air. "I still do not understand when kitchens and cookies became more important than parties, boyfriends and beautiful clothes!"

"Might be something to do with the fact the world is at war," Lily muttered. "If we at home can't step up to the plate and keep our businesses going, then how are we supposed to have a strong enough base to win the war?" She bit back her smile at the deliciousness of being able to quote Tom's words at her mom.

Victoria let out a sharp laugh. "Giorgio Conti is only employing women at Valentino's for that very reason—because we are at war and you are useful to him. Up until now, the only girls he hired in the restaurant were cigarette girls and coat checkers. And quite rightly, too." She narrowed her eyes, lowering her voice a moment. "My concern is not unfounded, Lily. I read an article in the newspaper recently, raising questions and concerns about women in the workforce and what they will do after the war."

Lily finished cutting her last pattern out of raw cookie dough. She cast her eye over the whole tray. Even though she'd done a full stint working with Julius, the pastry chef, when she'd forged her way up the *brigade de cuisine,* she was still more than a tad envious at the way Julius turned out his exquisite creations perfectly every time. She had worked like a demon to try and emulate him. Not quite as good as Julius, but not bad. *And he didn't have his mother breathing down his neck.*

Lily undid her apron with a flourish. "Well, Mother, Giorgio Conti has just offered me the chance to train as head chef. I'm hoping you'll give me your blessing and view that opportunity as the very opposite of servitude. As for after the war, well, I hope by then I will have proven myself enough that I will be a valued member of staff."

"Lillian!"

"Who would've thought?" Josie interjected quickly. "I'm proud of you, dear."

Victoria's face was puce. "Let me level with you, my girl."

Lily stepped nimbly around her to pop the cookies in the oven. She stared at the miniature round balls of dough for a moment. She'd long given up trying to argue logically with Victoria, because every time she did, her mother batted back with something that left Lily reeling. The only strategy that seemed to work was to avoid arguments, which was what Lily's dad had always done. For years, Lily had come to view Josie's house as her real home.

Lily shuddered at the memory of her mother's behavior after she'd applied for the role of trainee chef at Valentino's. Victoria had refused to talk to her for a fortnight, slamming doors and throwing tantrums that ricocheted around the apartment, while Lily's father ducked for cover and spent his evenings working late at the millinery.

"The minute the war is over, you marry Nathaniel. And you consider yourself engaged to him as of today."

After closing the oven, Lily slowly turned to her mom. She folded her arms across her chest. Cosmo yowled in the hallway, and the anger about Marco that had hounded Lily on the drive down here spurred into life again. "What next? Will you be going down on bended knee and pulling a diamond ring out of a glass of champagne? Or must that wait until you pay a visit to Fifth Avenue to beg for his father's permission and explain your prospects to him?"

Josie stood tall and straight and strong next to Lily. Slowly, she reached out and rested an arm across Lily's shoulder.

Victoria lowered her voice. "Either stay home and stop making a fool of your father and me or accept my terms. If you must remain in that ridiculous kitchen playing chief cook and bottle washer," Victoria brought her hand to her forehead, her diamonds glistening under the basement lights, "I will continue to explain to our friends that you are doing your bit for the war effort, that you are not content to pine for your fiancé, and that you want to contribute in a more meaningful way than just philanthropy. But you'll marry Nathaniel the minute the war ends. Your father retires then, and you will contribute to the family just as any dutiful daughter should. Family comes first. We will all have to pull together after the war so as not to lose everything we hold dear. We have supported you. You will support us. I trust you understand."

Lily took a deep breath, but her voice shook. "You are playing games with my future, Mother." Was Victoria threatening to cut her off? Despite Victoria's hugely difficult personality, Lily had never felt truly threatened before. *Because she'd always complied.* Until she took on this job. Now, fear as to how far her mother would go to get what she wanted drew a fine needle and laced a painful thread around Lily's heart.

Victoria took a step inside the kitchen, only to stagger out again, planting her feet firmly in the doorway. "If you won't help yourself, you cannot expect us to help you."

Lily gasped.

"How will the best families survive after all this upheaval if we don't pull together and secure our futures now? This is about preservation of the things that matter," Victoria continued.

"Have you told Father Simmons to put up wedding banns?" Tears glittered in Lily's eyes. "What century do you think I was born in?" Her voice quavered, but she sent her mother a glassy stare.

Lily felt the gentle pressure of Josie's hand on her shoulder.

Victoria raised herself to her full height. "We raised you in the right church. We just need to get you up the aisle."

Lily's mouth dropped open, and Josie took in a sharp intake of breath behind her.

But Victoria's tone was crisp. "Women working during wartime is acceptable. But I will not have you being a *career girl.*"

"I'm a sous-chef at one of New York's most famous restaurants, working for one of our most respected restaurateurs, Mom. Surely even you would not be ashamed of that." Lily swallowed hard.

Victoria pointed a finger at Josie. "Nothing gave you the right to recommend to my daughter that she apply to become the Contis' slave!"

"I do not see it as in any way demeaning for a young woman to work at Valentino's. And Lily loves her job." Josie raised her chin.

"It is impossible for me to consider quitting." Lily choked out the words.

"Fine. You've just accepted your father's and my terms."

Lily took in a sharp breath.

"Meanwhile," Victoria went on, "no liaisons with the pastry chef, no flirtations with the waitstaff, and definitely no associating with any kitchen types. You know very well that people worth knowing will talk about you. You'll ruin your reputation faster than you can whisk one of your horrid wooden spoons through a ridiculous bowl."

Lily's cheeks burned. "Mother, there is nothing wrong with the people who work with me." She closed her eyes. *This could not be happening.* The urge to run upstairs and bury her face in the soft pillows atop Josie's bed in her sunny white bedroom overwhelmed Lily. She took a step toward the staircase.

But her mother blocked her. She spoke in imperious tones. "Power for a woman lies in her ability to mix in the right social circles, meet her wealthy husband and then produce children who will carry these traditions forward. The right schools, then the right parties, and finally the cultivation of one's bridge and tennis circles. It is the way things will always work." Victoria tossed her head.

"*That is not for me,*" Lily said, standing, now, eye to eye with her mother, her gaze striking hard against her mother's blue-eyed stare.

And behind those eyes? There was nothing. Nothing but cold, hard ambition. Nothing but a determination for her daughter to comply.

"I'll earn my own way," Lily whispered, her voice husky, coming from some deep part of herself. "I'm getting paid." She earned forty-eight dollars a month.

"Try living on a woman's income." Victoria ground out the words. "*Just you try.* In fact, you can consider yourself cut off after the war if you persist in this nonsense."

Josie's tone was soothing. "For goodness' sakes, let's not rile her further…"

Lily stood unmoving, her fists clenched into two tight balls at her sides. And suddenly, everything whirled in front of her eyes. All of it. Poor, dear innocent Ettie, the girls at school, Victoria and her snobby, disrespectful friends who hardly spoke to Lily except to compare her unfavorably to their own daughters and ensure she didn't get in the way of their marriage plans.

No wonder Lily felt a new sense of home at Valentino's.

She *had* to get head chef. It was the only way she'd be able to win this battle, stand on her own two feet and prove she could be as successful on her own terms and did not need some completely inappropriate choice of a husband that her mother had made. To not even allow Lily the dignity to make her own choice!

"She is right about one thing. I did recommend you apply at Valentino's," Josie whispered. "I worry that this conflict is my fault."

Lily jumped at the sound of Josie's calm voice. "No, Gram," Lily whispered. "*Never.*"

The comforting smells of the scented orange cookies filtered from Josie's oven, only serving as a reminder of how Lily had learned to cook on a small wooden stool by her grandmother's side, laughing alongside her gram as their attempted creations became more complicated and ambitious over the years.

"Mother, I need to leave. I have an early start in the morning," Lily said.

"Girls like you marry boys who work in the Financial District and who dine at Valentino's. You don't work in the places that your equals frequent." Victoria's jaw was set, she swept her shawl around her shoulders. "I expect you to be on Nathaniel's arm at the Carters' luncheon party on Sunday." She blocked the door.

Lily ignored her mother. "Gram, the orange-scented shortbread cookies are a special wartime recipe I made up for your afternoon tea. The butter is replaced by shortening. I hope you enjoy them. Emmeline should check them in ten minutes." She grasped Josie's outstretched hand, closing her eyes at the feel of its accustomed, soft warmth, managing to send Josie a watery smile.

"Sweetheart, how clever of you," Josie said. "Congratulations, darling, on your opportunity to train for head chef."

"I am counting on this war to end *very* soon," Victoria growled.

Lily hugged Josie hard, burying her face in her grandmother's soft velvet shoulder. Without a word to her mother, she turned and rushed out of the kitchen, using the servants' stairs.

"What on earth is wrong with that girl?" Victoria's voice filtered up from below. "An unmarried cook for a daughter is an embarrassment beyond repair, sitting in church as an unwanted third wheel with us, hovering around like some wallflower at parties. Ugh."

Lily stopped on the top landing. She waited a moment, her chest heaving. And then a surge of indignation flew through her, and before she could contain herself, she hollered back down the stairs. "Mother?"

"Don't you shout at me!"

"You worry I will hover? Well then. I promise you that I will fly!"

"Well, good for you, Lily. I'll let Kitty Carter know that my daughter has come to her senses and wants to step into the role she was born to live—wife of Nathaniel Carter. There's nothing better than that!"

Lily pressed her fist to her mouth. In that moment, she realized what she must do. Her mother wanted to play games? Well then, she'd play them right back. She'd *pretend* she was going to marry Nathaniel, and hope like crazy he'd fall in love with someone else.

Chapter Four

Lily

The streets of New York were silent, dark and eerie just before three the following morning. With blackout restrictions in place, the war raging in Europe seemed strangely close and sinister. Lily fought the urge to hurry. The only company she had, other than Tom, were the sweepers, their carts scraping against the sidewalks, their calls to each other ghostly in the night.

They came toward Valentino's, the sound of the restaurant's Chevrolet refrigerator truck coughing and spluttering in the side street as it warmed up for the two-and-a-half-hour journey to the market gardens in Bridgeport, Connecticut.

Giorgio stood near the truck in a textured blazer suit smoking a cigarette. Lily gathered her cardigan around her against the chill air.

Giorgio patted Tom on the back. He crinkled his eyes into a genuine smile for Lily. "Good morning, dearests." He stamped out the cigarette with his tan leather shoe. "Now, which of you two would like to drive this lumbering baby of mine?" He patted the side of the truck. "She takes a lot of getting used to."

Lily blinked. She had hardly slept after yesterday's argument with her mother, and for fear of missing the sound of her alarm.

"Lily, how about you take the wheel?" Tom leaned on the side of the rumbling truck. "Show us how to drive."

"You want Lily to drive the truck?" Giorgio clicked his tongue.

Lily lifted her chin. "Well, I do love to drive." But she chewed her lip at the sight of the great thing. And all the time, Tom smiled at her encouragingly. Lily managed to send him a tentative smile back. It was unusual for someone else to have more faith in her own abilities than she did, that was a fact. Lily had grown up with her mom making light of the things she could do well, and, all the while, *never* encouraging Lily to undertake something that should be done by a man. Like driving this truck!

Giorgio shrugged. After what seemed like an age, he heaved open the driver's door.

Lily peered inside behind him at the single, red bench seat. The steering wheel that sat almost horizontal looked big and heavy. Her muscles would be tested turning corners, that was for sure.

She climbed onto the wheel cover and swung herself up into the cabin.

The two men slid in next to her, Giorgio in the middle, and Tom on the far side.

"Way above my pay grade," Lily said to herself, frowning at the controls.

"Here's the stick shift." Giorgio pointed at the long shaft. "And your clutch pedal is down there, dear."

Lily stood on her toes to reach it.

"*Madonna Santa*," Giorgio muttered. He crossed himself.

Beads of sweat pooled on Lily's upper lip. She sat right at the edge of the long seat, stuck her left foot on the clutch and her right on the gas pedal.

"First gear is as useless as a bunch of bananas, dear," Giorgio said. "Gun her straight into second and go!"

Lily pulled the shift into second, but the gears snapped, and the truck bolted forward and came to a slamming stop. They all jolted back in their seats.

"Holy cow!" Lily said.

"Easy to do, try again." Tom's voice was calm.

Giorgio mumbled what sounded like a prayer.

Lily gripped the steering wheel and planted her left foot on the clutch again, eased it up and pushed with her right foot. This time, the truck lumbered down the narrow street at about two miles an hour. Lily jammed on the brakes at the corner of the street.

"*Santa Maria*," Giorgio murmured under his breath. He'd start on a full Hail Mary next.

A lone car wove its way across in front of them. Lily waited to give it right of way. Once everything was clear, she clunked the gears into second again, the engine spluttering as she almost stood up on her heels to get the truck round the corner.

Next to her, Giorgio gripped the dashboard with one hand and, with his other, he held onto his hat. "Watch the pedestrian, dear!" he yelled over the engine's thrum.

Lily slammed on the brakes. An elderly man was crossing the street right in front of them in the darkness, not looking anywhere but straight ahead.

The truck rattled off again, and Lily fought to control the shaking steering wheel. Tom started chatting with Giorgio, asking him about his French wife, Vianne, whose fashion design house was further down Park Avenue, and soon, the older man was chuckling at the sound of Tom's low, relaxed voice.

"Oh, my darling Vianne is inundated with ideas, Tom. She is fascinated with the new fabrics that are going to grace our American women's figures during the war. Even though she has her atelier full of swatches already, the apartment is currently filled with swathes of rayon." Giorgio let out a loud laugh. "Yesterday, she rebuked me in a torrent of French for moving a swatch from my favorite reading chair in the sun. Apparently, she was studying the material's performance at different times of the day!"

"She is an amazing woman," Tom murmured. "Your marriage is truly modern, such a success."

Lily gripped the steering wheel, and dared not take her eyes off the road. She pushed out pictures of how *un-modern* a marriage to Nathaniel Carter would be.

"I adore her," Giorgio said. "And I have done so since the moment I laid eyes on her over twenty years ago. You know, her atelier brings in wealthy clientele to Valentino's, so many of Vianne's clients have become loyal guests, and friends. Yes, I am most fortunate with my beautiful wife. And Sidney! The moment one of Vianne's ladies steps into Valentino's, Sidney charms them from their pearls to their silk-shod feet. We must not lose everything we have worked so hard to build up during the war. We must not, Tom." Giorgio shook his head.

They drove out of the city as a glimmer of dawn appeared on the horizon.

When she finally turned off the engine, Lily slumped back in the seat, her back slick with sweat. But once she was out of the cabin, she felt a smile form on her lips at the sight that greeted them. In front of her, a tapestry of farmlands and orchards spread as far as the eye could see, farms belonging to folks who had come to America seeking a better life; Jewish people, Italians, Poles, Irish and Armenians who had settled here since the late seventeenth century, when they'd started by growing tobacco in the well-drained soil.

Now, in the opaque morning light, rows of fresh veggies were tucked into the earth.

Tom brought over coffee and a fresh buttered roll from a table. "Well done. That was tough, but you were great."

"Well, thank you. It was fine, but, I confess, I'm starving after all that driving." She closed her eyes at the taste of the warm coffee and took a bite of the freshly baked bread.

Trucks of all sizes started pulling up and older men stepped out, patting each other on the back in greeting. Giorgio was in the thick of it, fanning his face with his felt hat.

"Giorgio's in his element out here," Lily chuckled, the warm coffee tickling the back of her throat and the sound of men's low conversation strangely companionable.

"Seems to be quite the social occasion for him." Tom smiled across at her.

Giorgio strode back with three gray-haired men in tow, who looked to be in their fifties. "Tony, Raffaele, Ernesto, I'd like you to meet two of my most talented chefs. Tom Morelli and Lily Rose. I'm training Lily up to replace Marco, in case Tom here gets drafted."

The three men shook hands with Tom, turning one by one to Lily and, one by one, raising their eyebrows, but she stuck her hand out and shook theirs with a firm grip.

"The market gardens are Tony's, and his cousins Ernesto and Raffaele know the ropes," Giorgio explained.

"*Jumpin' Jehosaphat!* You're going to be an asset, sweetheart." Raffaele nudged Ernesto and both men let out a guffaw.

Lily placed her hands on her hips. "I believe I have a good eye for top-quality produce. That's why Giorgio trusts me. To ensure you give us only the best for Valentino's. *Especially* during the war." Out of the corner of her eye, she saw Tom smile down at the ground.

Raffaele took his hat off and held it to his heart. "She's gonna do you proud, Giorgio!"

Next to her, Lily swore she saw Tom reach his hand out toward her shoulder, just for a moment, before pulling it back. She quirked an eyebrow and smiled. Giorgio's eyes twinkled with genuine warmth.

"Time to get down to business, gentlemen. And ladies." Giorgio pulled out a leather notebook. "For today, we want fresh mushrooms, iceberg lettuces, tomatoes, beans and the best baking potatoes you've got to go alongside our prime ribs, plus fruits for our fruit cup and apples for our apple pie."

"All right then. Let's show these two what we've got," Tony grinned.

Giorgio waved Lily and Tom forward. He placed a hand on Raffaele and Giorgio's backs and the three of them returned to the groups of chattering men.

The sun rose in a glorious golden arc, lighting up the timeless potager with its glistening rows of produce. Lily was certain there was nowhere she'd rather be.

Two hours later, Lily heaved the loaded truck toward the Chelsea Meat Markets. In the parking lot crowded with trucks, she took a few tries to maneuver the Chevrolet into place, but by now she was used to the huge vehicle, and Giorgio stayed quiet while she eased into a spot.

"You did well out at Bridgeport, but the meat markets will be more of a challenge, my dear. You can wait in the truck if it's upsetting for you." Giorgio placed his hand on the dashboard, his gold signet ring gleaming.

"If only you knew how fascinated I am by this; you'd have me come to the markets with you every day," Lily said.

"Well, all right then, Lily," Giorgio said. "But don't say I didn't warn you, dear."

She felt a new type of thrill at the sounds and sights surrounding them as they made their way under the sidewalk overhangs into the busy, bustling meat markets, with vendors shouting out their wares into the morning air. Hand-lettered signs decorated the purveyors' stalls, and Lily fought the urge to stop and stare as they passed open barrels of pigs' ears, carpet-sized rolls of tripe and jugs of pork bellies.

Giorgio strode along ahead of them, clearly heading toward his favored butcher, passing entire cows, hogs and sheep carcasses hanging from hooks in the ceilings. Ham hocks, pigs' snouts, cows' hearts and sheep's brains were all on display, along with chicken tails and turkey butts.

"You all right, Lily?" Giorgio came to a halt under a wooden painted sign that read "Master Purveyors."

"I'm sticking to what I told you in the truck," Lily said. "Don't you worry a fig about me. I'm busy thinking up recipes!"

Tom eased his hands into the pockets of his blue jeans alongside her.

A slim, bald man in his forties excused himself from talking with another customer. He came right around and grasped Giorgio's hand, then Tom's, before finally turning to Lily. "It's a rare day when we see pretty girls here." He spoke in a lilting Irish brogue. "What brings you along? Are you visiting with family?"

"I hope you'll realize how honored I am to meet you," Lily said. She reached out her hand, and, a puzzled expression on his face, the butcher shook it. "But, I am pleased to tell you, I'm here working."

"Well, I'll be," the butcher whispered. "I'll be."

"Lily, Tom, this is our master butcher, Paddy Jackson," Giorgio said, stepping aside while Tom shook the older man's hand. "Paddy's a third-generation purveyor of fine meats, and the only butcher Valentino's will deal with."

"I'm sure you've got some beautiful cuts to show us for Valentino's," Tom said.

Paddy shook his head as if he were waking himself from a dream. "That I have. Come in back with me," he said, ushering them in and around the back of his stall. "We get all our meat straight from the slaughterhouse, Tom and Lily," he said. "All our beef comes from the steer, just as you would expect." He led them into a locked, refrigerated room.

"For sure," Tom said.

"One of the first things Marco taught me was that the castration makes them develop the optimal combination of muscle and fat for the best texture and flavor," Lily added.

Paddy eyed her with respect.

Giorgio started inspecting the hanging carcasses, his thumb pressed to his lips.

In spite of her former confidence, Lily wrinkled her nose at the sight of the dead animals so close. She took in a slow breath. "Paddy, you obviously still have a robust supply, but how do you see the proposed meat rationing that we might be facing next year affecting your stock?"

"Ah, well. That's where butchers will have to look after old customers." Paddy dropped his voice down low. "When it comes to Valentino's, we will certainly be after takin' care of you, unless our supply chain gets completely severed—and heaven help us if that happens. Heaven help us, my dear."

Lily tilted her head to one side. "Yes, I understand. You would never disappoint us."

"No, we would not. Now, as for the present, we have fifty steers arriving each morning, quartered into two-hundred- to two-hundred-and-fifty-pound sections, then we hang them here on these bars attached to the rollers, and we stamp every quarter, see?" He showed them a red stamp proudly displayed on the flesh, with "*Master Purveyors*" written in clear red ink.

Lily glanced toward Tom. He was concentrating hard on Paddy.

"In the rare case that a customer ever complains about my meat, I ask them to show me the stamp," Paddy said. "After we add the stamp, we cut the quarters into ten pieces, and my butchers, supervised by me, cut the pieces into sirloins, ribs, briskets and so forth. When it comes to supplying Valentino's, my benchers take the meat from the coolers out front and cut the pieces into the finest-quality filet steaks and sirloin steaks. You choose what you want, and then we stamp the meat order with the special Valentino's insignia."

"That's Giorgio for you," Tom said, a slow smile spreading across his face. "No one else gets his meat. Everybody's happy."

Giorgio let out a laugh.

"But of course," Paddy said. "We value Giorgio's business. We'd never let you down." He led them out of the cool room, and they followed the butcher over to the glass counters in front of the stall.

When Giorgio and Paddy asked her opinions on the finest-looking cuts on display, Lily assessed every piece of meat for texture, color and touch, gave her considered thoughts and chose the very best, freshest steak she could see.

Tom chuckled softly. "I agree with your choices. They will be grand today."

Once they were done with talking to Paddy, Giorgio asked Tom to maneuver the truck around back of the stall to collect the meat. Lily was happy to take a break from driving.

"I've been impressed with you this morning, young lady. Surprised, but impressed," Giorgio said, while they waited for Tom to bring the truck. "I never thought I'd see the day when a woman chose my Valentino's steak." Giorgio fanned his face with his hat.

"Well, let's hope I'm the first of many more," Lily said.

The sun was up in a cerulean sky and their truck was filled with beautiful ingredients. Lily wound down her window, reveling in the sight of New Yorkers moving about the streets, crowding the subway entrances, rushing down the avenues, the sidewalks awash in a sea of hats and suits. Lily couldn't help it. She hugged herself. Because, for this one moment, she felt part of things more than she'd ever done before, not marginalized, not halfway the socialite her mom wished she'd be, halfway a cook sweating below Valentino's, but a girl who had a real purpose in her life.

*

Late that afternoon, after luncheon service, Lily sat between Martina and Tom, poring over plans for Valentino's winter menu. They'd offered to assist Giorgio in sourcing ideas, so that at least when it came to the entire season, he didn't have to start from scratch.

The remains of Martina's exquisite flourless chocolate Barozzi cake sat on the desk, a recipe that she'd learned from her immigrant grandmother and adapted for Valentino's. The addition of the Modena region's famous balsamic vinegar to the bittersweet roughly broken chocolate, almonds, coffee, cocoa powder, butter and sugar was something special that they might only be able to serve for a little while longer until their supplies of the famous vinegar ran out.

"This really is delicious, you know, Martina," Lily said. "Your grandmother must have been an excellent cook, and she's certainly passed her talents down to you."

Martina curled her lip. "But, of course. My nonna taught me everything I know. But, no matter how much my nonna likes to remind us all of my Modena heritage, I pride myself on the fact that I'm a third-generation American. I view America as my home country as much as anyone else—in fact, perhaps more so." She settled back in her chair, eyed Lily and crossed her legs.

"Of course," Lily said.

Martina returned to her notes.

"How about you, Lily?" Tom asked, leaning his chin on his hand and watching her in the soft light. "What's your ancestry?"

"Oh," Lily chuckled. Given the war, it would hardly do to say that her great-grandparents on her father's side had been German immigrants, fending for themselves down in the Lower East Side in a tenement, eventually moving to the German community in the Upper East Side, which is where Lily's late grandfather had been born.

During the last war, he'd quickly anglicized his name from Heinz Rosen to Hank Rose, channeling his meticulous sense of perfection and his creative talents into an exquisite millinery boutique serving the wealthy clientele of the Upper East Side, eventually expanding it to the bigger business down in the Lower East Side that his son, Jacob, ran now, delivering hats to the major department stores, and selling them from the front-of-house shop in Millinery Row.

"They're just business folk, nothing much else to tell." Lily knew she'd reddened. She sensed Tom still watching her as she hurriedly bent over her notes.

"The menu plans I came up with this morning were perfect," Martina said. "The idea was for you to look over things, not change them, Lily."

Lily placed her pen down. "But I had not seen a pre-war Valentino's menu before. I am astounded by the scale of it, and I wanted to note some of the more exciting dishes on the old menu, because I would love to try and modify them for wartime."

"Good idea, Lily," Tom said.

"I want people to see Valentino's as a haven, somewhere they can come to escape and to shut the war out, even for one evening of their lives. I'm interested in bringing back a sense of peacetime luxury to the restaurant, while not exhausting what are going to be limited resources," Lily said.

"Oh, so while your fellow Americans fight waist-deep in mud, or fly over far-flung oceans risking their lives every day, you want the guests to come here and forget there's a war?" Martina glared across the table.

Lily gritted her teeth. *Why did Martina have to make things so difficult between them?* It seemed crazy, given they were both dealing with enough antipathy from the older male chefs in the kitchen every day, already. Surely it would be better for the two of them, two young women in a sea of experienced men cooks, to band together and support each other?

"Ridiculous," Martina said. "Clearly, you have no idea about anything outside your rarefied world."

"But if you'd... lost someone, imagine how precious coming to Valentino's would be." Lily took a breath. "For me, Valentino's is like a family." She caught Tom's eye and he smiled at her in the soft lamplight.

Martina inhaled sharply. "*Madonna mia.*" She pushed back her chair. "I need to go. All the way home to *Queens.*" She looked pointedly at Lily. "My mama is sick, and I have to check on her." Martina stood up to her full five foot two, her curls catching under the light.

"I'm sorry to hear your mother is unwell," Lily said.

Martina held Lily's gaze a moment, and then gathered her coat.

Lily attempted to smile at her, but Martina adjusted her sleeves with exaggerated movements, and only sent Lily a curt nod in return.

"Tom," Lily said, under her breath, once Martina had swept out of the office. "Look at this."

"Homemade ravioli with Giorgio sauce." She tapped her fingers on the desk. "Sounds intriguing. I wonder what on earth that could be."

Tom grinned. "You've forgotten; I've worked here a while. You hungry?"

She felt a stirring of excitement. "Well, I haven't eaten dinner, if that's what you're asking."

Tom stood up. "Okay then. Follow me."

Lily giggled. "You know what Giorgio's sauce is?"

"Honey, Marco and I made up the recipe."

Out in the quiet kitchen, Tom pulled out a ball of fresh pasta dough wrapped in waxed paper from the fridge. "You want to do the honors with the ravioli while I make the filling?"

Lily's eyes lit up. "I'm starving!"

"Good."

Lily cut the dough into four large pieces, rolling it out through the old pasta maker, thin enough so she could see her hand through it, but not too thin that it would break when cooked.

Next to her, Tom had cooked and peeled chestnuts from the store, ricotta, parmesan cheese, egg, nutmeg and a tiny bowl of fennel seeds. He mashed them together and spooned the mixture onto the pasta that Lily had laid out ready on the table, before brushing some egg white around the filling, and folding the dough.

Lily trimmed the sheet of pasta with a wheel cutter and separated each ravioli.

Tom had a bowl of salted, boiling water ready, and he popped the delicious morsels in until they were cooked. At the same time, he whipped up a sauce of melted butter and fennel seeds.

"And voila!" he said, serving the ravioli onto two white plates, tossing it in the butter and fennel sauce, and handing a plate to Lily. "Homemade ravioli with Giorgio's sauce."

"Why, thank you," she murmured, bringing the spoon up to her mouth. "And that is perfection."

Tom leaned down into a cupboard, pulling out a beautiful bottle of Tuscan Pinot Grigio. He poured two glasses and handed one to Lily. "Here's to the longevity of Valentino's."

"And to you coming back safely, if you must leave us," Lily said, her tone serious. Her eyes locked with Tom's, and when she took a sip of the wine, her hand shook.

Chapter Five

Victoria

Her old school was exactly as Victoria remembered it. From where she sat on the stage, not a thing had changed in twenty-six years. Girls giggled behind their hands, shooting covert glances under their eyelashes at the stage, where Victoria sat with her legs crossed at the ankles and her pencil skirt pulled down demurely over her knees.

The gray-haired headmistress moved to the old wooden dais, her regal appearance causing a hush to fall over the crowded room. Victoria's gaze swept over her audience, her eyes meeting with a headstrong-looking girl who stared right back. Victoria smiled, recognizing something of herself back in the day.

But now, she stood graciously, allowing herself to send a little smile to the girls, when the headmistress introduced her by her name.

"Mrs. Jacob Rose was a scholarship recipient. We are delighted to have her back here to address you all."

Hateful, hateful word. *Scholarship.* She'd spent every ounce of effort during her first year here trying to wash that image away for good. From the very first moment she'd entered the school gates, her head filled with a love for her dear mathematics, the shock had hit. She'd been hopelessly naïve to think she'd be treated as an equal.

Her teachers had delighted in her, of course they had, encouraging what they called her "extraordinary mind," and sending her home with advanced workbooks and problems to solve that senior girls struggled with. But Victoria's classmates had taunted her, laughed at her strange love of "puzzling" with numbers, and left her out of their games, invitations to parties, sleepovers, camp-outs, and trips to Fifth Avenue to shop in the department stores. No one wanted to associate with the person who had committed not one, but two cardinal sins. First, Victoria was far too clever, and secondly, she came from a family who could not afford the school fees.

After a full year of suffering in these hallowed halls, of exclusion, ridicule, derogatory comments made to her face, behind her back, and not one invitation to another girl's home, Victoria had discarded her love of numbers like an old frock. She'd focused her formidable energy instead on winning a calculated battle to become "in" with the popular girls. Girls who wore bright, silk ribbons in their beautifully brushed hair, who never stepped foot on the train, but were driven to school by their fathers' chauffeurs, girls whose daddies did not own small businesses, or—heinously—drugstores in Brooklyn, like Victoria's father. No, these girls' fathers headed entire construction companies, with factories spreading West, railroads that traversed the continent, steamships that roamed the world, department stores that studded cities from one end of the United States to the other. They went home in the afternoons to mansions on Fifth Avenue, with retinues of servants dressed in black and white. They slept on soft feather beds at night, with silken sheets and down pillows, had wardrobes that were delivered from Paris twice a year, and ate dinners served on porcelain plates embossed with fourteen-carat gold.

The only way to survive in these overwhelmingly fabulous new surroundings, where all that mattered was wealth and prestige, was to do one thing: fit in.

So that is what Victoria had done ever since.

To her teachers' bewilderment, she gradually reinvented herself, suddenly affecting an inability to do math, forcing her teachers to move her from the top class to the bottom ranks, taking up dressmaking, replacing science with home economics, and making sure her results sat firmly in the middle of the class.

She'd discovered the art of manipulation, and she'd never looked back.

"I gave Mrs. Rose free reign today to talk about any topic she chooses." The headmistress dropped her voice accordingly, leaning forward as if addressing an intimate audience of one. "So, let's see what she wants to talk about, shall we? Hmm? So far, our past scholarship recipients have included a prize-winning novelist, a noted research scientist into childhood disease, a Broadway theater director and a philosopher!" She stood up to her full height again, running a hand through hair that was cut so short, it could be a man's.

The girls clapped, half-heartedly, Victoria thought, but she ignored that. Because she knew what these girls really wanted to hear.

"Good morning, my dears," she said, affecting a delightful smile, and waving her hand across the room. "Today I would like to bring a breath of fresh air into this old place." She leaned forward, just as the headmistress had done. "I want to tell you all about new plans to bring back debutante balls after the war."

Victoria sensed a ripple moving across the room. One girl covered her mouth with her hand, she seemed so impressed, and a whole cohort of pretty girls' heads shot up, their eyes alight with real interest.

Ha.

"Girls," Victoria trilled, "I have it on good authority—very good authority, indeed. One of my friends, a socialite and philanthropist, has a marvelous, exciting plan. How lucky you girls will be, because you will be just the right age. Apparently," Victoria dropped her voice even further, leaning towards them conspiratorially once more, "the balls will be held at the Plaza, and the organizers will encourage international applications from European royalty and daughters of heads of state, and will be preceded by a number of dinners and parties for those lucky girls who are chosen."

There was an outbreak of excited whispering.

Victoria held her finger up, knowing she had the entire audience entranced. "We hope to bring the world together after the war with an international debutante ball that will only help to restore world peace!"

She paused for dramatic tension, just as she had learned in deportment and etiquette classes. Every eye in the room was upon her. The headmistress let out a little cough.

"Now." She dropped her voice. "Each young lady will have to bring their own young man. Young men of distinction will be your escorts, scions of The Families, so that we, in New York, can hold our heads high and mingle with the best international society, and you and your escorts will be greeted by a thousand guests. Can you imagine?"

You could hear a pin drop.

"Those who are accepted will be from a close-knit, social world. You will be dressed in white, but the ballroom in the Plaza will be decorated in gold and pink."

A pretty young blond girl in the front row grabbed her neighbor's arm. Victoria smiled beneficently.

"You will receive a pink invitation, if you are chosen. You will all be waiting for the mail with such anticipation, you cannot imagine. But here's the best part…" Victoria waited, a substantial pause seeming like such a good idea right now. "You can start preparations now. Because, to be considered, you need to raise funds for the US military. You need to prove yourself to be a young woman of distinction. Only the most special girls will be selected for the Plaza Debutante Ball. It will be life-changing. I encourage you all to prepare."

Victoria stood back, smiling at the room, and waving her hand across them all.

A hush fell over the hall for a moment, and behind her, the headmistress took in an audible breath, until, suddenly, the silence was broken by an explosion of applause.

Victoria slipped back into her chair, and let out a gratified sigh.

An hour later, Victoria pulled on her gloves and placed her navy felt hat on her head. She wove her way through the corridors of the school, passing underneath the American flag that hung proudly above the school's front door, and left it all behind for the crowds on East 95th Street, passing by the elegant apartment buildings that lined the street, moving expertly onto Madison Avenue, and pushing open the glass door of Jacques'.

Inside, she let out a sigh of relief at the familiar sight of the bright, airy café, with its counters and sparkling glass cases that displayed all of her favorites: marvelous meringues fashioned with curlicues, sponge layers filled with butter cream, tartes Tatin, melting cookies and Florentines made with almonds, chocolate and candied fruit.

Behind the immaculate counter, Jacques bustled in a white apron, his eyes kindling at the sight of Victoria standing there.

"Chérie," he murmured, coming out to greet her, taking her gloved hand and bringing it to his lips, before leaning in for a French double kiss on each cheek. He eyed his busy café. "Your usual table, *Victorine*. Your friends are already here. Come with me, come with me."

Victoria felt a frisson of joy at his delightful pronouncement of her name, and a sigh of relief to be away from that dreadful old headmistress.

"Prim. And Adeline." She leaned down to plant a perfect air kiss near two of her oldest friends.

Jacques seemed to hover a moment. "Oh, my dears," he said. "We all must pray for my homeland."

Adeline and Prim's eyebrows shot up.

"Oh?" Victoria said.

Jacques rested his hand against the back of Victoria's chair. "*Oui.* The Germans have marched into Vichy France, after the French navy scuttled the Vichy fleet in southeastern France, to stop it from being used by the Axis powers in North Africa. Hitler says it's a violation of his agreement with Pétain. So, Vichy France is useless."

Prim reddened, and popped a tiny macaroon into her pink lipsticked mouth. Her blond hair was curled with immaculate care under her jaunty green hat, and she folded her hands on the table. "What is Vichy?"

Victoria pressed her lips together, but Adeline turned to Jacques, her perfectly arched reddish brows sculpted in an expression of even more eternal surprise than usual. "Oh, dearest Jacques. You know we abhor the news of war. I don't read it, and I forbid my daughters from filling their heads with such nonsense. Go and get Victoria her coffee and do not mope about like that. You will spoil your éclairs!" She gave a tinkling laugh.

Jacques shook his head and turned around to disappear.

Adeline clutched Victoria's hand, her beige painted nails gleaming under the lights. "Vicky. We have news that is far more delicious than that!"

Victoria turned to Prim. Because everyone knew that one did not announce news oneself. One told one's best friend, and then had them do it for you. If you had a best friend.

Jacques arrived with Victoria's coffee and a chocolate swirled meringue. "Oh, perfect, dear Jacques," Victoria said, reaching for the café crème and taking her first, invigorating sip. She laid a hand on his arm, as if in concession to the relentless Germans marching in on his beloved France. The last thing she wanted was for him to think she didn't care.

Jacques sighed, pressing his hand onto hers before walking off.

"Now, what is it, dear?" she asked Adeline.

"Eleanor," Adeline said, sitting back in her chair, her green eyes twinkling. "Prim's daughter has gone and got engaged to Harvey Lawrence."

Just then, three more friends swung in, and in a flurry of kisses and coats whipping off and chairs being drawn in close, the news was repeated.

"Marvelous." Victoria beamed, reaching across and clasping Prim's hand in her own. Prim beamed with pink, pure pleasure, her famous dimples crinkling delightfully. "Congratulations, dear."

And when the others whooped into exclamations of joy, all wanting to know every single detail, Victoria sat back and narrowed her eyes.

She waited.

When the lull came, and the gasps of delight and chatter about diamonds, and churches and the lack of pure silk, and white roses died down, Victoria played the perfect card.

"Well," she announced, in her cut-glass tone, with not an ounce of Brooklyn left in it, just loud enough for ladies at the neighboring tables to hear, just loud enough for the grapevine to gather the news and unfurl it, spread it, and let it grow little buds of fruit as it trailed through Manhattan. "Lily," she said, "is engaged to Nathaniel Carter."

The silence that followed was worth every diamond in the room.

Chapter Six

Lily

Lily's alarm pealed on Sunday, waking her from a heavy, unaccustomed sleep. After three mornings doing the market rounds, she'd become used to waking well before dawn, and last night after dinner service at Valentino's, she'd fallen into bed and not stirred once. While she was tired, she was also grateful that Giorgio had accepted her offer to work longer hours, giving her the chance to be away from Victoria's constant machinations. It was a relief.

She padded across the cream carpet in her bedroom to the window to throw open the thick silken drapes. Outside, the early-morning sunlight glistened on the gated gardens. She never tired of the view out to Gramercy Park.

"Lily?" Her mom was right outside her bedroom door, rapping on it. "I won't have a girl who's slovenly in the mornings. Are you up?"

"Morning, Mother." Lily stared out the window. A young man in uniform was already out walking with a pretty girl in the park. Lily reached down to the window seat for the notebook that she'd started for Valentino's wartime recipes, turning to the first page. *"Giorgio's Chestnut Ravioli with Ricotta- courtesy of Tom and Marco,"* was her inaugural entry. She let her fingers run over the ingredients and the methods.

"Get dressed. You need to be fully awake for the Carters' luncheon party."

The soldier bent down to kiss the girl.

Lily turned away from the open window.

*

"There's something wrong with you," Victoria said at breakfast. She poured tea through a strainer into a delicate porcelain cup. "You're looking peaky. She's looking peaky, isn't she, Jacob?" Victoria nudged her husband.

Lily's father peered over the top of the *New York Times*. He pulled off his reading glasses and regarded Lily, his gray hair oiled smooth and his kindly blue eyes smiling at her. "If you were rising at two o'clock in the morning for three days straight, then you'd be tired too, Vicky."

Her mother sniffed and patted her white napkin against her mouth.

Lily took her first sip of coffee, closing her eyes at its evocative, rich aroma and taste. Adjusting to the current rationing with an allowance of only one cup per day had made that one coffee a thing to truly savor. "I am a little tired, but I'm relishing the opportunities I'm getting, Dad."

"Well," Jacob said, "young Nathaniel is bursting to see you, from what Matthew Carter tells me at the Yale Club." His eyes swiveled to Lily's mom before, quick as a flash, he mouthed to Lily, "*Keeping the peace, darling.*"

Lily sighed at him. She stood up to go to the sideboard to help herself to a fresh plate of scrambled eggs. "Since we all know I'm not Nathaniel's girlfriend, I have no idea why he expects me to be available to see him at all."

Victoria glared at her husband. "One has to strike while the iron's hot when it comes to suitable husbands. I worry that our leniency in allowing Lily to work, even during the war, might put dear Nathaniel off."

Lily's dad held up his hand. "If the boy is pining, it won't do him any harm. Might increase his appreciation." He caught Lily's eye again.

"Oh, for pity's sake, Jacob. You don't hold any truck with that old idea," Victoria said.

"The harder he has to work, the better."

"Oh, you are so old-fashioned," Victoria chided. "Surely a modern woman can express interest without being considered fast. I say we make our position, our enthusiasm, about the engagement very clear today." She twisted the napkin into a ball in her fingers.

Lily's eyes widened. "*Mother—*"

But Jacob cleared his throat and shook out his newspaper. "Now, then. Hitler has issued a directive calling for the execution of all British commandos who are captured by the Nazis." He peered at the print. "And Canterbury in England has suffered terrible damage in retaliation for the bombing of Milan. And oh, my darlings, France. Unthinkable."

Lily stared at her food, her appetite dimmed as she thought again of Marco.

"Must we have this examination of the war every morning?" Victoria said. "I do not believe it is tasteful talk for the breakfast table. I say we should cast aside the papers and focus on more pleasant things. Surely, the *New York Times* is overplaying the real events."

Jacob placed his glasses down on the breakfast table. "I have to go down to the factory now. I've ordered a shipment of pins with patriotic messages to adorn our hats."

"Oh, not on the day of the Carters' party!" Victoria threw her hands in the air. "Surely not. Does the war not stop on a Sunday?"

"I'm sorry, my dearest. I want to be there for this important delivery and not leave all the work to my loyal staff who are coming in on their day off to help." He stood up and took his leave.

Victoria leaned forward once he was gone. "I've got the most fabulous frock in mind for you today, and you are going to wear it and knock that boy's socks off. Dearest Nathaniel will have absolutely no hope against you when he lays eyes on you in this dress."

Lily listened to the sound of her father's footsteps on the wooden floorboards until they disappeared. "Donate the money you've set aside for my wardrobe to the war effort, Mom. Please, don't go buying me clothes at this time. I can't bear it."

Victoria stood up. "The dress is bought. The invitation is accepted. You're not letting this family down."

"I don't believe I am letting anyone down."

"I will remind you that I told you days ago about this. We are going."

The sound of Jacob closing the front door resonated through the apartment.

Lily tipped her head back, slugged down her coffee down, and reminded herself how much she loved her job.

On Victoria's pink painted wardrobe in her private dressing room, a white chiffon dress decorated with green polka dots and a velvet flower pinned to the waistline hung on a padded hanger. The skirt flared out and fell in soft folds beneath a low-cut, fitted bodice.

"Go on, put it on." Victoria stood with her hands on her hips.

Lily pulled the dress off the hanger. "I'll put it on, just this once." *Because I can't bear the fuss if I don't.* "But afterward, please sell it. And donate the money to the war."

"Oh, fiddlesticks." Victoria sat down at her dressing table and admired Lily. "That will drive him delightfully insane. There. See what you're missing? Why not dress up every day like other girls do?"

Lily stared at her reflection in the mirror. "I can't imagine," she said, a little sardonically.

"Thinking about the style of engagement ring he'll give you?"

Lily dug her fingernails into her palms. "Believe me, it's the last thing on my mind."

"You're blushing." Victoria lowered her voice. "I'm so glad we reached our agreement."

Lily stood stock-still. "Mother—"

"Nathaniel will want to rescue you from that dreary job."

"But you said, a modern woman wouldn't want to be old-fashioned."

"Not quite what I said." Victoria arched a brow. "We'll have to drive to the party with*out* your father. Men. They have no idea. That's why we have women in the world. If you have any brains, you'll stand beside your future husband and make sure he increases his fortune for your own benefit and for that of your children. Just as I am *trying* to do for you!"

As Victoria left the room, Lily slumped down on her mom's velvet stool and put her head in her hands.

An hour later, her hair swept up off her face in carefully crafted soft waves courtesy of Victoria's maid, Lily stared out the window in the back seat of the family's car. The beautiful polka-dot dress fanned around her long legs and she felt like one of Giorgio's beef steaks going Uptown to be put on a plate.

Victoria kept up a consistent chatter about nothing the whole way to the Carter mansion on Fifth Avenue. Outside the window, Midtown gave way to the mansions of the Upper East Side. Nannies paraded with prams, and smartly dressed folks strolled with poodles and walking canes. The fall sun dappled through the trees onto the lawns and the pathways.

"You know, Katherine Carter hinted to me that they'd give Nathaniel the Fifth Avenue mansion for a wedding present," Victoria said, dropping her voice in confidence, the way she always did when she was revealing intimate details about Katherine and her husband. Nathaniel's father owned thousands of miles of railroads and factories all over the Midwest.

Lily lay her hand on the armrest. "Good for her."

"Katherine would adore to see the gilded mansion filled with children. And, after the war is done, you will be the one to produce them."

"I can hardly wait."

Victoria flicked a glance at the silent driver. "Keep your voice down, Lily."

Lily took a deep breath and held it in.

The driver pulled over outside the Carters' famous imitation French chateau on Fifth Avenue. The double front doors were discreetly half open, and their butler stood at the top of the marble steps.

Lily tapped her fingers on the polished handle of the car.

"Katherine tells me that the squash courts on the fourth floor could easily be converted to roller-skating rinks."

"How delightful."

"And you could host such glittering fundraisers in the magnificent rooms on the second floor. As for maintaining the garden, it's getting to be quite a thing for Katherine to oversee and manage, dear. I told her, Lily, that one benefit of your working at this ridiculous job with the Conti family is that you will be comfortable with staff and have developed a good eye for a dinner party menu. You'll be such an asset to Nathaniel when he has to entertain his business associates and the family's wide circle of friends."

"It's a limited circle," Lily said. She stepped out of the car.

"They know half of Manhattan." Victoria stepped graciously up the wide front steps.

"Only the upper half."

"Mrs. Rose, *Mademoiselle* Rose." The Carters' butler opened the door wide for them.

Lily sent the man a curt nod. Her brow darkening, she stepped inside with her mother.

The smell of fresh flowers saturated the Carters' grand foyer. Lily's feet started to pinch in her shoes and her footsteps seemed to echo strangely on the black-and-white marble floor. The sounds of glass tinkling and laughter drifted down the magnificent sweeping staircase from the family's famous salon.

"Pre-luncheon drinks are in the ballroom," the butler said. "But Mrs. Carter particularly asked me to notify her of your arrival."

"Oh! How delightful of dear Kitty," Victoria said.

Lily heaved out a breath.

"Of course." The butler looked around behind Victoria. "Is Mr. Rose here?"

"He had to go into our hat factory," Lily said, narrowing her eyes. "In the Lower East Side. It's a millinery business. He's ordered a batch of patriotic pins. For the war, you know." Victoria curled her fingers around Lily's arm and pressed.

The butler raised his refined pointed nose.

Just then, Katherine Carter came sweeping down her staircase, in soft, pure silk that fell to the floor in a flow of shell-colored pink. She took in Lily's green-and-white dress and a slow smile spread across her pearly painted lips. Her golden hair was done up in a timeless French roll. "Ah, I see Jean Michel has kept you here for me," she said. "Just as I asked, just as I asked."

"Hello, Katherine dearest," Victoria said, her voice dripping with supercilious relief.

"Do come into the drawing room, Victoria and Lily." Katherine leaned forward to give Victoria an air kiss.

They paraded back across the marble behind Katherine.

Lily braced herself. *Heaven help me.*

Once they were in Katherine's drawing room with its silks and Gainsborough portraits and pale Turkish rugs and exquisite velvet drapes, Katherine arranged herself in front of the windows on a Louis XVI sofa and insisted Victoria and Lily sit down. She adopted a pained expression.

"Matthew would be here too, but, unfortunately, he is stuck in an important conversation about supplies for the war. Lending... you know... *things* to the effort. One must do one's bit..."

Victoria made a sympathetic noise. "Yes, dear. Jacob is similarly inconvenienced today; he, too, has been called away to do what he can. We are all doing what we can, darling. I am exhausted with it, you know."

Lily rubbed her brow.

"Oh, Victoria. Lily, the thing is, I have some news that will affect... things, I'm afraid."

Lily sensed Victoria stiffening. She leaned forward on the edge of her seat. *Please, tell me that Nathaniel has fallen for some other suitable girl. A far more suitable girl than me, because there are plenty of them right in this darned mansion upstairs!*

"We have some news about Nathaniel."

Lily clasped her hands tight. *Come on.*

"He's done the right thing, the brave thing—Nathaniel has enlisted and is leaving us. I would expect nothing less, but I confess, dears, it's still a shock." Katherine raised her hand to her throat.

Would that give Lily a reprieve? Surely, even her mother would not expect her to tie herself down to a boy she didn't love, right on the eve of his departure for war. And then... what if he didn't come back? Lily's brow furrowed. Nathaniel was an old family friend, and she hated to imagine anything terrible happening to him. *But it could.*

"Oh, how devastating," Victoria said, grasping Katherine's hand.

Katherine sighed loudly. "He's awfully caught up in the fact that Hitler is persisting with this march toward Stalingrad. Nathaniel gets out his maps and talks over the news on the radio. Of course, it's all about oil, he says. He positively gives me the shivers with what he says might happen in Europe and the rest of the world if Russia falls. Anyway, the upshot is that he cannot stay here. He simply must go and do his bit."

"You must be proud," Lily said. "Good for him."

Katherine sagged in her chair. "Yes, well, I am proud, I suppose." She sighed. "Lily, dear, you look more exquisite than any other girl here. As usual. I've always said it. You are incomparable. You will bear the most beautiful children."

"Thank you, Katherine." Victoria crossed her legs and sat back in her chair. "She is a beautiful girl."

Lily felt like an ornamental bird, trapped in a cage.

Chapter Seven

The chandeliers glowed in the salon. Framed by priceless works of art, the Carters' guests looked like they'd stepped straight from the pages of *Vogue*. Diamonds sparkled, champagne glasses clinked and conversation drifted above the strains of a string quartet.

Lily had hardly stepped inside the room when a familiar man dropped a light kiss on her fingers. Lily let her arm fall back down by her side and sighed at the sight of Nathaniel standing there.

"Lily." His green eyes scoured her face, his blond hair was combed neatly with Brylcreem, and he looked down at Lily from his full height of well over six feet. He adjusted the sleeves of his cashmere sweater and took her arm. "How are you?"

Victoria floated off, raising her hand in a triumphant wave.

Desperately hoping to thwart my mother's plans to ruin both our lives. "Good day to you, Nathaniel." Lily glanced at the grandfather clock that rested against one heavily decorated wall.

Nathaniel reached for a glass of champagne from a passing waiter and handed one to her. "You look stunning. The most enchanting girl in the room, as usual."

Lily heaved out a sigh. "Oh, Nathaniel. Your mother says you've enlisted."

Nathaniel picked up her free hand and tucked it under his arm. "She can talk of nothing else."

Lily's high-heeled pumps pinched, and she opened her mouth to protest, but he'd led them right into a group of girls from Lily's schooldays.

"Oh, my, it's Lily! We haven't seen you anywhere in an age!" Elizabeth O'Connell, her brunette curls brushed into soft waves, threw herself into Lily's arms. "You're causing quite the stir. Gossip abounds. Do tell." She glanced from Lily to Nathaniel and winked exaggeratedly.

Nathaniel's eyes crinkled at the corner, and he turned away to the closest group, leaning in, his blond hair shining under the lights, standing a head taller than most of the other men in the room.

Lily winced, champagne glass midway to her lips. "No need to alert the media. Absolutely nothing to report, Elizabeth. But it's nice to see you."

"Nathaniel's enjoying keeping us guessing," Eugenia Thomas, another girl from the Uptown circles, said. "You both are, you delectable things. Don't they make a divine couple? Aren't I correct? Aren't they lovely?"

Lily took a couple of tentative steps away, only to feel Eugenia's cool but determined hand on her arm.

The girl whispered in Lily's ear, enveloping her in a swathe of Coco Chanel. "Don't forget to have me as a bridesmaid. I expect you'll have to have at least ten. You must be excited beyond measure. What a lucky girl you are. That man is sublime. Imagine. All this will be yours." She waved a hand around the crowded room.

Lily stared openly at Eugenia, but across the room, Victoria raised a champagne glass in her direction. Lily put on a rictus smile and raised her glass back. If only there were one person in this room who could see how utterly wrong this all was. If only, when surrounded by the people who were supposed to be her family and friends, Lily didn't feel so awfully, hopelessly alone. It was as if she were speaking a different language to everyone else here. Not one of these people had an inkling of the truth of what was really going on behind closed doors with her mother. And that was the problem. It was all smoke and mirrors. Just the way Victoria wanted it to be.

"Elizabeth and I can't *wait* for things to be made official," Eugenia confided. "All the people will be quite wild with excitement.

Weddings are about the only decent thing to talk about with this boring war. Can't wait for all the boys to come home."

Lily spoke in a quiet tone. "But we don't know how many American boys will be killed."

Eugenia looked at her as if she were absurd.

Lily stared out at the broad terrace, serene beyond the rows of ornate French doors that lined the ballroom wall, her eyes wanting to rest on the gracious old trees that dappled lace patterns against the blue sky. It was a chilly, but sunny, clear fall day. No one would be out there at this time of year.

Before she knew what she was doing, Lily excused herself and, head down, wove through the crowded, chattering groups. Outside, she leaned her arms against the stone balustrade, arching her back and gazing up at the sky, before bringing her gaze down to the shaded circular gravel pathways that were all lined with flower beds, roses and lavender encircling a wide, lush green lawn, freshly mowed, the grass meticulous in strips of darker and lighter green. Around the edge of the lawn, hanging over the pathways, great English trees, some evergreen, spread their glossy branches and lent ample shade to stone benches dotted along the paths, and in front of the terrace, a marble fountain, decorated with fishes and shells and other sea creatures and nymphs played into the crisp fall breeze.

Lily eased off the impossibly tight shoes her mother had insisted she wear today, her poor toes pinching beyond belief and her heels already red and raw.

"I lost you."

Lily closed her eyes.

Nathaniel came and stood next to her. "Darling. All those people. And no chance to spend time alone with you."

Lily let the shadow of a smile pass across her features, but she didn't turn to look at him. She couldn't bear to face the expression of adoration she knew would be on his face. It wasn't fair. She knew that.

Because what she'd been thinking lately, after that awful, ghastly row with her mother at poor, dearest Josie's house, was this. What her mother was doing was cruel toward not only Lily but Nathaniel as well. He deserved to be loved. If only Victoria hadn't made Lily's job at Valentino's contingent upon an agreement to toe the line with Nathaniel, because what made it so terribly awkward was the fact he was in love with her. Lily had known it for a while, and so had her mother.

Lily had lived with her mother's machinations all her life, but instead of loosening up as Lily grew older, she had only tightened her grip until it was as secure as a vice. And, Victoria had powerful connections. Whether she would use them or not was something she didn't dare put to the test. But Victoria could have Lily fired if she refused her mother's terms. Her friends lined Sidney's pockets, and Giorgio relied on Sidney as his second-in-command. No, the best thing would be to get herself so established in the restaurant industry that she was beyond touchable when it came to her mother's schemes.

Nathaniel laid a hand on Lily's arm. "Darling, I have something I can't hold in before I leave. Especially now—"

She stared at the fountain below. An elderly gardener stopped trimming the white rose bushes, tipped his head at Nathaniel and moved out of earshot. Lily heaved out a sigh. How many times had she run around these gardens, she, Nathaniel and their childhood friends, enchanted with these magical, rarefied grounds in the middle of Manhattan, while their mothers had sat right here on the terrace, sipping pink lemonade and eating delicate chicken sandwiches, strawberries and cream?

In fact, she'd known Nathaniel as long as she could remember. Had worked him out when she was about five years old. Lily could convince him of anything and he'd accept it, following along with her ideas for games. There was no mystique about him. No allure. Perhaps, in her own way, she did love him. As a brother. As her childhood friend. What you saw was what you got: a charming, well-educated young man who fitted perfectly into the lifestyle expected of him.

Problem was, Lily didn't. And she never would.

Lily looked up at him, her eyes softening as she thought of what he was facing. "When do you leave?"

"Three days. I've enlisted for officer training in Georgia." He stopped, and his expression darkened. When he spoke, he rushed out the words. "You know how much I'll miss you. Please, darling, make me the happiest fellow in the world before I leave for the war. Marry me."

Lily scraped a hand through her hair. She risked a glance into the salon. The chandeliers glistened, and a woman threw back her head and laughed near the open French door. It was extraordinary. These people were carrying on as if there wasn't a war at all.

She turned back to Nathaniel. His blue eyes scoured her face. Her mother's words rang in her head. *Marry Nathaniel the minute the war is over, and consider yourself engaged to him as from today.*

Lily turned away from him and pressed her hands into the balustrade.

"Nathaniel," she said, staring out at the floating water droplets from the fountain in front of her eyes. "We've known each other all our lives. I do respect your feelings. However, I don't reciprocate them. And the last thing I want is for you to get hurt by me. I regard you as a family friend. And that is all. It can't ever be anything more." She winced. She couldn't lie to him.

But Nathaniel reached forward, gripping her kitchen-roughened hand between his smooth fingers. "I have no idea where I'll be posted after training. I want to go to Russia, but I worry they'll just send me to the Pacific. It's going to be lonely, and hard. I understand you're not ready to accept a proposal just yet. It's too rash, too soon. And amidst the war. Write me while I'm gone. I need you to promise to do that for me." He picked up both her hands. "Or it won't be bearable for me. Lily, you've always been there for me. Always. I… think of you as home."

Lily pressed her lips together. Unlike her he had no place to run. He had no Josie. She turned to him. "Dearest Nathaniel—"

"You are all I think about. Constantly." His eyes darted over her face, entreating her.

Lily stiffened and she angled her body away from him. Slowly, she opened her mouth to speak. And she felt her own treachery weighing on her shoulders.

"I will write you," she said. Her heart beat wildly, and she pulled her slick, wet palms out of his grip. She held her chin up, "Of course I will. You know that."

Silently, he leaned close to her and dropped a kiss on the top of her head.

"I take that as hopeful."

Lily stood next to him, while the fountain played. She watched how the spray threw itself upward only to disappear into nothing in the air. And, despite everything, she leaned her head on her old friend's chest, and only hoped that he'd come back safe. At the same time, she prayed for forgiveness. The last thing she wanted to do was lead Nathaniel down his own garden path.

Lily escaped the moment Nathaniel was swept up into conversation inside. She hovered outside the ballroom, on the landing near the grand staircase, and the discreet click of a door closing served to remind her how the Carters' butler was always around.

Her mother would be looking for her. And yet, there was no way she could set foot in that party again. She'd made her truce with Nathaniel, and the fact that he'd taken that as hope for something she couldn't give him would have to be sorted on his return. She'd let him down when the war was done, and by then, her position at Valentino's should be secure.

If she got the job.

Lily stood there for one second longer, bent down and pulled off the horrid, painful shoes her mother had bought for her, and then turned around and fled down the stairs like the very opposite of the demure debutante everyone seemed to think she was, out to the sidewalk, where the Carter family saloon was waiting in the street. The driver was leaning against the car, smoking a cigarette.

She came to a halt on Fifth Avenue, a girl in bare feet in a polka-dot dress.

"Miss Rose?" the driver tilted his hat at her. "Can I take you somewhere?"

Lily's chest heaved with short breaths. "If you're not needed, that would be awfully kind."

"Well, I'm not required by the family for at least another two hours, and then it will be to drive Mrs. Carter's mother home." He ground out his cigarette with his polished black shoe and held the car door wide for her.

Lily slipped into the luxurious interior and closed her eyes. Once they were out of sight of the mansion, she leaned forward and spoke. "Greenwich Village, not Gramercy Park. And, can you be a dear and not tell anyone where you took me, not even my mother?"

The chauffeur's eyes caught with hers in the rear mirror. "You have my word, Miss Rose."

"Thank you." Lily sat back in her seat and wrapped her arms around her waist.

Nathaniel was not the only one going to war, and, perhaps, she was going to have to fight for them both.

Chapter Eight

Lily

Lily slipped down Josie's basement steps in Greenwich Village, the polka-dot dress she'd worn to the Carters' luncheon rustling against her legs. The moment she was at her grandmother's kitchen door, hovering by Josie's tumbling collection of potted geraniums and roses that were a riot of color during the warmer months, Lily pulled her hair out of its restrictive updo and let it swing in loose dark waves down her back.

"Gram?" She pushed the door open, only to come to a standstill in the entrance, holding her shoes.

Her mouth fell open in shock.

At the kitchen table, looking as at home in Josie's deliciously warm basement kitchen as he did behind his stove at Valentino's, legs encased in his favored blue jeans, sat Tom Morelli. Sleeves rolled up, dark hair brushed back, eyes laughing at some story Josie was clearly halfway through telling him, he held a cup of coffee to his lips. And stopped dead.

He put the cup down with a thump on the table. Coffee flew over the rim. He sprang up, sending his chair clattering to the floor.

"Oh, my!" Josie said, her eyes lighting up wickedly.

"*Tom?*" Lily took a step backward, self-conscious in the party dress, with her hair tumbling all down her back. She took a swipe at it to push it away from her face.

Tom hurried around to set his chair back upright. He wiped up the spilled coffee with a cloth from Josie's deep enamel sink. "Sorry about the chair, Mrs. Rose, and the coffee," he said. "Lily…" He put his hands in the pockets of his blue jeans. "Hey."

"Hey."

Josie's dark eyes crinkled with warmth.

Lily threw her grandmother a tense look.

"Tom helped me carry my shopping home from Bleecker Street today. His mom and sister work at Albertina's—you know, the deli that I favor, dear—and Tom sometimes helps out there on a Sunday."

"Oh." Lily was still unable to move. Josie's voice warbled on, but her eyes were stuck on Tom, and his on her.

"He gave me a tasting of a wonderful deep-fried *arancini*, the risotto inside fairly melted in my mouth like you wouldn't believe and the crispness of the breaded coating? Well, I tell you, this man's cooking made my taste buds wake up. Magnificent. And when such a talented young cook offered to carry my bags for me, what could I say? I simply had to ask him in for a cup of coffee. It was the least I could do! Now, I'm insisting he tell me all about his family's delectable Sicilian food." Josie leaned forward, resting her chin in her hand. She crossed her legs in their wide-legged, cream velvet trousers, and tapped her black booted heel on the floor.

Lily gaped at her gram, sitting there so innocently, framed by one of her beloved abstract paintings on the wall.

"I didn't mean to intrude." Tom leaned against the back of his kitchen chair and brushed his hair out of his eyes.

Josie waved his concern away. "Seems Tom and I share a love of cooking, and… Valentino's."

Lily narrowed her eyes at her gram.

"We've been having quite the talk."

Tom looked at Lily, his expression sheepish. He gave her a crooked smile.

With Tom's attention diverted, Josie threw herself into a mighty swoon behind his back.

Oh, how Lily adored her gram. If her mom were here on the other hand… Lily tried not to laugh.

"I wasn't expecting you to be here. I would never have come unannounced," Tom said.

He wasn't expecting *her?*

"Well, thank you for helping my gram with her shopping bags, Tom." Still, she was stuck on the spot, her eyes dancing toward her gram. And a thought hit her. If Josie liked Tom, was there really good reason for her not to let her attraction to him have free reign?

He stood there, hands in his pockets.

Lily forced her delectable thoughts aside.

"What I did learn," Josie said, "is that it is Tom here who makes Albertina's fabulous cannoli. I adore it. He was just telling me about that particular family recipe that has been passed down for generations." Josie held up a plate of rolled pastries filled with custard cream, her eyes sparkling. "Why on earth are you in bare feet, dear?"

Lily held up the horrid shoes and tore her gaze away from Tom. She allowed herself to feast on the sight of Josie's pretty blue-and-white plate that was filled with a selection of delectable pastries decorated with icing sugar, the sweet creamed ricotta cheese filling piped into them.

Josie settled back in her chair, eyes twinkling, folding her arms.

"I haven't had any lunch, not one bite, despite having just come from a luncheon," Lily blurted out. The sight of those cannoli was sending her appetite into a spin.

"What, are the Carters taking the war seriously at last? Are they applying rationing to their luncheon guests?"

Lily's hand flitted across the table, reaching for a piece of cannoli. She let the sweet, deep-fried pastry linger in her mouth. Its crispness was the perfect foil for the soft, ricotta crème, with just the right hint of vanilla. The feel of its deep velvet on her tongue was heaven-sent. She heaved a sigh of pleasure. *Oh, he could cook.*

"You keeping this recipe a secret from the restaurant, Tom?" She kept her tone mild, but her taste buds were filled with the cannoli's delicious taste.

"Not sure that it's grand enough for Valentino's," he said, eyes narrowed, right on her.

Lily held her cannoli halfway to her mouth. "But it transcends class." She sent him a coy smile.

Tom sent her a slow grin in return.

Lily slid down into a chair. Tom was still watching her.

"Mmm-hmm," Josie said. "Now, you can see why I got this boy to walk me home. I'm not silly, darling. If a handsome man offers to carry your shopping, well then. It would be impolite to refuse him. Plus, when I heard he makes the cannoli…"

Lily couldn't hold back her laugh. Her gram was impossible!

Tom grinned.

Josie cleared her throat. "Darling? Why aren't you flaunting that dress around the Upper East Side? Surely you're not supposed to be swinging around down here below Fourteenth." She turned to Tom and lowered her voice as if revealing something the entire family didn't know already. "My daughter-in-law thinks folk will catch the plague if they travel below Fourteenth, Tom."

"Well, phooey to that, because I love the Village," Lily said, the cannoli kicking in and giving her a new lease of life. She reached for a second. "Especially since you moved down here, Gram." She sent Josie a wicked glance of her own. "You know I've always preferred walking in your footsteps to those of anyone else."

A soft smile passed across Josie's face. "Well, I'm honored, darling. You know that."

Lily was achingly aware of Tom's gaze passing from her to Josie and back.

"I didn't realize you were partial to my favorite part of New York, Lily," Tom said. "Living in Gramercy."

Lily leaned forward in her chair. "The Village is *life*. In every sense of the word." She frowned a moment, serious now. And that was what she wanted. Life. To live her life in every sense of the word.

There was a silence.

"Well, sweetheart, it sure seems you're already breaking part of that deal you made with your mom!" Josie burst out laughing. "What was it? No liaising with the waitstaff, no fraternizing with—"

"Gram!" Lily was certain her very ears had turned red, now. From under her eyelashes, she saw Tom cock an eyebrow, his eyes dancing.

"The Carters' luncheon can't be over yet, dear." Josie looked at her watch. "How did you get away from their son and heir? Did he propose?" She turned to Tom. "Definitely a man who can't cook. Probably never stepped inside a kitchen in his life!"

Tom sent her a winning smile.

Gram. Lily let out a giggle. She whipped over to the pantry and opened it up. She grabbed eggs, shortening, salt and pepper and grated cheese. "I'm hungry and I can't eat all your cannoli."

Tom stayed where he was.

"You hungry at all?" Lily avoided looking up at him, or at her gram, who was clearly more outrageous even than *she* was, Lily flurried around with her supplies. "I feel bad about using your ingredients, Gram, but I'll replace them."

"Oh, don't mind about that." Josie waved the voluminous sleeve of her beaded top in the air, her multicolored rings glinting in the light. She sat there, tall and elegant, her gray hair sitting perfectly in thick waves on her shoulders and her deep blue eyes as sharp as a young girl's.

Lily shot her a warning glance.

Josie just faked another swoon right back.

Lily buried herself in the refrigerator.

After a few moments, Tom rolled up his sleeves. "I can swing by the deli anytime to restock ingredients for Mrs. Rose, if you like."

Lily started grating cheese. "Am I keeping you from Albertina's?" Her heart was racing, but her hands were working with their usual deftness, grating a soft buttery mound of Cheddar cheese.

He was next to her, breaking the eggs into a bowl. "In theory, I only work at Albertina's on a Sunday morning when folks come in after church. But, it's past noon now, and everyone's back home having lunch. They have plenty of staff on for the rest of the day."

Tom whisked the eggs and Lily built her pile of fluffy yellow grated cheese by his side. She nodded furiously. "Oh, great. That's just grand." She threw herself into the familiar rhythm of preparing food.

Josie picked up a newspaper from the table and started leafing through the pages, popping her reading glasses on the bridge of her nose.

"My sister and my mom are both working at Albertina's until closing time," Tom continued. "It's just a way for me to help out and spend time with them. I don't get to see them much during the week with all the long hours I work at Valentino's. And I don't mind cooking some of my family recipes on a weekend for folks around here, after working with French and Northern Italian cuisine all week."

"I didn't realize you had a sister."

He nodded. "We've been close since my dad died."

Lily's hands stilled. "I'm sorry, Tom."

"It was a long time ago. My mom's had to work extra hard ever since, and so has my sister."

"They're not the only hard workers in your family."

He handed her the bowl of blended eggs and sent her a smile.

"Cooking isn't work to me," he said, his eyes searching her face.

Slowly, Lily nodded. "I know," she said, eyes locked with his.

"Let's get this omelet cooking. Shall I do the honors?" he whispered.

"Go right ahead, Chef," she murmured, feeling her cheeks burning. Knowing she was breaking her own rules, forget her mom's!

He chuckled, holding her eye a moment, and she stood close by him, wanting to stay close, while he deftly took the egg and grated cheese mixture to the stovetop, spreading it into a film in the pan. Holding the pan just over the gas burner, Tom turned it and tilted it until, with a flick of his wrist, he flipped the omelet in the air.

"There." He slid it onto a plate and folded it in half, sprinkling extra pepper on top.

"I always wanted to marry a man who could cook," Josie sighed, as Lily brought her plate to the table.

Lily shook with laughter.

Tom's eyes danced with hers, and he returned to the pan.

"There you go, Gram," Lily said. She popped the delicious-looking golden eggs in front of Josie. "You are incorrigible," she whispered, waving her forefinger at her gram.

"Well, thank you," Josie said out loud.

Tom whipped up another omelet in no time. "Care to share this one with me?" he asked Lily.

She hovered over his shoulder. "Sure!" she said, the word coming out with far more force than she'd intended. She reddened again.

Josie raised her fork in the air. "Beautiful, dearests! As light as air!"

Lily rolled her eyes at her gram.

Tom brought the omelet over to the table. Lily sat down next to him. He held out a tiny taste on a fork for her. Leaning forward, she let him pop it in her mouth. The eggs were so very fresh, and he'd handled them like a dream. They were cooked to perfection. Lily ate alongside him in companionable silence for a while.

When she took the empty plate over to the sink and washed it, it was Tom who let out a laugh.

"What?" She turned around.

"You. You're a humdinger of a girl. Anyone ever told you that?" Tom said.

Lily paused, holding her plate above the sink. Soapsuds dripped from it. "Humdinger? Well, I'm not sure about that, Tom Morelli."

Josie leaned forward and cupped her cheeks in her hands like a girl.

"In that dress, cooking in a basement on a Sunday afternoon," Tom said. He smiled at her. "I'll miss... New York if I have to go to war."

Suddenly, the room felt cold.

Lily put down her plate. "Tom..."

"*Cara,* I'm only still here because I'm considered useful on the home front. I've been helping the local Italian communities build up produce gardens, and I help support my sister and my mom, but I guess I'll be drafted sometime, and when I am... well, I'll miss Valentino's too. So very much..."

Lily started. *Cara.* He'd used the Italian term of endearment. She stood, rigid, unable to move, unable to blink. Eyes locked with his. She'd thought he'd only been joking with her. But could he feel something deeper for her as she was beginning to feel for him?

"Sorry. I didn't mean to be too familiar, Lily." He shot a glance toward Josie, his cheek tightening. "I get emotional about... the war."

Lily frowned down at the floor, and right then, it was as if Josie blended into the backdrop of the room, and Lily was so aware of Tom that, if she breathed, the whole kitchen might disappear.

She raised her eyes to his.

He came a step closer. "I take it your mother isn't championing you working at Valentino's? That's not something I could imagine having to deal with. My family mean the world to me."

Josie stayed quiet. A breeze picked up outside, and the basement door rattled.

Lily let out a sigh.

His voice dropped to a whisper. "You don't have to tell me anything you don't want to." Lily sensed him shooting a glance toward Josie. "How about I take you to Albertina's? Would you like to meet my mom and my sister, since I've made this unexpected appearance at your grandmother's house?"

Lily lifted her chin. "That would be grand. I'd love to meet them, Tom."

"You'll love them," Josie added. "Tom's mother is an incredible woman. Beautiful."

Lily didn't dare look at her gram.

"Let's tidy up this mess we've made and go right on up," Tom said, his expression still soft.

"And I am going upstairs to take a nap." Josie stood up, came forward, pulled Lily into a hug, and held Tom's hand a moment. "Far too much excitement for an old woman for one day." She disappeared in a swirl of velvet.

Lily stood there for a moment.

"Let's tidy up this kitchen, Chef," Tom whispered.

And slowly, she nodded, her pulse racing while she collected up plates and cutlery, her hands feeling light as a pair of soufflés, her knees wanting to buckle down on the nearest chair.

Chapter Nine

Lily stepped out of Josie's Bank Street home with Tom into the crisp fall afternoon, a breeze swirling around them, a reminder that, in spite of the sunshine, winter was on its way. The pair of espadrilles that she kept at Josie's house felt like clouds on her feet compared with those other awful pinching shoes, and she'd borrowed a soft cashmere shawl from Josie, which she wrapped around her shoulders.

Tom took her arm, and Lily's heartbeat quickened as she walked alongside him in the surrounds of the charming old New York townhouses in the area that she so loved, the classic facades looking down on them kindly.

"Your gram is terrific, you know," Tom said, his eyes crinkling at the sides.

"Oh, she is." For a moment, they walked in companionable silence toward Bleecker Street, Lily focusing determinedly ahead, still uncertain as to what had passed between them at Josie's house, still uncertain as to whether Tom's repartee was just in fun, or meant something more. And yet, at Josie's house anything seemed possible, and Tom had fitted in so well in the place Lily saw as her true home.

She walked alongside him, and he greeted a couple of other local folk out for a stroll. Lily smiled at a middle-aged woman passing them in a smock smattered with paint. Oh, things seemed entirely *possible* in this part of the world.

They turned right into Bleecker Street, Bank Street's classic townhouses giving way to vegetable carts, their awnings up, revealing what brightly colored produce they could get these days.

Women peered over the stalls, selecting pumpkins and oranges, their hair gathered in fashionable waves at the napes of their necks, and bicycles whizzed by, bells ringing into the afternoon air, as well as the occasional produce truck and the odd car.

"All the talk this morning at the deli was of meat rationing starting next year," Tom said, eyeing the produce stalls. "It made me wonder whether Paddy Jackson will really be able to cover for Valentino's."

"I've been thinking about the sugar problem too," Lily said, slipping back into talk of restaurants and produce easily with him. "Giorgio says that sugar from Hawaii and the Philippines isn't coming through anymore, and our signature desserts are going to be even more challenged. And then there's coffee. But yes, I fear our main problem will be lack of meat, no matter how loyal Paddy is to Giorgio, and no matter how determined Giorgio is to keep things going."

Tom stepped aside to let Lily pass by an elderly couple, and then pulled her arm back towards him, his fingers flickering against Lily's, sending a thrill through her insides.

"This morning," he said, moving on again, her hand still tucked in the crook of his arm, "my mom and I were talking about using more processed meat at Albertina's to make up for the shortages. Hot dogs. Sausages. My mom is experimenting with different types of sausages at the deli, using herbs. How we convince the Valentino's clientele to take on processed meat is a different matter."

Lily looked up at him. "Can you imagine Giorgio allowing sausages at Valentino's? How adorable for the illustrious clientele."

Tom grinned, coming to a stop opposite Albertina's, its picture window filled with displays of olives and hams, prosciutto and yellow and white cheeses. "We Sicilians know how to make the best out of any situation," he said, a twinkle in his eye. "We can conjure something out of nothing. Come on inside."

Lily paused a moment outside the narrow doorway, her fingertips skimming across the soft cotton of his shirt. Truth be told, she didn't want the walk to end, she didn't want to pull away.

But the door to Albertina's opened wide, and an elderly couple walked out. Tom stepped aside to let them pass. Inside, conversation buzzed, high-pitched Italian voices bargained, and at least ten staff bustled behind the high glass counter. Folks chatted, their baskets full of cheeses and olive oils and bread. Preserved tomatoes and olives sat proudly on display under the counter, along with stuffed chili peppers, and roasted eggplants.

Lily was drawn to a delicious-looking tray with small parcels fried in breadcrumbs set out on the counter.

"Ever tried Sicilian swordfish?" Tom picked up the tray and offered one to Lily. "These deep-fried breadcrumb rolls are made with them."

Lily took a bite.

He waited, head tilted to one side. "What do you think of my inherited cuisine?"

She allowed her taste buds to experience the intense flavors, letting the sounds of people chatting and laughing in Italian swirl around the store.

"Raisins and pine nuts, and olives. I'm sitting in a café on an island, looking out over the blue Mediterranean Sea," she said, looking up at Tom.

"Of course you are," his voice was soft and close.

A flush spread up from her throat, and she looked up at him. They were so close in the crowded room that she was almost pressed against his chest.

A tall man wearing a white apron wound his way toward them and rested a hand on Tom's shoulder.

"You cannot bring such a lovely young woman in here without telling us who she is, Tom. We need an introduction!"

"Lino, this is Lily Rose from Valentino's," Tom said, gently placing a hand on her back.

"I confess, I don't usually dress quite this formal to go to the stores," Lily said. Thank goodness no one could see her espadrilles in this crowd!

Lino held out a hand. "Hello, Lily Rose from Valentino's. Albertina's my particular baby."

Lily shook Lino's outstretched hand. "I'm glad to meet you, sir."

Lino was called back to the counter, but he sent Lily a wide smile. "Tom! Is this *the* Lily Rose?"

Tom grinned and looked down at the floor.

Lily's eyebrows arched, and she turned to find herself face to face with a young woman, equal to her in height, her lustrous black hair pulled back into a bun, and her green eyes taking in Lily curiously—the mirror images of Tom's.

"I'm Natalia," the girl said. "Tom's sister." She threw an arm around her brother's shoulder.

Lily took a step back, almost bumping into a group of women chatting behind her. The girl was arresting. "I'm charmed to meet you."

"Mama and I have heard a lot about you."

"I never know whether that's a compliment or not!" Lily said above the noisy crowds.

Slowly, a smile lighted up Natalia's gorgeous face. She called to a woman who was serving at the counter. "Mama! Come and meet Lily Rose from Valentino's."

Lily gasped. A beautiful woman in her fifties was weaving her way out from behind the counter. Her chestnut hair was tied in a chignon, and her own eyes were framed with the same long dark eyelashes as Tom's. Natalia maneuvered her way back to the counter.

"Mom, this is Lily. Lily, this is my mom, Gia," Tom said.

"Welcome to Albertina's. We're a bit less formal than Valentino's here." Gia wiped her hands on a cloth and held her hand out to shake Lily's.

"Everything in this store looks amazing. I'm already inspired," Lily said. "I'd love to pick up everything in sight and show it to Mr. Conti." She attempted to send Tom's mom a winning smile. Her gram had fallen for Tom, head over heels, and suddenly, Lily wanted Tom's mom to like her just as much.

Gia smiled, her soft laugh lines crinkling. "Well, I think our Southern Italian cuisine is the best in the world, but then, I'm biased."

"When it comes to Valentino's, we're going to face every challenge under the sun getting produce with the war intensifying. Giorgio might just be inspired by you," Lily said. She tilted her head to one side. "You know, my gram, Mrs. Josie Rose, loves Sicilian food."

"Mrs. Rose is your grandmother?" Gia said. "I had no idea. We all love serving her!"

"She'd be delighted to hear that." Lily bit on her lip. What a day this was turning out to be. She turned to Tom, trying to catch the expression on his face, and as she did so, he looked down at her, his face breaking into a gentle smile.

"Tom. Why don't you show Lily our kitchens? I need to get back to work." Gia indicated toward the increasing queues of people lined up at the counter. "You should come over for dinner sometime, Lily. We can talk more." Gia disappeared off behind the counter. "Next!" she shouted to the customers.

"Head straight for the back door," Tom whispered, close behind Lily.

Achingly aware of him right behind her, Lily dodged barrels of olive oil stacked in the cement-floored corridor. The smell of wine and garlic and cooking tomatoes scented the air.

"Lino opened Albertina's two years ago," Tom said. They came to a halt at the end of the passageway. Tom pushed open a swing door. "It's been a mighty success for him. As you can see, people have embraced it. Come on in." He held the door for her.

Lily stepped into a room filled with spotless, gleaming countertops and neat rows of imported Italian ingredients lined up on shelves.

Tom pulled a string of sausages out of a fridge. "Let's put these babies in the pan. Once we've had a taste, we can slice up the rest and hand them out to customers. You up for that, Lily?" He sent her one of his famous grins.

Lily gazed around the immaculate kitchen, her keen eye taking in every detail. "You bet I am." She faltered. "Only thing is, if I come home with sausages staining this dress, I suspect I'm going to be in more trouble than I've already managed to cook up."

"Well, then, why don't you try wearing one of Lino's great big aprons?" His eyes danced and he held out a man-sized cooking apron.

"All right then." Lily let out a giggle, but she raised her hands in the air and Tom slipped the apron over her head.

"There now," he whispered, gently taking her shoulders and turning her around while he did up the tapes. "This look would knock the whole of the Upper East Side set off their perch, don't you think?"

She looked up into his eyes.

"Okay, Chef, let's get cooking," he whispered.

She stifled her smile, moving over to the stoves, where, a few minutes later, he held out a slice for her on the end of a fork.

"Pork sausages with cheese and fennel. Have a taste."

Lily bit into the juicy meat. "Oh, that is quite tasty. Cheese and fennel…" Right now, she was more than glad she could slip back into Lily the chef mode, because Lily the young woman was sure having her head turned by her handsome co-chef today.

Tom sliced up the other sausages and laid them out on two white plates. He popped toothpicks into each slice.

"Who says you and I can't convince the folks out on Bleecker that these are the very best thing for them right now?" he said.

"Best things I've tasted today," she laughed.

He raised a brow.

"Well, apart from the cannoli, and the omelet, and the sword-fish," she giggled.

He chuckled, holding the door open for her to go first. He turned around once they were outside in the sunshine, holding the plates aloft like a waiter. Lily couldn't help it, she snorted with laughter.

"Something funny?"

"Thinking about how my mom would react to me selling sausages out in Bleecker Street."

Tom narrowed his eyes at the folks lining up already. "Bet you'll get more people in the store buying sausages than I could in six hundred years," he murmured.

Lily sent him a smile.

A man with a little boy was first in line.

"You haven't eaten a sausage until you've tried this special recipe from Albertina's," Lily said.

The man popped the morsel into his mouth and the young boy took a slice from Lily's plate.

"They are a specialty," Lily went on. "If you go in and buy some today, talk to Gia, she will look after you personally."

"I just think I might."

Folks queued and tasted, nodding their heads and going into the store.

Lily bent down to give a small girl a taste.

But when there was only one piece of sausage left, a curvaceous young woman sidled up to Tom as if from nowhere. Lily stiffened.

"Tom Morelli? What on this earth are you doin' handing out sausages?" The woman twirled her long black hair in her fingers and looked up at him from under her lustrous eyelashes.

"I'm showing folks how grand Albertina's wares are, Elena," Tom said.

Lily chewed on her lip.

"Well, look at you, standing out here on the street looking all handsome as usual." Elena picked up the last piece of sausage, her bright painted nails pinching at the toothpick, and popped the morsel in her mouth.

"Elena, this is Lily Rose. Lily, this is Elena Di Maggio. Elena's my neighbor."

"Hello, Lily Rose," the girl said. She held out one of her beautifully manicured hands. "Charmed to meet you, I'm sure."

Lily took Elena's outstretched hand, but in a jiffy, Elena let Lily's hand drop.

"Tom. I want to go to the movies. Are you free tonight?" Elena smiled up at him, showing her pearly white teeth.

A truck blared its horn at a pushcart.

Lily felt constricted on the sidewalk. Of course he had a girlfriend. How could a man as good-looking and funny as him be single? And yet she'd let herself get carried away.

"You know, Tom; I should get home." Lily handed Tom her empty tray and pulled the apron over her head.

Elena laid her hand on Tom's arm. "Are we catching the train or a bus to the movies? Which picture theater do you fancy?"

"Goodbye, Tom," Lily said. "I'll catch up with you tomorrow at work." She took a step away.

"Lily?" He reached out, his hand resting on her arm. "Give me two minutes."

"Flippin' sakes, Tom," Elena said. "Come on. The afternoon's nearly done."

In the pit of Lily's stomach, something uncomfortable unfurled.

"Thank you for showing me Albertina's. I'll see you at work." She turned on her heels, did her best to smile at Tom and walked off.

*

A few minutes later, Tom was next to her, the trays and the aprons and Elena nowhere in sight. "Lily? Wow, you can move fast. Didn't you hear me calling out to you?"

Lily stopped. She folded her arms across her body. She had to be more careful. She was a hardworking, professional chef who was trying for a big promotion, and already, her mom's recriminations rang in her ears most days. The last thing she needed was to get carried away with a co-worker.

But she'd had more fun with Tom today than she could remember in a long time. The green space of Washington Square Park spreading ahead of her seemed like an oasis, bringing her back to reality.

She frowned, stepping out into the street.

Tom grabbed her by the elbow. "*Cara!* Careful!"

A car came to a screeching halt.

She stepped back onto the sidewalk, shaking her head, her arms folded. She tapped her espadrilles on the sidewalk. He should stop calling her *cara.* That was not okay if he had a girlfriend.

"You okay?"

"I'm just peachy," she said, focusing ahead on the square, with its winding pathways, its famous arch. Josie had told her only recently that there was a graveyard buried underneath Washington Square Park. A super old one. Wasn't that *fascinating?* Apparently some nights, there was a thick green miasma floating above the square. Ghosts from the past. "Absolutely grand. Just heading home. Thinking about how I'm going to put those sausages in my wartime recipe book. That's all."

She looked both ways this time and set out to cross the road again. Tom was quiet next to her. They wound their way through the park, where a lone busker with his saxophone was playing jazz near the arch and students lay around on the lawns, catching the last rays of fall sunshine after the earlier breeze had dropped. The trees were throwing long shadows onto the ground.

Lily headed straight on to Park Avenue, carefully keeping her pace up to keep in time with the crowds. The old buildings of the Village gave way to the grander stores and apartment blocks, up toward the skyscrapers in Midtown that pointed the way home. She chatted with Tom about nothing consequential: recipes, work, who was going to the market on what days this week. Finally, she turned into Gramercy Park and stood still, her arms hanging by her side. She had no claim to ask who Elena was, but the girl's face was stuck in her head like a demon.

Until she let out a breath at the sight of the car that was parked right outside her parents' apartment building. Lily brought her hand to her mouth when Nathaniel climbed out.

"Oh, jeepers," she whispered. "Tom, I—"

Nathaniel came straight toward them, hiding behind a bouquet of flowers so huge that a girl could lose herself in it and never come out. A woman passing by stared at him in his herringbone jacket, with a cream cashmere V-necked jumper underneath, and his checked trousers and polished shoes.

Lily screened her eyes from the lowering sun. "Nathaniel."

Tom cleared his throat next to her, and for a brief second, Lily swore his hand brushed against hers, just like it had in the shop, but this time, Lily pulled her own hand away.

Nathaniel came to a stop, reached in and kissed her on the cheek, handing her the flowers. "I didn't want to leave without saying goodbye, sweetheart."

Only then did he stand back and register Tom.

Tom shoved his hands in his jeans pockets.

Nathaniel's face fell.

"Nathaniel, this is Tom Morelli. Tom, this is Nathaniel Carter."

Abruptly, like a picture coming back into motion, the two men shook hands.

Lily tapped her foot on the ground.

"Hello," Nathaniel said, confusion passing over his face.

Lily fought to peer over the top of the flowers. "Tom works with me at Valentino's," she managed. "Nathaniel's… a family friend."

She pressed her lips together. Neither man spoke.

"Well!" Lily kept her voice bright. "I'm going to have a real early night. I think I should go in now."

Tom brushed a hand over his hair. "You want me to meet you here before we catch the train at 2.30, Lily?"

She kept her focus locked ahead. "Sure. Thank you." She winced at her clinical words.

"The train?" Nathaniel said. "Is that a good idea?"

Lily sighed. "Oh, Nathaniel. Don't worry. I'll be fine. I can't, in all honesty, drive around Manhattan for much longer, with gas rationing. It's not the right thing to do. Dad is going to put the car up on blocks, and anyway, it's so early, no one will be riding the subway except us."

Tom stood tall and straight. "I'll take care of Lily."

Nathaniel narrowed his eyes.

"Goodbye, now." And with that, Tom turned around and walked off, his footsteps ringing into the quiet afternoon.

Lily stole a glance at Nathaniel. She was quiet a few moments, resisting the urge to sneeze at the great bouquet that was pinned under her nose.

"They're from our garden," he said. "Mom arranged them especially for you. She said you were poorly."

Lily hovered. "Oh, Nathaniel. I'm sorry. I'm feeling ever so much better."

"So it seems."

There was a silence.

"He works with you?"

Lily stared out at the park. "Yes," she said. And she needed to remember that was all.

"Darling?"

She switched back to Nathaniel. *Please, don't call me darling. Just don't.* And the way Tom had called her *cara*… the two endearments were the same and yet quite the opposite.

"I brought you a photograph of me. I hope you'll remember me when I'm gone." He pressed a black-and-white photo into her hand.

Lily nodded. The games her mom was playing were not fair on him. Not fair on either of them. "Nathaniel…"

In an instant, what had seemed so light and fun and, well, full of hope this afternoon was all coming crashing to a staggering halt. Who was she kidding? They were in the middle of a war. Nathaniel, who clearly had feelings for her, was going off to fight, while she had been off joking with a man who seemed to have a girlfriend.

Lily drew her hand up to her mouth. Admitting the impossible truth to herself was a shock. But the fact was, she had fallen for Tom. She'd had a crush on him for months. Oh, what a potential mess she was creating for herself.

"Oh, darling." Nathaniel reached forward, pulling her into an awkward embrace around the side of the flowers. He rested his head on the top of hers. "Think of me thinking of you every day."

Lily forced herself to take deep breaths into his woolen jacket, the flowers hanging from her rigid arm. She should tell him.

"Goodbye, Lily," he murmured. "You know I'll live for every letter you write."

He held her at arm's-length. Could she, in all honesty, let him go away, thinking she cared for him as more than a friend?

"Stay safe," she said, wincing. Meaning it.

He reached out, his hand resting on her arm a moment, before, giving her one final glance, he went back to his car.

Lily stood on the sidewalk, so shocked at her burgeoning feelings for Tom, at the way she was treating Nathaniel, so aware that she might never see him again once he'd left for war, she could barely move.

Out of the corner of her eye, she saw the curtains in her parents' second-floor living room twitch. Her mom appeared, and Lily stared wide-eyed at her.

Victoria raised her hand, and if Lily weren't mistaken, her mom gave her the thumbs up.

Chapter Ten

Lily

Fall, 1942

A haze hung over New York City for days after Nathaniel left. Three more men from Valentino's went off to war in a swirl of excitement and emotional goodbyes. The basement kitchen was enveloped in a steaming, sweating fog and there was not a forehead that wasn't slick with perspiration, a cook who wasn't sweltering over their station, a temper that did not run short.

Waiters rushed up and down the stairs, running into the kitchen, sashaying out again with trays of food held aloft. Giorgio employed a woman *entremetier* as the new vegetable cook and put the lower kitchen staff on a roster as *communards* to cook the daily meal for the staff. He struggled to find a *tournant* who was experienced enough to run around and help at any station, and it looked like they were going to lose their commis chef.

Rosa, the new dark-haired vegetable chef, was so fresh to the kitchen that she couldn't wrap her head around anything.

"Too much oil there," Lily told the sweating Rosa right when they were in the middle of a particularly busy luncheon service, keeping her tone calm and kind.

"Lily, you have to catch the cooks *before* they mess up." Martina whisked up behind her. "You can't figure it out as you go up and down the line."

"Well, Martina, I'm teaching all the time. Part of learning is making mistakes. If new staff don't mess up every now and then, how will they learn?" Lily said.

Out of the corner of her eye, Lily saw Tom raise his head. Leo, the grumpy *rôtisseur,* stopped working and folded his arms. Lily sighed. She motioned to Leo to get back to work, but he curled his lip at her. Rumor had it that he was frustrated at not being able to get away to the war, being too old, instead, he was stuck here, and to add insult to injury, he was being bossed around by a woman. But everyone was giving Leo some leeway in the kitchen, because while he couldn't enlist, his three adult sons were off to Europe and it was clear his heart was in his mouth every day.

Lily returned to the station in front of her. She would try to be understanding toward Leo. If he didn't make it impossible.

Rosa frowned at the pan of new onions she'd tried to roast into delicate petals in the oven. The scarf she wore to cover her hair was wet with perspiration. "Oh, why did I come to New York? I had the perfect life back in Iowa; engaged to the best beau ever. All I had to think about was choosing wedding gowns!"

Lily laid a hand on Rosa's shoulder. "Believe me, after a few months working at Valentino's, wedding gowns will be the last thing on your mind. Working here tends to have that effect."

Martina stayed where she was. "Rosa, all you're supposed to say is '*Yes, Chef, no, Chef.*' You're a line cook. We don't want to know anything else."

Rosa's eyes flew from Lily to Martina. "Yes, Chef," she said, her eyes wide.

Lily pulled down the outside layer of one of Rosa's onions. "When I do this, I see a nasty, slimy piece of onion. Try again."

"Yes, Chef," the girl muttered.

"Hold any roast chicken until I give the go-ahead," Lily called out to the kitchen at large.

"Yes, Chef," came the call back, and Tom nodded his acknowledgment at her.

Leo placed a platter of perfect roasted meat onto the stovetop. "If the new hire can't keep up, why don't you send her back home where she belongs?"

Lily spoke quietly. "That was out of line, Leo. Rosa is only learning."

Leo folded his meaty arms. Button eyes flashing, he glared at her. "This is why we've kept women out of here. You can't control your emotions. And if you can't take a bit of honest criticism, then you should get back to your sewing circles."

"Back to work. I don't want to hear any more of that nonsense again." Lily forced herself not to say anything further.

Leo's gaze bored into her back.

A half-hour later, Lily was back by Rosa's side. The girl was trying to peel back another set of fresh roasted onions now. "You've undercooked them this time," Lily whispered, keeping her voice low so that no one else could eavesdrop. "You want even browning. Just a little oil."

The girl nodded, but she wiped a telltale hand across her face.

"Cooking is an exact art, Rosa, but it's an art. Go with your instincts. If you think it is time to take vegetables out of the oven, then chances are you're right. Better to check things than burn them. Now, here we go. See, just a touch of olive oil. *Piccolo.* Always, always, a smidgen of olive oil. You'll get there." She rested a hand on the girl's back.

"I hope so," Rosa whispered. She threw a panicked glance around the kitchen, her brown eyes wide. "Thank you, Chef."

"Oh, no point in getting upset over a bunch of onions," Lily said.

Lily moved up the line to Leo's *rôtisseur* station. Giorgio had not employed a new grill chef or a fry chef when the men who had been in those positions had left for war. And now, Leo was sweating it out to cover all the meat dishes, roasting, frying and grilling. So that was adding to his rancor.

Lily stepped in to help him pull a platter of prime ribs of roast beef out of the oven, the meat crackling on the outside and perfectly pink in the center.

"This is evenly cooked, right on temperature. Well done, Chef," Lily said.

"What did you expect?" Leo muttered, wiping a hand over his reddened face. "Burnt prime ribs that remained stubbornly raw in the middle? Come on, woman! This is why we should not be employing more women in this kitchen!" he shouted to the room at large.

"Leo," Lily said, straightening her back. "You've lost more staff this week again. I'm aware it's difficult." She lowered her voice. "But don't take it out on the new hires."

Leo thumped the roasting pan down on the long central bench. "Why don't you go back to your society family and leave the kitchens to us?"

Lily's cheeks burned. "Who is the sous-chef, Leo? You, or me?"

Leo's face shone in the heat. "I have worked here twenty years. You tell me who knows more about this place."

Lily drew in a slow, steady breath and counted to ten.

The kitchen stilled.

Leo ground out his words. "Playing at some job while the war's on? Planning on running back to Mommy and Daddy, finding a suitable man to keep you in the custom you're used to once the men are home? You don't belong here, *Miss* Rose. None of you darned women do. And the sooner Giorgio realizes that, the sooner we can get things back to the way they have always been!"

Rosa stiffened, catching Lily's eye.

But Leo jabbed a finger at Lily's chest. "Once the likes of you women are done messing up honest enterprises, we can go back to having some proper supervision in the kitchen!" He scowled at Rosa too, and she brought a hand to her mouth.

Lily was aware of footsteps coming to a halt by her side. Tom was right next to her, a towel thrown over his shoulder, his own handsome face covered in a fine film of sweat and his chest heaving under his white chef's top.

Others downed their utensils across the bench.

Tom towered over Leo, but before either of them could open their mouths, Lily spoke. "When have I ever told you I'm not serious? When have I ever said I'm not here for the long haul?"

Leo's nostrils flared. Even over the sounds of the bubbling pans and the steaming pots, his breathing was heavy and loud. "You women think you can just waltz off the dance floor into the kitchen and tell us what to do, as if we're staff at one of your fancy tea parties. You'll be well served to get out of here and go have children."

Lily used a carefully controlled tone. "You have children. And you still work."

She'd hit the right note. His mouth worked. He wiped his forehead with a cloth. Finally, he bowed his head.

Lily kept her tone even. "We *all* have folks we love who are gone, Chef. That's why we need to work together back here at home. The divisions that might have once separated women and men no longer mean anything now we're all fighting for a common cause."

Leo stared at the ground. He shrugged, and wiped a hand over his eyes. "Sending women barely out of finishing school in to run the likes of Valentino's is something I never thought I'd see while I drew breath."

"Well, you'd better get used to it, because I'm here to stay."

Leo's mouth twisted, but Lily held her ground, and finally, he shrugged and went back to work.

The kitchen hum started up again, but Lily stood still a moment. This sort of thing was everywhere. She'd read about men disparaging women in every wartime occupation, from volunteerism, to the

Auxiliary Armed Forces, to munitions factory floors. And there was no other reasoning behind their derision other than the fact they were talking to a woman, nothing else.

Fortunately, Giorgio did not model such behavior when it came to this restaurant, and Leo would be well served to take a leaf from his employer's book.

"Lily?"

Lily rounded at the sound of Giorgio's voice right behind her. *How much had he heard?*

She loosened her tight chef's collar. "Giorgio."

"Have you got a free moment to talk with me about something?"

Lily took in a deep breath. "Yes, Giorgio."

Giorgio led her toward the head chef's office. Inside, he leaned on the desk. "After service, I have an important supplier I want you to meet. Are you free to stay after luncheon is done?"

"Yes, Chef." Lily was running on reserves of energy she never knew she had after her early trip to the markets this morning, and she'd spent most of the previous night on her window seat with a selection of Josie's old cookbooks scattered around her, scouring for ration-friendly recipes using a torch to read so her mom wouldn't march in and demand that she stop.

Giorgio's own tired brown eyes were ringed with purple bruises from the long hours he always worked. He called out to the busy kitchen where Martina was working to join them, and the other sous-chef was there in two seconds flat.

"I need you to stay too, Martina, and Tom will be joining us. This particular supplier has to feel comfortable working with you, so I want you to meet him. All of you. How you will work with our valued suppliers is one of the things we'll assess when establishing which one of you two women will be chosen as head chef."

Martina whirled around and left.

"You are doing well, Lily," Giorgio said. "I know there is much pressure placed on you, and on Martina."

Lily caught the gaze of the man who had given her the job she loved. "Thank you, Giorgio," she said. "I'm thankful for all the opportunities you've given me."

Giorgio's kind eyes crinkled under the harsh lights.

Once the kitchen was immaculate again, Lily made her way up to Giorgio's office. He was right. The next head chef had to get to know every supplier. Lily was starting to realize how important all the relationships Marco had built up over the years were to the smooth running of Valentino's, from the restaurant's suppliers to Giorgio, and, vitally, the male kitchen staff.

Lily, Tom and Martina sat down opposite Giorgio's desk, and he flicked on a lamp in the office.

"I'm keen for you all to meet Joe Martinson tonight, our coffee supplier," Giorgio said. "Joe's a character, and someone we don't want to lose. Whoever is head chef will have to know how to keep him onside." Giorgio's expression held a hint of amusement, but his words were deadly serious. "Joe comes in regularly to taste a cup of our coffee. Insists on checking each one of his customers is brewing his beans the right way." Giorgio ran a hand over the stubble on his chin. "Now, more than ever, Joe is vital to us. Our civilian coffee supplies have shrunk with rationing. But some of our guests come to Valentino's for the coffee alone. We change our coffee, we could lose clientele."

Next to Lily, Tom's expression was alert and fixed on Giorgio. Lily forced herself to focus on Giorgio as well. But had Tom really felt something more than friendship for her at her gram's? Had she blown his seeming warmth toward her out of all proportion? Was she just getting carried away?

"Some suppliers are starting to add chicory to their roasted beans, but not Joe," Giorgio went on. "He sells the most expensive coffee on the market, and even though prices were boosted back before Pearl Harbor, Joe was able to stockpile."

"It's excellent coffee," Martina said. "The best."

Lily nodded her agreement.

"Joe migrated to the United States from Latvia and, at the age of sixteen, started roasting several high-quality types of coffee beans separately before blending them, which is incredibly labor-intensive, and not something many people do."

Lily leaned forward in her chair, intrigued by the tale of the artisan manufacturer and his meticulous attention to detail as Giorgio spoke again.

"He began by selling his blended coffee out of a pushcart, going around to folks' houses in the Lower East Side, before moving to a small factory and converting a fleet of Rolls-Royces into delivery cars in the thirties. The back seats are removed and filled with his tins of roasted coffee."

"Sounds marvelous," Lily said.

"I couldn't agree more," Martina said, almost under her breath.

Lily sent the woman a surprised look.

"Joe Martinson's a legend," Tom added. "And an inspiration. I can't wait to meet him, Giorgio."

"All right then, you just wait until you see his Rolls-Royce." Giorgio reached for his suit jacket and waited for them to go out the door, but just as they all stood up, the head waiter, Sidney, appeared at the entrance to the office.

"Giorgio," Sidney said. Sidney's highly polished shoes gleamed under the office lights, and he wore a perky carnation in his buttonhole.

"Sidney?"

"I need to borrow Lily Rose for a while," Sidney said.

"Well, not now, Sidney. I am working, as you can see." Lily turned to follow Giorgio.

Sidney's brow furrowed. "We have an emergency with the party in back. Guests wanted a good-looking girl to sell Lucky Strikes, and unfortunately, I wasn't informed."

Giorgio's face clouded. "The Bank of America group? You say they want a cigarette girl and we haven't got one for them?"

Sidney nodded. "They're recreating old Hollywood at the movies. Everything else is in place. I've hired fake palm trees, mirrors, and leopard-print rugs. The menus are on old Hollywood cinema tickets and we've got a selection of movie theme tunes." Sidney looked at Lily. "No one else in the building can play the part. And they'll all want to smoke."

Lily's gaze flew from Sidney to Giorgio. If she had a dime for every time she fought the urge to snap her cap at Sidney, she'd have a suitcase full of cash, but this took the cake!

"You can't be serious," Lily said. It was vital she met Joe Martinson. If she didn't, she'd be steps behind Martina. "I'm busy, Sidney. Get someone else."

But Sidney took a step closer to Lily. "Oh, but I am serious, Lily. In case you haven't noticed, all my waiters are men. You going to let Valentino's and Giorgio down, Lily Rose? Or are you going to play your part and help us out with one of our most important corporate guests?"

Lily turned in shock to Giorgio. "Surely, not, Giorgio."

"Lily's been working since half past four this morning," Tom added.

"She's a chef, not a cigarette girl," Martina said.

Lily sent Martina a grateful, surprised smile. "Seems that's sorted, Sidney," she said. "I trust you'll fix the problem in a more appropriate manner."

"Wait." Giorgio held up a hand.

Lily stood face to face with her boss and his oldest, most loyal employee. The two men exchanged a look. Sidney nodded at Giorgio, and Giorgio ran a hand over his chin and sighed.

"Lily, dearest." Giorgio sounded genuinely exhausted. "I'm afraid you'll have to go help Sidney tonight." He attempted a smile. "Dearest, it's the war. We all have to do things we wouldn't normally undertake. Me included."

Lily's shoulders sagged. "Yes, I understand that, Giorgio, but still—"

He held up a hand. "I hope, at least, you'll enjoy the atmosphere, see what we can do outside the regular restaurant service. I am sorry—so very sorry—but we cannot let the Bank of America down."

Sidney turned on his heels. "Snap, snap, Lily!" he called down the hallway. "You'll need to get changed, put your hair up properly, and wear red lipstick, rouge and powder. We've got an old costume from the twenties. It will fit you just fine."

Lily stood, open-mouthed, as Giorgio followed Sidney out of the room, leaving her with Martina and Tom.

"Even I'm sorry for you now," Martina whispered. "Sidney's gone too far."

Slowly, Lily turned to the woman. "Thank you," she said, simply.

Martina sent her a nod. "One step forward, two steps back for us women," she murmured.

"Yes," Lily agreed, smiling sadly at Martina.

Martina just sighed and followed Giorgio.

"Lily?" Tom said. His eyes roamed her face. "I'm *so* sorry," he whispered. "I'll wait until you're done. Walk you out? And I'll make sure that Joe Martinson knows we have a fabulous other candidate for head chef."

Lily stared at him. "I can't believe it," she whispered. "Sidney, yes. But Giorgio?"

"*Cara,* if I could put on a cigarette girl costume myself, so you could be spared this, you know I would."

"Tom, please. You have a girlfriend. Don't call me *cara.* Just don't."

His brown eyes darkened. "Girlfriend?" He frowned.

She stood tall.

"Elena?" he whispered.

Lily held his gaze, imperceptibly she nodded.

"Oh, no," he said, his voice barely audible. "Elena's just a neighbor. A friend of Natalia's. She's one of the gang we grew up with, that's all. She was just bored. Saw me and wanted to do something, go to a movie with other friends too. That's all. You didn't think…"

Lily let out a deliberately quiet exhale. She bit on her lip. Now, had she made a fool of herself? Now, had she admitted her feelings?"

Tom cracked a sad, crooked smile. "You'll probably meet some businessman at that banking party who'll sweep you off your feet. And that guy with the flowers on Sunday? He seemed to like you a lot."

"If I'd wanted to date a businessman, I could have already done that." She paused a moment. She lowered her voice. "But I don't."

"Well," Tom said, his voice barely audible. "Then that's good," he whispered and winked.

Lily bit down her own smile, and slipped along the corridor to Sidney's office, feeling extraordinarily lighthearted all of a sudden.

Chapter Eleven

Lily pulled off her chef's outfit, her fingers fumbling with the buttons. She put on the ridiculous cigarette girl costume—short skirt, fitted jacket with a peplum waist and high-heeled shoes.

It was hard to say who she was most annoyed with, Sidney or Giorgio. Giorgio for holding his bossy head waiter in such close confidence, and because he'd made the classic mistake of considering her as a woman first, and a professional second, and Sidney, for seeming so smug at the idea of Lily dressing up in such a demeaning way, and not caring a twig if she missed out on an opportunity that was vital to her training.

And then, Tom... *had* she heard him right? Had he said that he'd be disappointed if she dated someone else?

Lily stared at her unmade-up face in the mirror, dug around in her handbag and found the lipstick, powder and rouge that her mom always insisted she carried, and made up her face. But as she circled her lips into an "O" shape, she had to fight to stop herself from giggling, had to frown sternly at her reflection to settle the sparkle in her eyes. Because both the idea of not dating some cold businessman, *and* dating Tom were equally grand in her books.

Lily paused at the double doors that led into the main dining room, still glowing from the exchange with Tom, determined to get this party out of the way so she could get back to her proper role, and put this escapade behind her.

The beautiful space was being prepared for dinner service.

Someone started switching on the lights, and one by one, the geometric art deco lamps cast a soft glow over the room. Around the rich, wood-paneled walls, the lights came on in turn, their tiny bulbs as delicate as fairies.

Lily breathed in the beauty of Valentino's and remembered everything she loved about this place, remembered how its magic had first inspired her. It was so easy to forget that all the work they did down in the kitchen ended up in this elegant environment, and that the plates of food added as much artistry to Valentino's as did the stunning decor and the warmth that pervaded from Giorgio Conti when he greeted each and every guest by name.

Now, waiters moved discreetly, hardly making a sound on the parquet floor as they set the tables dotted around the room, and the intimate leather banquettes, with two layers of freshly ironed linen tablecloths, the finest soft white napkins, monogrammed porcelain tableware and silver cutlery laid with a ruler. Finally, they set down Baccarat crystalware, turning the beautiful glasses in their white-gloved hands to inspect them for blemishes.

Lily watched while the waitstaff carefully replaced each individual candle on every table, their cream silk shades topping a sterling silver base. A member of staff scoured the floor for marks or traces of anything untoward, even though they had been vacuumed twice today: once in the morning, and again after luncheon service was done.

Nothing was out of place.

More waiters lined up the chairs so that they were arranged just so around each table. Maids carefully dusted the paintings that graced the walls, and staff came in and out with green watering cans for the palms in each corner of the room.

As if in a perfect choreography, a second round of waiters appeared with tiny silver bowls for the breadsticks that would be served to guests.

And, in the middle of it all, like a conductor orchestrating a perfect symphony, Giorgio stood, his pocket handkerchief catching the light, gently checking that everything was just so, supervising his loyal waitstaff with the utmost care, measuring the angles of the cutlery, and lining up his waiters to check that their appearance was on par.

Sidney was nowhere in sight. Lily frowned in annoyance. *Where was he?*

When a head popped around a side door and called her name, Lily turned around.

"Lily?" Vianne Conti, Giorgio's wife, tilted her head to one side and beckoned Lily into the small sitting room she kept at the restaurant.

Lily smiled at Giorgio's beautiful wife. While Vianne did not spend much time at Valentino's, every one of Giorgio's staff adored her, and Lily had to confess that she admired Vianne as well. She listened hard when Giorgio spoke of his talented, independent wife.

"Good evening, Vianne," Lily said.

Vianne's smile was tinged with sadness, her fingers playing at the string of pearls around her neck. Her blond hair was dressed in an exquisitely classic French roll, and faint traces of Chanel No. 5 lingered in the air in her sitting room, decorated with navy-blue sofas with cream piping, and white roses in crystal vases on coffee tables set with table lamps that lent a soft hush to the room.

Lily couldn't help but admire the sharply cut, navy suit Vianne wore, its stylish Eisenhower jacket bloused around her upper body and fitted at her slim waist with a belt.

"Dear Lily, I see you are helping us tonight, thank you. Believe me, dear, I understand that this goes far beyond the call of duty." She reached out and took Lily's hand. "I'm sorry. We had a last-minute *disaster.*" She lengthened the last word and lingered on the final syllable like the true Frenchwoman she was. "Please, take a seat."

Lily sighed and sat next to Vianne on a sofa. "Well, I'd rather ask about your outfit than discuss what I'm doing in this cigarette girl garb." She caught Vianne's cornflower blue eyes with her own smile.

"Ah! The fabric?" Vianne let out a delightful laugh. "But of course. This is one of Giorgio's old suits retailored for the female form. My seamstresses are flat out producing them, and I've managed to do something with the only fabric we have available for blouses: rayon! You know, I never took silk for granted, but I cannot wait until the war is over and we can work with it again."

"Amazing what you can do with lesser-quality fabrics, and without wasting anything that might be to hand."

Vianne nodded, her bow-shaped lips forming a quiet smile. But then she sighed. "Oh, *chérie*. I am so worried about my beloved France. Paris… I have so many dear friends there, Lily. And I have no way of knowing if they are alive."

Lily looked down at the floor. How selfish she'd been, worrying about the silly peplum skirt she was wearing for one evening when Vianne had friends whose lives were at grave risk living under the Nazi regime. "I'm sorry, Vianne. I'm afraid now that Hitler has overtaken Vichy France—"

"Not that the Vichy government under Pétain was any use." Vianne settled on a sofa, crossed her elegant legs at the ankle and held up a silver coffee pot. "Oh it is too terrible to talk of. Coffee? The Valentino's special blend for you?" Her French accent was lilting and soft. "At least I can offer you the dignity of a break before you have to take on this ridiculous assignment." She eyed Lily. "Giorgio asked me to apologize for him, dear."

"Well, I admit, this is not in my job description." She only hoped she'd live it down. If Martina got talking with the rest of the *brigade de cuisine*, telling them all how Lily had been forced to dress up and entertain the clientele, she'd lose any hard-won respect from the older male kitchen staff that she'd managed to earn so far.

But even Martina had seemed sympathetic tonight, showing a side of herself that Lily had never noticed before. If they were to work together closely, presumably one of them as head chef, and the other as *chef de cuisine*, then they had to get along. And, at least Giorgio had asked Vianne to apologize. That was something.

Lily folded her hands in her lap, eager to learn more about the mysterious, wonderful Vianne, keen to talk of the older woman's wild success in the fashion industry, about her fashion atelier further down Park Avenue, and the way she managed to blend her career with a perfect modern marriage. Vianne and Giorgio were legendary in New York, often gracing the covers of magazines, or featured in double-page spreads in their lovely apartment on the first floor of the building that housed Valentino's.

But Lily also knew the woman sitting opposite her had a dramatic, private story after the last war, but no one spoke of it. Lily admired Vianne's strength and resilience, her rise in the New York business world, so very dominated by men, and hoped that a tiny part of it would rub off on her.

Vianne handed over a cup of perfectly blended coffee. The flavor was exquisite, fine and yet with deep notes that were rich and satisfying. They *had* to keep Joe Martinson on board.

When Vianne offered her a plate of biscotti, Lily took one and placed it on her saucer.

"Lily," Vianne said. She looked out the window a moment, where crowds dashed up East 63rd Street, many of them working women amongst the older men. "You see, while Giorgio and I are working day and night to try and adapt to wartime conditions, some folk, some wealthy New Yorkers, our customers, well…"

"They still wish to carry on as if there is no war at all?"

Vianne nodded. "Sidney, as our host, knows many of our most valued customers, *chérie*. He relates to them quite well and he brings in people who are valuable to us."

You mean he's a snob.

Vianne drew her coffee to her lips. "And, tonight, we have a contingent of Broadway-loving bankers and their guests wanting to recreate the atmosphere of the theater in Valentino's, complete with cigarette girls. We need all hands on deck, and we appreciate you coming on board to help us. Our waiters will be working overtime, and you, dear, will be paid handsomely for helping out. I'm sorry if Sidney offended you in any way." Vianne shook her head. She drew her eyes downwards. "He is not sometimes subtle in his approach."

Lily raised a brow. "Well, you know my loyalty is to you and Giorgio, and if you need me to help out tonight, then I'm here, Vianne."

Vianne nodded. "Thank you, dear." She shifted in her seat. "I also want to talk to you of a matter of some... delicacy."

Lily placed her coffee cup down. Was Vianne about to take her into her confidence? Lily smoothed her hands over her embarrassingly short skirt. Why would a woman of Vianne's importance want to confide in her?

"Your mother is holding a luncheon in one of the private back rooms, tomorrow, Lily. I want you to be aware so that you do not get—how shall I say it—a shock?"

Lily rolled her eyes and crossed her legs in her seat. "Mother has not said anything to me about luncheons."

"Your mother phoned the restaurant today and booked a private room. She is, however, concerned that her guests may be upset if they happen to bump into her daughter. She says it may offend them to see you dressed as a common working girl."

Lily held her hand to her mouth at her mother's arrogance. "I can assure you that I never treat my job here as anything other than a privilege. I'm sorry about my mother's attitude. It is in stark contrast to my own."

Vianne's expression was kind. "Several ladies from the Upper East Side set are her guests. She told me in complete confidentiality that if Katherine Carter sees you, it would be displeasing for her, given your close relationship with her son, Nathaniel."

"No." Lily stabbed out the word.

Vianne frowned. "Is there something that you have not told us? You are not engaged to this boy?"

"I am not engaged to Nathaniel Carter. Nothing of the sort." Lily's teeth pierced her bottom lip.

Vianne spoke in a more intimate tone. "I value my independence above all else and I fought hard to keep it and have a wonderful marriage. However, if marriage plans are being made with a family as established in their traditional ways as the Carters, then they may well restrict your availability to work. No doubt, as his fiancée, Mr. Carter would expect you to be available to spend time with him several evenings a week. We would need you here six nights a week were you to be chosen as our head chef. As wonderful as you are, you could not be two places at once."

Lily let out a loud breath. "Oh. Honestly, I will ensure, specifically, that I am out of sight of my mother and her guests tomorrow, and I am utterly committed to training as head chef. I have no arrangement with Mr. Carter and I have no feelings for him, nor any desire to enter into anything other than a family friendship. My mother has hopes that things will be otherwise, but I assure you this is a fantasy on her part."

Vianne nodded. "Giorgio asked me to talk to you. He felt that it would be best handled from one woman to another."

"In the instance that Tom should… be called to war," Lily managed, her voice barely a whisper, "you can rely on me entirely if I'm fortunate enough to be chosen as head chef at Valentino's."

Vianne's beautiful eyes locked with Lily's.

Lily flinched. Did Vianne notice how she'd struggled when talking about Tom? "I have no desire to get engaged. Please, understand that."

"If you ever change your mind about the Carters, let us know, Lily. We will support you, but with a family like his—"

"*Lily Rose?*" The unmistakable sound of Sidney hollering in the hallway outside the door cut Lily off. "Where is that Lily Rose?

I told her I needed her immediately, and she is not here where I need her to be."

"I will not let Valentino's down, Vianne," Lily said. "I promise." On an impulse, she leaned forward and squeezed the woman's soft hand. "Valentino's is my home. And everyone here is family to me. Including—"

"Sidney." Vianne smiled up at the man.

Sidney burst into the room. His eyes landed on Lily and he cracked a smirking smile "Ah, perfect," he said. "You will do so very well."

Lily caught Vianne's gaze and the older woman shook her head and raised her hands in a shrug that could only be regarded as French. As she made her way out of the room, she placed a hand on Lily's shoulder. "Thank you, *chérie*," she said.

"Sidney." Lily held the waiter's beady gaze. "I will do this on one condition."

He folded his arms.

"It never happens again, you don't start any rumors in the kitchen about it, and from here on, you remember you are not my boss, and if you want to speak to me, you consider me as Giorgio's trainee head chef, Marco's possible replacement and every bit as skilled as yourself in my profession, not as one of your inferiors, not as some waitress you can boss around."

"But I don't have any waitresses," he said simply. "We only hire men for the restaurant."

Lily held her ground.

His eyes glittered a moment, but then he sighed. "That was more than one condition."

"Yes, it was."

He held the door open for her.

"No, after you," Lily said.

She did not move and made him leave first.

Chapter Twelve

Lily

The private room in the back of Valentino's glinted with diamonds by the yard. Women compared their Harry Winston necklaces and their earrings by Cartier. Seafood platters sat, resplendent, on polished mahogany tables decorated with silk lamps and white linen. Waiters stood discreetly in the shadows.

Sidney had Lily checking in all the sable coats when the guests arrived. She had neatly labeled them all and stored them in the anteroom next door. Now, at half past ten, cigarette fumes thickened the air and, outside the window, a storm had begun. Rain poured down in sheets and thunder boomed over Manhattan. Lily trudged around the heated room in the red skirt, the matching tight red satin jacket and the pillbox hat. The Lucky Strike box filled with cigarettes made her shoulders ache and her neck hurt. No one was bothered by the weather, and the snippets of conversation that Lily heard were nothing to do with war. New York heirs and heiresses mingled with bankers and businessmen and the latest Broadway stars.

Just after midnight, a shriek came from across the room. The group of guests whom Lily was serving turned stone silent and a girl in a honey-colored silk dress that flowed to the floor and looked to be worthy of a thirties Hollywood premiere pushed her way through the crowd, coming to a breathless halt opposite Lily. She placed her hands on her hips and wiggled her fingers. "Hey, cigarette girl, I swear you're the spitting image of someone I once knew!"

Lily's hands curled around her box. She was staring at Penelope Hudson; a girl she'd met at debutante classes. Around Penelope, a few guests whispered behind the backs of their hands. If Lily's mother ever found out she'd been spotted by a girl they knew in this get-up, she'd forbid Lily from setting foot in Valentino's again.

"Oh, my," Penelope gave her a wide-eyed look before dissolving into laughter again. "Well, hi-de-ho, Lily Rose. Honey, I hate to ask, but do tell me. What on earth are you *doing?*"

Lily's hands were clammy on the box. She swiveled her head around to see what other folks had heard. One of the waiters gave Lily a worried look and trotted over to the gramophone. The room swelled with Glenn Miller's "I've Got a Gal in Kalamazoo."

"Hello there, Penelope," Lily said. The sooner she could get out of this outfit, the better, but the party was showing no signs of slowing down. Taking a deep breath and holding back the retort that wanted to bounce right out from her lips, Lily forced herself to focus on how delicious Joe's coffee was instead, and how she'd ensure that next time he came by, she'd meet him and learn all she could.

"Well, I'll be…" Penelope whistled. "Look where *you* ended up. Guess all that education was wasted on you, dear."

"Oh, you know how it is, Penelope," Lily said. "*Dearest* Giorgio wanted me to help out for a lark. So, what could I do but be a good sport?" And, of course, this was as close to the truth as could be. She was helping Valentino's out tonight. She lifted her chin.

Penelope placed her hands on her hips. "Is that right?"

Lily stepped closer. "Dear, don't tell anyone you discovered me. We're trying to fool people that I'm the real deal. And Giorgio will snap his cap at you if he thinks you know who I really am."

Penelope pursed her lips.

"He might not allow you to come to Valentino's again either, honey, if you let the cat out of the bag," Lily said.

She waited.

Penelope cleared her throat and stood a while. "In that case, I'm off to find someone around here who wants to jitterbug." She eyed Lily up and down, curiously. "Nice to see you, dear. Glad you haven't lost that sense of humor we all loved back in debutante school." Penelope attempted a smile.

"Charming to see you too," Lily murmured. She tipped her hat to the girl. Sense of humor? Ha!

It wasn't until the early hours of the morning that the party began to wind down, and Lily finally had the chance to unstrap the box from her aching, heavy shoulders. Abandoned Baccarat crystal, monogrammed plates and silver ashtrays loaded with cigarette butts adorned the coffee tables. Outside, rain slivered down the windowpanes and the sound of thunder rumbled in the distant sky.

Lily bent down to pick up a couple of stray champagne glasses that were tipped over on the thick carpet. She poured all traces of bubbly liquid into a metal bucket and took the empty glasses to the bar. Just as she was doing so, a hand landed on her shoulder. She turned around to come face to face with a well-dressed gentleman in his sixties. His eyes twinkled, and he pointed at Lily's cigarette box.

"Hello there. Don't suppose you'd give me one last packet?"

In spite of the tiredness and irritation she felt at this whole escapade, Lily reached for her box. "Certainly, I can, sir," she said. "I haven't a huge selection left, but you can take your pick of what's here."

The man selected a box, and he lit up, contemplating Lily, his eyes narrowing in the smoke. "Forgive me for saying this, but you speak very well for a cigarette girl." The man had a slight accent himself: Eastern European.

"Well, that's because I'm not, strictly speaking, one at all."

"If I hazarded a guess, I'd say that's a very social accent you have there." He placed his free hand in his trouser pocket and jiggled some coins around.

"I cannot wait to get out of this costume, I confess."

He shook his head in sympathy.

Lily sent him a smile. The need to remind herself that she was returning to the job she loved seemed overwhelming, and the gentleman standing next to her had kindly eyes. "I'm actually training to be head chef," she said, rubbing her shoulders.

Those eyes widened.

"I was supposed to be meeting our coffee supplier tonight, but the Contis asked me to help out here instead. I'm Lily Rose."

"Well, the coffee's very good around here," the man said. "If I don't say so myself."

"I think it's the best in New York."

The man fluttered his cigarette in the air and sent her a smile. "Well, what do you know. I'm Joe Martinson," he said, holding out his hand. "And I supply the coffee beans."

Lily took a step back. Oh, what a night this had been! If she tangled herself up in one more awkward situation before she made it out the front door, she swore she'd go and bury herself in the cloakroom and never come out. "Oh, you are kidding me. Mr. Martinson? I was absolutely looking forward to meeting you this evening, and I'd promised myself that I'd make sure I got the chance to talk to you next time. But here you are!"

"Here I am!" He waved his cigarette in the air.

Lily thought fast. "Of course, I may have missed out on meeting you tonight, and I was awfully sore about that, but I had the chance to sample some of your coffee with Mrs. Conti before I came up here, and guess what?"

"Do tell."

"It kept me going all night. I haven't yawned once." Lily placed her hands on her hips and smiled straight into Joe Martinson's eyes.

"Well now, I'm glad you appreciated it, and I'm sorry I didn't get to see you demonstrate how you would make a cup of my coffee, but I saw the other two trainees, and they both did a fine job."

"Oh, good…" Lily sighed. "I did learn tonight how you went to all the extra effort of roasting different types of high-quality coffee beans individually before blending them together. And I learned how important it is to do your work uniquely, in a way that no one else does, and I also learned that taking that extra effort makes all the difference if you want to get ahead."

Slowly, Mr. Martinson nodded. "If you took that in, then I think that Valentino's will be in good hands with you in charge. It was a pleasure meeting you, Lily Rose. And good luck with your training."

Lily shook the man's hand and sent him the brightest smile she could at nearly two in the morning.

"Evening, everyone."

Lily turned sharply at the sound of the voice.

Tom was framed in the doorway, one hand on the brass handle, chef's top still on and legs encased in those faded denim jeans. He started at the sight of Lily in her cigarette girl outfit.

"Hello there, Tom," she said.

Oh, lovely Tom. He'd promised he'd wait for her, see her home safely, and here he was. Lily sent him a grateful smile, a thrill uncurling at the fact that he'd done that for her.

One of the last remaining guests in the room let out a low whistle. "Right on the beam," the girl murmured. "Hello, baby… Carlotta and I were just sayin' how we needed some company. You want to bebop with us in a club? We're all decked out and ready to go."

"I'm sorry. I really can't." Tom's tone was mild. He came over to help with the heavy tray Lily was carrying and took it to the bar for her.

"*Cigarette girl!*" one of the women hollered. The sumptuous, decadent room turned dead still. The remaining waitstaff stopped moving, and everyone stared at the drunk society woman. "Fix your superior chef a whiskey. Hurry up, cigarette girl!"

Lily's nostrils flared. "Excuse me?" She pinched in the words that she wanted to hurl back.

"I don't think so," Tom said. He came back to stand next to her, wiping his hands on the cloth he still had thrown across his shoulders. Had he been cooking downstairs all this time?

Lily risked a glance at him. His expression was hard to read, but he touched her hand softly with the slightest movement, his fingers feathering her palm.

"Oh, come on. Have a drink. And afterward, the clubs will be a gas. Carlotta and I are all fired up. Why else did you come here except to play with us, handsome?" The woman tilted her head at Tom.

"I came up because I've been working," Tom said evenly. "And Lily, the woman you're calling *cigarette girl*, has been here nearly twenty-four hours straight. Since she went above and beyond to work this party after her full regular shift as *sous-chef*, I thought I'd offer her some food and a safe ride home."

Lily looked doubtfully out the window. Rain continued to pour in sheets down the glass.

Through the smoke haze of her cigarette, the woman's eyes narrowed into two slits. "*Cigarette girl*," she hissed. "Go back to your dingy, drab life and leave the good-looking guys alone."

Tom slipped his hand downward and curled his fingers around Lily's.

Lily's eyes rounded, and she didn't even try to hide her grin. His hand was warm, fingers soft.

As she stood there holding Tom's hand like a schoolgirl, a middle-aged man with a cashmere scarf across his shoulders appeared at the door to the private room. "You coming out now? We've made a real dent in Giorgio's cigar collection, and we're off," he called to the women.

The women shrieked and staggered out of the room.

"I should speak to Giorgio about them," Tom muttered. "In fact, I will. That was disgraceful. Giorgio would be appalled."

"No," Lily said. "Don't."

"Why?" Tom's jawline was set.

The waiters bustled around them, and Tom picked up a tray and started collecting dirty plates. Lily worked alongside him.

"I can't afford to complain, Tom. I don't want to risk upsetting Giorgio. You know how he values his guests, and he may not see things the way we do. Believe me, he'd probably just think it was a joke."

Tom turned to her, his dark eyes serious.

Lily lowered her voice. "If I lose my job, my mother will ensure that I never work again." She softened her tone. "Tom, you've got to understand, working at Valentino's is my only ticket to freedom."

"Your parents are giving you a hard time again. Why do they do that?"

Lily stacked four dirty plates on top of each other. "Like Josie said, I'm supposed to be moving to the Upper East Side, anything below Fourteenth is out of bounds." She glanced at him under her eyelashes.

Tom placed his tray on the bar and he looked at her. His eyes bored into hers. "What do you want, Lily?"

She held his gaze. *You... but I can't have you. I shouldn't let this go any further, because my mom will interfere, and I'll lose you. She'll make sure of it.* "Something real," she whispered. "To be with someone who understands what it is to live with passion, to have your life wrapped around both a career you love, and the person you love all at once. That's my dream. Nothing more, nothing less."

"Sounds good to me," he whispered.

Lily held her breath. She swayed as Tom's velvet gaze met hers. Lily closed her eyes.

She felt Tom's arms wrapping around her waist. He scooped her up in his arms and carried her down the hall.

"You are exhausted, *cara*," he murmured.

Lily half heard him, but the hallway was swaying violently. Further down, he opened a door into a room. Lily's eyelids drooped. She just managed to realize that she was looking at one of the Contis' luxurious private salons set up for guests from out of town. In the middle of the room, there was a huge bed with a sweeping art deco wooden feature set into the wall behind it, and deep golden covers with a collection of soft pillows a girl could sink her head into for hours.

"One of the Contis' guest suites for family," Tom whispered. "Yours tonight."

She yawned deeply, rocking on her heels, and the room spun.

"It's pouring outside. If anyone says anything, I'll tell the truth. That you were exhausted."

"Tom…" She wanted to fall onto the huge bed and never climb out.

Gently, he took her arm and led her over to the bed. He reached forward and turned back the soft, silky sheets.

A wave of exhaustion engulfed her. "But you need to sleep too." Her words were foggy, indistinct.

"Don't worry about me. Lily, can I ask, do you keep a change of clothes at work? Because if you do, you can shower downstairs and then get straight on with your day in the morning."

"Always. Don't you?" Unable to keep her head upright, she slipped off her shoes and sank down onto the bed.

"Of course," he whispered. "Go to sleep."

"Tom?" she said.

He stopped, halfway to the door.

"Where are you going?"

"I'll make a pile out of the lost fur coats from the cloakroom," he said. "I'll sleep outside your door. You can lock it if you like."

"No, you can't do that," she whispered, managing to send him a warm smile. She stretched, and the sound of rain beat on the windows. Lily pointed at the chaise longue in the far side of the room. "You've been here since three a.m. too."

He stopped, hands in his pockets. She saw the ravages of tiredness on his face. "Are you sure?" His eyes lingered on hers, darkening.

Lightning flashed outside. Thunder rolled overhead.

"Don't you know there are ghosts all over New York? You can fight them off for me," she whispered. "I can have something of an imagination in the middle of the night."

"Is that right?" he whispered.

Lily closed her eyes. "Goodnight, Tom," she said.

She heard him lay down on the chaise longue. "Night, *cara*. Sweet dreams."

"Sweet dreams, Tom." Lily sank back on the soft feather pillows and everything turned black the moment she rested her head.

Chapter Thirteen

Lily

Sunlight gleamed through the gaps between the rich velvet curtains that adorned the guest suite the morning after the party for the Bank of America and their wealthy guests. Lily sat up in the bed to which she was unaccustomed. She glanced around the beautiful room. Tom was gone, and everything was quiet. She sank back down on her soft pillows, lifting her wrist to check the time: eight o'clock.

A silver tray with a glass of orange juice, a fresh croissant, and little dishes of jam and butter sat on the side table by the bed. Lily's eyes softened. Next to the tray was a note on creamy paper, folded into a rose. She bit on her lip as she opened it.

> *You were sleeping like an angel when I left this morning. Enjoy your breakfast, and don't rush downstairs. You've worked your heart out for Valentino's. I've told Giorgio you slept here, and he is absolutely glad you did. I didn't mention those awful guests, but I think they are lucky I didn't! By the way, Giorgio mightily appreciates your help last night. He told me so himself. And I admire you for it, cara. Although I still think you're the best chef we've got.*
>
> *Tom x*

Lily read the note twice, hugging her knees, and grinning like a fool. Finally, she stretched, and reached for the breakfast tray he'd left her, cherishing every bite of the buttery croissant. Once she was done, she slipped out of the bed, searching for her shoes.

She made up the bed deftly, ensuring the room looked just as it had when she'd practically fallen into it last night. Lily picked up the tray and was almost across the room when she heard the sound of a familiar voice coming through the panels in the wall.

Sidney.

And her mother.

Lily froze. Victoria's luncheon. The one Vianne had warned her about. The one where she was not supposed to show her face. Lily shook her head. While it was acceptable to her boss for her to sell cigarettes in a pillbox hat to his wealthy clientele, her own mother couldn't face laying her eyes on her own daughter doing the job she loved. There was something mighty wrong with both of those situations, but right now, it was all too hard for her to fix.

"The fresh flowers will arrive mid-morning, and we've set up the room with the table configuration exactly as you requested for your luncheon, Mrs. Rose."

Lily took tentative steps across the floor, willing everything to stay in place on the tray and not make a sound.

"It looks utterly perfect. Everyone will be delighted, I'm sure. Given it's a delicate occasion for Mrs. Carter, I think the pale pink roses will do very well. Shocking red would be too much for a woman whose son has just gone to war."

Sidney's murmured reply was inaudible, but at the sounds of footsteps coming closer, Lily staggered backward into the room.

She stared in horror as one of the wooden panels in the wall opened with a jolt.

For one horrible second, she was face to face with Sidney. His gaze roamed from Lily's bedroom hair to the tray with the rose in its dear little vase in two seconds flat. Eyes gleaming, he pushed the panel shut with a firm click.

Lily sank back further into the room and closed her eyes. No one in their right mind would tell gossipy Sidney a thing. He lived for talk of New York's upper echelons. And the fact that he'd just seen her with a romantic breakfast tray in a private room? Lily could only hope and pray it was not going to come back and bite her.

Lily was in the kitchens by half past nine, freshened from a quick shower in the ladies' changing rooms, and in a clean chef's uniform from her locker. The sight of the busy cooks stirring up rich sauces, whipping up pastel-colored confections and chopping fresh produce from the markets was enough to inspire her again, even after being up half the night. Tom glanced up at her from his station, his hands working deftly. He winked at her.

Lily shyly returned his smile before glancing around the room. A filmy haze had set in the kitchen. The heating that Giorgio was so proud of was on, sunshine or not. Everyone's faces were slick with sweat up and down the line. Last night's storm had given way to a sticky morning.

Martina was already bustling up and down the line, checking the quality of market produce. She came to a halt in front of Lily. "Morning. I…" she lowered her voice. "The way Sidney spoke to you last night was horrible."

Lily stilled. "Oh?" Martina had shown some compassion toward her when Sidney had spoken to her so dismissively yesterday afternoon, but Lily was not confident enough in that to assume her co-sous-chef was warming to her. After all, Lily's efforts to try to be friendly had failed for months. And the fact that they were now in competition had seemed to render the possibility of them ever seeing eye to eye even more remote.

But now, Martina threw a gaze around the crowded room. She seemed to be weighing up her options.

Lily waited. Truth be told, she hated the bad blood between them. To that end, she sent Martina an encouraging smile.

The other girl fiddled with her cuffs. "I didn't sleep last night after what he did to you." A multitude of expressions passed across her face before she spoke again. "The truth is, I'm sorry if I've come across as kind of rude to you. It's the pressure in here. I don't cope with it that well. It's not your fault." She compressed her lips. "Even if, deep down, I think you're a mighty talented cook and I worry that you're better than me. There, I've admitted it."

Lily nodded hesitantly.

"Sidney should not have treated you that way," Martina went on. "Just because you could be a fashion model yourself, you didn't deserve it and it made me think about how I was treating you. Not well, I'm afraid, when you've been nothing but friendly toward me. And," she glanced around the busy kitchen, "to be honest, I'm sick of the way Leo is speaking to you as well. Don't be afraid to stand up to him." She narrowed her eyes.

Lily chose her words with care. "You know, I hate that we two women are pitted against each other."

Martina sent her a flicker of a smile. "Well, perhaps we should stick together a bit more. Not add fuel to the fire."

On an impulse, Lily held out her hand.

Martina shook it, a faint dimple appearing on her cheek.

"Chef?" Jimmy appeared next to Lily, his face decorated with stubble and his green eyes patterned with red train tracks. "Can you come over here a moment?"

Lily wove her way around the main bench, past the sweltering line chefs, to Jimmy's station.

Jimmy stopped filleting fish. "Nearly every appetizer on the menu is seafood today, Chef. Cape Cod oysters, Blue Point oysters, littleneck clams, and shrimp cocktail, along with sole. I don't know who went to the markets, but they sure fell in love with the darned seafood."

Lily pored over the menu that Jimmy had next to him, her eyes lingering on the picture of a soldier, and the sign saying, "*Support the people defending America.*"

"Well, Jimmy, in that case, I will fillet sole alongside you." Lily rolled up her sleeves, with a feeling of lightheartedness and positivity after her chat with Martina. It was a relief, to be sure, and, last night, things had not been so bad. She'd met Joe Martinson. *And Tom…*

She hid her own secretive smile and boned and filleted, concentrating on the soft flesh of the white fish. The more she got to know Tom, the more she was coming to fall for him.

"Chef?" A few minutes later, Leo was next to her. He was puffing and panting, his face already flushed.

"Leo."

"Giorgio wants *boeuf bourguignon* on the restaurant menu for luncheon. But all I have is mutton. Mutton! I will not work with it. I take it you are responsible for this fiasco?"

Jimmy worked on beside her, his brows drawing together.

Leo regarded her. "These days, I may as well be a housewife making dinner for her husband."

"This is not a dialogue we are going to have," Lily said, remembering Martina's words, feeling strangely even more confident in standing up to the difficult man beside her knowing that she had more support amongst the senior staff in the kitchen. "Go back to your station, Chef. We all have to make do."

But Leo stayed right where he was. "Five years ago, we were serving sauerbraten of beef with potato pancakes, English lamb with bacon and *vert pre,* filet mignons…"

Lily closed her eyes. "I know, Chef. But now, you need to get back to work."

"You mark my words, Miss Rose. Mussolini will bring order back to Europe. And we will have our roast prime ribs again." Leo stood tall.

Lily raised a hand to her head. "For goodness' sake, Chef."

But Leo's jawline was set. "You would never have gotten this job in my old country. If we had the likes of a proper leader like Il Duce, you'd be at home where you belong."

"*What?*"

"Sirloin steaks, steak minute, roast prime ribs of beef au jus, imported Prague hams. These are the things we have lost since you sailed into this kitchen! The world has gone mad and it will right itself again. Mark my words. And Italy will shine once more."

Lily fought to maintain her own calm. "Well, you can be thankful to President Roosevelt that we still have French lamb chops, minute steak, spaghetti with meat sauce, and *boeuf bourguignon* on the menu in spite of the *atrocities* Il Duce is overseeing in your homeland. Back to work, Chef!"

Leo thrust out his chest. "How *dare* you speak like that about—"

But Lily held her ground. "When I said this wasn't a dialogue, I meant it. It's a monologue. I'm talking, you're listening. Now that's enough and get back to work, Chef!"

Leo's hands dropped to his sides. He reddened, opened and closed his mouth and stalked away.

Over the steaming table, Martina's expression was warm.

Half an hour later, after she'd done helping Jimmy, there was a ready pile of delicate filleted sole for her mother's society luncheon. The shrimps were peeled, the oysters shucked and the littleneck clams rinsed.

Lily noticed the young commis chef, Paul, wandering around. She took him up to the top of the line.

"Tom?"

"Yes, Chef?"

"Paul will help you this morning. You have a heavy round. Jimmy will be sending a lot of fish your way."

"Yes, sous-chef." Tom winked at her.

Lily rolled her eyes at him and then sent him a grin, but next to her, Paul sighed with delight.

"Gee, I'm honored. Thanks, Chefs, I won't let you down," Paul said.

"Come on then, Paul." Tom turned back to his prep.

"Here we are!" Giorgio came through the door from the air-controlled rooms with two waitstaff, looking as cool and suave as ever. "Who says we can't impress upper-class ladies during wartime?"

The waiters placed a beautiful ice sculpture on the main counter. Jimmy and Leo stood back to make way for the stunning creation, a life-sized swan, her wings carved intricately and tucked into her sides.

Giorgio started to clap, and the kitchen staff followed his lead. "My friends, I salute Julius, whose talent is insurmountable, both with pastry and with ice. I've asked him to take over as my official ice sculptor, since I lost Henry to the war."

Lily clapped with the rest of the staff. Julius must have been up since well before dawn to create this beauty, while managing to oversee his staff to ensure that all the day's baking for the restaurant was done. Suddenly that buttery croissant she'd had for breakfast felt even more indulgent.

"I would like to say one more thing, my dears," Giorgio said.

The room was silent, only the sound of pots bubbling and the low rumble of the ovens piercing the quiet.

"You are the heartbeat of Valentino's. And this," he indicated toward the swan, "is an example of what our wonderful team can do when times are difficult."

A cheer rumbled through the *brigade de cuisine*.

"If we can create beauty in the ugliest of times, then we are surely achieving something worthwhile."

Compliments flowed from the ladies' luncheon. The plates sent up with the filet of sole bonne femme came back elegantly clean with not a scrap of food wasted, and Tom's delicate raspberry ice earned him charming messages from the society women.

Lily was helping Julius with the final touches to a Chantilly layer cake when the kitchen quietened.

Sidney was at the doorway, clearly searching the room before he spotted Lily.

"Kitchen staff?" Sidney called. He clapped his hands. "We have a visitor. Lily Rose? Back up in the kitchen, now, I trust?"

Lily's hand floated up to her mouth.

Katherine Carter was magnificent in a white mink coat. She swept across the kitchen and clasped Lily into a close hug, brushing her red lips against Lily's cheek and assailing her with Guerlain Shalimar.

"Mrs. Carter, please." *What horror was this?* Surely her mother had not encouraged Katherine Carter to swan in here like a mermaid into a dank pool of swarming fish?

But Katherine held her at arm's-length, and everyone stared, the male cooks' jaws dropping to the ground at the sight of the beautiful woman, her coat swinging open to reveal a tantalizing pale pink dress, and legs that went on forever, encased in forbidden silk.

Lily bristled with embarrassment. The silk should have gone toward parachute making for the war. She tried to flinch away. Her mother and her friends' attitudes to the war, and to the people working so hard down here, seemed to horribly mirror the stance of the women she'd encountered last night. Lily felt a deep sense of shame pass through her, and she was not able to say a word because Katherine was an important Valentino's client. Lily could only stare in horror at the floor.

Sidney. He'd seen her with the remains of her breakfast in a guest suite and he'd served his revenge.

"Darling," Katherine said, impervious to Sidney's satisfied, simpering smirk. "Darling girl." She turned to the kitchen at large, putting on a voice that was worthy of opening exhibitions or of charming presidents. "I am so pleased to say that this girl, this vision of beauty, is doing her bit for the war. By being here with you all, by gracing you with her presence, you have no idea what she is giving up."

A flush crept across Lily's cheeks, her body freezing in place, and she cast about wildly for the nearest exit, only to have her eyes fix, unmoving, on Martina's confused face. *Oh, no, please no. Let's not ruin my inroads with Martina before they've had a chance to get underway.*

Lily swallowed, but her throat stuck.

Katherine strengthened her grip on Lily's arm. "My son," she said, dropping her voice to dramatic effect. "My son, Nathaniel, went away to war yesterday. And as for this delightful creature, whom we are all hoping will be closer to the family than anyone could have dreamed of, when Lily and Nathaniel were walked around Central Park by their nannies in their prams... well, let me just say that it is Lily's letters that my son will be waiting for while he's at the front."

Lily sent an entreating glance around the room. Tom! Where was Tom? She couldn't bear it. But Sidney folded his arms, tilting his head toward Katherine, sending a frown Lily's way.

"Here she is, working away in the kitchens with you all, while my dear Nathaniel goes to war. Who would have thought I would be standing here addressing you in a basement, while my friend's precious daughter works as one amongst you folks?"

Leo dissolved into silent laughter and Lily shrank back into herself, still unable to locate Tom amongst the gathering of chefs around the long bench, tall hats obscuring her view, dishwashers with tea towels thrown over their shoulders, prep staff faces red, hands roughened from chopping, washing, scraping peelings into trash bins, staring in open-mouthed wonder at the woman, the likes of whom they probably only saw in the society pages they used to wrap fish and chips, their faces drawn with the endless, day in, day out sweat of working down here. Steam clung around them all in a close, matted fog above the steam table with its dishes holding prepared food, while pans bubbled on stovetops, sauces needing to be stirred, desserts baking in ovens. She'd ruin the rest of service.

"Mrs. Carter, I thank you, but we all need to get back to work," Lily said.

But Katherine only turned her innocent wide blue eyes toward her. "I just hope that you all realize what a wonderful, talented girl you have working with you here. That lunch was just delightful. Charming. You've all made my day—which, I can tell you, should have been one of the very *worst* and *hardest* days of my entire life."

"Shall we bow?" Leo muttered.

A murmur went through the kitchen staff.

Lily pulled at the high collar of her chef's top. Wildly, she cast about for a friendly face.

And then it happened. She caught Tom's eye. He was standing to the side, by himself, and for one split second, he held her gaze, only to turn away from her. Head down, he went back to his station.

Katherine turned her shining eyes to Sidney. "May I borrow Lily to come up and say goodbye to her mother's guests?"

And then, Lily held up a hand. "I can't. I'm working, Katherine. Please." Her eyes fought through the seemingly overwhelming crowd of people, her staff, her workmates, people she had to face again and again every day. Her privacy shattered. Everything she'd fought to hide emblazoned for everyone to see. And all the while she sought out Tom. But in the awful, interminable silence, she couldn't see him. She could only hear him. Hear him working, tossing a pan about.

Lily was overcome with a feeling of lightheadedness. Her chest tightened, and her face, neck, ears felt impossibly hot. She found herself fighting back tears, fighting the urge to run right out of this room, up to Central Park, where she'd sit on a bench and throw crumbs to the pigeons. Because they would not judge her, would not regard her because of where she came from. And that was clearly too much to expect when it came to human beings.

Katherine squeezed Lily's hand. "I understand, dearest," she said. "And, actually, we don't want to upset your mother, do we? I know how sensitive dear Victoria is to the way you've chosen to grace Valentino's kitchen with your presence as a working girl for the duration of the war. That is, until Nathaniel returns."

Lily closed her eyes, and in the face of the silence from the entire kitchen staff, Katherine and Sidney paraded back out the door.

Leo came up behind Lily and spoke in her ear. "Mommy doesn't approve of Lily dearest playing cook in kitchens? Thought so. Wonder if Giorgio knows this is only a temporary thing for our Lily."

Lily's stomach hardened, but she stood there, just like she used to, when her mother needled her at home.

"She's not like the rest of us. I knew it. And here it is. How on earth could we possibly rely on her to be head chef, when she's going to scamper off the minute the war ends?"

With a start, Lily turned to Leo, pushing her way past him, rushing up the stations toward Tom. She no longer cared who saw her. What did it matter? All her secrets were laid bare now. But she could not, would not, lose the friendship, the deepening relationship, she had with Tom. And, right now, the fact that this mattered more than anything else was abundantly clear.

Martina ordered everyone back to work, told them to get on with it and not ruin the rest of service. The party was over, Martina said. Lily, barely aware of this, thankful, in some strange way, for her co-sous-chef's ability to take control, came to a sudden halt by Tom.

But he only turned back to his station, the expression in his brown eyes clear. He looked like she had broken his heart.

Chapter Fourteen

Lily

Lily raced out of the kitchen the minute the excruciating service was done. The afternoon was a nightmare. Leo had swept around, head high, imitating Katherine Carter's soft accent at every turn. In the end, Lily had told him to be quiet again, but he'd laughed in her face. Tom had been silent, but Martina had maintained a seemingly respectful silence, focusing the staff, once even laying a hand on Lily's arm.

Outside in the corridor, Lily backed up against the wall, waiting for the rush of departing staff to pass her by. Once things were clear, she dashed into the changing rooms, pulled off her cook's outfit, threw on her blue suit and rushed out the door to find Tom.

But in the wine room, she came to a skidding halt.

"Sidney," she said, marching up to him, her fists clenched into balls of steel.

He lifted his head from where he was inspecting the aged wine collection.

"Ah, Lily," he said, looking as innocent as a puppy in a park.

Lily's breaths hitched. She glared at him, painfully aware that she needed to find Tom, and fast. She had to catch him before he left for home. "I never want to have that happen again," she said, grinding out the words. "You have no right to bring my family friends down to the kitchen, in front of my staff, humiliating me like that. It was unprofessional, and rude. I should report you to

Giorgio. However, since he is so busy doing at least three jobs, my warning will have to be sufficient."

But Sidney just folded his arms. His eyes crinkled in amusement. "So, engaged to Nathaniel Carter, Lily? Do have us plan the wedding breakfast. You know, everyone down there will be cooking for you soon, so I don't see what the problem is, darling. Only thing is, I'm not sure what you were doing last night in that suite with handsome Tom Morelli?"

Lily lurched backward, aghast.

Sidney leered closer to her. "Let's get one thing straight, Lily Rose. When you are married to Nathaniel Carter, you get to tell me what to do. Until then, I am your superior, and your elder, and I have Giorgio's confidence in all matters to do with the restaurant. If a guest as illustrious as Katherine Carter wants a private tour of the restroom facilities, we will give it her. Do I make myself clear?"

Lily folded her arms. The cool, muted room had emptied and was quiet. "And let me make one thing clear. I am *not* engaged to Nathaniel Carter. I never will be, and as a trainee head chef, I am more than your equal here. And if I become head chef, I will say who is admitted to my kitchen, and you will ask me first before you bring guests into the working part of the restaurant. Because my staff are not show ponies for you to put on display!"

"Oh, funny you insist so hard that you are not engaged to Nathaniel." Sidney pulled back the cuffs of his black jacket and looked at his watch. "Because, this morning, I heard that you were."

Mother.

Right then, the sound of Tom and the young commis chef Paul's voices filtered from the stairs.

Lily glared at Sidney. "My private life is no concern of yours."

She swept off to the sound of Sidney's chuckle. And as she clattered up the stairs, she swore she heard him humming a tune.

Tom was halfway up the stairs to the staff entrance, talking with Paul. The young man's voice rang out, high-pitched and excited, over the clatter of shoes on wood.

"Tom!" Lily called, once she was out on the sidewalk and Paul had disappeared.

Tom stopped.

Finally, he wheeled around.

Lily came to a standstill next to him, her chest heaving, horribly aware of strangers jostling around them. A couple of folks cursed as they pushed their way past.

"Hey," she said, breathless.

"Hey there, Lily." He sounded perfectly polite, but he strode on down the busy street only stopping when he came to the corner of Park Avenue, his eyes darting to find a gap in the crowds.

Lily pulled up next to him. "None of what she said about Nathaniel is true."

He turned the corner and stopped by the pillars outside Valentino's main entrance. "It's fine. No need to worry."

Lily kept an eye on the double oak doors of the restaurant. She'd rather run all the way to Josie's house than endure another encounter with someone from her mom's entourage. "Nathaniel Carter is the last person I want to marry, Tom. I have no feelings for him." She wrung her hands.

Tom frowned.

The sounds of buses and cars seemed to make an awful din.

Lily's pulse pounded and something drove her on. Something strong was unfurling within her, something she could not control. She could not live with herself if she'd hurt Tom today. She could not live with herself if she'd lost his friendship. Because he was a man she needed to believe in as deeply as she believed in herself. His friendship was growing to be so important to her that she would fight for it and she would fight to convince him that her regard for him was genuine. Her feelings for him were growing and she could not bear him having the wrong idea about her.

Lily rubbed her hands down her skirt. "*Tom.*"

He glared at the ground. "You shouldn't limit yourself. He could offer you a life beyond compare."

Lily's mouth went dry.

Dense gray clouds shifted in the sky way above the tall buildings. The atmosphere was loaded. It needed to rain.

Lily chose her words with care. "The other day, when you and I cooked together at my gram's house, well, that meant more to me than anything."

He jerked his head up to meet her eyes, only to swing off down the busy avenue, striding toward the elegant lampposts that heralded the subway entrance. He skipped down the stairs, fast.

She kept pace with him, jerking her arms away from other commuters, pushing her hair out of her eyes, her forehead slick with sweat.

He swept along to his platform. His eyes raked over her face, and she looked up at him. "Tom, if Katherine Carter's speech meant anything to me, I'd be following her, not you." Lily clenched her fists. She meant it.

He shook his head slowly, but she finally seemed to be getting through to him. "*Cara?*" he croaked.

She almost sagged into the grimy train station wall.

But despite the crowds surging around them, the shouts, the whoosh of incoming trains, it was as if they stood in a bubble. And right then, Lily knew that she wanted to make something of what was between them, because, for the first time in her life, she felt the stirrings of an affection for a man that was real.

His face furrowed with concentration. In the middle of the crowded station, his words came out as clear as if they were in an empty room. "It's not just Nathaniel. I can see you don't have feelings for him. But what about after the war? Men will come back. Wealthy men of your own class who can give you the life you've always had, or more."

"I hate that idea." She whispered the words. "Don't insult me. Please."

"What are you trying to say to me, Lily? Because I—"

"I'm trying to be myself." Her voice cracked, and she attempted a smile, but his eyes raked toward the incoming train.

"You deserve the best, *cara*. I can't give that to you." Swiftly, he pulled her toward the incoming train, taking her hand and weaving through the crowds to make the doors. "You going to the Village?" he shouted.

She threw up her hands and nodded. *Yes, if you're going there.* Hardly knowing what she was doing, she squeezed in next to him on the train.

Closing her eyes, her body swayed and jolted in time with the train, keeping her close, sandwiched next to him, her head next to his shoulder. She took in a ragged breath, only aware of his body so close to hers, the steady pulse of his breathing, the feel of his navy-blue coat, the lure of his hand right by her side. She remembered the feel of his hand in hers just last night, when he'd held it while those other women had humiliated her.

And now, here they were.

Once the train came to a juddering stop, Tom eased his way through the other commuters onto the platform. Lily stumbled and he caught her, tucking her arm into his, and her whole side burned at the feel of his hand on her arm, as if it were electric, on fire. He led her along the crowded streets, and she walked with him, wanting to shout her feelings for this man. For that was the truth of it, even though she could only admit as much to herself. And all around them, folks rushed home from work, women, men, everyone wearing dark coats and felt hats, their faces heavy with war, work, worry.

When they came to Washington Square Park, Tom wheeled around to face her. "*Cara*," he said.

She searched his face.

"Come and sit down with me." He indicated a bench under the Square's biggest old tree.

Lily nodded. When he sat down, he rolled up the sleeves of his coat, and his breath curled in the cold afternoon air. He stared at a pigeon on the path, frowning as it picked and pecked at a small crumb.

"There's no easy way to tell you this. I've been selected by the draft board. My mom called the restaurant this morning. She was wired at eleven o'clock."

Lily gasped, the warmth she felt at Tom's touch disappearing in an instant. "No." A coldness hit at her core.

"I have to report to a military induction center in a few days for my physical. I'll find out which training camp I'm being shipped to once I've sworn my military oath."

"Oh, Tom." She brought her fingers up to her lips.

"It's been eating at me all day." He turned to her, gently pulled her hands from her mouth, and held them in his own, his fingers caressing hers. "I probably should explain why I'd put off enlisting." A muscle tweaked in his cheek, and his brown forearm rested on his leg. His eyes were the color of rich honey today, and they held unfathomable depths. "The reason I hadn't enlisted was because of my mom."

"Go on," she whispered, she wanted to rest her head on his shoulder, but instead, her eyes roamed every contour of his face. A face she might not see again for months. This war was dragging on. "Tell me everything." She let out a sardonic laugh. "It's not as if I have any secrets that haven't been laid bare today." *And false ones, at that.*

A cold breeze stirred the leaves in the great old tree. "My family came from a long line of fishermen, and the women were the passionate cooks, but my grandfather, Mom's dad, owned a restaurant in a little seaside village called Marzamemi, on the southern tip of

Sicily. When my mom was born, her mother died, so Mom grew up with her older twin brothers, whom she adored, and her dad."

"Marzamemi," Lily breathed. "What a lovely name, Tom. How awful about your grandmother."

Tom heaved out a sigh. His expression clouded. "After my grandmother's early death, my grandfather threw himself into running his restaurant, and into raising his three children. He was determined to make the restaurant the best in the region, and he was proud of his two handsome boys and his beautiful daughter, Gia. When the First World War began, Mom worked at the restaurant from the age of thirteen, replacing her brothers. She learned fast, soon perfecting famous smoked swordfish, Sicilian pesto made with ripe tomatoes, basil and almonds, croquettes made with cheese and mint and our arancini made with ham and cheese."

Lily sat back. In Italy, food could have a bible all of its own.

"In the local town square, the Piazza Regina Margherita," Tom went on, his voice low and calm, "my grandfather's restaurant had white linen-covered tables, and chairs painted blue, with huge pots of geraniums dotted about. In the end, people came from all over for his cuisine, including his *panelle,* his delectable crispy fritters which, apparently, only Gia can master."

A couple of kids ran around playing with a dog on the lawn in front of them, their hands encased in bright mittens.

"But then," Tom's voice darkened, "the twins were killed in the war."

Lily's eyes rounded. "Both of them?"

He nodded, his jaw tightening, staring straight ahead. "And, in 1918, my grandfather died of a broken heart."

"Poor Gia," she whispered.

"She was eighteen, and deeply in love with my father," Tom said. "After the devastation of war, he married Mom and carried her off to America, with big dreams of his own."

"And then he did not live a long life," Lily whispered. She turned to Tom, but his eyes were fixed straight ahead and yet were far away.

"No," he said, his voice soft. "He died far too young." He was silent a moment. "You see; I didn't enlist because my mother has already endured so much loss. I couldn't bear to do that to her. Natalia and I are all she has."

Lily was silent. A shiver passed through her.

He turned to face her. "Come home with me." He punched out the words. "Come and meet my mom properly. Now. Because you might not—"

Lily's heart skipped. She held a finger up. "Don't," she whispered, her heart full for his mother, for all she had endured. "I would love to come and talk more with Gia."

He stood up, waiting for her, holding out his hand, and they walked, fingers entwined, Lily feeling more at ease now that everything was out in the open between them.

Chapter Fifteen

"Welcome to the street where I live. MacDougal Street. An Italian family on a street with a Scottish name," he said.

She walked next to him, out of Washington Square Park toward MacDougal Street, in the part of New York that was as familiar and beloved to Lily as the palm of her own hand. And now, as well as being Josie's home, the Village held a special place in her heart because of Tom.

Around them, the sounds from people's wirelesses and chattering filtered out onto the sidewalk from the typical row houses of the old Village, some of them with wooden artists' studios perched on their rooftops.

"I love it," she said.

Tom tipped his hat to a couple of passers-by, who looked at Lily with interest.

A little way down MacDougal Street, he pulled out a set of keys and opened the front door of one of the row houses. Inside the tiny foyer, a stairway only just wide enough for two people to pass through rose up to the floor above.

"After you," Tom said. "This is where we live. Go right on up to the top floor."

Lily's insides fluttered with nerves as she moved up the narrow stairway.

But the moment Gia answered the door wearing a cooking apron, her face spread into a beautiful smile. "Lily," she said. "What a wonderful surprise." And as they stepped inside the kitchen of the Morelli home, she kissed Lily on the cheek. "It's good to see you again," she said, but then her pretty black eyes snapped straight to her son, her chestnut curls loose.

Gia moved to Tom, pulling him into a tight hug, holding him and closing her eyes. When she pulled back, Lily saw the quick, telltale way that the older woman wiped her cheek.

"Making *caponata*?" Tom's lilting accent seemed more pronounced here at home.

"Yes, *Tesoro*." Her gaze swept once more over her handsome son, before she turned back to her cooking.

Lily folded her hands in front of her now, not knowing where to put them, not wanting Tom or Gia to see how they shook.

Behind Gia sat two fat purple eggplants, an onion, garlic, olives and a bunch of bright red tomatoes on the narrow kitchen counter. Pots filled with green herbs lined the freshly painted windowsill, and canisters of ingredients were stacked neatly underneath. A scrubbed wooden table sat in the middle of the room, so like Josie's big wooden table. Lily felt at home.

"Lily?" Gia asked. "You are very welcome to stay for dinner."

Lily felt Tom's eyes on her.

"We'd love you to stay," he said.

"As long as we won't get in trouble with your folks for keeping you away from your family?" Gia added.

"I don't imagine my mom will be up for a huge dinner tonight," Lily said, and then blushed. The last thing she wanted to mention was the embarrassing events of today. She focused on the feast of colors in the kitchen.

"You interested in cooking with herbs, Lily?" Gia asked.

"My grandmother lives near here, and she introduced me to them a while back."

"Why don't you show Lily our garden, Tom?" Gia said.

Tom leaned on the countertop. "Sure."

Lily stared at the gorgeous ingredients. She needed to focus on something else. Food. The last thing Tom or Gia needed was her panicking about his leaving for war when Gia was so obviously trying to make her feel welcome and focus on normal family things. "Mrs. Morelli?"

"Call me Gia, Lily."

"Gia, would you mind if I watched you cooking *caponata* when we come back up? I'd love to learn how to make it."

"It's one of our favorite Sicilian recipes." She eyed her eggplants. "I'll begin the preparations, while you go down with Tom."

Lily nodded. She could barely trust herself to speak. This home, this loving mom. "Thank you," she whispered. "I appreciate it."

"My pleasure," Gia said.

Once they were outside, sun shot through the deep gray clouds of the late afternoon, bathing the plot out back in the last bright light of the dying day. Rows of neatly tended vegetables spread out: peas, parsnips and potatoes were planted in neat lines, along with acorn squash and pumpkins.

Lily shaded her eyes against the sun, looking out at the garden. "Oh, Tom," she breathed.

He stuck his hands in his pockets. Lily bent down to run her hands over a fat pumpkin.

"The garden belongs both to this house and the one next door. We knocked down the fence and made a communal vegetable and herb plot in '39 when war broke out in Europe."

"I love this," she said. "It's magical."

"Every family in these houses is Italian. We put our heads together and knew we had to do something to make what was happening in our home country more bearable. Elena, whom you met outside the deli, lives next door. You're in the Italian heartland of America here. And this is our own victory garden."

Lily tensed slightly at the mention of Elena, but she couldn't let that ruin her appreciation of what was in front of her eyes. The possibilities… What she was looking at seemed richer than anything she'd seen in an age.

"Every family in the two buildings is self-sufficient when it comes to vegetables," Tom added. "We all have our own sections of the garden to take care of."

"What a wonderful idea." There was a large communal garden behind the apartment building where she lived with her own parents. It was all lawns and neatly tended shrubs. What would her parents say to the idea of a produce garden?

"I know there's animosity in some parts of the country toward us Italian Americans, not to mention German Americans and Japanese Americans, but, as you see, we are doing our bit to be patriotic." He lifted his head, his expression serious.

Lily bent over a row of herbs outside the back door, reaching out to stroke the swaying parsley, the sprigs of oregano. "Just like Giorgio."

"Lily—"

Lily stood up. Her eyes searched his face, taking in his features. Imprinting them on her memory while she could. "Oh, I hope it's only weeks until the war's done. If I had my way, it would be days and you would not be leaving."

He spoke in a quiet voice. "The fact is, we've already lost two Italian boys from these houses."

She turned away from him, crossing her arms, closing her eyes.

His voice behind her was soft. "There are a lot of mixed feelings about Mussolini in this neighborhood. He divided us during the thirties." He heaved out a sigh. "To be honest, when I'm drafted, I hope that I end up in Italy somehow. I've never been there. *Cara,* I want to see it for myself."

Lily drew her cardigan closer around her body. "It's suddenly cold out here." She turned to him.

He stood there a moment, his eyes intent on her. "Let's go back inside."

Upstairs, Gia was adding the finishing touches to a round dining table in a cozy room off the kitchen. Natalia stuck her head around the kitchen door. She wore a light blue cotton dress, and her black wavy hair hung softly around her shoulders.

"Hey, Lily," she said, her eyes flashing to her brother. "Tom?" she said, her voice softening. She reached out toward him, resting a hand on his arm. "Mom told me," she said. "I... don't know what to say." Her eyes averted back to their mom.

The expression on Tom's face said everything. *Don't upset Gia.*

Natalia sent Tom a sad smile and lingered in the doorway, as if unsure where to go.

"It's good to see you again, Natalia," Lily said, touched by the genuine emotion she had toward her brother.

"I'm going to freshen up," Tom said.

Gia's eyes followed her son as he disappeared down the hallway a moment. She straightened herself. "Come and I'll show you how to make *caponata.*"

"Thank you, Gia." Lily followed her into the kitchen, and Natalia moved over to the window to look out at the street.

Gia's hands moved quickly. "I don't like to overdo the olive oil." She poured in a couple of small glugs into a cast-iron pan and placed it over the heat, before adding the eggplants, now cut into chunks, and some chopped oregano, seasoning with a pinch of salt. "Otherwise, you end up with a caponata that's swimming. I've eaten that, and it's not good. And I also don't like my eggplant to be diced too small, otherwise, the pieces soak up the olive oil and you don't get that lovely creamy flavor and texture that's so important in this dish."

Lily watched intently, moved and inspired by the way Tom's practical mom was able to focus on her cooking. Maybe, it was the one thing that helped her escape, just like it was for Lily. As Gia shook the pan, turning the eggplant nice and golden, Lily realized that once again, cooking, her love of food, of creating beautiful recipes that made people happy, was going to have to be the thing to get her through while Tom was away at war.

Gia added onion, garlic and black pepper and kept cooking another couple of minutes.

"Next, you add a few capers and olives to add depth to the flavor," she said, while adding a drizzle of vinegar.

"I loved your garden," Lily said. "I can smell the fresh ingredients coming out in the cooking."

Gia stayed focused on her sizzling pan. "It was a necessity with the war."

"Yes."

Gia sighed. "We Sicilians know how to survive in hard times, Lily." She stopped stirring a moment. "Tom's grandparents, my late husband's parents, are still there."

Lily brought a hand to her face. "I didn't realize."

"Tom's dad and I migrated to America more than twenty years ago. Things were… complicated back home in Sicily. Then along came Mussolini, and now, the war. I hate to think of all our fellow villagers, cousins, living under the fascist regime."

"Oh, it's impossible for us to imagine, safe back here." Lily shuddered.

Lily watched over his mom's shoulder while Gia added the chopped tomatoes to the *caponata*, letting it cook a while longer and sprinkling it with parsley. "I suppose Tom has told you he wants to go to Italy if and when the Allies finally invade. It seems ironic, you know? We come here for a better life, and my son could go full circle to fight in the country we left behind. Sometimes, fate moves in ways we would never have imagined."

"He did tell me," Lily said. "I would imagine you never thought he might even have an inkling of returning under circumstances of war." The last word came out soft, and she held the older woman's gaze a moment.

Gia tossed a green salad. "Yes, well, it's something I've seen before."

Lily helped Gia and Natalia bring a ceramic bowl of crisp salad greens into the dining room, setting out the warm *caponata* on a huge colorful dish. Natalia sliced a loaf of crusty white Italian bread and set it out on the table.

Tom came back in a pair of fresh jeans and a white shirt, looking as if he'd showered. His dark hair was combed, and still damp.

Lily had to force her eyes away. All she wanted to do was look at him.

"Sit down, Lily," Gia said. "You too, Tom. Natalia and I will serve. You have a guest, my son." She swatted him playfully with her tea towel.

Tom dodged her, his face lighting up in a boyish grin, breaking the more serious mood back in the kitchen.

Gia tossed the salad with a little olive oil and vinegar. On the table, there was a plate of bright red cherry tomatoes and basil.

"In Sicily, we'd eat this salad with buffalo mozzarella," Gia said, "made with the milk of the Mediterranean buffalo, but, sadly, there are some things we cannot get here."

"It's gorgeous," Lily said, savoring the explosion of fresh flavors that burst onto her tongue. Even the bread tasted exotic. "Your produce is incredible," she said to Gia. "And your cooking is wonderful."

They tucked into the delicious food for a while.

Tom poured them glasses of red wine from a carafe. "Lily is facing a huge challenge at Valentino's. She and our other sous-chef are having to fight it out for the role of head chef. Lily could be singlehandedly running the restaurant just as our access to good produce diminishes and people's wallets become increasingly tight. Not only will she have scores of jobs at stake, and staff to manage, but this is one of the finest restaurants in New York we're talking about. If the food isn't up to scratch…"

"Folks have already been talking of a black market for poultry. But how Valentino's is going to do without enough meat is anyone's guess," Gia said.

"Meats and fats are just as much munitions for the wars as tanks and airplanes," Tom agreed.

Lily took a break from eating, the exquisite food waking her taste buds and intensifying her appetite. "I think the only way forward is to gradually introduce organ meats to the clientele of Valentino's, to be honest."

"Good luck." Natalia wrinkled her nose.

"My daughter, the American." Gia gave Natalia a playful swipe on the arm.

"Americans are going to have to be convinced more and more to eat livers, kidneys, hearts, brains, stomachs and intestines," Tom said. "And that includes you, Nat."

Natalia finished her plate of food. "Well, excuse me, but I'm going to get dessert and leave this charming conversation to you."

Gia reached up, her hand brushing her daughter's, while Natalia collected their empty plates. "Lily, I don't begin to think I could be of any real help to you, but, if there's anything I can do while Tom's away, I'd love to help."

Lily caught Tom's eye, his expression full of encouragement and warmth. Seemed Tom's mom shared not only Lily's love of cooking, but her need to keep busy when things were tough.

"That would be wonderful," Lily said. *If I get the job, which, based on my current performance, and today's little escapade in the kitchen, seems less and less likely.* She bit on her lip uncertainly and turned her attention away to Natalia, swaying back into the room holding a creamy ricotta cheesecake dusted with icing sugar, its crust made of golden baked biscuits.

"Have some of Mom's ricotta cake. Enough talk of organs in the American diet."

"Well, that looks stunning," Lily said, genuinely fascinated by the delectable-looking dessert.

Natalia placed the tart down, and lifted a knife, addressing everyone. "I'm planning to sign up as a radio operator somewhere in the Pacific, so I'm outta here. I could not do what you are doing, Lily, that is for sure."

"Oh, I'm sure the food will be delectable where you're headed, Nat," Tom said.

Natalia sliced the tart and grinned at him. "Don't remind me," she said. "That's why I'm making the most of Mom's cooking before I leave."

Lily thought she'd quite gone to heaven when she tasted the rich biscuit crust and the ricotta filling that melted in her mouth. "Gia," she said, "I can in all honesty say that I am in awe of your skills. The texture of this is sublime. The crunch and the heavenly rich center is something truly special. I wonder if Giorgio knows about this Sicilian dessert."

Gia's face lit up into a smile. "I am honored, dear." She turned a shade of pink. "That really is a compliment from a chef like you."

Natalia coughed, and from under her eyelashes, Lily caught the expression on Tom's face. He was grinning at his mom.

And in that moment Lily realized, breaking into a smile herself, that was quite something for a man who was about to go away to fight in a war.

After they'd had coffee, Lily hugged Gia, who urged her to stay in touch. Outside, people strolled in the twilight, families out walking, couples arm in arm.

"The *passegiata*," Tom said. "People walking out in the evening. Just like in Italy."

"Tom?" Lily asked, standing below the house on the sidewalk.

He stood in his doorway with his hands in his pockets.

"I'm of a mind to walk all the way home this evening. I don't want to get on the train."

He hesitated a moment. "You'd like me to walk with you, *cara?*"

She smiled at him and nodded.

He stepped onto the sidewalk, looking down at her, reaching out and tweaking one of her curls that had fallen across her cheek. "So beautiful," he whispered.

"Oh, they always go astray," she said, barely aware of her voice.

Slowly, he drew his hand back and turned, walking next to her. When they came to the end of the street, he reached out again, and took her hand in his. And Lily walked the whole way home next to him in silence, in an aching, wonderful, unbearable silence, his warm hand enclosing hers.

Once they came to the edge of Gramercy Park, Lily looked up at him, the dark shapes of trees tantalizing beyond the locked gate of the old square.

Tom's eyes darkened a little, and she brought a hand up to her cheek. Silently, he took it, and held it a moment.

"I have the keys to the gated park," she said. "Would you like to walk in there with me?"

"I'd love that, *cara*," he whispered. "As long as your parents won't shoot me."

Lily sent him a grin. She turned, moving toward the park. Her hands surprisingly sure and steady, her heart hammering, she unlocked the gate.

Lily stopped at the end of a familiar winding path, standing at the foot of a grand tree, its branches curling overhead, the only sounds were the soft clips of people's feet on the pavement outside the high wrought-iron fence and the breeze rustling through the trees. The soft twilight lent a magical feel to the garden, the trees and the flowers that lined the winding gravel paths glistening after the recent heavy rains.

The air turned still.

Lily focused on the trees, their silhouettes fading into the night. The sound of her own breathing seemed louder than anything else.

"We'll miss those blue jeans of yours in the kitchen, Tom," Lily said, all at once shy.

He raised his head, meeting her eyes. "I'll be doing a lot more marching than cooking over the next few months, and I'll be learning how to clean guns rather than frying pans."

Lily shivered. *He was a cook, not a soldier.*

He took a step closer. "The whole time I'm away, just remember one thing. I'll be fighting for… what I'll be leaving behind, *Cara.*"

He reached down and took her hand and she raised her head to look up at him. Their eyes held, a question in his. She tilted her head back, leaning closer. Reaching out, he tucked his hand under her chin. Lily's arms moved up around his neck, and he leaned down, his lips meeting hers, ever so soft.

"Write me, *cara mia,*" he whispered into her hair.

She squeezed her eyes shut.

Tom stroked her hair with the tips of his fingers, his head resting on hers, and they stood still while soft breezes whispered the secrets that only fate knew through the trees.

Chapter Sixteen

Josie

November, 1942

Josie swished her breakfast dishes around in the soapsuds and then polished them with a fresh tea towel until they shone. That would lessen Emmeline's daily chores when she arrived at ten o'clock.

Josie sighed at the sight of her empty, silent kitchen. Back in the twenties, there wasn't an evening when this room was quiet. Most nights, her warm kitchen was filled with the laughter of friends. By six o'clock, she'd have a happy group gathered around her scrubbed table, sipping wine, nibbling on crackers and delicious olives and cheeses, before Josie pulled a luscious, hot bubbling meal out of the oven for them all, and then off they'd go, out for the evening to the local theaters, the comedy acts or the Village jazz clubs.

What a renaissance they'd all had, thinking they would never get old.

Josie gathered her navy-blue cape from its hook on the wall, and adjusted her felt hat, her shoulder-length thick gray hair hanging lustrous below its brim. Her blue eyes in the mirror on the wall were still as bright as her granddaughter's. On her way out, she smiled at her father's self-portrait by the basement door. He seemed to wink right back at her, rakish, even though he'd long departed this world.

She'd put him there, right where she'd see him each day, to remind herself that she had him to thank for the life she enjoyed now. A struggling artist all his life, eking out an existence here in the Village, he had finally hit the jackpot in his eighties, when a serious collector fell in love with his entire body of unsold work, bought it all, and sold on one of his stunning modern canvases of Manhattan to the Met. After that, Peter Quigley's paintings had become collectors' items.

Josie's father had left everything to her, and thanks to the proceeds of his estate, she'd been able to sell the rather formal apartment that she'd lived in with her husband Hank, who had died young. She'd bought her very own Bank Street house, right smack bang in the middle of the Village where she'd grown up. It hadn't taken long to reconnect with old friends, nor had she had any trouble making new ones. It was as if she'd picked up where she left off when she married Hank and moved to the Upper East Side. Problem was, now many of her old friends had passed away. So, things were quieter these days.

Josie clicked her basement door closed behind her, and trotted up the stone steps to the sidewalk, gathering her cape closer around her body against the swirling winds that scattered brown leaves down the street. She strode through Washington Square Park, reveling in the cold air on her cheeks, in the magnificent golden colors of the trees against the blue sky, her feet in their lace-up boots crunching on the gravel paths.

Rushing to the subway, she ignored the slight breathlessness that seemed to dog her these days, swinging into the train, her sharp mind taking in her fellow travelers. They looked worn, worried.

In Midtown, Josie swept through Grand Central Terminal, head high, the lofty marble ceilings ringing with muffled announcements, people still rushing to go someplace, despite this dreadful war.

And that was it. Something to do, someplace to be. That very idea was what had sustained her in the face of aging. While her remaining friends were starting to lose the energy she still seemed to possess, Josie had soul-searched, and come to the conclusion that in order to cope with old age, she needed a purpose, because if she didn't have one, then she may as well be dead.

During her marriage, she'd not had a purpose. All those years seemed to blend into a whirl. And if Victoria had her way, her darling Lily would suffer the same fate. Josie knew that, were Lily to marry Nathaniel, she'd be as good as locked up in a gilded cage. The rules would be rigid, and she'd never achieve a thing for herself.

But the problem was, Josie knew, as she pushed on out to 42nd Street, that she refused to overtly interfere. Jacob adored Victoria, and Josie had maintained a strict rule of no unwanted interference in their marriage. What she had done was try to give Lily all her love, because she recognized so much of herself in that gorgeous girl.

Josie marched toward Bryant Park, coming to a halt, quite puffed, outside the grand New York Public Library, where the usual group of smiling volunteers stood around outside the building's majestic facade. Josie flipped her cape behind one shoulder and made her way to the wooden stall that was set up for the Books for Victory campaign.

"Good morning, Mrs. Rose," a young woman said.

Josie sent the women her most winning smile. It didn't bother her a fig that she was nearly eighty and working alongside a team of women Lily's age.

"Mrs. Rose, rather than sorting today"—the young woman intercepted her as she approached the expansive piles of books already stacked just outside the library's heavy front doors—"could you man the booth? Inform folks who drop books off, or who want to inquire about us, that books in poor condition can be accepted for scrap paper, that we will take rare books to raise money for the Victory Book Campaign, and that we are not requesting children's books, or books on women's subjects."

"Oh, what a shame."

The girl smiled. "If folks do want to donate those books, we will give them to families in industrial communities where manufacturing for the war effort is being carried out."

"Excellent," Josie said. She accepted a warm cup of coffee from another young girl who looked all of seventeen and who was operating the urn today, curling her gloved fingers around the mug, and thanking her. She took a reviving sip. "Very well," she said.

"Any books appropriate for our men in the military will be sent to warehouses," the girl went on. "After that, they'll be distributed to nearby army, navy and merchant marine bases." The girl shook her head. "So far, we've had to turn down thousands of books. Totally unsuitable, I'm afraid."

Josie felt her lips twitch. *Totally unsuitable?* It was what she'd been all her life.

In fact, as a mother with two young boys approached with a bag of books, and Josie leaned forward to greet and direct them, she worried that her history, her story, had been quite wiped clean from the family's slate. She knew that Victoria had not informed Lily of Josie's less-than-wealthy background, of her struggling artist father, of her mother who took in ironing to pay the bills. Nor was Lily aware of what Josie's marriage had been like. Perhaps it was time she rectified that. *But how?*

Only one thing was certain, she would have to strike when the time was right.

Chapter Seventeen

Lily

Lily took the day off when Tom left for the war. She made her way through Grand Central Station to meet him, the crisp, cold New York afternoon air sending chills through her bones. Troops swarmed the concourses, the voices of folks saying goodbye to their loved ones ringing through the echoing station. Grand Central's huge windows were covered with blackout paint, and buttons gleamed under the artificial lights, highlighting the skinny, uniformed chests of boys, boys who were being forced to become men before they had time to figure out who they were.

Lily loosened her own coat, a wave of nausea assailing her, the familiar worry that had kept her tossing and turning last night beating the same tune in her mind, over and over again. *What if she never saw him again? What if he never returned?*

When Tom pulled her into a hug, holding her close, Lily tried to smile bravely at Gia over his shoulder, standing behind them, pale and uncertain, while Natalia tried to keep up a steady chatter to stop her mom from breaking down.

Tom held her in silence, his heart beating against her chest, one hand running through her hair.

"Stay safe," she whispered into his shoulder. "Come back to me, Tom."

He dropped a kiss on the top of her head. "*Goodbye, cara mia.*" He ran his finger across her chin a moment, his eyes intent on hers.

"Cook to your heart's content, sweetheart. I'll be imagining your beef Wellington, and before you know it, we'll be together again."

She managed a watery smile.

Right then, everything came to a standstill. Every person in that crowded, eerie station terminal turned to the sound of the organist swelling to the strains of the national anthem. Tom circled his arm around Lily's back, holding her close and firm, while the music swelled through the halls, and Lily swiped a hand over her eyes. Other women around her openly cried into their handkerchiefs.

Once the music stopped, there was a moment of silence, and Tom enfolded his mom in his arms.

The train whistled, loud and deep, and an empty feeling settled in Lily's stomach. She pasted a brave smile on her face. She was aware of Natalia moving to stand closer to her.

"Oh, I'll miss him," Natalia said, clutching Lily's arm.

Lily held Tom's sister's hand as if her life depended on it. "And so will I," she managed. "So will I."

"Darling, oh, my boy!" Gia's eyes scoured her son's handsome face, looking up at him, beseeching, as if drinking him in for the last time.

Lily shuddered, and felt Natalia tighten her grip on her arm.

"*Goodbye*," Tom mouthed to Lily, once he'd hugged Natalia and Gia all over again.

Lily blew him a final kiss right in front of everyone, letting the tears fall unchecked down her cheeks, and when the train let out another long whistle, she followed him with her heart and closed her eyes at the unbearable inevitability that he would become just one of all the thousands of troops, no longer the Tom whose calm presence and kind demeanor added something to the kitchen, but just a number. Just another soldier at war.

Only yesterday he had told her that his head would be shaved, and all his clothes turned in. She'd made him promise to leave his favorite blue jeans at home with Gia, so they'd be there when he came back to New York.

Gia let out a low sob. Natalia was right next to her, her arm around Gia's shoulder, her free hand now clutched in Lily's. Lily stared at his retreating back, fighting the urge to run to him for one last kiss before he boarded the train and disappeared inside.

When the train departed, its deep, unfathomable engine rumbling along the tracks, Gia lifted her hand in a frail wave. Natalia stayed close, holding her mom's other hand, and Lily dug in her purse for a handkerchief, which she waved a moment, before blowing into it, hard. *What was he about to endure?*

Gia's face seemed to collapse as the train pulled away. Tom's mom, helplessly having to give over her son for this battle, like so many other mothers, turned and enfolded both Lily and Natalia in her arms.

"Keep in touch with me, Lily," Gia managed, before she gave way, properly, to the sobs she had held in bravely, for her son.

Lily nodded. "Of course I will, Gia," she said. And in that instant, Lily knew that, were she and Tom to stay close, she and Gia would become friends, because this moment had drawn them together, two women both saying goodbye to the man they adored.

Natalia pulled back, holding Lily at arm's-length. "My brother is fond of you. And I like you too."

Lily squeezed Tom's sister back, trying to glean the last sounds of the departing train, while she held onto the lingering sensation of being held in Tom's arms to bottle the memories, as if knowing that, many times, she'd look back to this moment in the months, in the years, to come.

Lily stumbled out of Grand Central Station, pulling Gia and Natalia into a last, hopeless hug in the swirling crowds outside, before digging her hands into her coat pockets, and walking, blindly. She had no destination in mind. She took a right turn up Fifth

Avenue, head down, brushing past women out for a stroll, their hands filled with shopping bags from the fashion houses and the elegant stores that lined the beautiful boulevard. Lily didn't even glance at the sumptuous boutiques, mannequins dressed in the latest wartime fashions posing in the windows.

What did it all matter? Lily almost barked out a laugh. What did all this mean when the country was about to lose another generation?

She strode on, more purposeful now. The anger she'd felt at Marco's death flickering within her, growing, until she couldn't bear it. She gritted her teeth, all the way to Central Park, where she turned left and stood outside The Plaza, her chest heaving. She had to cross the road. She needed to sit down.

Lily marched into the park, and by The Pond, she found a bench, and slumped down into it, gathering her coat about her in the afternoon cold. Winter seemed to have arrived all at once now Tom had left. She clasped her hands together, staring at the inevitable way the water drifted forward, the tall buildings of New York gleaming on the surface, only to shimmer and disappear into nothing at the slightest breeze.

When Lily finally stood up, huddling against the cold afternoon, she took one lingering look at the park in the fading light, the trees strange and dark against the silhouetted skyscrapers beyond, before turning around and making her way to the train.

But she didn't alight at Gramercy Park. She went straight down to the Village, hands in her pockets, head down against the roiling wind that whistled in the trees in Washington Square Park. Lily hurried forward, determinedly not thinking about the hundreds of old graves buried under the lawns where she walked, didn't focus on the stories of ghosts and a green miasma that had been seen floating above the park after dark.

Instead, she hotfooted it to Bleecker Street, a sense of sadness dragging her down when she thought about the last time she'd walked through here on Tom's arm, when she thought about how empty this area would feel, knowing he wasn't here anymore.

Pushing the door open to Albertina's, massaging her hands against the cold, she bought chicken thighs, fresh eggs, and olive oil, cheering up a little when the owner, Lino, recognized her and said hello.

Back outside in the cold, Lily stopped automatically at her gram's favorite fruit and vegetable stall and collected ingredients for a fresh salad, and then she grabbed a couple of warm salted pretzels.

By the time she made it to Josie's basement door, Lily's teeth were chattering and she was certain her hands were red, despite the leather gloves she wore. She took one off with her teeth, pulled out the key that Josie had given her years ago, and pushed the door open, popping her shopping bags down on the kitchen table.

"Gram?" she hollered, tripping up the stairs.

Her gram's muffled reply came from her bathroom. "In the bath, darling."

Lily grinned. How she always loved coming here.

She went back downstairs to cook.

A half-hour later, having released some of her anger on the pretzels which were now perfect crumbs, she'd coated her chicken thighs with seasoned flour, beaten egg, and rolled them about in the batter. She pulled them out of the oven, drizzled them with a mixture of mustard, honey and vinegar, and placed them on two plates with her fresh, crisp green salad.

Josie came down the stairs, resplendent in a deep blue kaftan, with a pair of velvet trousers underneath.

"Darling." She came forward, pulling Lily into an embrace. "How you spoil me."

Lily whipped off Josie's cooking apron and popped the two plates onto the table either side of a bowl of bright yellow roses.

Josie had her contacts in the Village; she was never without flowers in her house.

Josie reached for a bottle of white wine from her refrigerator and poured two glasses.

"Sweetheart, are you quite all right?" she said. "I don't want to pry, but you look a little pale."

Lily didn't confess that she'd have to force herself to eat tonight, but at least the chicken was light, the pretzel coating crunchy, there was some comfort in that. She leaned on the table and rested one hand in her chin. "Tom went to war today," she said. There was no point beating about the truth with her gram. Josie would have it out of her anyway.

Josie took a sip of her wine and placed it down on the table. "I see," she said and reached across the table and placed her hand atop Lily's. "Oh, he is charming, darling," she said, her words rushing out. "I liked him very much. I really did." She rested her chin in her hands in the way Lily adored. "And I would have been a fool if I hadn't seen the sparks flying between the two of you that day he was here."

Lily nodded, unable to stop her mouth from working. "I love him, Gram. I'm sure of it." The relief of telling a member of her family the truth, and knowing she could do so without being judged, was too much. Lily sent Josie a brave, watery smile. "So, there it is," she whispered.

"I'm not surprised. I fell for him before you arrived at the door in your green polka-dot dress," Josie said. "You know," her tone grew intimate, "I know how you feel, sweetheart."

Lily shot up her head.

Josie's smile was small and sad. "When I was young, oh, about your age, I fell in love."

Lily's eyes rounded.

"Oh, he was a painter. A student of my father's. My mother wouldn't have a bar of me marrying him." Josie chuckled, but her beautiful eyes were tinged with sadness. "She wasn't going to allow me to marry an artist. Not another one in the family."

"I had no idea…"

"And, when your grandfather came along, well, he was meticulous, and creative, a hardworking, successful man, and his millinery business was quite the rage in the Upper East Side. He was the sensible choice, dear."

"And the young artist?"

"I don't know what became of him. The only way to deal with the loss was, unfortunately, to let go and hope he'd find happiness with someone else."

"But you loved him." Lily's blue eyes bored into Josie's.

Josie tilted her head to one side. Slowly, she nodded. "I never fell in love that way again."

"So fleeting, though," Lily whispered. "How could you bear it?"

"I only wish I'd stood up to my mother. Been stronger." She eyed Lily. "Worked somewhere myself, so that my husband's income was not the only means of support."

Lily took a sip of her wine. She pressed her lips together.

Josie sighed. Victoria, she knew, had never divulged to Lily how poor Josie's father had really been, how he'd struggled to pay the rent, the bills, to even make ends meet and put food on the table while insisting so stubbornly on focusing on his art. Lily only knew that he'd taught art, and had been successful and famous. *For five minutes before he died.*

Josie wasn't about to tell Lily what she'd really endured as a child, cold November nights like this one with no food on the table at all, her parents arguing, her mother rushing her up to her cold, bare, room, freezing and hungry. It was the reason she adored food, never took it for granted and never wasted a crumb on her plate.

Josie was not about to infuriate Victoria by revealing her side of the family's poverty to Lily, a part of the family story which had been so cleanly wiped off the map, but she was darned if she were not going to warn Lily that giving up love for security would not result in a happy life.

Because Lily could well support herself. She did not need a man to provide for her. She was building up her own skills, and like a true modern woman, she could contribute, and therefore have more choice in a partner. Josie truly believed that.

"You know, things will be very different for you," Josie said carefully. "This war, while taking men away, is giving women opportunities they've never had before. Make the most of it, darling. Because the more you build your own career up, the more you can contribute to your household income down the track. You will never be fully reliant on a man to provide for you. And that means you can make the right choice for you."

Lily held her gaze, and just then, she reached out a hand and covered Josie's with her own.

"Throw yourself into your passion while he's away," Josie whispered. "Be a trailblazer in the restaurant industry. You've worked hard. You'll also inspire other women. I'm inordinately proud of you, you know that."

The flame flickered back into Lily's eyes.

Chapter Eighteen

Lily

December, 1942

The following Sunday, Lily yawned her way to breakfast at home. She slipped into place at the table beside her mother. Victoria was sipping black coffee in a pale blue dress, make-up perfectly done, hair dressed, pearls in place.

"I'm counting on you *not* to entertain us with any talk of that kitchen today, Lily. I need you in the parlor straight after church to help us prepare care packages for the Red Cross. Remember who you are, and don't embarrass yourself, or your father and me."

"I'd planned to do some research into possible wartime recipes for the restaurant after church. Giorgio Conti will be deciding soon whether I or Martina will be head chef." She avoided mentioning that this was because Tom had gone. "I'm sure you'll understand, I want to show how keen I am, by presenting some ideas as to what I can do."

"I was not giving you a choice."

Her father placed his newspaper down and regarded Lily over the top of his reading glasses.

"I heard from… another chef at Valentino's," Lily said, taking her father's seeming interest as encouragement, "how Sicilians use organ meats in their cooking. I need to work out exactly what they use, so I borrowed some cookbooks from Valentino's. I'm going to have to scour them today."

"*Organ meats?*" Victoria drew her napkin up to cover her mouth. "Do you hear where this family is going, Jacob? Organ meats!"

Lily shot a glance at her father and went on. "I worry that Giorgio Conti would be appalled at the thought of them, too. I just need to figure out how to make the dishes palatable to Americans." She frowned. "It's going to be a matter of re-educating people's palates."

"For pity's sake!" Victoria threw a glance across the room to where their maid stood in her starched apron and black dress, staring straight ahead. "We are not tramps. We will not eat like peasants, even if the country does have to tighten its belts for the boys."

Lily's dad winked at Lily. "Yes, but the point is, the restaurant is going to require some innovation if it's going to survive the war, my darling Victoria. Goodness knows, we're seeing it in the fashion industry. You should see the rules. The War Production Board has insisted that there be no tucking or pleating, no hoods, no more than one pocket and only two buttons per cuff on a dress. Thank goodness I'm not in shoes. I think they'll be fashioned out of hemp and raffia soon enough. Hats, so far, are unaffected. But maintaining standards is becoming a major challenge in this war, across the board."

Lily leaned forward. "Yes, that's it, Dad. It's about keeping standards as high as we possibly can in the face of wartime austerity and rationing. It's also about being patriotic, Mom. And, if we all have to eat organ meats for a while, well, that's hardly a huge sacrifice, compared to what our boys are doing for us all."

"I know about patriotism, Lillian. I wound bandages in the last war." Victoria thumped her napkin on the table. She waved the maid away.

Lily did not miss a beat. "I thought of something else we could do as a family."

Her father shook out his paper and cleared his throat.

"Mother, Dad, there is a whole garden in our backyard."

"I have noticed," her father said.

"Don't you see?" Lily asked. "I think we should turn it into a victory garden."

Victoria dropped her coffee cup in its saucer with a clatter. "Mother…"

Victoria's voice was high and tremulous. She reached out a hand and laid it atop her husband's. "It is my dearest wish that once you and Nathaniel finally get engaged, we hold your engagement party in the garden. Goodness knows, the last thing I want is the Carters thinking we cannot afford suitable wedding celebrations. But what are you going to do with that dream of mine now? Throw a wrecking ball through and pull up all the flowers as well? I don't think so. I do not think so, my dear."

Lily stared at the ceiling.

But her father placed his newspaper flat. "I've been reading about such gardens. Tell me more, Lily."

Victoria gripped the table. "I will not countenance this. You will remember your priorities, Lily. You are throwing away everything."

"I saw a wonderful victory garden down in the Village, recently, Daddy. Two houses shared it. They were sustaining themselves and growing all their produce. It was run by a group of Italian families."

"I blame your mother, Jacob!" Victoria said. "Why did Josie move to the Village after your father died when she had a perfectly fine home in the Upper East Side? I tell you, Jacob! Your daughter shares the same madness as your mother. It's in the genes." Victoria's eyes flashed.

"The garden I saw was nothing to do with Josie," Lily continued. "It was a pair of tenement houses. I'm friends with one of the tenants." *That had slipped out!* But, overcome with a rush of affection for Tom, for Gia and Natalia, Lily sent her mother a determined glare.

Victoria brought her handkerchief to her mouth. "Are you *insane?*"

Her father patted Victoria on the back.

Victoria stood up and marched to the window. She stood there, her shoulders rigid.

"*Tenement houses?* What tenement houses? What is our daughter doing in row houses?"

Lily's words tumbled out. "Going out to Bridgeport to the market gardens has made me realize how much of our produce is going to have to go toward feeding our servicemen and women abroad. If we grew our own produce, then we'd be making a small contribution toward freeing up supplies for the war, don't you see? While we all feel so helpless in the face of all the conflict, this is something we can do to help."

Jacob nodded.

"With… friends going to war, it's made me realize how we should do everything we can back here."

"You could well be running the kitchen in one of New York's most significant restaurants," her father pointed out. "I'm already proud of you."

"*Jacob!*" Victoria threw her arms in the air. "Honestly. Am I the only sensible person in this family?"

Lily rushed on, encouraged by her father's words and ignoring her mother. "Imagine if we could turn some of our parks and gardens into victory gardens, produce bowls for the city, Dad, while the markets focus on supplying our servicemen. The more we do, the higher we keep morale. And depriving people of their fruits and vegetables, well, we don't want that, do we?"

Victoria raised her gold and diamond wristwatch. "I'm not turning the back garden into some market stall." She swept toward the door. "Talk to your daughter, Jacob. Make her see sense," she said. "I'm not even going to dignify this with my presence anymore."

Lily's father waited until Victoria had disappeared. He leaned toward Lily and dropped his voice. "I don't want a civil war in my house, but I have another idea that just might work, dear."

"My heart is in the idea, Daddy."

He lowered his voice, throwing a glance toward the empty hallway. "Yes, but how about this? Why not suggest that Valentino's start up a victory garden instead, somewhere in Manhattan? You'd be doing exactly what you aimed, and it would do wonders for the Contis' business. If you want to bring some of the produce home for us here, I have no issue with that. Think about it."

Lily clasped her dad's hand. "Daddy, you are a genius."

He cleared his throat and folded his napkin. "Darling? Please help me. Go and get ready for church."

Lily squeezed his arm. "I'll make up victory garden plans in my head while I'm there. Along with wonderful recipes for organ meats," she added, her eyes sparkling.

Her father waved her away, but sent her a smile.

Once she was upstairs in her room, despite her mother's instructions being hurled down the hallway at her, Lily pulled out her notebook for Valentino's, the front section already filled with her adapted recipes and ideas. Settling herself in her window seat overlooking the square, she started drawing sketches of plantings based on the victory garden out back of Gia's house.

Lily drew her pencil to her lips. What if Valentino's were able to grow its own produce and meet its own demands? What if she could ask Gia to help and what if she put her suggestion to Giorgio, along with her growing list of recipe ideas? All she needed to do was find a site for Valentino's victory garden. And the idea of working with Tom's mom made her heart soar.

"In fact," Lily said to Giorgio on Monday morning, sitting opposite him at his desk, "I've got an idea as to exactly where we could grow our own Valentino's fruit and vegetables, and I've spoken with someone who is willing to help turn it into a victory garden."

Giorgio tapped his fountain pen on the desk. "I have long-standing relationships with my suppliers, with Tony, Raffaele and Ernesto. While your idea of us growing our own produce has merit, I can't afford to upset these good men. I'm sure you understand. We must keep things stable for Valentino's, not make changes that are going to anger our loyal suppliers."

"But changes are here whether we like them or not, Giorgio." Lily took in a breath. "I've thought about our suppliers. I would propose that Tony and his cousins' supplies that are meant for Valentino's go to feed our servicemen instead during the war. This could be a philanthropic gesture. With petrol rationing, the two-and-a-half-hour commute to Bridgeport is also going to become very challenging until the war is done."

"I am all for philanthropy, but my suppliers are key to the success of the restaurant."

"If Valentino's becomes self-sufficient," Lily pulled out her final card, "that will be good publicity for you, Giorgio. Don't you see? People will read about how Valentino's is not helping itself to wartime supplies but is growing its own produce instead. I think folks who might have frowned on indulgences such as dinners at fine restaurants during a time of war and food rationing would be more likely to keep coming here if they knew you were doing your bit and then some. And there would be no question of compromising quality."

Giorgio fiddled with his tie.

Lily rolled on. "If the press knew that we were not harming the much-needed supplies for the troops, then, they might write about it favorably too."

"There is a problem." Giorgio frowned.

"Yes, Giorgio?"

"Where are you proposing to find this space you are talking about to grow a garden big enough to supply Valentino's? In

Manhattan?" He threw his hands in the air. "It is one thing to have grand ideas, but the execution of them is even more important."

"The Schwab mansion." Lily pulled out a letter and placed it on the table. "The house covers an entire block of land on Riverside Drive."

Giorgio leaned forward to survey the document that Lily had placed on his desk.

"Since Charles M. Schwab died in 1939," Lily said, "the garden has grown wild and the property has fallen into disrepair. There is talk that the mansion will be knocked down after the war. But I've spoken with the current administrators already this morning and they are interested in my plan. We would need to employ a team of women gardeners, but you'd only be doing them a service. I am certain they would work the land. And I know a woman who could plan and design the whole thing for you and oversee the changing needs each season. She works but has offered to do this in her spare time. I've spoken to her too."

Giorgio picked up the information about the Schwab mansion.

"I'm trying to keep us one step ahead," Lily said. "What's more, what is left from the victory garden could be donated to the war."

Giorgio cleared his throat. "This is innovative, Lily, my dear. I have to say, I like the thought of it. It would be a matter of working out practicalities, though. I need to think about it."

"Of course. Thank you, Giorgio."

He tapped his pen on his desk. "If you end up running the restaurant and are going to introduce sweeping ideas like this, Lily, then Valentino's is either going to boom or bust during the war. And I, for one, know the latter is not on the cards."

"Well, you know what I say?" Lily asked. "I say we boom."

He shook his head and smiled. "All right, Lily. We're watching you and Martina today. No final decisions have been made as yet."

"Yes, Giorgio." Lily pushed back her shoulders and stood up.

*

Out in the corridor, waitstaff bustled around carrying trays of cutlery and glassware, hurrying into the restaurant.

Downstairs, Julius had a tray of scented warm apple pies already set out and the vegetable chef was sorting through the day's vegetables on the long side table. When Giorgio strode in and called everyone together for a meeting, people slipped to the long staff table where the basement luncheons were served without the usual scrabble and gossip. Instead, everyone's focus was on Giorgio.

Lily pulled out a chair next to Jimmy, the chair that Tom usually occupied conspicuously empty opposite hers. She swallowed hard and forced herself to look toward the head of the table.

Giorgio scanned the kitchen staff, his eyes lingering on Tom's seat too, for a moment.

"My friends," he said, "today is a sad day for Valentino's. In the several years he's been with us at Valentino's, Tom proved himself more than capable of excelling at every aspect of his role as our *chef de cuisine*." Giorgio looked down a moment, gripping the back of a chair. "But we must accept that he had to leave us. Without warning. Called up… another young man."

"May Tom return safely," Leo murmured.

Muffled sounds of agreement filtered up the table.

"Now, to that end, as you will be aware, we have two candidates for the role of head chef."

Lily pushed up her white kitchen sleeves.

"Either Lily or Martina will be leading the kitchen from here on."

A heated sigh passed through the team. Lily kept her head high, ignoring the looks that she knew were passing among some of her male counterparts.

"I will be making my decision as soon as possible in the light of Tom's departure. I'd like you both to deliver a few words to your fellow chefs as to how you would run the kitchen for us all, please. Martina first."

Lily barely heard Martina's speech as she tried to collect her thoughts. When it was her turn, she stood. "We may be down in the basement of Valentino's," she said. "But we, the kitchen staff, are the heartbeat of this restaurant. Together, we are all united in our passion for food. As your head chef, it would be an honor to lead you all as we share our love of cooking and our commitment to producing New York's finest cuisine." She paused, lowering her voice. "When you walk into the restaurant, with the lovely art deco design it's the magic that captures you, it's as if you've walked into another world. War or no war, we need to continue to capture that magic in our food. Because that is why folks will come to Valentino's, because no one else can do exactly what we do."

A couple of the kitchen staff leaned forward. The room was quiet.

"Giorgio drove Valentino's through Prohibition, the Depression, and now, he will bring her through this war. I have been working behind the scenes to develop new, innovative recipes to ensure Valentino's thrives, in spite of war, and in spite of increased rationing. To that end, I've started a wartime recipe book for us to use and for any of you to add to, should you have an idea. If I am head chef, I will strive to help Valentino's continue to adapt. I would be honored to lead the kitchen so that Valentino's remains the jewel of New York, while we continue to move forward, to innovate, to *lead* the way for food in Manhattan."

After a moment's silence, Jimmy started a slow clap, and soon the rest of the staff joined him.

"Very well. Thank you, Lily, thank you, Martina." Giorgio looked thoughtful. "Time for you all to go in for preparations."

The kitchen staff started pushing chairs back. Lily's heart beat in her mouth. She had no idea how that had gone. She knew she must not allow Leo's constant attempts to belittle her curb her enthusiasm for trying new things, but she worried that if she stuck her head too far out and came across as wanting to march ahead too far, she'd lose the support of everyone who loved things the way they were.

And the war was dictating everything these days. Running a kitchen would prove to be a fine balancing act. Lily only hoped she'd got the tone right in her speech.

Giorgio's voice rang out across the room. "Leo will cover for Tom today. And I will make my decision after this shift."

For Lily, the service could have lasted a lifetime. She didn't want to hear the inevitable bad news, but all too soon, Giorgio was right at the door.

"Ah, Martina, Lily," he said.

Lily nodded. "Yes." She scoured Martina's face.

But the girl only frowned at the floor.

Giorgio smiled. "I have come to a decision. Lily, I would like to speak with Martina first. When I'm done, I will call you in."

Lily nodded, ducking her head down to hide the swell of emotions that coursed through her. And the fact that Giorgio wanted to talk to Martina first, well, surely that only meant one thing. He was going to give Martina the chance to accept the position of head chef before he spoke to Lily.

Her cheeks burning, she averted her eyes from the curious stares of all the kitchen staff as she passed down the line. *Well, at least her mother would be pleased!*

With all the energy of a wooden doll, she started chopping mushrooms for the vegetable chef. He sweated over a pile of tomatoes alongside.

In five minutes flat, Martina gently patted Lily on the shoulder. "He's ready for you," she said.

Lily scoured Martina's face. Joy flooded the girl's features, and her eyes sparkled. She whisked away, calling out instructions to the kitchen at large.

Lily's fingers curled around the handle of her knife. She placed it down, precisely. "They are all done," she said.

"Very good, Chef," the chef said.

Lily glanced around the kitchen and slipped out of the room.

Giorgio was at Marco's desk. "Well, my dear. Do sit down."

Lily slid down into a chair.

"Congratulations, Lily," Giorgio said. "You are to be Valentino's next head chef. Martina has happily accepted the role of *chef de cuisine.* It became obvious to me that your skills, Lily, are more suited to managing staff, to designing and creating recipes, and sourcing ways to obtain our produce and designing menus, while Martina is best employed following instructions and cooking. I am delighted to have come to a decision, and welcome you to this most important, highly valued position. I am certain that you will do us proud."

Lily covered her mouth with her hand. Slowly, a smile spread across her face. "I cannot tell you how much this means to me," she said. "I promise you this. I will never, ever let you down!"

Part Two

Chapter Nineteen

Lily

Late summer, 1943

Lower Manhattan slumbered through yet another sweaty, humid night. Lily sat alone in her office at Valentino's, her now bulging journal of wartime recipes lying open next to her on the desk. Memories hung in the air, of times spent poring over recipes with Tom, discovering the first entry in her book, Giorgio's special Chestnut Ravioli. Those days seemed so long ago now.

Outside Valentino's, New Yorkers were joining together, buying war bonds, donating blood, but Lily couldn't tear her eyes away from some of the darker local stories, stories of terrible racism endured by New York's black GIs in the training camps of the South, spawning riots that had devastated Harlem in the last weeks. She'd read with horror of an outfit called the German American Bund, a pro-Nazi organization based in Yorkville, Manhattan, where Lily's own grandparents had lived. And, at the same time, Irish-Catholic gangs attacked Jewish youngsters and vandalized synagogues while the police seemed indifferent.

Each night, she left the desk tidy before switching off the light and saying a heartfelt prayer for her adored Tom. Since he had been drafted to Italy, she followed the news of war there with increasing angst.

Ever since the Allied troops—more than a million men—had invaded Sicily back in July, she'd scoured the newspapers every day. After driving Rommel out of North Africa—the campaign in which their head chef Marco had been lost—the Allies had moved into Sicily, and now they faced a far bigger challenge: Italy.

It was where Tom had wanted to go, and now, all she could do was hope and pray that the land of his ancestors would keep him safe.

There was very little good news being reported, but it was impossible not to follow it. She'd sicken at the sight of photographs of American boys trudging along ancient, dusty tracks in Sicily, their faces cloaked with dust and flies as they pushed on. Tumbling villages soared behind them and the destruction of war laid waste to a timeless, brown landscape.

But now, as the American and British forces pushed onward into mainland Italy, the papers warned that the strongly defensible terrain was going to make their advances much, much harder. She and Gia together pored over newspapers full of proclamations about deep valleys, east–west spurs across the peninsula's central spine that provided secure, fortified lines for the Germans, for Field Marshal Albert Kesselring, who was regarded as a master of defensive warfare. Everyone knew that conquering Italy was going to be a bitter and costly campaign. By all accounts, the battle for Tom's home country was going to be a long and tragic slog.

And Tom was in the heart of it. He was somewhere in the march onward toward Rome. She had secretly hidden away Tom's letters to her, in a box concealed in the office. Now, she had two new letters, one he'd written a full six months earlier, that had arrived today.

North Africa, February 1943

Cara mia,

> *We've been here three months now, and the way things are moving, we should be finished soon. While I'm here in body, my heart is across the world, with you.*

Here, deep in the midst of war, we are witness to the very worst of human behavior, and I am seeing things I will never forget, but at the same time, we are seeing the ways in which people bond together, and that is heartening.

I still dream of that beef Wellington you promised me. I can tell you, thinking about that is a welcome distraction from our rations—sausages, beans, canned fruit, cigarettes and, if we are lucky, a little chocolate and processed cheese with dry crackers.

In this part of the world, events move fast. I'm becoming proud to be a part of the American forces pushing the Nazis into the sea!

But, most of all, I hope you are thriving back at home, and that the victory garden of yours is green and delicious. Give my mom a hug for me, and I send you all the love in the world.

I miss you, my love, and dream of the day I can hold you in my arms again.

Your Tom

Sicily, summer, 1943

Cara mia,

How are you? The thought of coming home to you keeps me going, as the days blur around me. I often think of summer in New York—the green trees, the hot humid nights, Central Park, ice creams. And you.

My arrival in my native homeland of Sicily was moving, incredible, and rang with the sound of gunfire and the lurch of the sea propelling us to the coast. I was overwhelmed with emotion as we invaded the southern coast of the island.

The relief on the locals' faces, some of them on that beach to greet us, was testimony to the terrible suffering they have endured. I was overcome with heartfelt sadness that I was seeing my homeland for the first time, under circumstances such as these. Every person I saw, every child, old man and woman, left me wondering, are these my relatives?

The old town of Gela had been heavily bombed by the Axis forces, the streets were rubble and the old houses damaged and dusty, the whole town filled with destruction. To see the haunted remnants of once grand buildings, defaced with painted slogans celebrating "Il Duce," was something I will never, ever forget.

For days we bumped through Gela in a small jeep, on the lookout for stray Axis forces who might be hiding. As we drove along the ancient alleyways, even driving down staircases at times, I wanted to shout that these places were precious and centuries old, but no one cares about such things anymore. Then we started the long march to Messina, our engineers going ahead of us to detonate landmines.

I cannot tell you what it meant to me to march through the countryside of Sicily. I fought the wild urge to stop and lay my eyes on the distant hills, to linger in the ancient villages where my ancestors may have stepped, eking out an existence in this hot, dry dusty land.

At the moment, everything around me seems so active, so alive, so full of the rash, chaotic, yet systemized tempo of war. It is as if life is exploding all around me, and at the same time, I have this deep sense of home.

My darling, stay safe and well.

All my love, always, cara,
Your Tom

Lily placed his letters in her cardboard box and hid them all behind a pile of old recipe books on Marco's shelf. At home, she kept another stack of letters in a box in her bedroom. Nathaniel's letters. She read his missives from the Pacific dutifully. She wrote back as best she could and followed the Allies' push back toward Japan, but her first thoughts were always toward Sicily.

Now, Lily forced her thoughts back to New York, while her heart yearned across continents. She raked a tired hand over her eyes. While she was thankful that she was able to do something worthy to keep the home front going, she had run herself into the ground in the process. It had become clear that she needed to employ at least one sous-chef. Until now, she had been taking care of her old role as well as that of head chef and each job needed to be carried out properly.

Last week, Paul, the enthusiastic young commis chef who had become so adept at assisting at each station, and who had endeared himself to everyone on staff, had finally enlisted to train as a pilot. Lily knew she had to add more people to her team.

Every application on her shortlist was from a woman. Like most restaurants in the United States, Valentino's would soon be staffed by a team of women, with only a handful of elderly and older middle-aged men to round out the team.

Lily stuck her head out of her office door. Martina was still in the kitchen, tidying the *chef de cuisine* station and polishing Tom's pots until they shone.

"Martina?" Lily asked. "Can we talk a moment?"

Martina set down her polishing cloth and approached Lily's office, a slightly exhausted swagger in her walk.

Lily watched her *chef de cuisine*, frowning. She'd seen hints of attraction between Martina and her fish chef, Jimmy. While he was twenty years older than Martina, Jimmy's sense of humor and kindness would be a wonderful foil for the hardworking, passionate woman who stood opposite Lily now. A romance for Martina would be grand, and Lily only hoped that, in time, something came of what she sensed was happening between them.

It was hard to imagine that they had once been rivals. Lily had no idea how she would have managed to get through the last few months without Martina. Her real flair and passion for cooking, along with her unshakable work ethic, were invaluable assets to Valentino's, and Lily always made sure that Giorgio realized what a gem he had in Martina.

"Come in, Martina, have a seat."

Lily handed Martina a sheaf of papers.

After a few moments, Martina handed Lily three applications and folded her arms. "I think this one. And these two," she said. "They look just what we need. And we do need more staff." Martina held Lily's gaze a moment.

Lily looked over the pages. "Exactly," she murmured. "When it comes to the two sisters, Meg and Ellen Anderson, I was thinking of taking on both of them as sous-chefs. And my heart went out to Agnes Romano, what with losing her husband in the war and having three children to support on her own. Her experience in the restaurant in Brooklyn looks strong. She's worked every station."

Martina yawned hugely.

"Go home, dear. Get some rest."

Martina stood up, but halfway to the office door, she paused, sending Lily an odd look. "Lily?" she asked, almost shyly.

Lily raised her head.

"Do you think Jimmy is handsome?"

Lily downed her pen and tilted her head to one side. "Jimmy is lovely." She waited. Was Martina going to open up to her, and confirm what she hoped was true?

Martina hovered. "Well, I think so too."

Lily sent the girl a warm smile. She looked out to the empty kitchen, to Tom's vacant workspace, sitting like an aching hole in the otherwise quiet space. "There are, and were, some other lovely men here at Valentino's too." Her words came out softly. Perhaps because she'd been so absorbed in Tom's letter, she was suddenly overwhelmed with a sense of missing him.

Martina's eyes rounded. "Anything you're not telling me, Lily?"

Lily stood up and gathered her coat. She patted her *chef de cuisine* on the arm. Unfortunately, she'd had to keep her feelings for Tom a secret. If Sidney were to find out, the whole of Manhattan would know, including her mother, Katherine Carter, not to mention Giorgio, and Vianne. For now, her romance with Tom had to be her delicious secret, but, hopefully, Martina would not have to bear such silence if anything came of her feelings for Jimmy.

"Not really, Martina. I'm sure Jimmy admires you. How could he not?"

As she whisked past the other chef, Lily saw that Martina's cheeks were flushed.

Chapter Twenty

Fall, 1943

Lily's pinned-back hair clung to her damp forehead as she walked with the wave of workers heading to the train station from Gramercy Park on Friday morning. They had endured a hot, humid summer and even now, in September, the newly fashioned wraparound dress that she wore, made to save fabric without covered buttons, seemed to cling to her, the wartime viscose fabric not allowing her skin to breathe. Every newspaper on every newsstand on the streets screamed news of the Italian campaign, and the sight of the relentless black-and-white headlines lifted the hair on the nape of Lily's neck and her arms.

She was glued to the news every morning. The new government of Italy had surrendered to the British and to the USA, and Italy had agreed to join the Allies, but the Germans had taken control of the Italian army, freed Mussolini and set him up as head of a puppet government in Northern Italy, blocking the Allies from their attempted advances deeper into the country. It seemed the liberation of Italy from Nazi Germany was going to be a long and arduous affair. Where Tom was, Lily did not know. But every night she wrung her hands and prayed for his safe return.

The moment she stepped inside the staff door, Giorgio called her into his office.

He looked up from the newspaper he had spread out on his desk. "God help my country," he murmured.

"Amen to that," Lily whispered. She forced herself not to panic about Tom. There were no guarantees for any soldier fighting a war.

Giorgio rubbed his hands together and stood up. "The first round of our interviewees is in the foyer. Will you sit down next to me, please, while I bring them in."

Lily plumped down on the chair. A black fan whirred in the still room, sending a welcome breeze over Lily's face.

"We'll interview the sous-chef applicants together, then I want you down in the kitchen. I'll handle the commis chef position and send the successful applicant straight down to you."

"Yes, Giorgio."

Giorgio adjusted his bespoke suit. He paused a moment. "You are doing well as our head chef, Lily."

Lily pressed her lips together. "Thank you."

He turned around and left the room.

Lily tried to tidy the newspapers, but as usual the images of American boys being soldiers amidst dust and tanks leapt out at her. Scanning the photographs in the crazy way she'd adopted to see if any of the boys were Tom, she grimaced, and placed the papers on a table at the back of the room.

"Miss Rose, here we have Miss Meg and Miss Ellen Anderson." Giorgio swept back into the office, leading one tall blond woman and a short woman with wavy fair hair. "Sisters," he announced. He regarded them. "Although you wouldn't guess it."

"Oh, I know," the short woman called Ellen said. "Folks always get confused when we say we're related. When they'd come into Father's restaurant, they'd never be able to tell."

"Please," Giorgio said. "Sit down."

Ellen sank down. "Oh, my what a blessing. My feet are killin' me, you know. These shoes, I am not used to them. I won't ever work in them; don't you worry about that!"

Lily covered her mouth with a hand, stifling a laugh.

When Ellen smiled, a dimple appeared on her cheek.

The taller sister, Meg, lounged back in her seat, crossing her legs. She pulled off her gloves and a diamond engagement ring sparkled on the third finger of her left hand. Lily noticed Giorgio's gaze homing in on it and staying there.

"Well, we're just honored to be here and we're more than excited about the job," Ellen said. "We love cooking. And we know restaurants inside out."

Meg fiddled with her ring.

"Is that right?" Giorgio folded his hands on the table. "Can you tell us more about that?"

"Oh, well, you see, our father owned a restaurant in Midtown nearly all his adult life, and he hired us when we were just twelve years old," Ellen said. "We started with responsibility for the pantry, you know, keeping it neat and tidy and running errands for the cooks. Then, we worked our way up to chopping vegetables, and then Father had us filleting fish. He insisted we learn how to debone and how to cook every type of fish to perfection. I tell you, that was fun when I was fourteen. Then, he moved us to grilling, frying and sautéing, before teaching us at night how to cook everything from pastries, to chocolate éclairs, to Boston buns. That was my favorite part. The desserts!"

Giorgio sat stock-still. "Go on."

"We were takin' it in turns running the whole kitchen as sous-chefs by the time we were eighteen. One night each. The nights we weren't on duty as sous-chefs, Father made us cook wherever we were needed, on whatever station was required. We've lived and breathed restaurants since we were born."

"So, ten years' experience, then," Lily said.

"Oh, yes. And more. We started cooking on stools at our father's side when we were wee girls. But after Pearl Harbor… well, you see, our father is a real patriot. And he sold the restaurant and got a job in the War Office. He spends all his spare time volunteering."

Giorgio tapped his fingers on the desk. "Do you speak, Meg Anderson?" he asked, addressing the quiet girl with the engagement ring.

Meg shrugged. "Yeah, it's just that Ellen talks enough for two."

Lily bit back her smile. Something told her that these girls would add something to the kitchen. From what they'd said, they were more than confident around food. And she suspected that they'd stand no nonsense from the men! Ellen would come back with a mighty one-liner of her own if Leo tried any rudeness, and she suspected Meg would give him a surly look, ignore him and carry on. No, these two would be a splendid addition to the kitchen.

Ellen flushed pink with pleasure. "It's always the way it's been. One of us talks, the other's silent. But I can vouch for my sister. She won't let you down. She's as passionate about food as I am, and we'd both be honored to work at Valentino's."

"That was what I was going to ask," Lily said. "How do you feel about working at a restaurant with such cachet as Valentino's?"

"Oh, we're excited," Ellen said.

Lily's eyes danced. Ellen spoke of their feelings as a pair?

"The chance to be sous-chef somewhere as famous as this? Why, it's a dream come true and we won't let you down. I know we can run your kitchen, with no problems at all."

Lily's expression turned serious. "The kitchen runs smoothly, but the pace is intense," she said. "How do you handle pressure?"

"Ellen here is always as good-natured and cheerful as she appears in front of you," Meg said.

Giorgio looked at the girl with something that approached respect.

"And Meg is as quiet and steady as she appears. Her fiancé is away in the Pacific for the duration of the war. With us, what you see is what you get. Meg might be quiet, but she works hard," Ellen said. "Our dad taught us that there's no way to get anywhere but by good, honest work."

Lily shot Giorgio a look.

"Well," Giorgio said. "I'd like you to wait outside for five minutes while I convene with our head chef."

Half an hour later, Lily had Meg and Ellen down in the kitchen on trial as sous-chefs for the day. She'd been pleased at the way the girls had immediately split up, Ellen going to the top of the line and Meg starting down with the pantry chef. Lily smiled at the sound of Ellen's cheerful laughter ringing through the kitchen. The girl was a breath of fresh air.

Lily went back to her office, only to find Giorgio standing with another woman wearing a blue coat and a matching hat in her doorway. "Agnes Romano," he said. "Your new commis chef."

"Welcome, Agnes." Lily shook the woman's hand.

"I'll be popping in from time to time throughout the day as my other responsibilities allow," Giorgio said. "If you have any questions, please direct them to Lily, or Martina, our *chef de cuisine.*"

"Very well, Mr. Conti," Agnes said.

"Would you like to sit down?" Lily asked the new hire.

The short, practical-looking woman with dark brown hair nodded.

"I read something of your background," Lily said. She'd been moved by the woman's account of how her husband was killed in November last year in French Morocco. "I'm sorry for what you have been through. I was moved by your application. But, of course, I wanted to hire you for your experience and obvious work ethic."

Small lines grazed the sides of Agnes' eyes, but she held herself steady. She blinked a few times. "I have three children to feed and all I know how to do is cook. This job is a real step up for me. So, here I am."

"I'm so sorry for your loss."

Agnes jammed her hands into the pockets of her coat. "Yes, well, there are plenty of women in the same boat as me. Just means we have to work outside the home to bring in money for our kids, you see."

Lily nodded, warming to this woman. "Well, let's get you suited up and set to work. I'm going to rotate you around the stations, depending on who is most in need." Lily smiled at Agnes. "Today, I need you to start with Rosa, our vegetable chef. In fact, we're going to be using more and more vegetables in our dishes as we go on," Lily said.

"Mr. Conti told me about your victory garden run by a woman," Agnes said. "Valentino's is getting quite the reputation for employing us girls."

Lily chuckled. "Ah, yes, we have a veritable team of talented women here. Welcome to Valentino's!"

She stood up and ushered Agnes to the changing rooms. As she walked through her kitchen, Lily felt a rush of excitement about her growing team of women chefs.

Chapter Twenty-One

Victoria

At precisely twelve noon, Victoria tidied her bureau, closed the lid, and locked it, tucking the miniature key into her clutch purse. She pulled on her white gloves and matching hat and slipped out the door into the lift, stepping out into the shady street.

All the way down to the East Village, Victoria sat upright, hands folded in the lap of her yellow frock, her thoughts a whirl with wedding gowns, caterers, florists, cake decorators, the church, which was non-negotiable, guest list, mother-of-the-bride costume, wedding gifts and, of course, a venue for the breakfast after the charming ceremony, which would move everyone to tears.

The folders she'd created in preparation for Lily and Nathaniel's nuptials were brimful of fabric samples, glossy pages cut out of fashion magazines, memos on scented paper jotted down after conversations with prospective suppliers, and even some sketches, which she had contrived to fashion herself. Of these, Victoria was especially proud.

Planning Lily's wedding was becoming a full-time occupation, and while Jacob was spending extra hours at the millinery, and Lily was rushed off her feet at Valentino's, Victoria at last had an enterprise, something that she believed in with all her heart, and something for which, she knew in the end, Lily would be grateful.

Victoria stepped off the train, weaving her way through the crowded streets of the Lower East Side and dodging past children playing out on the sidewalks, running around her in rather ramshackle groups, all skinny legs sticking out of shorts and cotton frocks. *Honestly.* Victoria walked by delicatessens and drugstores and butcher shops. At least all the market trolleys had been removed in the last decade! What a racket this end of town would be otherwise.

On she marched to East 7th Street, toward Rose's Hatworks and Millinery.

While making an appearance at Jacob's workplace every now and then was important, the best way to support one's husband was surely to be wearing one of his bespoke hats. She'd always believed in wearing Rose's millinery designs while socializing with her friendship circle, because everyone knew it was women who'd ask who your milliner was.

But Victoria did draw the line at some things. She recoiled with horror at the recollection of Jacob trying to convince her to walk around wearing one of his latest visored caps, not to mention one of his ghastly cone-tipped berets that he'd designed for working women during the war. She'd sternly made him promise not to induce Lily to wear such a thing, simply because Victoria was certain that if Jacob asked her to, the ridiculous girl would!

Victoria stepped up onto the wooden stoop and pushed open the polished glass door to Rose's Hatworks and Millinery's combined retail store, wholesale trade, workroom and offices. Last year, Jacob and his staff had designed nearly 20,000 hats. His hats cost upwards of $20, which lent them a certain refinement.

She pulled off her gloves inside the doorway, sweeping her gaze over hat blocks stacked on shelves and finished hats sitting on mannequins' heads, all played out against the faint sounds from the workshop behind drifting out into the store.

Since the four shopgirls were all engaged in attending to custom-ers, Victoria busied herself examining the ready-to-wear collection that was on display on wooden shelving around the edges of the store, a small smile on her face as she took in one of the sales girls telling a customer most eagerly that, of course, they could alter the hats on-site, or create one from new.

Victoria's eyes raked over the selection, from trilbies to fedoras. The French velvet trimmings, corded laces, ribbons, softest wool felts, straw braids, feather details and jewel-like colors were such a feast.

When one of the girls finally spotted her, flushing beautifully with embarrassment at the sight of Mrs. Rose, Victoria sent her a small, condescending smile. The girl disappeared into the back, where Jacob's workers labored with their traditional tools, bent over their old sewing machines and molding the hats on Hank Rose's original blocks of all shapes and sizes, as well as some more recent blocks of Jacob's own design.

Victoria couldn't shake the feeling that she'd stepped back into another century when she came to visit here. She felt rather like a Victorian lady when the shopgirl informed her that her husband would be out in a few moments, and would she like a cup of coffee in the meantime?

Victoria refused the coffee, waved the girl back to work, and continued to amuse herself by working out which designs might best suit a grand wedding in the Upper East Side. Soft pastel confections for the bridesmaids, something more striking for the mother of the bride.

When Jacob appeared, peering at Victoria over his half-moon glasses, and sending her a disarming smile, his brown eyes lighting up, Victoria flushed and gave him a little wave.

He held out his arm, coming forward and kissing her on the cheek. Victoria tucked her gloved hand into his, and he pushed open the door and led her outside.

"My darling," he said, swinging his cane as he strolled down the busy street. "I want to take you somewhere unique and very special today."

"Hmm." Victoria narrowed her eyes and dodged a hula hoop that was running wild down the sidewalk.

She still found her husband most intriguing. To be honest, she still loved him. That was her problem, and her defense, she knew, especially when she found herself so often comparing her life to the splendors of Katherine Carter's.

Victoria had spotted Jacob Rose at a beach party in the Hamptons at the home of one of her friends. Those twinkling eyes, that amused smile, the way he came out of the sea in a bathing costume, black hair all glistening and quite six foot three. And the heir to a successful, well-known New York millinery business.

It had not taken Victoria long at all to convince Jacob Rose she was perfect for him, and even though she became frustrated at times with their daughter, who took after Jacob in so many ways, the fact was, Victoria knew she was always right when it came to marriages and affairs of the heart. In fact, she'd say she was an expert.

If only it was as easy to convince Lily that the gorgeous Nathaniel was the right choice for her, as it had been to convince Jacob that Victoria was the girl for him! But Victoria also knew that Lily took after her when it came to determination, and that was what she had to get around.

And get around it she would.

"I hope we are traveling Uptown."

Jacob pressed her hand. "Trust me. You'll love what you're about to see."

"Well. We'll see about that." Victoria pressed her lips together against the smell of hamburgers and fries wafting out from luncheon places, workers crowding the sidewalks while they waited to place orders. Girls with skipping ropes scooted up and down the street. Victoria reminded herself why she only visited the Lower East Side on rare occasions.

On Houston, Jacob stopped right outside the old facade of a shop, its pink and green sign flashing in the heat: Russ and Daughters.

Victoria cast her eye up at the painted sign. *Daughters?* "I trust you are not proving a point, Jacob."

A line had formed outside the shop. Jacob chuckled. "Inside," he said, "is paradise. Just you wait, Vicky."

Victoria heaved out a sigh. She'd been looking forward to a train ride back to Midtown and some charming French bistro where they could share a carafe of wine and chicken confit, followed by a small slice of hazelnut dacquoise. She could fairly taste the layers of nutty meringue and the rich whipped filling. But, instead, here she was.

Victoria drew away as folks stepped out of the appetizing shop, balancing bagels spread with shining pink lox, and cream cheese on slips of translucent paper.

Jacob nudged her. "That, my darling, is the greatest sandwich you'll ever see."

Victoria bit on her lip.

Once they were finally inside the store, Victoria cast her eye down the counter that ran the length of the store. Smoked salmons were arrayed in the glass cases, along with dishes of caviar and a variety of roes, cream cheeses and herrings. Servers and slicers worked, white coats on, taking orders and chatting with regulars.

Family photographs lined the wall at the back of the shop. Jacob busied himself schmoozing with one of the servers behind the counter.

"How is your daughter at Valentino's?" the man asked.

"Oh, she's marvelous," Jacob said.

"Shall I make you your sandwich?"

Victoria gathered her clutch purse to her chest.

"Two toasted bagels with cream cheese and a slice of smoked salmon," Jacob said. "And two caramel macaroons."

In a flash, the man handed over the sandwiches, and Victoria couldn't help it, her stomach grumbled.

Jacob linked his arm through hers again, leading her out of the shop to a park around the corner. Settling himself down on a bench that overlooked a manicured square of lawn, he handed her a bagel. "The flavors of life are here, my darling," he said.

"Oh, honestly, Jacob." Victoria eyed the crisp toasted bagel with its satiny smoked salmon and cream cheese. She took a bite. The flavors swirled around her taste buds, and she vowed that she would never tell Jacob that this was the most delicious thing she'd tasted in her life.

Chapter Twenty-Two

Lily

Fall, 1943

Lily slipped out of the restaurant straight after luncheon service on Saturday. She sat up straight on the train all the way to the Schwab mansion victory garden, perched on her seat holding her letters from Tom. She couldn't help grinning like a fool.

As the train rolled on, Lily unfolded the latest letters that Tom had sent by V mail and read them for the millionth time.

Pantelleria, Italy, Summer, 1943

Cara mia,

You have no idea how much I miss you. I can't write about it properly, because I feel it so deeply that it is too much to put into words. We all feel that way, all of us soldiers, because we are away from our families.

My darling, I've received a slight shoulder wound in action, nothing to worry about— please don't tell Mom. For my services, I received the "order of the purple heart." Outside of that, everything is in pretty good condition.

For a short duration, I am in hospital, manned by men from a big western university back home, intelligent men, who are swell. I'm surrounded by other injured GIs, but I consider myself lucky as I'm strong as an ox.

Other than that, cara, a little about this island. Here the houses are made of stone so thick that they keep the rooms cool in summer and warm when it gets cold. Italians live off the land, growing grapes, tomatoes, onions, wheat. The children often go barefoot, or wear slippers with wooden soles. They love candy, and ask us for it all the time! We give it to them, because there is no candy on the island, and no stores at all. The children swim in the sea and just love it. One day, in better times, we will come back to visit, and I will show it all to you, my love.

I feel like this is a forgotten place.

Cara, you are in my heart and thoughts constantly,

Your Tom

Italy, summer, 1943

Cara mia,

Now I'm out of hospital, I find myself dreaming about you. Last night I dreamed I was back in Valentino's. You were fighting with Leo, and I was admiring your gumption, hoping no one would notice me smiling about you to myself. It's both beautiful and heart-wrenching to think of home, and especially, cara, of you.

Talking of home, we all get homesick, and my outfit is mostly Midwestern, from Wisconsin and Illinois. The men from Wisconsin are swell. Two of them are cheesemakers. We talk of marble peppercorn cheese, which makes my mouth water and has the chef in me working out ways I could use it in my cooking. We even have a burger chef here. He insists that you should add a pat of butter to the top of your

burger and the others back him up and tell me that pat of
butter makes all the difference! My mouth is watering at
the thought of a pat of butter!

I hope the censors have not cut too much of this, and,
cara mia, thank goodness they will not censor my love for
you, and that, right now, is all that matters. Perhaps it will
always be all that matters, in the end, for the rest of my life.
I love you, my darling.

Cara, my beautiful Lily Rose, here it is. I can't hold it
back anymore. I want to marry you. I want to spend the
rest of my life with you, loving you. It's a fact and I want
us to enjoy the sweetest life. I would be honored to spend
the rest of my days with you. But, most of all, I want you
to be happy, so please, whatever happens, remember that.

My love,
Your Tom

Once she was off the train, Lily clutched Tom's proposal tight
in her hand all the way along 73rd Street toward the Schwab
mansion, too scared to put it in her handbag in case it fell out and
fluttered away in the wind. The moment she could, she'd taken a
fifteen-minute break this morning, rushing outside and walking
around the streets of Manhattan in a wondrous daze, heart beating
wildly, knowing that her face was flushed, eyes sparkling. All she'd
needed was an umbrella or a cane to twirl in the air!

Back in the kitchen, she'd forced herself to be professional
during her luncheon shift, when all she wanted to do was go and
sit in her office and whirl around and around on her the wheels
of her chair like a little girl.

Marrying Tom? It was the dearest, sweetest dream. She loved
him. Loved Tom with all her heart, and, as Josie had always told
her, that was the most important thing there was in this world.

Lily was not going to allow anything to stop her from being with him. Even if it meant keeping her engagement a secret, close to her heart, only shared with those she could really trust. And the first person she knew she had to talk to was Tom's mom, Gia. The sense of love that she felt for Tom, for his family, for the fact that she was going to be lucky to be a part of it alongside them from hereon, was more than she had ever dared dream of in her life.

She'd imagined the cosy apartment they'd live in, both cooking, going home from their jobs at Valentino's and eating delicious food, inviting Gia, Natalia, their chef friends over, enjoying New York with them all. Oh, it was all so perfect. So heavenly! She could hardly breathe for excitement.

The street carts with their colorful umbrellas selling cold drinks looked mighty tempting in the sultry heat that still lingered in the city even though summer was over, but Lily marched straight past.

The streets around here rang with the sounds of newspapermen shouting about production in the United States skyrocketing, and how Nazi Germany was unable to protect its cities from the Allied bombers that were being made on home soil.

The imposing Schwab house with its turrets and spires took up a whole block of land running toward the river. Lily rushed around the corner to Riverside Drive, stepping through the elaborate iron gates that marked the entrance to the palatial old estate, with its ornate fountains and gravel walks reminiscent of New York's Gilded Age. The whole place was as romantic as Valentino's, and Lily adored the fact that the restaurant was making use of this lovely old property for their vegetables.

She went straight to the huge victory garden, where women in light sundresses with scarves wrapped around their heads hoed the earth under the beating sun.

In the Valentino's plot, Gia worked alongside one of her volunteer gardeners, looking up from weeding around a patch of beets, a green pile of waste spread alongside her knees. "Lily," she said, reaching up to take Lily's outstretched hand and standing up.

"Hello there." Lily leaned in to give Gia a hug.

Gia wiped a hand across her brow. "I'm glad to see you. Giorgio Conti was keen to clean us right out of tomatoes this morning. I had to work hard to convince him to leave some for Valentino's weekend menus. Told him I had important connections with his head chef!"

Lily took in the last of the tomatoes in the rich soil. "Everything you grow flourishes, Gia. Giorgio probably thought you'd conjure him up a fresh crop by Monday. You're a magician, I swear."

Gia took off her gardening gloves. "I often come here in the evenings. And I'm here anytime I'm not working in the deli." She glanced over the garden, her expression serious. "With both Tom and Natalia gone, I need distractions. Thank you for allowing me to take part here."

Lily squeezed Gia's hand. Telltale shadows bloomed around the older woman's eyes. With Tom so deep in the Italian campaign, and now with Natalia away at the Women's Auxiliary Army Corps as a radio operator in Asia, Lily knew that Gia was working hard to stop herself from constant worry.

"Giorgio did say he was delighted with my mint." A gentle smile passed across Gia's face.

"It's a beautiful crop. And it's going to be served with the tomato soup appetizer tonight," Lily said, before adding nervously, "Gia, could I talk with you quietly a moment?"

Gia smiled. "Come and wander with me through the herb patch."

Lily tucked her hand into Tom's mother's arm. She wanted Gia's blessing and she could not live through another week without sending an answer to Tom. "Tom has asked me to marry him."

Slowly, Gia turned to Lily. "You're getting engaged to Tom?"

Lily handed Gia the letter.

"I love him," Lily said. "I love your son, and I want to spend the rest of my life with him, but I also would love... that is, it would mean a lot to me to have your blessing."

Gia scanned the last paragraph. Slowly, she brought a hand up to her mouth. "Lily. I adore you, you know that." She looked up, fanning herself with the letter. "But will your parents accept Tom? And, I hate to say this, but we are poor. Tom can't give you what you are used to, dear." Doubt flickered from Gia's eyes, but she held Lily's gaze.

Lily spoke in a whisper. "I love Tom, Gia. To me, that is all that matters. We are both chefs. We love each other. Who has what means nothing to me. My love for him runs deeper than that. I want to get engaged to him with your blessing."

Slowly, Gia nodded. "You know that I am very fond of you, dear Lily. I know how much Tom cares for you. Both of you deserve every happiness, and I can only give my blessing, dearest girl. But I do hope your family will be as liberated as you are."

Lily pressed her hand into Gia's. "Gia, I will keep my engagement a secret for now. I understand your concerns, and I'll wait until Tom gets home to introduce him to my parents, because I know that they won't be able to help but love him once they meet him."

"I am *thrilled* to hear your news," Gia whispered into Lily's shoulder. "But, please, think about what you are giving up in marrying into our humble family." She stepped back.

Lily hugged Gia hard. "Giving up nothing, and gaining everything," she whispered. "I'm the lucky one."

Late on Sunday afternoon, Lily curled up on her window seat in her bedroom. Golden streaks of late summer sunlight beamed through her window.

Dearest Tom,

I miss you at every turn. You have no idea how much. My heart goes out to you every day and I love reading the detail in your letters. The ones from Sicily only just arrived today, and I can see what you describe so perfectly.

Oh, I can't hold this off any longer. Of course I will marry you! One thing this war has taught me is that every day is a gift. I choose to spend the rest of my days with you.

I feel such a thrill at saying those words! What excitement they bring me, what joy, dearest Tom. I am filled with such happy anticipation for our future and I can't wait for your return. You must stay safe. Please, promise me that. We have so much to look forward to, when the sun rises over the world again.

I am doing fine, making some interesting decisions with menus. You won't believe how I am anticipating the reactions of our illustrious clientele. The latest charmer is going to be creamed chipped beef on toast—doesn't that sound entirely delectable? You can imagine how they will love that. But, so far, folks are pulling together and not complaining too much.

Your mother is doing a marvelous job with Valentino's victory garden. We have cauliflower, celeriac, chicories and fennel, parsnip and shelling beans growing now.

I told your mom about our engagement. I'm thinking that I'll wait until you're home before telling my mom and dad our wonderful news. That way, they can see you face to face. I know that once they meet you, they won't be able to resist you. Josie certainly can't!

In the meantime, I don't want them finding out about us from some third party, so I'll keep our wonderful news between us until you're safely back.

A secret engagement! What a thrill! It makes it seem more real, more special to me. Especially without society gossips pulling us apart while you're not here.

No, I will keep you close to my heart. So close, it almost hurts.

As for my job, I worry that Giorgio might intimate that me being engaged could interfere with my ability to work. So, let's tell him together, too, when you come back.

My love is with you, and it always will be.

Please, stay safe, beef Wellington will be cooked to perfection, just you wait.

Your Lily

Lily read the letter over, frowned at it, and stared out the window at the setting sun. At the sound of her mother pushing her bedroom door open, Lily slipped her letter under the cushion she was sitting on, and stood up, folding her hands in front of her.

"Well," Victoria said. "I have good news."

Lily eyed her mom.

Victoria fidgeted with her pearls. When she spoke, her voice rose in pitch. She cleared her throat and thrust an envelope into Lily's hand. "Here. This arrived. It's quite splendid."

Lily frowned at the letter, turning it over in her hands. Nathaniel's sloping writing ran across the envelope. Neat, upright. How she couldn't help comparing it to Tom's endearing, scribbly penmanship.

Victoria folded her hands behind her back. As she did so, Lily frowned. Were Victoria's hands shaking?

"Mom?" she said. "Are you quite okay?"

Victoria nodded. But she hovered.

"Is there anything else?" Lily asked. How she hated this. How she hated the fact that the only interaction she'd had with her own mom this weekend had been her bringing a letter in from Nathaniel. "I'll read it, of course," she said.

Victoria's eyes rounded. "Shall we read it together, dear?"

Lily slumped back down on her window seat, sure to land on the cushion that hid Tom's proposal. She sighed, picking up her letter opener, which was still to hand, thankfully, and sliding it under the envelope's rim.

If she didn't know better, she'd swear the letter was damp, as if it had been touched with steam. She narrowed her eyes. Surely, not even Victoria would stoop so low…

But Victoria's eyes drank in the neat writing across the thin paper. "Why don't you read it? Come on, Lily."

"Why are you so keen that I do?"

"Oh, for pity's sakes." Victoria snatched the letter, her eyes darting across the page, her chest heaving underneath her cream blouse, her painted nails trailing across the paper as fast as her eyes. She read it aloud in the same strangely tremulous tones. "*Dearest, Darling Lily, Oh, I can't wait any longer…*"

Lily stood up.

Victoria continued. "*Let's make our engagement official. You know how happy it will make everyone concerned—me to the utmost, Lily. You can't imagine how knowing I'll have you to come home to will make these long days and nights on this infernal ship worthwhile, or at least bearable. Knowing that you'll be waiting for me, that you, at least, are having fun planning our wedding, will give us both something wonderful to focus on.*

"*Please say you'll marry me. I can't bear the thought of not coming home to you. Whenever I think of New York, it's you that's in my heart. I think being away from you has made that state of affairs even clearer. You know, you didn't give me a photograph when I left, when I said goodbye to you over a year ago in Gramercy, but I had one of my own. One that was taken when you were eighteen and a debutante.*

"Such a stunning girl. I knew even then that I was in love with you, that there was no one else for me. But I couldn't get near you with all those fellows around. And you just seemed to ignore them all, which only made it worse! Or gave me hope. Hope that I might be the one you were really thinking of. I'm sorry I left it so long. But for four years, I've been in love with you. It's taken a war for me to get the courage up to propose. Oh, Lily, please just say yes this time. Make me the happiest man alive. We've been writing for more than a year now, and I think that it's time we went official, my love. Please, just send me word. A telegram, a letter. In the meantime, I'll wait, but know that it's getting impossible. I need something to keep me going! All my love, always, Nathaniel."

"My dear," Victoria whispered. "You cannot say no to that."

Lily lowered her eyes to the floor. How much easier this would be if Nathaniel were not in love with her. The last thing she wanted was to hurt him, but to lead him on any further, that would be even crueler.

"Mother," she said, her voice sounding far away. "Why were you so keen to read me that letter?"

"Well, dear, you haven't been here all weekend. Out at the restaurant, and then at that garden of yours. I hardly see you. I wanted to share it with you."

Lily folded her hands. When her voice came out, it was deadly quiet. "It had been steamed open, Mother."

Victoria's eyebrows raised to the roof. She shrugged. "Censors. You know what they're like. The war has turned our country crazy!"

Lily's smile was tight. "I have to go to bed. I have an early start, and, you know, all of a sudden, I'm not hungry. If you'll excuse me." Lily moved toward the door. She'd have a bath. Right now, she was full of everything: shock at her mother's audacity in opening her mail, love for Tom, relief at her acceptance of his proposal, desperation to be by herself so she could think about their future and make plans, while guilt bit at her about Nathaniel...

Victoria's grip on her arm was firm. "Darling, accept him. You're dragging this out. And that is making everything so much harder on us all."

Lily pressed her lips together. The urge to shout, to just tell her mother the darned truth about her life, threatened to explode. But a dark voice inside her held onto the truth. If she did come clean about Tom, she'd risk her job, risk losing Valentino's, and deep down, she knew she might even lose her family. Because her engagement to Tom could well estrange her from her mother, and in turn, that would break her father's heart.

No one chose secrets unless they had a better option. But, for now, she had no choice but to hold Tom close to her own heart and keep quiet about it.

Lily rested her hand on her mother's arm a moment, stayed silent, and turned on her heel and walked out of her room.

Lily hovered outside Giorgio's office on Monday morning, clutching a folder of recipes to her chest. Recipes she hoped that Giorgio would approve of as an Italian, but not, she suspected, as an American. She'd rehearsed and rehearsed the speech she was going to make.

"Lily." Giorgio held the door to his office open. "Why, you look like you've seen the Valentino's ghost."

Lily sank down opposite him and fanned herself with her notes.

His brow furrowed. "What can I do for you, dear?"

Lily chewed on her lip. "I have some proposals to get us through the coming autumn and winter, but I fear our Upper East Side clientele will not take to them."

Giorgio got up and shut the door. "They will chew me up and spit me out, not you." He slid back into his chair. He shuffled some papers around on his desk and handed a couple of pages to

Lily. "Right now, I'm dealing with the issue of no rubber for the truck's tires."

"The refrigerator truck?"

Giorgio sighed. "I've had the tires recapped, but they won't last much longer. I can't put the truck up on blocks, you know, we are too dependent on it. This rubber shortage is causing me great concern."

Lily scanned the notice in front of her. It had been over a year since everyone had handed in their old galoshes for the rubber drive, but that sort of rubber was no good for tires.

Giorgio went on while she read. "Then, there's gas. Even though we get a decent ration allotment for our essential shopping because we are a business, that is no use to us when gas stations are running dry. How are we supposed to get around?" He rested his head in his hands.

Lily had read about Germans operating off the East Coast, sinking gas tankers as fast as the US tried to bring them up from the Caribbean oil fields.

"Well, we surely can't be waiting in line for hours to get our gas every morning," she said. Her Bantam had gone up on blocks ages ago, as she and her father had planned. She'd only had an A card, allowing her three gallons of gas a week.

"We can hardly lug an entire day's worth of produce from the markets on the train," Giorgio said.

"I only wish I had something useful to say, Giorgio."

"Well, we can be cheered, dear, by the fact that coffee rationing has been lifted. Joe Martinson has kept me in good supply, and I don't want to know how, but that is something, at least. Seems they have an awful lot of coffee in Brazil."

Giorgio reached for his ration books, the rows of red stamps for meats, cheese and fats getting smaller and smaller as the months went on and the stamps came close to expiring.

He threw a glance toward the closed door. "Hundreds of businesses are violating the rationing systems even though the Office of Price Administration are carrying out inspections. Between you and me, I *might* have bought some supplies under the table, not to mention gas when I could, cash on the side, paying above the ceiling price, but I'm not the only one. You understand?"

Lily nodded.

He clasped his hands together. "I'm not overbuying. But I need to keep the restaurant alive, and keep all the people here employed."

"I'm keen to help and that's what I wanted to talk to you about." She frowned at her folder of recipes and opened them up. "Giorgio, I'm thinking people may be more likely to eat different foods when they look like something they are familiar with."

Giorgio watched her, tapping his pencil on the desk.

Lily screwed up her nose. "I'm thinking of shaping mincemeat like a steak. I know it sounds mad, Giorgio. But, right now, I'm hoping the restaurant guests will run with it."

Giorgio let out a loud laugh. "You're cheering me up already. The wealthy New Yorkers are hardly making a dent in their lifestyles, and if we can't supply them with what they want, we have to come up with alternatives. I like your approach."

She lowered her voice. "I struggle with their attitudes, Giorgio. Some folk hardly seem aware we are at war." Her mother. She could not throw stones.

"*Santa Maria,* that is so very true," he murmured the words, and something shifted in his voice.

"Take a look." Lily handed him a wad of her recipes. "I'm thinking of turning liver into meatloaf, and using kidney in our pies with a tiny portion of beef."

He scanned the page. "Smoked Beef Tongue à la Madeira…"

Lily glanced at him and continued. "I will use cans of dried beef and mix them with shortening, flour, milk and cayenne pepper and call it 'creamed chipped beef.' I'm adapting it to make it seem more appealing, adding some spices and pepper. Tom told me they had something similar a few months back in the army."

Giorgio raised his head at the mention of Tom.

Lily reddened.

"You have heard from him?"

Slowly, she nodded. "Yes. Yes, I have."

He stared past her a moment. "Lily, go now and try out those recipes. You'll have a job convincing the chefs."

Lily let out a long exhale. "I know that. I'm having to convince everyone of everything right now, but at least I know what I want."

Giorgio's eyes flew up to meet hers, but she stood up and turned to go out the door.

Chapter Twenty-Three

Lily

November, 1943

On a still fall afternoon, Lily hovered in the restaurant by the Valentino's bar. Giorgio scanned the sketches that Jimmy had made for tonight's seafood platter. It was a feat to conjure up in wartime, but, between them, Jimmy and Lily were proud of what they'd designed after an extremely early visit to the Fulton fish markets to beat the other chefs to the catch.

"This is good." Giorgio handed back the diagrams of tumbling oysters, clams, and shrimps, along with a drawing of an ice sculpture, a free-form rock that they had worked up with Julius late into the previous night.

Lily smiled with relief and slipped the drawings back into her growing collection of wartime recipes.

"Thank you, Giorgio," she said. "I'll get Jimmy onto this straight away."

Giorgio patted her on the shoulder and drifted off. The sound of the telephone burst into the foyer.

"Valentino's. May I help you?" the maître d' enunciated with great clarity into the telephone on his desk. He looked up sharply at Lily, his hand over the receiver. He beckoned to her.

Lily's hand fell to her side, Jimmy's sketches dangling in thin air.

The low whoosh of the Hoover vacuum cleaner hummed in the background, and maids chattered like sparrows as they polished and dusted the foyer after luncheon service.

No one had ever called Lily on the restaurant telephone.

The maître d' held the phone out to her. "Strictly two minutes."

Something dark unfurled through Lily's insides. She took the receiver, holding it away from the bouquet of flowers that took up most of the restaurant's reception desk.

"Hello? This is Lily Rose."

"Lily." The voice was faint and far away.

"Gia?" Lily cupped her hand over her free ear to block the Hoovers and the chatting maids.

"Oh, Lily." Gia's voice shook. There was a sharp intake of breath.

Not Tom. Please, not Tom.

"I've had a telegram."

There was a shaky pause. Lily gripped the phone cord.

"Tom's been reported missing in Italy… it was during the Allied landing at Salerno. They've lost him." Gia's voice rose on a terrible, high sob.

Lily grabbed for the polished table. Her journal of recipes fell to the ground and loose pages filled with all her notes pooled on the floor. "When? What happened?"

"I don't know. All I know is that he's disappeared."

Lily's hand shook on the receiver. "Well, missing does not mean…" she could not say the word. Her voice quivered and she jerked her head up toward the ceiling, trying to focus on the plaster, on the lights. *Not Tom. No.*

"My son, my boy…"

"Dearest, Gia," Lily whispered.

"Lily… we will keep in close touch."

Lily placed the receiver down.

The maître d' looked down at her, the expression on his face one of barely disguised disapproval. He pulled out a cloth, went to the telephone and wiped the receiver she'd just held.

Lily drew her hand to her mouth, uttered a sob, bent down to gather all her work from the floor and fled back toward the corridor, but as she reached the doorway, she walked headlong into Vianne.

Giorgio's wife caught Lily's shoulders. "Lily, dear?"

The maître d' came toward them. "The matter of staff calls on the telephone, Mrs. Conti."

"Not now, Howard. *Attendez*," Vianne said, fluttering her hand at him. "Lily? Would you like to come and sit down?"

Lily let Vianne lead her. The corridor's solid walls seemed to flow either side of her like two watery streams.

Tom would not receive her acceptance of his proposal. What if he never had a chance to know she would have spent the rest of her life with him?

Vianne pushed open the door to her sitting room.

Lily stumbled on the threshold.

"Giorgio says you've been in your office very late after dinner service six nights a week. Are you all right, my dear?"

Lily drew the bound journal containing her own wartime recipes toward her. The book was now filled with all the ideas she had sketched out late at night, transferred from her mind and her heart to her pen. The thought of the war ending, and Tom coming back had been keeping her going.

Vianne stood quietly opposite her.

Despite the war, despite rationing, she'd pushed on and thought up ways of adapting corned beef into fritters, of creating an eggless sponge, of cooking lovely fried breaded balls using day-old Italian-style bread, shortening, onion, herbs and stock. She'd worked so hard to keep things going, and now… It was unthinkable.

She looked up at Vianne. "I'm sorry. It's just that…" She couldn't confess that she knew. She could not tell Vianne that she'd been the first person to hear that Tom had gone missing, because the Contis would guess that something was going on.

And yet he was her fiancé!

Lily swallowed, but her throat stuck hard.

Gently, Vianne touched Lily's shoulder.

"Lily?"

Lily shook her head, her throat tightening again.

"Would you like me to take you home in my car? I have a bit of petrol for my business, and we could say it was essential."

Lily brought a hand to her mouth.

"I think you need to go home."

Not home. Home was not home anymore…

"Lily, dear. Please know…" she looked away for a moment, her lovely eyes settling on the floor. "I understand. I lived through the last war, too, and I was only young."

Lily pressed her lips together and looked off to the side. She stifled a watery smile. "You are so very inspiring, Vianne," she said. Lily shook herself. She pushed back her chair and stood up. "Are you sure that Giorgio can do without me tonight?"

"I am certain. You need a rest, dear." The older woman's intelligent blue eyes scanned Lily's face.

"There is someone I have to go and see."

"Lily, whoever he is, he's a lucky man."

Lily stared at Vianne for a moment, then she turned around and rushed out the door.

Hardly knowing what she was doing, Lily hurried out of the train station at Greenwich Village, gathering her coat close against the swirls of wind and falling leaves that flurried through Washington Square Park. She walked with her head down under the arch to MacDougal Street, trying to pinch back the flood of memories that assailed her from the last time she walked down here, arms linked with Tom's and local folks tipping their hats to greet him, smiling at her with interest. She'd felt like she was his girl. Now, only a few stray kids played in the street, and women and elderly men went about their business with their collars turned up against the cold air.

Lily stopped to catch her breath outside the house where Gia lived. The front door to the building was slightly open. Her chest pounded as she trudged up the staircase to Gia's apartment. She stared a moment at the closed white painted door, peeling in places, before reaching up to knock.

Gia was on the threshold in a flash.

Tom's disappearance seemed so very real and threatening standing here, face to face with his mother. Her pallid face was streaked with tears.

Lily stared at Gia for one helpless second, before, somehow, they fell into each other's arms. Lily hid her face in Tom's mother's shoulder, breathing in the smell of fresh linen and perfumed soap, the scents of home and peace and love and comfort. She hated the thought that Tom could be stuck in some dank place, a prison cell... or worse.

"Lily, sweetheart," Gia murmured. She loosened her grasp and held Lily at arm's-length, speaking in a halting voice. "Tom is a fighter. He has a reason to survive."

Lily's arms hung, slack at her sides.

"And that reason is you."

Slowly, Lily nodded. She had to be brave for Gia. She knew it was right to come here. "And, he has you. You and Natalia. We have to pray that we are enough for him to hold onto, to keep his spirit alive."

Gia scraped back a cluster of curls from her forehead. "Come inside and I will make coffee."

A few moments later, Lily took her shoes off and curled her legs underneath her on Gia's soft sofa. When Gia came back with two cups of coffee, Lily plonked her legs back on the ground. "I'm so sorry. I hardly know what I'm doing."

Gia placed the cups of coffee down. "Honey, those are old sofas. You've slipped your shoes off. Curl up as much as you like."

Lily bowed her head and stared at the ground. "It seems so long since he left. And yet, I feel as if it were last week that we were sitting here together with you."

"Yes."

"Coming to your house is like coming home for me. I feel his presence here so strongly, Gia." She whispered the last words, her face reddening at the confession that had slipped from her tongue.

"It is hard, difficult, when you have held a child in your arms, to imagine something like this. I know I am only one of so many mothers." Gia put her coffee cup down and stared out the window.

"Natalia is all right?" Lily asked.

Gia nodded bravely. "Oh, yes. Brave, breezy letters about the other girls, the camaraderie, only with vague descriptions."

Lily's voice broke. "We have to be brave ourselves about Tom. Don't we, Gia?"

"If he's alive, I have hope." She spoke with a quiet assuredness.

Lily pulled out a piece of paper from her handbag.

Gia took it absently.

"I made some plans for our late-winter plantings, for beets, cabbages, onions and parsnips, and winter squash. I'll help you plant them." Her voice broke, but she wavered on. "Tom would not want us to stop what we are doing to help, would he?"

Gia shook her head, her eyes filling. "The garden we built is a *victory* garden. I believe if we hold out, that is what must happen. It *must*."

"You are right," Lily whispered. "We have to focus on victory. On freedom and a better future for us all."

Later, back in Gramercy Park, the enforced darkness of the blackout seemed to enfold the street. The gated park was still and quiet and inside her parents' apartment, there was no sound but the ticking of the grandfather clock.

"Lily!"

The lights in the hallway flashed on.

Her mom stood in a long-sleeved navy silk dress that hugged her bodice and flared out to her knees. A cream silk flower was pinned to her breast. Diamonds sparkled around her wrists and at her earlobes and her dark hair was elaborate and exquisitely styled.

Victoria's lip curled at the sight of Lily's ensemble. "Remind me when I encouraged you to dress like a man?"

Lily looked down at the trousers she'd put on this morning in the darkness as if hardly registering them. "Women are starting to wear trousers now. It's far more practical with so many of us working."

Victoria threw her gaze to the roof. "Hurry up. You know we have a dinner engagement."

Lily scraped a hand over her hair. "No, Mom. Not tonight." She stared off to the side, at the familiarity of the wall lamps that lit the long hallway of their apartment. The heating was on, and the carpet was soft underfoot. Tom could be starving, hiding in someone's barn in the cold, not knowing if he'd ever walk out alive.

Lily wrapped her arms around her body. Why couldn't she fall into her mother's arms like any other daughter and confide?

Victoria closed her eyes. "We have accepted an invitation. We are going to the Carters, and that is final. This exhaustion of yours is becoming tiresome."

"What?" Lily barely registered the crack in her voice.

"I told you a week ago. It's not big, just around twenty or so people. You can't pull out now. It would be rude and ungracious."

"We have had a terrible day at Valentino's." Lily clenched her fists by her side.

"Well. All the more reason to come out with family and get your mind off things." Victoria turned down the hallway. "Come on."

Lily swayed. She reached out for the polished table in the hallway, her fingers fumbling to catch the edge of it. "Our... *chef de cuisine* has gone missing in Italy. In the Allied landing at Salerno." And tomorrow, everyone would know at work. Gia was informing Giorgio over the telephone tonight. Lily would have to pretend that, just like the rest of the kitchen staff, she only mourned Tom in a professional capacity. Lily scoured her mom's face for a trace of understanding. "Mom?"

Victoria's smile was tight. "Lily, just get dressed, and behave like a normal girl."

Lily fought back the tears that threatened to spill down her cheeks.

Victoria rushed off to the sitting room. Lily followed her, dragging herself through the house.

"Honestly!" Victoria grimaced. "For goodness' sake, get a grip." Victoria bustled over to her bureau, making a big deal of tidying papers, notes, folders, cutouts from magazines.

Lily clenched her fists at her side. Maybe she should tell her mother. What if the fact that Tom was missing might just bring her around? "Mother..." But just then, Lily caught a glimpse of the papers her mother was so busily tidying away. Slowly, she moved across the room. And stopped behind Victoria. "Mom?"

Spread in front of her was an array of pictures. Wedding dresses, lists of caterers' names. A letter from the Church of the Heavenly Rest.

Slowly, Lily reached out a hand toward the letter, saw her name. Nathaniel's. Confirmation of a date: September 25, 1945. She staggered backwards. "*Mom?*"

Victoria turned around, raised a brow and placed her hands on her hips.

Lily wanted to form words, but they simply would not come out.

Her father came into the sitting room, looking fresh in a formal dinner shirt and black trousers. He held out his arms for Victoria to fasten his cufflinks.

"Dad?" Lily felt the rush of blood to her cheeks. She brought a hand up to cover her mouth. Pointed with her other hand at the bureau.

Her parents exchanged glances. The lights seemed to throw strange shadows on the wall.

"It is such a pleasure to me to think that you will be well looked after once the war is done," Victoria announced. "Dear, later, this will all make perfect sense."

Lily stared at the desk.

"Katherine and I are all anticipation."

Lily's head shot up.

"The only way to survive this war is to plan ahead for when it's done. In fact," Victoria murmured, "if we weren't planning this wedding, I think I'd go quite mad with worry about you."

"Excuse me," Lily said, knowing her face was scarlet, her hands shaking. She pulled away from her father, too distressed to enunciate her words.

"Just think! Silk will be available again, dear. Lovely. The occupation of Paris has had such a dreadful effect on the fashion industry."

Lily swayed out of the room. Outside in the hallway, she leaned on the white painted wall. How had things come to this? How had everything split itself into two? Her job, her family. Nathaniel, Tom. The Village, Gramercy Park. Gram, her mother.

Her eyes fixed on her favorite photo of Josie, staring out directly at her, with blue eyes clear. Lily swung back around toward the sitting room.

Her father was pouring himself a whiskey.

Victoria was settled on the sofa, her legs crossed at the ankles. She raised her face to Lily, her gaze as innocent as a child's.

Lily met her mother's gaze. And right then, it came to her. The answer. Lily stood up tall, her words strangely even. "Mother, father. It's time I moved out of here."

Victoria blanched. Her gaze flickered toward Jacob.

And then, fists curled at her sides, Lily ground out the words that she should have uttered months ago. Well before Nathaniel left for the war. She took in a breath. "I cannot marry Nathaniel, and I'm not going to do so."

Her father leaned against the bureau, shadows falling across his features. "Darling—"

Lily's chest heaved up and down. "I want you to stop planning a wedding that will never happen. And I'm going to move out, pay my own rent. All I ask is that you respect my decision to do so. As you would any other adult."

Victoria folded her arms.

The room seemed to close in around Lily, but her thoughts were crystal clear. "This is not your life, Mother. It is mine. I would love to have your blessing, your respect for all my hard work that has led me to where I am. But it seems as if I am unlikely to get it."

She held her mother's eye for one interminable second.

And then, Victoria's mouth working, her cheeks red with rage, her hands gripping and tugging at her pearls, she shook her head, glared at her daughter, got up and left the room, slamming the door behind her.

Her father ran a hand over his tired face, his eyes locking with Lily's a moment, the agony he felt so clearly displayed on his features.

But Lily stayed resolute.

And, after one agonizing moment, he sent Lily a sad look, shrugged at her, and he went to Victoria, clicking the door softly behind himself, his feet treading a steady beat up the hallway.

Lily walked, slowly, to her own bedroom. In ten minutes, she had a bag packed.

Out in the street, she hailed a cab. "Greenwich Village," she said, the moment she slipped inside.

And in the dark interior, she stared out the window, tears coursing down her cheeks.

*

Dawn broke over Bank Street. Lily sat, awake, in the window of the spare bedroom in Josie's house, looking out at the sky, staring at the pearled, gray light. Cosmo was curled in her lap. After Josie had made her hot chocolate and plied her with biscuits last night, Lily had sat up, her thoughts a whirl, praying that Tom was somewhere, anywhere, safe under the same sky, disappointment swirling through her at her mother's refusal to accept her as she was, sadness that her father would not stand up to Victoria, wishing that things could be different. That Tom would come home. She held an old thin, folded letter from him in her lap.

Winter, 1942

Cara mia,

I don't want to pretend that things will be the same when I get back. You will have changed. I will have changed. We both will have experienced things that neither of us might ever understand. I am seeing things that… well.

I am enjoying the camaraderie of the others here. We are keeping each other going. In the end, sometimes, it is all we can do. Having such people around you, surrounding yourself with those who prop you up and don't pull you down is the most important thing in life. Promise me that you will do the same to get you through. Surround yourself with friends, with those who genuinely care about you.

But, cara, know one thing. Know that despite what either of us may experience, what will not change is my love for you. Despite our enforced separation, the tender feelings I have for you are unfolding inside me more and more every day. They say that the heart grows stronger with distance. Think of me as your faraway fortress, just as I think of you as mine.

When things are tough for either of us, we must remember that you and I are not alone, that our love will get us through until we meet again. It doesn't matter where we are, who we are with or what we are doing, we are always together, no matter what might happen.

Keep this with you, always,

All my love,
Your Tom

Chapter Twenty-Four

Victoria

"She'll come around," Jacob said. "It's Lily we're talking about."

Victoria stared out at the park. In Lily's room, sitting on her daughter's window seat, she closed her eyes and remembered that young girl who'd run around the park while she sat on a bench and watched, her hair in two long brown plaits. The memories burned so hard that they hurt. But as Lily had grown older, more independent, she'd pulled away from her mother, always running to Josie's house when she needed to talk. And Josie had encouraged it. Every time Lily fell in or out of love at some school dance, she'd gallop down to the Village to tell Josie all the gossip, all the news. When her grades came in, straight to Josie, all the friendship problems, dress decisions... Victoria had been entirely left out.

The fact was, Josie and Lily were a club of two, joined at the hip.

Truly, Jacob's mother had fashioned herself as some sort of elderly member of the *avant-garde,* refusing to age graciously ever since poor Hank had died, flitting out to the theater, associating with those Village types! It was hardly the behavior of the Upper East Side widow she was supposed to be. There were rules, and Josie seemed intent on breaking every one of them.

She, Victoria, would have to be the one to bring her daughter around.

Victoria sighed. Now, when she was *trying* to do something that would result in Lily becoming one of the most coveted girls in New York, when Nathaniel, who was a dear, upright man, a good man, was in love with her, why was Lily insisting on running off to Josie's, not to mention idolizing a woman like Vianne Conti, of all people?

Last week, Lily had carried on for ten minutes about how she so admired the French fashion designer for her commercial success, her creativity, her drive and her passion to succeed. Why could Lily not understand that she should be going to Vianne's for her dress fittings, not aspiring to *be* the woman?

The notion was ridiculous.

"If my mother had encouraged me to marry a man like Nathaniel Carter," she said to Jacob. "I would never have—"

"You would have married him like a shot." Jacob sat down on the dainty chair, covered in floral fabric, that sat empty in front of Lily's dressing table. He looked at her, his brown eyes clear.

Victoria's hand floated to her mouth. "I didn't mean that," she whispered. "Not exactly, dear."

Jacob tilted his head to one side. "Is it really so bad?" he asked. "Our life together?"

"No." Victoria's words were soft. "But, for Lily. What an opportunity. Come on, Jacob. Don't be daft."

He tilted his head to one side. "You know I adore you, and even your schemes, but don't let this obsess you, darling."

Victoria pressed her lips together. "I should go and supervise lunch."

As she passed by her husband, he caught her hand, and held it a moment. "I love you," he said.

"And I you." Victoria sniffed, shook her head, and walked right out of the room. And outside in the hallway, she paused a moment, the memories they'd created in this life together staring her in the face. Everything they'd done had been around Lily, and now she had lost her daughter. Lily had slipped right out of her hands.

Oh, Victoria had often felt envy toward Katherine and her diamonds, her European holidays, her furs and her priceless works of art, often worried that she couldn't possibly keep up with some of Katherine's other wealthier friends, with their husbands' spending capabilities, had always tried to urge Jacob on. But then, he'd always remained, quite stubbornly, himself. And she had to admit she respected him for it.

She'd seen this opportunity for Lily and jumped at it. Transferred her energies to her daughter. If she couldn't have all the riches in the world, why not her beautiful daughter?

Victoria shook her head, and made her way down to the kitchen to supervise the maid.

The following morning, Victoria pushed aside her half-eaten breakfast and went upstairs to her bathroom, passing Lily's silent, empty bedroom, ignoring the gnawing pain that slunk through her insides. She freshened up, dabbed a few drops of perfume on her wrists, collected her things, and went out.

She caught the train to Josie's house.

"Is my daughter here?" she asked, standing like a ridiculous fool and asking the obvious question on her own mother-in-law's front steps.

Victoria flushed as Josie simply regarded her, her wide blue eyes as clear as a girl's, standing there in an utterly unfashionable flowing cream cardigan over a hopelessly dated checked skirt.

Josie opened the front door wide, standing aside for Victoria to enter. The smell of baking filtered up from the kitchen.

Victoria turned to her mother-in-law, opening her mouth, a tirade that she'd tossed and turned all night over fighting to come out, only to find herself staring at Josie's back. Jacob's mother had the gall to turn her back on Victoria and was trotting down her basement stairs.

"Coffee, Victoria?" Josie called. "I've just put some on to brew. So lovely of you to drop by and see me. I was *hoping* you'd come, you know."

Victoria's brows knitted and she headed down after her mother-in-law, unpinning her hat, pulling off her gloves, removing the fitted green jacket of her up-to-the minute suit.

Josie poured coffee, slowly, into two cups, and handed one over. The expression on her face was unfathomable.

Victoria pulled out a chair and thumped down at Josie's kitchen table. She stared around the room while Josie busied herself with biscuits. Biscuits Lily probably baked before rushing off to Valentino's early today.

Victoria sat as stiff as a pole. "She's here, isn't she? You have her."

Josie was quiet while she pulled out a chair, settling herself down at her table. "Lily is not a parcel, Victoria."

Victoria raised her head and let out a laugh.

Josie took a sip of her coffee, before slowly placing it down again. "Victoria…"

"You think you can sweep in and infiltrate my daughter's mind with your ridiculous ideas. Well, I won't have it. I won't have it at all."

"I'm doing nothing of the sort. Lily can make up her own mind," Josie said.

Victoria clenched her teeth. Oh, this woman was always confounding. So confident. Victoria tapped her nails on the table.

"Can I ask you something?" Josie said.

Victoria glared at her mother-in-law.

"It seems to me that you are intent on being noticed, Victoria. You are intent on being someone."

Victoria pressed her lips together and frowned. Finally, she gave a shrug.

"You know, you don't need to use your children to be noticed," Josie said, her voice gentle.

Victoria's mouth dropped open. "How *dare* you. You have never had any idea how things are done."

"Ask Lily," Josie replied. "She knows exactly how things get done."

Victoria downed her coffee, pulled on her gloves, placed her hat on her head, and marched right out of the basement door.

Chapter Twenty-Five

Lily

Lily hovered over an oven in the Valentino's kitchen. The aroma of savory pie filled the air, while, outside, rain streamed down the misted windows. The moment Lily instructed her, Rosa bent down and pulled out a bubbling, experimental dish. She turned to everyone, a shy smile spreading across her face.

"This is exactly the sort of thing we want," Lily said. "Well done, Rosa!"

"I hope that when I cut into it, you don't all change your minds, Chefs." Rosa held a knife over the bubbling dish.

"It looks tempting," Ellen said. The cheery sous-chef bent closer to inhale the vegetables covered in melted cheese. She smiled, her cheek dimpling with delight.

"Oh, there's nothing to it," Rosa said. "I used whatever vegetables I could find, put them into this pie dish, and seasoned them with lots of pepper and a dash of salt. Lily gave me some herbs from the victory garden."

"Sounds like a cheery pie," Leo mumbled.

Agnes cleared her throat. "Why, Leo, Lily and Gia Morelli have done a wonderful job with the victory garden." She shot Lily a glance. "And, if they had not done so, Rosa would not have these wonderful vegetables every day."

"*Sicilianos*," Leo muttered under his breath.

Agnes stiffened. "What did you just say?"

Slowly, Lily raised her head from Rosa's dish. She'd heard the way Northern Italians looked down on their southern counterparts, when Giorgio sometimes let slip a few jokes with Tom. But Leo's attitude was something more sinister.

Leo's nostrils flared. "Gia Morelli is a *Siciliana*."

"Leo." Lily lowered her voice. "Petty prejudices have no place in my kitchen."

The chefs were silent.

"Now," Lily said. "Why don't you tell us about your new recipe, Rosa?"

"Well, I made a gravy with fat, cornstarch, vegetable stock and seasoning. I poured that gravy over the vegetables, then I placed a thick layer of mashed potatoes over the top. I sprinkled it with cheese, and I hoped like mad that I ended up with a good nourishing lunch at the end of it."

"Martina, I'm thinking we could serve it in small pots as a side dish," Lily said. "What do you think?"

Martina's eyes were focused on the dish. "I think it's an excellent idea. Well done, Rosa."

Ellen laid a hand on young Rosa's back. "I have to say, that pie looks mighty fine. How about we share it for lunch together?"

Rosa turned pink.

"It looks like a grand staff luncheon dish to me," Lily added.

Rosa started cutting into her pie. Martina took the slice Rosa handed to her and the others lined up for theirs.

Ellen dipped a spoon into the satisfying-looking dish and took a bite. "This is delightful. All velvety and lovely." She smiled, her dimple showing up.

Next to her, Meg made appreciative noises.

Rosa beamed.

A noise startled Lily. She turned to find herself face to face with Vianne, in a fitted red woolen dress with a pearl brooch pinned to her breast. A fur stole rested over one shoulder.

Rosa turned to Lily, a question in her eyes.

"Go on," Lily mouthed.

"Excuse me, madam, would you like to try some of my pie?"

"*Oh, la, la,* but of course. If you can spare a slice!"

And Rosa flushed again as she cut a generous slice for Vianne.

"Rosa is becoming a wonderful vegetable chef," Lily said.

And she smiled from the heart when Rosa turned pink with pleasure.

"Ma'am, this pie will stretch for miles and miles," Rosa said, genuinely beaming at Vianne now.

Leo wandered over.

Leo peered at the pie, shrugged his shoulders, and reddened at the sight of the beautiful Vianne.

Vianne took a bite and held her fork up to them all. "Well, my dears, I think you have a gratifying meal here. I'll encourage Giorgio to put it on the menu! It's perfect Valentino's wartime fare."

A cheer went through the kitchen.

"Lily?" Vianne said as the staff started going back to their stations. "Are you doing anything after luncheon today, dear?"

"We're trying more recipes out," Lily said. "I've asked my girls here to come up with a slew of fresh ideas for the coming winter months. I've scoured Gia's Sicilian cookbooks."

Vianne's frown was only slight.

"Martina?" Lily called.

The girl stopped, her hands poised above her station.

"Why don't you tell Vianne the ideas you've had."

Martina lifted her chin. "I'd love to. I've been thinking about *cotechino* served with lentils and mashed potatoes."

"Yes?" Lily prompted.

"I could make the sausages using pork skin as well as the meat, just like they used to in Modena. *Cotechino* was created in Modena in the sixteenth century to preserve the meat of the pig during a siege. My mom told me about it."

"And what else, Martina? Please tell us more," Lily said.

"Well, I was wondering about using cheap cuts of stewing beef and bacon instead of the sirloin that Marco used to insist on, standard onions instead of pearl onions and no mushrooms, with plenty of rosemary, thyme, parsley, and tomato paste for a beef bourguignon, war style. Fresh carrots and celery."

Vianne's lips curved into a small smile.

"The other idea I came across was mock duck." Martina's eyes lit up. "I thought we could take sausage meat, onions, apples and fresh sage, spread the sausage meat into a layer, top it with fresh grated apples, onion and sage and turn them into a duck breast shape, then cover it and bake it. It's actually very tasty."

Vianne stood with her spoon poised in the air. "I'm sure Giorgio would like to hear more of that sort of talk from you."

"She's making us men redundant!" Leo muttered.

"Oh, get over it, Leo. We girls are geniuses at making something out of nothing," Vianne said.

Leo flushed as he looked down at the ground.

"And that's a real skill," Agnes said quietly next to Lily.

Lily squeezed Agnes' arm.

"Meg's making up an eggless sponge," Lily said. "Ellen's taking on mock cream, using dried milk powder, sugar, milk, and shortening, and Agnes is looking into a wartime apple pudding, using breadcrumbs and almond essence with no flour, and maple syrup."

Vianne turned to Ellen. "Could you run this little wartime cooking session, Martina? I want to take Lily out somewhere special this afternoon."

"Why, of course I could," Martina said.

Vianne tapped the long prep bench with her red painted fingernails. "Can you meet me in the front foyer at half past three, Lily?"

"Are you sure, Vianne?"

"Have you got a good dress here with you?"

"Well, I suppose you could say that." Lily dropped her voice. "My mother does not tend to buy clothes for me that are not good quality, if you know what I mean."

Lily was certain that Vianne gave her a wink.

Vianne turned and went out of the kitchen, leaving a waft of Shalimar perfume behind her, and the basement hummed with the sounds of preparation for lunch.

Several hours later, Lily changed into the dark-green woolen suit that she hardly remembered putting on at four o'clock that morning. Her mother had complained when Lily had chosen it last year, because, like many other women's wartime fashions, it was the color of military attire, but Josie had complimented her on it when she laid it out on her bed last night. Lily checked that the rayon blouse underneath sat just so, and that her shoes were polished to a sheen that would pass even the test that Giorgio applied to his waiters.

Vianne was already in the foyer. She had replaced her fur stole with a full-length mink coat. "Our driver is outside in the car." She sailed out through the main entrance, the doorman holding the double doors open for her.

Outside, Lily caught her breath at the chill early-winter air. The doorman held open the door of Giorgio's Pontiac, and she slipped into the interior with its smell of leather and polish.

Vianne chatted with the driver, an elderly waiter who seemed to be doubling as a chauffeur, and Lily contented herself with looking out the window at the skyscrapers and the new sight of working women in coats, hats and trousers, hurrying down the Manhattan streets and disappearing into subway stations just like men used to do.

The saloon car glided up into Midtown, coming to a stop at Herald Square.

"I hope the drive was acceptable, ladies?" the elderly waiter turned to Vianne and Lily. He cracked a cheeky smile.

"It was charming," Vianne said.

"Thank you sincerely," Lily added.

He winked at them, before coming around to open the car doors. The famous five-story store that took up almost an entire city block loomed in front of them.

"Ah, Macy's," Lily breathed.

Beautifully dressed women came in and out of the doors that were held open by doormen, just like at Valentino's. Lily smiled at the tiny drop of nostalgia she felt for the pre-war shopping trips she'd taken here with her mom.

"I made the decision that you needed a break," Vianne said, waiting for Lily to catch up with her. Vianne thanked the doorman, tucked her patent leather handbag over her arm and wandered into the charming ground floor. "I also thought you might like to see something outside of that kitchen."

Lily smiled shyly at her, surprised that Vianne would take an interest in her.

Vianne flashed her ravishing smile. "And, the truth is, I want to ask your opinion on my latest collection. As a professional working woman, you are just the sort of customer I'm hoping to attract. Macy's have asked me to design a special line for them, and today, I'm having a final look at the wartime fashions I designed over the last few months."

A gale of warm air greeted them. Vianne sailed along. People stared at the fashion designer with Lily in tow.

Lily accepted a spray of perfume from an exquisitely turned out store attendant, while Vianne went to the concierge's desk to announce that she had arrived. Lily couldn't help sighing at the sight of the magnificent store with its wooden-framed, glass-paneled counters filled with gloves, scarves fashioned of rayon and lavish stationery. Escalators flowed smoothly to the upper floors, and the female staff chatted charmingly with customers, popping cash payments into pneumatic tubes.

When a man in his sixties appeared in a black tie and formal suit, he took Vianne's hand, raised it to his lips and kissed it, his white fingers with their square-cut fingernails gently holding her red painted nails. There was something about her that was delicate, and yet, Vianne was one of the strongest women Lily knew. A hush fell over the room.

"Why, *bonjour,* Mr. Straus," Vianne said. She waved in the vague direction of Lily. "You must meet Lillian Rose, who is the epitome of the new working woman that I want to try and target with my new collection: *Vianne at Macy's.*"

Lily came forward and the man held her hand, examining her face for a moment, before nodding and letting out a sigh. "Delightful," he breathed.

"I'm charmed," Lily said, feeling somewhat overwhelmed by the attention.

"Back to work!" he called to the gaggle of store attendants who had stopped entirely and were staring at him, mouths open wide. The high-ceilinged room resumed its buzz and chatter.

"Jack Straus owns Macy's," Vianne told Lily. "The attendants are somewhat star-struck to see him here."

Mr. Straus moved through the store. "I grew up with Macy's," he said. "I was here, aged two, when the Herald Square store opened!"

The staff bustled around their counters, sending Mr. Straus furtive looks as he led the way to a wood-paneled elevator at the far end of the store. A female attendant in a navy uniform took them inside.

"Private viewing rooms, Diane," Mr. Straus told the woman, who pressed the button for the relevant floor. The elevator doors closed.

The elaborate doors swept open a few moments later, leading straight into a room where the floor was covered by a swirl of velvety floral carpet. The huge windows were dressed with flowing silk curtains and pale roses sat in crystal vases on polished mahogany tables around the edges of the room. A group of Louis XV sofas were grouped at one end. Mr. Straus invited them to sit down.

Once Lily and Vianne were settled, another woman started pouring coffee. She handed Vianne a cup, gave a half-curtsy and waited while Vianne sipped.

"Ah, perfect." Vianne smiled and leaned back, crossing her legs at the ankles. "Lily, dear, would you like coffee?"

"Oh, thank you," Lily said. She accepted a the dainty cup of espresso, sighing with pleasure at the taste of Joe Martinson's special blend.

A woman in a wide-collared silk blouse with a tight-fitting black skirt that flared around her knees appeared from a wooden door. "Are we ready, sir?"

"We are, Beryl," Mr. Straus replied.

Beryl came to stand beside the sofa and, for the following half-hour, a parade of fashion models strolled into the room. Vianne examined the outfits, asking Lily for her opinion, while Glenn Miller's "Moonlight Serenade" accompanied her proposed new Macy's line. They started with pleated, shorter skirts to minimize the use of fabrics, and jackets with masculine shoulder pads, tailored to show off the waist. Next came long-line coats with fur collars and matching skirts, topped with stylish hats with netting that covered the face in the most flattering way for moving between business meetings in New York.

One girl came out in blue jeans with a scarf tied around her head, and Vianne turned to Lily, a question in her eyes. "For the practical working woman," she said. "Girls working the land, keeping us stocked with fruit and vegetables. The point is to feel comfortable and right for one's role in the workforce."

"Mighty practical," Lily said. She chuckled. "I only wish Giorgio would allow us women to wear blue jeans in Valentino's!"

"Well, you will have an uphill battle there, dear." Vianne squeezed Lily's hand. "But war or no war, I feel a surge of excitement for women's daily wear in the coming decades."

Next there were winter dresses in satin with only the wartime regulation numbers of covered buttons, scalloped bodices and sleeves, bows pinned to breasts and jewelry that sparkled for afternoon wear, costumes with small woolen capes and jaunty tilted hats for afternoon drives and, lastly, the evening wear.

Lily allowed herself to be swept away. She could not help but imagine going out somewhere special with Tom wearing the swathed viscose low-cut dresses that trailed to the floor or the pretty gowns with diamanté brooches and peep-toe shoes.

Vianne consulted with Beryl, and then came back to Lily's side. "How did you enjoy that, Lily?"

"It was lovely." Lily let out a sigh. "Although, I feel a bit guilty sitting here while the others are working."

Vianne eyed her. "You are allowed to take a break occasionally, you know. In fact, it's important you do."

Lily bit on her lip. Could she confide in this stunning, elegant woman—a woman who had a successful career and who might understand more than Lily thought? She took in a breath and plowed ahead. "I confess that I want to move closer to Valentino's," she said. She would have to choose her words carefully. "It would save me my daily commute."

Vianne picked up a rose-patterned plate of colored macaroons and offered it to Lily. Lily took one and stared at it, hit with worries about Tom. *Where was he? And if he was alive, did he have access to food?* She felt so helpless. If she could jump on a boat and go to Italy to try to find him, she would. And she hated to think what Gia was going through.

"What do your parents say? I'm sure they would not want you to move out?"

Lily bit on her lip. *She already had.* "It is for practical reasons."

Vianne was quiet a moment.

Lily placed her macaroon back down on the plate.

"You know you could take one of the apartments above Valentino's. Giorgio and I own a few in the building, and there are two that are empty right now."

Lily's heart skipped a beat. She glanced around the opulent, beautiful room. She'd had a look at what she could afford on her chef's salary in this morning's paper, and had ended up folding the paper and putting it aside. Giorgio paid her one third less than what Marco had been paid for doing the same job. If she was being paid what she deserved, she could afford a home that was worthy of a head chef. "Thank you, Vianne," she said.

Vianne laid a hand on Lily's arm. "I will talk to Giorgio. It makes sense, dear."

Lily smiled at the older woman. Her offer was wonderful. If she could catch the elevator upstairs after work, and relax in her own home, that would do a great deal to distance her from her mother's ministrations and wedding plans. It wouldn't be fair to stay with Josie in the long term. She adored her gram but didn't want to burden her by being a long-term guest. And it would allow her to focus on the life she wanted to build for herself, on the career she loved, and the man she adored. Lily was certain Josie would be proud of her.

"Mrs. Conti." Beryl swept back into the room, a nervous-looking girl behind her with a measuring tape around her neck. "Would you like to come and have a final look at your garments?"

Vianne rose.

Lily stood too. "Vianne, thank you for bringing me with you."

Vianne dropped her voice. "You enjoyed today?"

"Of course," Lily whispered. "I confess, I loved it."

Vianne leaned out and pressed Lily's hand with her fingers. "You would look beautiful in my clothes. I hope one day to dress you, perhaps when you marry some handsome man of your own. Someone successful like my Giorgio."

Lily sent her a tight smile.

"Thank you for coming with me today, my dear." Vianne pulled Lily into a hug, before turning and taking Beryl's arm.

Lily made her way out of Macy's with its magical atmosphere, back into the wartime streets of New York.

Chapter Twenty-Six

Josie

Josie stepped out into Bank Street. Only the last remnants of warmth lingered in New York, and were Josie honest, she was not looking forward to another freezing wartime winter. She wrapped her shawl around her shoulders against the cool breeze and headed down Bank Street, dropping a dime into an old man's hat and stopping to chat with him for a few moments. He grinned at her, his rheumy eyes shining like a young boy's, before Josie trudged on to where she was heading today.

The doctor. A place to be avoided, as much as possible. She had been so certain that the odd chest pains she'd been feeling lately were nothing. But after a while, after the niggles had escalated into outright burning, she'd done the right thing, gotten tests done, and last week the doctor had talked for an age about heart conditions, and had said something about Josie's Maker "knowing when it was time."

She'd known her doctor for many years, but was not impressed. Surely, his job was to cure illnesses, not to talk about makers. And yet, she'd lain awake in recent nights, fretting that, should things be coming to an end for her, she didn't want her family becoming anxious. That was not the way she wanted to finish her life.

To that end, she would not say a thing to them about her illness.

Josie pushed open the door to the surgery, just a few steps down from Albertina's. She'd pop in there and pick up some cannoli from lovely Gia Morelli after this was done. The sooner it was over, the better. The sooner she could get back to doing all the things she so loved.

The doctor looked at her test results. "I think you should move in with family. The medicine I have given you will help alleviate the symptoms of your heart condition, but I don't want you on your own anymore."

"The last thing I want to be is a burden to my family," Josie said to the aging doctor opposite her.

He regarded her over his half-moon glasses. "I'm not sure I know what you mean."

Josie leaned forward. "They are all busy. I won't worry them with this."

"Your son? Could you not move in with him and his wife?"

Josie snorted. "I'd be dead in a week."

The doctor folded his arms. He sat back in his seat. "You cannot have anyone come and live with you?"

Josie regarded him. And slowly it dawned on her. "Emmeline."

The doctor nodded. "Your granddaughter?"

Josie shook her head. "Oh, no. Lily's only staying with me temporarily. I won't stop her moving out, being independent and living on her own as soon as she wishes to do so. But, if and when that happens, I will confide in Emmeline, who helps me in the house these days, and only Emmeline, because this will upset my family too much. Especially Lily. I'm sure I could make a room comfortable for Emmeline, though." Josie sent him a level gaze. "I only hope that living with an old woman like me would not be deadly dull for her, poor thing. At least she will be paid to do so."

A hint of a smile passed across the doctor's face. He finished his notes, screwed the cap back onto his gold pen, eyes serious. "Josie.

We've known each other long enough for us both to know that the last thing this Emmeline is at risk of with you is boredom."

Josie raised a brow and chuckled out loud.

Ten minutes later, Josie walked into Albertina's, only to stop and stare at the sight of Gia Morelli behind the counter. The usually upright, bright-cheeked woman looked pale and drawn, and instead of chatting with customers in her usually friendly manner, she sliced ham and scooped up olives with the energy of a sad old hound.

Josie refused the attention of another sales assistant, waiting, instead, for Gia to turn her way. "Gia," she said, when Gia was finally free. "Is everything all right, my dear?"

The beautiful woman's lip began to quiver, and Josie instantly scanned the room for Lino, the charming owner of Albertina's. On seeing him, she marched up to him, told him she was taking Gia home with her before the poor woman collapsed, and had Gia leaning on her arm, with a white box filled with cannoli and Italian biscotti clutched firmly in her spare hand.

Once back home, she settled Tom Morelli's mother down in the warmest spot at her kitchen table where the sun poured in through the basement window, made coffee, and placed the cannoli and assorted biscotti out on a brightly colored blue-and-white striped plate. She added a selection of Lily's homemade biscuits for good measure and put her handbag with the wretched heart pills out of sight.

"Has Lily told you?" Gia's eyes were huge.

Josie reached out a hand, placing it over Gia's reddened fingers, the nails clipped short. "Yes, she's told me your Tom's gone missing, my dear. I'm afraid she's worried sick. I was fortunate to meet him, and I can tell you, he was one of the most charming, dear men I've ever met."

Gia buried her face in her hands.

Josie settled herself down. "Better out than in," she said, rubbing Gia's arm.

Gia nodded, swiping at her cheeks. "I hadn't been able to cry until now," she whispered.

Josie handed her a cup of coffee, and Gia heaved a sigh, sipping at it.

"Cannoli," Josie insisted, and Gia managed a watery smile.

Gia took a bite, even in the pain of her worry over Tom, she closed her eyes against the heavenly taste. And then she folded her hands on the table. "Mrs. Rose."

"Oh, there's no need for Mrs. Rose. Call me Josie. Everyone does."

"Josie, I worry about Lily's parents. I hope they won't hold Tom's position in life against him. I see how deeply Lily and Tom adore each other, but I understand these wartime romances can be viewed as aberrations by some folk."

Josie sat up in her seat. "Well, I view this in quite the opposite way. I see love affairs like Tom and Lily's as something so special that they must be cherished, Gia. I would hate to see either of them look back with regrets."

"Mrs. Rose… Josie, I hope Lily's parents are as open-minded and as gracious as you."

"Well, dear, Lily's mother and I take opposing views to just about everything in this world, but I've never let that hinder me." She eyed Gia.

At this, Gia's black eyes crinkled, lighting up and sending a hint of how beautiful she was. "I think that you and I are going to be firm friends."

Josie gathered her cardigan around her. The air in her usually warm kitchen suddenly seemed a little cold. "I'm sure of it," she said.

If she had anything to do with it, she'd remain on this earth as long as she could for one reason only: to stop Victoria making a terrible mess.

Chapter Twenty-Seven

Lily

Cold air misted across the Hudson River, blanketing the victory garden in a pale white fog. Winter was coming on thick and fast, and Lily tucked straw around the turnips, bedding the winter vegetables, the old Schwab mansion looming, like a gray ghost, in front of her. Next to her, Gia worked, her fingers red and raw. Around them, parsnips, winter squash and potatoes sat perky and healthy in spite of the cold. Somehow, there was consolation in the fact that nature pushed on, no matter what destruction humans could bring.

Gia sat back on her haunches, tightening the red scarf that she wore to keep her thick hair away from her face. "We should stop for coffee."

"I think so," Lily said. She glanced at the older woman next to her. "Oh, I do worry you are working too hard, Gia."

Gia stood up, arching backward, the heels of her hands pressed into the base of her spine. "I'm fine." She peered down at Lily. "You know it's a distraction, Lily. It stops me from thinking, and at the moment, that is a good thing."

Lily followed Gia along the neat, lovingly tended rows, their feet crunching against crisp golden leaves. Even though much of the garden was taken up with wartime vegetables, the old trees still soared over wide lawns with their stone seats and hints of long-ago fancy rose gardens, reminders of an age that had disappeared now.

Gia stopped at the basket she'd left at the end of the row, pulling out her tall coffee flask and pouring the hot coffee into enamel mugs. Lily cupped her hands around the delicious warm drink, letting her fingers thaw out a few moments before she took her first sip. She was thankful for the trousers that she'd put on today. The thought of being out here with bare legs when stockings had all but disappeared and girls were stenciling black lines down the backs of their legs was not attractive, not one bit.

Gia reached out and handed Lily a currant bun. "Eat this, Lily," she said. "You are looking too thin."

Lily took a bite of Gia's home-cooked rock bun. She was eating, but the weight had fallen off and was continuing to do so as her stomach churned with nerves and she struggled to sleep. Late at night, even in the warmth of the room she'd always slept in at Josie's house, she fought nightmares of Tom in the worst of scenarios, trapped and lost in the European cold.

Gia glanced across the freezing patch to where Giorgio stood talking with a couple of Gia's volunteers. Despite the pressure he was under, Giorgio still cut a fine figure in his navy coat and cherry-red scarf.

Gia's free hand fluttered to her own cotton scarf. "What if he doesn't come home?"

"No!" Lily leaned away from Gia. "I'll always wait for Tom. I love him, Gia." She missed him every day, the way he sauntered around the kitchen in his blue jeans, the way he threw himself wholeheartedly into his cooking, the way he cared about her and talked to her in the way no one else did. She closed her eyes.

"You know; I was worried that Tom will not be able to afford to keep you in the way you are used to." Gia stared out at her garden. "So, I spoke to your grandmother about it."

Lily turned to Gia. "You did? I can only imagine what my gram had to say about that."

"I really liked her, and she put my mind at rest. You both share a strong conviction about things." Gia stared out at the river. "I wish I could share it. I wish I hadn't already seen so much of war."

"I know," Lily whispered. War didn't care whether a dear man was loved at home. It showed no discrimination in who it carried away.

A light rain started to fall from the leaden sky, and Lily closed her eyes and sent up her thousandth prayer.

Two days later, Lily sat on the train to Valentino's, her gloved hands resting on the two suitcases either side of her. She'd hugged Josie fiercely, holding her gram and telling her how much she'd cherished staying with her these past weeks, but now it was time for her to move on. Giorgio had readily agreed to her staying in one of the apartments at Valentino's and for all she would miss her gram, she knew it was for the best.

The train hurtled Uptown. In the midst of the turmoil of living on her own for the first time in her life, it was thoughts of Tom that plagued her.

Oh, please. Send him back safely.

She leaned her head against the window of the train. In the pit of her stomach, she knew this was a one-way trip, and she'd never go back to living at home.

The following morning, Lily raised the blind in the studio apartment Vianne had prepared for her on the third floor above Valentino's. Gray light filtered through the window and her suitcases sat empty in a corner on the floor. All her clothes were already in the mahogany wardrobe and she'd laid a couple of novels by her bed. In pride of place was a silver-framed photo of Lily and Josie,

Josie sitting in her cherry-red chair, Lily standing behind, leaning over her grandmother's shoulder, arms wrapped around her beloved gram, both of them smiling at the camera. They were like a pair of peas in a pod, born decades apart.

Lily stroked the frame for a moment, before picking up her chef's outfit from the chair where she'd laid it out last night and gathering the things she needed to wash in the bathroom.

She showered quickly, and when she stood on the threshold of her first home away from home, her body tingling from the warm soapy water, the room seemed to float around her. Winter sunlight had broken through the clouds outside and the sounds of New York coming to life filtered into the apartment.

She strode into the restaurant kitchen, greeting Julius, who was already at the larger oven he used for baking, pulling out fresh hot rolls for the day. Lily fixed herself a coffee, accepted a warm roll and butter from him, and took the newspaper that had been set out early for the kitchen staff into her office.

She'd sent Martina out to the markets with Giorgio this morning, aware that she must start to promote her loyal team if she were to be an effective leader. She was determined to give them new opportunities to thrive.

Chapter Twenty-Eight

Lily thumbed through the paper. In Russia, the Soviet Army were working toward lifting the siege of Leningrad. Stalin, Roosevelt and Churchill's plans for a simultaneous squeeze on Germany were in place, along with an agreement on post-war settlements. Stalin did not want any diversions further east. While Churchill did not trust Stalin, Roosevelt wanted to show that he would not stand against Russia. Lily frowned.

She took in a deep breath and read on about Italy. Nothing new: the Allies were focusing on trying to liberate Rome from the Germans. Even though Mussolini had been deposed in September, he still remained head of the puppet government in Northern Italy, and the Germans also retained control of the Italian army.

The sound of Ellen and Meg arriving in the kitchen was a welcome distraction. Lily folded the newspaper and brought it back out with her. Their cheeks were pink and the basement lit up with Ellen's laughter, while Meg busied herself taking off her gloves. Julius cracked a joke and Ellen chucked him on the arm.

Jimmy strode into the kitchen, unwinding his scarf, his expression keen. "Good morning, Lily." He nodded at Ellen and Meg. "Last night, the three of us had a conversation…"

"Oh, we did." Ellen grinned at the affable *poissonier,* and Jimmy winked back at her.

"Do tell." Lily placed her clean plate on the dish rack by the sink and straightened her chef's hat.

Ellen brought a hand to her mouth.

Lily stretched, fully awake now. "I'm all ears."

"We thought we should go out as a group, Lily," Ellen said. Her eyes darted from Jimmy to Lily and back. "You know, out dancing?"

Martina and Rosa came in, followed by Leo.

Lily stared at her little team of lead cooks.

Ellen squeezed Meg's arm. "What do you think, Lily?"

Julius paused from kneading dough, sending the girls an indulgent smile.

"Lily, truth is, we all want to celebrate all you've done for us," Jimmy said. He clapped Leo on the back, almost tipping the rotund *rôtisseur* off his feet. "Don't we, eh, Leo?"

Leo ran a hand down his chin. "Maybe."

"Oh, come on, Leo. We menfolk could deceive ourselves that we're twenty-six again," Jimmy said, the traceries around his eyes wrinkling, his eyes dancing. "And take you girls out. With all due respect, Lily." He threw her a wide grin.

Martina raised her brow.

And Lily saw the way Jimmy winked at her. Martina blushed, her dimple showing as she smiled down at the floor.

"Martina?" Lily said. "Why don't you choose where we all go?"

"Well, here's the thing." Martina cleared her throat, looking shyly toward Jimmy now. "You know I've never been out in the Village before. Living in Queens, with my mom. It's just not something I've done. But I've heard about the clubs down there."

"Well, dear, you've found just the right girl for that," Lily said. "I can't tell you how fond of the Village I am."

Jimmy leaned on the bench behind Lily. "You talkin' about a jazz club, there, Martina?"

Martina nodded, her eyes round. "You bet I am, Jimmy."

Jimmy winked at her again and Martina blushed.

"Jazz clubs are up on 52nd Street," Jimmy said. "The best ones. But they're mighty fussy who they let in," he went on, his eyes still on Martina. "They'd never let me set a foot inside, you know. Might let Martina and Lily in, but I'd fear for us men."

Lily bit down a smile. "I've long been interested in going to hear Billie Holiday at Café Society in Sheridan Square."

"That's the place Barney Josephson owns," Julius said. "The wrong place for the right people?"

Ellen giggled. "Sounds like we'd fit right in!"

Lily couldn't help but grin.

Julius shook his head. "Never thought I'd say this, but all right then, Martina and Lily have it. Let's go down to that basement in Sheridan Square. Men in suits, girls in hats and dresses. You in, Leo?"

The rotund cook threw his hands in the air and nodded his head. "I guess so."

"Saturday night after service?" Lily said.

"That's tomorrow!" Ellen squealed.

"I'm in," Agnes said.

"We all are," Jimmy said. "Tomorrow night."

Julius raised his rolling pin above his head. "I cannot wait, my friends."

Everyone hummed their way through dinner service on Saturday. Martina and Rosa twirled around the kitchen once the main bench was all cleaned up.

"Right, meet back here in half an hour!" Lily said.

"Dunno if that's enough time for me to get all dolled up." Jimmy winked at Martina.

Martina took a swipe at him with a cloth. "Oh, yeah? Well, if I can do it, you can."

"But you're gorgeous," he said.

Lily grinned at Jimmy and rushed out with the other girls, only to come to a standstill on the stairs. For one moment, she stood there. Tom would want her to go out and have fun. He would hate her to stay in the whole time.

She took in a breath and made her way downstairs. Lily had brought a dress to the changing rooms that morning, so she could get ready along with the others. She didn't want to waste time running up and down stairs to her studio, when everyone was getting in the mood down here.

She tore off her chef's outfit and pulled out her red evening dress. Ellen fastened the long row of covered buttons that slid up the back of the low-cut gown. Lily turned and Ellen brought a hand to her cheek, her mouth falling open. Meg and Agnes gathered around.

"Why, you're one of the most good-looking girls I ever saw," Agnes said. She reached forward and straightened the right shoulder of Lily's dress, standing back and admiring the way the jeweled bodice gathered under the bust, before flaring into a flirty skirt.

"You're all the most beautiful creatures in the room," Lily said, her voice softening.

"Well, we have to do our make-up and hair before any of us can admit to that," Agnes replied.

Lily giggled at the practical woman beside her. She applied red lipstick, powdered her nose and sprayed her wrists with some precious Chanel No. 5. She brushed her hair until it shone, before pulling it up and elevating it fashionably.

"Wow," Ellen breathed. "Not bad for a bunch of chefs!"

They all stopped what they were doing and glanced in the mirror a moment. Agnes wore a dress with a black velvet bodice and a cream silk skirt, Meg was in bright blue with sheer sleeves, her blond hair pulled up and smoothed. Ellen was radiant in pale pink with a lace overlay patterned in roses and a netted skirt, while Rosa and Martina took Lily's breath away. Martina was draped in a slinky black dress, a gold binding running around her bust decorated with jewels. Her black eyes sparkled and her curls were swept up on her head. Rosa was also in black, her long eyelashes looking impossibly lush against her bright cheeks, while her dress sparkled with sequins and diamantés on the bodice.

"Wait," Meg said.

Everyone fell silent.

Solemnly, the girl reached inside her locker. She pulled out a screwdriver handle, a bicycle leg clip and an eyebrow pencil.

"Oh, ho, ho!" Ellen whistled. "Look who's organized for a party!"

Meg's eyes crinkled and she put the contraption together. "Right, who's first?" she asked.

"Well, me of course, honey," Lily murmured. "Who says we can't have stockings in wartime?" She stepped right up, placed her leg on the long bench that ran down the changing rooms, and let Meg attach the bicycle leg clip to her leg, wield the screwdriver handle and draw a perfectly straight line from her thigh to her ankle with the eyebrow pencil.

One by one, the other girls lined up, and soon, they all sported black lines that looked as sexy as any pair of silk stocking ever did.

"Well, let's go, beautiful girls," Lily breathed. "I say, the men will fall flat on the floor in dead faints. I can't wait to see Jimmy's face."

Meg snickered into her hand, but Lily was certain she saw Martina blush.

Once they were Downtown, Lily led the way to Sheridan Square. Ellen snapped along beside her, while Jimmy had kept steadily close to Martina ever since they'd left Valentino's. Now, they lingered behind everyone else. Leo and Julius continued to chatter with everyone in turn.

Lily trotted down the stairway to the basement, and true to form, they were let straight into Café Society.

Lily stopped a moment, her arm linked in Ellen's, while Meg was close behind. She adjusted to the dark and the cigarette smoke, before lifting her head to the stage and letting out a gasp.

"Wow," Ellen breathed. "Look at her."

On the tiny stage, surrounded by tables jammed right up to her feet, Billie Holliday crooned out a lilting version of the tragic song, "Strange Fruit."

"This song gives me the shivers," Meg said.

"It's meant to," Julius said. "Right, Lily, how fast can you go?" he said, eyeing a group leaving a table.

Lily took steps toward it, but Julius placed a hand on her arm. Lily stopped mid-stride. She brought her hand to her mouth. A well-dressed white man was confronting an African-American couple who were sitting quietly at a table next to the one that had just been vacated. And as soon as it happened, two men in black suits and bow ties were escorting the white man out. The rest of his group, all seemingly wealthy, were following them, incredulous looks on their faces.

Lily turned to Julius, eyes wide.

"Well, there it is," Julius said. "He must have insulted the black couple. But Barney Josephson won't tolerate discrimination. That's the difference between Café Society in the Village and the Clubs on 52nd Street." Julius threaded his way through the crowds. "Come on," he said. "Let's take advantage of those fools' departures and sit right up front to watch Miss Holiday here." He stood by the tables and waved his arm for them all to sit down.

Whether Billie Holiday had taken in the commotion or not, Lily swore that her face broke into a smile at the sight of Julius and their new group arriving, and she tipped her head back, showing off the double row of pearls on her throat. She started crooning, "They Can't Take That Away from Me."

A couple of hours later, Lily threw herself back down in her chair. She clutched Ellen's arm. "Oh, that was fun," she said. "I never thought I'd enjoy dancing with a whole heap of middle-aged men so much!"

Ellen clasped Lily's hand. "And look what we've got goin' on over there," she said, her dimple creasing.

Meg was bebopping with Rosa, Leo and Julius. Agnes had gone home a while ago to relieve her mom from taking care of her kids, Julius was across the table, and Martina's head was nestled on Jimmy's shoulder, and his chin rested on the top of her head.

Ellen blew Martina and Jimmy a kiss. "A pair of lovebirds, if I'm not mistaken. The first Valentino's wartime romance!"

Lily drew in a breath and a quiver flittered through her insides. She only just managed to give Ellen one of those brave, wartime smiles.

Once the night was done, Martina walked next to Lily in the darkened street, the others up ahead, laughing and singing, their voices ringing in the cool night air.

"Lily?" Martina said.

Lily stopped.

"I hope you're not grieving, or worried about someone special. I noticed you weren't with us the whole time tonight."

Lily stopped in the dark. A couple of girls hurried past her. The others were way up the street. Should she confide in Martina? Once, Martina was the very last person she thought she'd ever trust. Lily fiddled with her necklace. She tucked her arm into Martina's. One thing was certain, Martina did not gossip. "You see," she said, "I'm in love with Tom."

Martina kept walking. She did not skip a beat. "I guessed."

Lily bit her lip.

"It was obvious to me."

"Well, turns out I'm not so great at hiding my feelings as I thought."

"You know, I'm sorry about the way I treated you at first. I made an assumption about you. And I shouldn't have. You're nothing like some of those society girls."

Lily shivered. "No."

Martina was quiet next to her.

Lily sighed. "I never was, Martina."

"I hope you won't think class a barrier to friendship." Martina lowered her voice.

"Never," Lily said. "I never did think that, either, you know."

"I'm sorry if I once did." Martina's voice was soft in the dark. "And as for Tom and you, things shouldn't be complicated there, either."

Lily clutched her purse. "I know. I feel the same way. The simple truth is, I can't bear the thought of him not coming home."

Martina walked alongside her. She tucked her arm into Lily's, the sounds of the others' laughter filling the dark street.

Chapter Twenty-Nine

Giorgio strode into the kitchen on Monday morning, clearly searching for something, or someone. He started sniffing the air, looking for all the world like a detective on the hunt for a clue.

"Rosa," he murmured, finally landing at her station. "You know I love lobster bisque! And I'm certain that's what I can smell!"

Rosa's eyes lit up. "Well, sir, Lily told me to boil the tails in salted water for only five minutes to make a stock, and also to pre-cook the lobster and get as much flavor with reduced ingredients as we can. Why don't you take a look?"

Giorgio rubbed his hands together. "You clever, clever girl."

Rosa dipped a clean spoon into her bubbling pot. "You see, then it's a *mirepoix,* and a blend of fresh herbs from the victory garden, and some tomato paste and flour to thicken the bisque. And also, cayenne pepper."

"Perfect, Rosa," Lily said, resting a hand on Rosa's back.

Giorgio took the spoon and closed his eyes in delight. "This is mouthwatering, Rosa. Lily, can we have a chat in your office a moment?"

"Of course." She wiped her hands on a clean cloth and followed Giorgio into her room. Despite the turmoil with her parents, and missing Josie something dreadful, Lily was appreciating not having to commute to work. The extra hour's sleep each night was proving a godsend, and the studio apartment that Vianne had prepared for her suited her to a T.

Giorgio closed the office door. "I've organized something with Paddy Jackson."

Lily had a high opinion of their loyal meat supplier.

"I want to take hot dogs and coffee out to Staten Island, to Stapleton, to feed the troops who are about to embark for war, and to welcome those who are coming home. Paddy can supply the hot dogs, and I've bought a hot-dog stand. Would you and your team of women be happy to cook? Paddy can get the meat and bread to Staten Island, and I will sort getting the stand delivered there."

Lily clasped her hands in joy. "Of course, Giorgio. I'll talk to Martina and Ellen. We can take it in turns."

"Many of the departing troops will be familiar with Valentino's. Our little stand will be the last taste of America they have. And I want them to see my team of chefs smiling at them before they embark for war."

"I think it's a mighty fine plan, Giorgio."

Giorgio smiled, but Lily could see the worry lines that furrowed his brow. "I don't know what I'd do without you, Lily."

Chapter Thirty

A few days later, a freezing wind scurried across the decks of the Staten Island ferry and gray water churned below the boat. Lily pulled her cashmere scarf close around her neck, mighty glad for her warm winter trousers, and for the fact that her mom wasn't supervising her fashion choices today. The ferry heaved into dock, croaking and groaning in the mist. Lily cupped her hands against her mouth and breathed into her fingers to warm them up.

Ellen's cheek dimpled underneath her thick fisherman's woolen hat. "I never thought we'd be doing this, Lily."

Lily squeezed the girl's freezing hand with her own as they disembarked from the ferry.

The chain-link fence that surrounded the Port of Embarkation loomed up in front of them. Inside, scores of troops stood around at assembly points, their heavy boots sinking into the dark puddles that pooled on the cracked cement. A huge navy vessel was moored at the dockside. A steady flow of young men carrying kit made their slow way up the gangplank, their backs hunched, before finally disappearing into the mouth of the ship, its side pocked with rivets.

Lily couldn't tear her gaze away from the sight of the men alongside the huge troopship. She'd read in the newspapers how the ports of New York had become known as "Last Stop USA." While soldiers boarded troopships to Britain, the Brooklyn Navy Yard turned out these monstrous, looming battleships, along with aircraft carriers, and repaired thousands of Allied vessels. Coming down here made everything seem hauntingly real.

At the same time, New York had become a haven for thousands of refugees from Hitler. Some of Europe's leading scientists and artists and writers had fled across the seas to come here.

But the outgoing New York troops who were off to defend their home countries were only boys. If Lily looked closely, she could see the brave grins on their faces. For a moment, she stared at them, scouring the recruits for signs of one of the boys she'd grown up alongside. Boys who she once danced with, talking of their dreams and plans and hopes. None of those dreams mentioned going to fight in a war.

If only there was a chance she could see her Tom again, have even one more day with him, and hold him in her arms.

They made their way to the station entry box.

"Lily Rose, Valentino's restaurant," Lily said. "We're here to serve hot dogs to the boys."

The GI looked from the top of Lily's head to the soles of her shoes. "Do you have identification, miss?"

Ellen and Lily produced their IDs.

The soldier waved them in. "You'll have to report to the Port Commander's Office. It's the long white wooden building to your left."

The Port Commander's assistant took them to Giorgio's hot dog stand, and Lily got the steam pans up and running while Ellen put up the umbrella emblazoned with "Valentino's."

The three steam pans were full of Paddy's sausages, fresh from the meat markets, which Lily boiled for seven minutes exactly before pulling them out with tongs and placing them inside the buns that Giorgio had organized, along with mustard and tomato ketchup. Ellen busied herself frying onions in a pan on one of the hobs.

Soon an eager line of boys extended from the hot dog stand right across the cement strip on the foreshore, and Lily quickly made up jugs of fresh Valentino's coffee that Giorgio had organized with Joe Martinson for the day.

"Ah, Valentino's," a young GI said. "It's my parents' favorite place in New York."

"Well then, your folks have good taste. It's my favorite place too," Lily said, handing him a cup of steaming coffee. "What's your name?"

"William Day," the young man said.

"William, when you get back, you come and visit us and tell them that Head Chef Lily Rose will cook you lobster bisque."

William flushed with surprise, grasping his hot dog and warm coffee in his white-cold hands.

Ellen and Lily exchanged a smile.

Soon the air was filled with boys' chatter and the smell of coffee, sausages and warmed bread.

"You know what," Ellen said, next to Lily. "I never thought the war was going to be a time when I made so many good friends." She sounded shy. "And you are becoming a very important friend to me, Lily."

"Oh, Ellen," Lily said, her focus remaining strictly on her watch, not letting the sausages stay in over time. "I feel incredibly at home with our little family in the restaurant."

Ellen's expression clouded, before she turned to a painfully young-looking recruit. "You enjoy that, and you remember us when you get home."

"Oh, I will, miss, and I wish I could write you. I never seen such a pretty girl," he said, winking at her.

Ellen sighed. "I'm sure you've got flocks of girls to write to."

"Watch your onions don't burn," the young man said, and winked at her again.

Lily turned the sausages, keeping one pan warm and the other two boiling until they were nearly out and they'd fed what seemed like a thousand troops. The great ship let out a deep whistle. It was time for all these boys to leave.

Ellen was starting to tidy up while Lily fed the last of the waiting boys. A young man with cheeks and nose flushed red from the cold came to the front of the line.

"Miss," he said. "You have no idea how much I'll miss our American hot dogs."

"Onion?" Lily asked.

Behind her, Ellen whistled a lilting tune softly to herself.

"Yes, please, and ketchup, no mustard," he said.

Lily handed him his hot dog. She smiled when he took a bite and groaned in appreciation.

"Where you from?" she asked.

"Paris, Kentucky," he said, looking up at her, earnest as anything.

"And where are you off to?" she asked, her eyes grazing the last group of men still standing around the truck.

"I can't say," he said, his voice soft.

Lily's pulse quickened. Her freezing fingers curled around the photo of Tom that she'd kept in her purse. Knowing that Ellen was unlikely to hear with all the noise and commotion surrounding the stand, she leaned forward. "My fiancé," she said, "went missing during the Italian campaign. Would you mind… that is, if I gave you this photo, could you show it to people and see if anyone has heard of him?"

The young man frowned in concentration at the photo of Tom. "You want to give up this treasured possession?"

"I would give up anything to know my Tom was alive. His name is Tom Morelli."

The boy reached out for the photograph, taking it in his fingers that were red with cold. "I'll personally see what I can do." He looked up at her. "And if I hear anything? If anyone has word of your Tom Morelli?"

Lily glanced across at Ellen. "Then you get word to Lily Rose, at Valentino's on Park Avenue."

He held the photo of Tom close to his chest. "Tom Morelli," he said. "And Lily Rose." He nodded at her and gave her a mock salute.

"Thank you," she mouthed at him. She watched his departing back as he walked away.

Chapter Thirty-One

Lily

Spring, 1944

Winter drifted into spring, but the warmer air and blossom that spruced up the city brought another tragedy to Valentino's. One sunny morning, Lily stood with her head bowed in the kitchen, her team gathered around her with their eyes downturned. The tears fell freely down Martina's face, while others sniffed and dug for tissues in the pockets of their uniforms. Giorgio murmured words of quiet prayer until, finally, everyone lifted their heads.

"We will remember our young commis chef Paul with great fondness. He touched all our lives with joy," Giorgio said. He wiped a tear from his own worn face. "The dear boy served bravely in the Pacific campaign as a pilot. It was what he wanted to do. To contribute and to fly. And while we are gathered in memory of young Paul, we also pray for the memory of our dear Marco, and also for Tom," Giorgio added. "We pray that he may be sent back to us safely and soon."

Lily dug her hands deep into the pockets of her skirt. Next to her, Martina reached over and placed an arm around her shoulder for a moment. Still no news. Still, she and Gia kept a quiet, hopeful vigil that, somehow, there would be a miracle and he would be safe.

The kitchen staff returned to their stations.

Giorgio moved toward Lily. "Now that Leningrad is finally relieved from the siege, the next stop for our Allies has to be our beloved Rome, dear." He scoured her face.

Lily nodded, knowing she was pale. Not trusting herself to speak.

"I've seen a lot in my lifetime, but the toll of this war is becoming unimaginable. The German defensive lines around Monte Cassino are proving to be almost impossible to break. I am worried." He shook his head and turned on his heels.

The war was lasting longer than any of them had imagined.

After the long luncheon service was done, Lily looked up to see Vianne standing at the entrance to the kitchen. She wrinkled her nose at the latest creation she and Leo had conjured up: a recipe using Spam and potatoes. "I don't think this will get any further than the kitchen staff lunch, Leo."

Leo leaned against the station, where, a few years back, he'd created masterpieces as the grill chef for Valentino's. He threw his cloth over his shoulder and shook his head at the pink Spam that bubbled on his burner. "It's a calamity of a dish, Chef."

"I'll have to agree with you there." Lily heaved out a sigh. She wiped her hands and went over to Vianne.

Vianne took in the crazy action in the kitchen. "Lily, I've got a small party of friends coming to my apartment tonight, and Giorgio asked me if you'd be a dear and send us up some food?"

"Of course, Vianne. But, the only thing is, I have limited supplies."

Vianne nodded, her beautiful eyes serious. "I know that."

Lily raised a brow. "Well, I could send up some chicken consommé, organize a casserole out of some of the lamb we were going to braise with egg noodles, and an apple pie for dessert?"

"Perfect. Lily? Darling, why not come upstairs and have a drink with us? It's not natural for you to be cooped up working all the time. You are allowed a little fun, you know." She flashed a dazzling smile. "Come out with us, as my guest afterward. Please."

"Oh, Vianne. You don't have to do that."

"But I insist. Come out and see what a girl your age should be doing with her nights off, *chérie.*"

Lily smiled at the beautiful woman, and Vianne turned on her heels and left.

That night, Lily hesitated outside the door of Vianne and Giorgio's penthouse apartment on the top floor of the building that housed Valentino's. The black silk rayon dress with its diamanté belt that she'd chosen clung to her figure and fell to her knees. She'd pulled her hair up in front while letting the rest of it loose in rippling waves. At the last minute, she'd applied a touch of deep-red lipstick, some rouge, and then mascara to highlight her blue eyes.

When the Contis' maid opened the door to greet her, Lily stopped to stare. She followed the uniformed servant through a vast modern entrance hall, resplendent with a wide staircase leading up to a gallery with intricate iron balustrades overlooking the entrance.

A young woman, clearly a fashion model, was sitting on a pale blue velvet sofa, with an enlarged image of Paris behind her. The girl was surrounded by a host of glamorous young things. A pink beret was perched atop her head, and she wore a silk blouse in the same color with a bow tie in front, a nipped-in waistline with a thin belt and a pintucked silk skirt.

A couple of other women reclined on another gilt sofa, waving cigarettes in elegant holders, eyeing Lily in a lazy, sultry way and drinking champagne. Behind them, a row of couture outfits hung on a rack that looked like it had been sent express from Vianne's studio, and behind the women, Giorgio stood in a tuxedo, a white silk handkerchief peeping from his pocket, chatting with a couple of well-dressed elderly gentlemen.

"Lily, welcome." He strode across the room to her. "You look wonderful," he murmured. "Just wonderful."

Lily gasped at the beautiful room, silk screens and huge potted palms in the corners, Parisian jazz music playing from a gramophone and the soft sounds of sophisticated chatter. Perhaps she should have been a fashion model, not a chef…

"Champagne, dearest Lily?" Giorgio asked.

Lily swung her focus back to Giorgio. "I haven't had champagne in an age."

His lips formed a smile. "Why ever not?" He leaned forward. "New York's much more fun with champagne on board."

"Well, I have to say, you might be right, Giorgio." She sent him a winning smile.

"Don't you dare move." He rushed off, only to return with a crystal glass filled with champagne.

"Lily? Your food was a sensation," Vianne called across the room. "Thank you, darling."

Lily nodded, returning Vianne's smile.

Vianne eyed her over her glass of champagne, a cigarette dangling from a holder, only adding to the elegance of her dramatic floor-length deep-red dress that clung to her curves to perfection. "I have an idea, *chérie*," Vianne murmured.

"Vianne always has an idea," one of the models said. "Sometimes, they are expensive, but they are always grand. Actually, they're always expensive," the girl laughed. "P'raps that's what makes them so darned grand!"

A ripple of laughter passed through the room.

"Well, Lily's glamorous enough that she'll get into the Copa," Vianne said.

The room went quiet.

"The Copacabana?" Lily asked, something stirring inside her. "I haven't been there since 1940." It was true. She felt a pang of regret for some aspects of her old life. The life she was going to give up when she married Tom.

But only for a minute. Every time she thought of him, she wanted to hug herself and embrace all the possibilities of their future together. And she had a feeling that if Tom came to the Copa, he'd jitterbug better than any man she knew. If his dancing was anything like his cooking, she was certain he'd be a wonderful dance partner as well.

"Well, four years is way too long to stay away from the Copa," Giorgio said, his eyes twinkling.

"And it's going to be a most wonderful evening, my dears!" Vianne said. She winked at Lily. "A bit of jive bombing, darling, and you'll be a different girl. Don't worry, we will have you back by dawn, *chérie*."

Lily raised her glass. "Well, I confess, I do love to dance," she said to the impossibly beautiful woman.

"It's going to be a gas." Giorgio sauntered across the room, clicking his fingers and swaggering in his patent leather shoes.

Lily blinked at the glare of the photographers' flashbulbs outside the private entrance to the Copacabana, set right behind Hotel Fourteen on East 60th Street near Central Park. The electricity of the New York home front during wartime screamed from the very sidewalks.

She had heard tales of the bobby-soxers rioting outside the Paramount in the crush to swoon over Frank Sinatra, an adored substitute for the boys who'd gone to war. Here they were outside the Copa, lines of hopeful guests, defense-plant workers flush with cash, jamming the sidewalks like they did the Broadway theaters and the Times Square movie houses with their lavish stage shows.

Folks crammed together, queuing for the chance to get inside the famous nightclub down in the basement, but Vianne swept past them all, sashaying up to the doorman. She whispered in his ear and waved to everyone before sweeping her entourage of fashion models into the vestibule in a flurry of ostrich feathers, satin, and patent leather kitten-heeled shoes.

Giorgio took Lily's arm and strolled right up behind his beautiful wife to the front of the line.

"Mr. Conti!" The doorman's eyes twinkled at the sight of the famous New York restauranteur.

"Evening, Luigi," Giorgio said. "How are you tonight?"

"Mr. Conti, can we have a photograph?" A photographer in a gray felt hat pushed his way to the front of the lines of press.

Giorgio grinned. Lily drank in the exciting New York atmosphere. Since the war had begun, she'd quite forgotten what an exciting place Manhattan could be.

"Smile," Giorgio whispered. "Like it or not, we're going to end up in the society pages tonight, dear."

Lily plastered on the bravest smile she could. Tom would want her to be brave for him, she knew that.

"Who's tonight's pretty little lady, Giorgio?" A newspaperman pulled a pen out from behind his ear and held up a small notebook.

Lily opened her mouth and closed it, about to give the man a mighty piece of her mind, about his assumption she'd accept being addressed in that way, but Giorgio laughed out loud next to her.

"Why, this 'little lady' is no other than Valentino's head chef. I give you the delightful, and talented, Lily Rose!"

"She's a doll." The newspaperman tipped his hat at Giorgio.

"Publicity," Giorgio whispered. "Thanks for being so good about it, Lily."

Lily sent the reporters a dazzling smile. "Oh, no problem," she murmured, feeling warmly toward Giorgio.

The flashbulbs lit up a few more times before Giorgio held up a hand. "Excuse me, fellas. I have to go inside. My friends are in the club." He waved his white cashmere scarf and sent them a grin. The flashbulbs went wild and Lily ducked her head as they climbed the three steps into the vestibule and went down into the private entrance.

Once they were in the basement, a middle-aged host in a tuxedo came to greet Giorgio. "Mr. Conti," he said. "Your usual table?"

"Thank you, Riccardo."

"You have a regular table at the Copa, Giorgio?" Lily asked.

"Why ever not?" he said.

Inside, bright lights dazzled and the famous Copa girls jived on the stage in silver sequined ball gowns with tiaras on their heads. Behind them, a full jazz band belted out Dizzy Gillespie's "Groovin' High". It was standing room only around the hundreds of candlelit tables that took up the center of the floor. Folks hung around smoking and chatting in the pink and green space, tapping their feet under the giant white palm tree columns that were dotted around the club. Waiters wove through the restaurant area holding platters way above their heads.

Riccardo led Giorgio and Lily to a table near the front. Vianne's coat was slung over a chair, along with a couple of the models' jackets, but they were nowhere in sight.

"Champagne to start, Mr. Conti?" Riccardo asked.

Giorgio flicked his fingers in acknowledgment. "A bottle, Riccardo."

"And something from the menu tonight?"

Giorgio sat back in his gilt-edged chair and regarded her. "I want you to try something new here, Lily."

Lily refrained from admitting that her stomach was growling with hunger pangs. "Well, I'd be intrigued to see what the Copa's serving during wartime!"

"Riccardo? Lily's an epicurean. Bring us a platter of your famous Chinese food."

"You serve Chinese food now?" Lily turned to the waiter.

"Of course, miss. We specialize in it at the Copa these days."

"Well, I'll be," Lily whispered. "I did not know that. Chinese food in a Brazilian club? What a marvelous idea!" Her thoughts danced with possibilities.

Giorgio just grinned.

Their champagne appeared within the tick of a second and the waiter popped the cork and poured them both a glass.

Lily's eyes widened at the bottle: it was vintage Moët & Chandon.

"Chicken chow mein." A waiter lifted a silver cover off a huge platter bedecked with glistening noodles and vegetables and fat pieces of chicken. He opened Lily's napkin with a flourish and placed it on her lap.

"The Copa has five full-time chefs here preparing a list of Chinese dishes," Giorgio said.

Lily stared, entranced, at the wonderful food.

Giorgio picked up the pair of chopsticks that lay by the plate. Lily inhaled the exotic scents and took a bite. It was delectable.

A half-hour later, Vianne and her entourage of models turned up.

"You're being boring, darlings," Vianne said. She leaned against the back of Giorgio's seat and waved her cigarette at the dance floor. "Care to dance, Lily?"

"Well, why not!"

The crowds parted for Vianne as they walked across the crowded room.

The band played "People Will Say We're in Love" and Lily swung along on the dance floor, while Giorgio danced with Vianne, until the lights went down and the opening notes of Rudy Vallee's "As Time Goes By" swelled into the room.

Lily's chest was heaving after all that jiving, but Vianne was next to her, tugging her arm. "Watch the stage, *chérie.*"

Soon, a spotlight came on, and a slender blond woman in a figure-hugging white dress with a mink collar and diamonds dripping from her wrists and ears stood at the microphone. Slowly, she raised her head and the crowds roared.

"Peggy Lee," Giorgio whispered. "She's who they've all come to see."

A lone guitar struck up the opening notes of "Fools Rush In" and Miss Lee had the room captivated with her lilting, sensual voice.

"Isn't she marvelous?" Vianne said, linking her arm through Lily's.

And right there, with the music swirling around her in this fabulous club in the heart of New York, with the wonderful Vianne and Giorgio, Lily couldn't stop the smile spreading over her face. Because, in spite of this war, right now the world seemed to brim with more possibilities than she'd ever imagined. If only Tom was safe, there was no reason she and he could not live, work, love and laugh in exactly the same way as Vianne and Giorgio did, every day of their lives.

Chapter Thirty-Two

Lily

Summer, 1944

The humidity soared in Manhattan as the spring of '44 passed into summer. The streets were filled with barelegged women in rayon and viscose suits, society girls hardly distinguishable from working girls as styles and fabrics became more uniform and the only thing that was not rationed was hats.

Every now and then, when she was out, Lily allowed herself a wistful glance at the way girls sought individuality in millinery, sometimes sporting whimsical, colorful creations, and other times wearing quite small hats with a military look.

Even Josie had gotten into the look, coming in to eat at Valentino's regularly, always with a friend, and a jaunty hat perched on her head. Giorgio would whisk her to a table by the window, and Lily would send up the best plates on the menu. Weekly, Lily chatted with her gram on the telephone. Josie wouldn't hear of any protestations on Lily's part that she worried she was not visiting Greenwich Village enough. Insisting she was proud of Lily, Josie assured her that everything was fine.

Lily had hardly seen her parents and had avoided the topic of her father's retirement plans on the rare occasions she had a chance to go have an awkward cup of coffee with them. Sometimes, she'd pick up the phone to have a chat with her dad, only to put it down again, the horrid reality that her mom was hardly talking to her sinking in and turning her cold.

Instead, she spent her days sweltering over hot stoves, her evenings poring over recipes in her office before falling into bed late at night, too wired and too hot to sleep, her thoughts and feelings always turning to her adored Tom. Occasionally, she'd go out of an evening with Ellen, Meg and Martina, but Lily knew such distractions were never going to alleviate her fears for Tom, fears that she shared with Gia, who was wrought with worry about her only son.

In June, Rome was finally liberated from the Germans and the Allies launched an attack in Normandy, France. The newspapers printed stories about an expected quick end to the war.

The kitchen staff scoured the articles, and as 1944 progressed, Lily became good at acting out her joy at the broad scope of the progress in Europe. When Leningrad was relieved, she'd smiled and smiled along with everyone—of course she had. But, privately, when the kitchen was quiet, she searched the papers for any and every update about Italy.

Rome's liberation had come and gone with no further news of Tom.

"Lily?" Martina asked. The *chef de cuisine*'s eyes met hers across the staff table one hot night. "You all right?"

Lily rubbed a hand over her forehead. "Work is the best distraction from talk of war, Martina."

Martina nodded, her eyes softening, Jimmy sitting right next to her, chatting with Leo.

Lily was glad for the girl's quiet understanding.

Summer slipped into autumn and New York society returned to Manhattan from the Hamptons. Giorgio took the opportunity to increase his catering commissions outside Valentino's in order to build up business as food shortages became ever more dire.

For the fifth weekend in a row, Lily surveyed the latest enormous basement Upper East Side kitchen where they were catering a

Sunday-evening dinner. Ellen, Agnes and Jimmy were opening drawers in the oversized marble-clad space and inspecting the cooking utensils and the two huge English country-style ovens in the immaculate room.

Lily went through her menu and checked all the produce.

"Chef?" The owner stood in the doorway, wearing blue jeans and a crisp white shirt.

Lily looked up.

"Your menu looks like heaven: French pastries and French lamb chops, filet of sole bonne femme," he said.

Jimmy opened his fabric case containing his filleting knives.

"I'm pleased to hear it. We'll send up your shrimp cocktails as soon as we can," Lily said.

He sent her a grin and sauntered off again, champagne glass clutched in his hand.

Lily raised a brow. "Let's get started. All hands on deck. Shrimp cocktails to be ready in forty-five minutes, and after that, we'll send up each course on the half-hour."

"Yes, Chef!"

At the frantic stage, just when the first round of entrées was being plated, there was a knock on the kitchen door. Lily glanced up from where she was finishing pan-frying the French lamb chops. Ellen tossed her pans of steamed green beans and tiny potatoes from Gia's victory garden.

Lily frowned, her hands still shaking the pan while her focus remained glued on the man who'd walked into the room.

"Toot toot!"

Lily wiped a hand over her sweaty brow. "Continue with your work," she said to her staff.

The slim middle-aged man tipped the red beret he wore to Jimmy. "Don't mind me," he said. "Once you've sent the food upstairs, I'd like a little chat with whoever's in charge."

The room went quiet.

Lily turned off her gas burner. She was done with the last lamb chop.

"Anyone got a menu?" the man asked.

"Can I ask why?" Lily said.

"Don't you know?" He shrugged. "Haven't you seen my face before, sweetheart?"

Lily sent Ellen and Agnes a glance.

"Who's the boss?" he went on.

"Lily Rose is head chef," Jimmy spoke evenly. "Lily, this is Richard Parelli from *New York Dines*. Richard, Lily is also the head chef at Valentino's."

Lily wiped a hand over her brow. She narrowed her eyes. Of course. Richard Parelli had replaced a younger restaurant critic who'd joined the war. But Mr. Parelli looked nothing like the photo attached to his byline in the paper. For a start, he wasn't sporting a sardonic smile. And his hair was shorter. Perhaps he changed his appearance so he could write his reviews incognito.

Mr. Parelli turned to take in Lily slowly, his expression tightening. "Well, then," he whispered. "How fascinating. Valentino's run by a bunch of women. Maybe that explains why service is far below the pre-war level of efficiency and your menus are poor substitutes for the gastronomic savories that used to lend themselves so favorably to wonderful reviews."

Lily lifted her chin. "When was the last time you actually visited Valentino's, Mr. Parelli? Because I don't recall Giorgio Conti informing me you'd been there in the last two years?"

Ellen looked up from her bench. Lily folded her arms.

"Oh, I think I'm up to forming my own opinions without needing to visit the place, thank you, Miss Rose."

"Is that so?" Lily asked.

He ran a finger over the immaculate benchtop, checking it for non-existent traces of dust. "You see, I'm writing an article on catered house parties at the minute, and this one will be my entire focus for my next piece. Lucky you. First, I'd like to see your menu. And then, I'd like to talk through how exactly a woman has managed to prepare each dish."

Lily placed her dishcloth down. "I'd be happy to oblige. And I'm sure you'll find my cooking capabilities and passion for food are not inferior to any man's."

He paused, midway through pulling out his notebook, a slight smile spreading across his face. "Glad we've got that established," he said. "I thought, at least, if you had to be a woman, you'd have something special to offer to make up for it."

Lily glared at him. She marched over to the fridge and reached for the custards that she'd made that morning with Martina to go with the French pastries and the last of the strawberries from the victory garden. Richard Parelli remained leaning casually against the benchtop, but Lily knew that he was watching every single move she made.

Chapter Thirty-Three

Josie

The kitchen was filled with the aroma of Josie's eggplant parmigiana baking in the oven. She added the finishing touches to her tomato and homemade buffalo mozzarella salad, sprinkling it with cracked black pepper, and tossing some fresh basil leaves over the deliciously ripe tomatoes. She carried a crystal vase filled with summer roses and placed it in the center of the table set for three, a chilled bottle of white wine sitting in a silver ice bucket and her prettiest china ready to go. After all, it seemed an age since she'd had Lily here for a meal, and Gia was becoming family.

If only Victoria had settled down, Josie would have invited her and Jacob tonight, but that was impossible. Josie had tried talking to her daughter-in-law, tried convincing her again that Lily was doing the right thing for herself, but Victoria just refused to listen.

As for Emmeline, Josie encouraged her to enroll in a cooking course at Albertina's, having realized that the girl had a real talent, and a quickness about her that would do very well in a commercial kitchen. When Josie was gone, Emmeline would need a job, so tonight, she was in the kitchen behind Albertina's on Bleecker Street, and the light in the girl's eyes before she left had been something to behold.

Josie perked up at the sound of knocking on her basement door.

Gia and Lily were both on the doorstep, Lily clutching the tiramisu she'd promised to make for dessert, while Gia held a bunch of green herbs in her arms, and a brown paper bag filled with vegetables, fresh from the earth. Lily waited while Gia hugged Josie, only to fall into her grandmother's arms the minute Gia was in the door.

Josie's heart tightened annoyingly, which was a nuisance, as she'd had a good day today. It was excitement, of course it was, at seeing Lily again, at having her here. She closed the door behind her with a snap and sent a stern look toward her father's portrait.

Once they were all seated, with glasses of wine and the chatter flowing, the eggplant parmigiana bubbling and fragrant on the table in a deep blue dish, with Josie's tomato-and-mozzarella salad and plenty of homemade crusty bread, Josie sighed with pleasure.

She'd made herself a promise. If she was going to die sooner than she'd hoped, she'd spend every single day she had left living her life. She remained true to her conviction that she would not be an invalid, nor would she worry her family in her old age.

As if by tacit agreement, the three women avoided the topic of war while they ate, but worry about Tom hung over them, and Josie couldn't help but wish that he was here with them, right now, just as he had been on that lovely occasion when she'd first met him, the sparks flying between him and her granddaughter as they cooked omelets together.

"So, what's happening at Valentino's?" Gia asked. She rested her cheek on her hand. "I miss hearing all the gossip each day."

"Well." Lily reached down into her handbag. "I don't suppose you saw this? Either of you?" She handed over a newspaper clipping.

Josie and Gia both leaned in to read it, Gia clicking her tongue with disapproval, Josie letting out a long sigh.

Not only has the war deprived us of such staples as meat, butter and almost our entire male population under the age of forty, it seems that the latest casualty that the United States is facing is a lack of decent male chefs.

They say that anyone making a living out of writing New York Dines *for the* New York World-Telegram *is a lucky guy. But gone are the days when I could just walk into a restaurant, order a prime cut of meat, lick my chops and rattle out an article waxing lyrical about a piece of beef.*

No, these days your faithful food critic is subject to such gastronomic challenges as lamb chops, an entrée of sole—no doubt procured from the bottom of some old barrel at the markets, or torn from the hands of a doubtful fisherman in a dinghy on the Hudson—and pastries fashioned without butter, instead with powdered milk.

It's getting to the point that I may as well go test cat food as write this column these days, but that is not the fault of Valentino's, who were given the impossible task of hosting a dinner party somewhere north of Fourteenth recently. Your faithful critic was invited incognito, but I couldn't resist asking to encounter the person in charge of this impossible task. Readers will be shocked to hear that the moment I met the chef down in the kitchen, I not only almost fainted to learn that even our oldest fine dining restaurant has had to employ a woman, but that woman is none other than Miss Lily Rose of Gramercy Park, rumored to be engaged to Nathaniel Carter of Fifth Avenue!

What Miss Rose thinks she is doing wasting her time trying to cook when nothing is available that any decent person would ingest is beyond me, but all I can say is this reviewer is not going to have any job to speak of if we don't settle this war as soon as our illustrious leaders are hoping we might.

And while Miss Rose clearly has an admirable talent for turning terrible produce into dishes that are charming and worthy of keeping a fine restaurant afloat, may we only pray that she will be elevated from the bowels of our kitchens to her proper place as a society wife and hostess with a charming kitchen filled with servants of her own to manage sooner

rather than later so that the correct order of things can be
restored once and for all!

"Well, I hope you are not taking any of that seriously," Josie
said. *Honestly.* She shot a glance toward Gia, who was still frowning
over the article. "I suppose the reviewer never took the time to
learn how your cooking had contributed in a mighty way toward
keeping Valentino's going during wartime?"

Lily placed her chin in her hand and sighed.

"Don't worry," Josie said, eyeing her. "Those who can't do always
criticize those who can."

Gia was still frowning, her pretty face pale. "Who is this
Nathaniel Carter?" she said.

Josie threw Lily a glance.

Lily reddened. "My mom, well, she has this dream that I'll marry
Nathaniel. But, Gia, you know that's never going to happen." Lily's
voice softened, "You know how much I love Tom."

A troubled expression passed across Gia's face. "I see."

Still flushed, Lily stood up to clear away the plates, and Josie
moved to help her, but Lily shook her head. "Sit down, darling
Gram. I insist."

Josie reached out a hand to cover Gia's. "Lily?"

Lily swung around, holding her glistening tiramisu in both
hands.

"I want you to know that I think you should definitely marry
for love. In fact," Josie lowered her voice, "darling, I insist."

Josie threw Gia a glance, her eyes twinkling, and in spite of the
looming worry of no news about Tom, Gia managed a brave smile.

Lily set the tiramisu on the table, sprinkling extra shards of very
precious, indulgent chocolate over it, and holding up a shining
silver spoon. "Here's to love and good food," she said.

And Josie and Gia clapped as Lily dug the silver spoon into the
beautiful creamy chocolate and espresso dessert.

Chapter Thirty-Four

Lily

Winter, 1944

Christmas of 1944 approached in a flurry of cold, wintery storms. A bittersweet feeling hung over New York. People still decorated their homes for the festive season, and the Allies were gaining ground, but at the cost of heavy casualties when Hitler launched his brutal Battle of the Bulge in their drive toward Germany during frigid weather conditions, attacking fatigued American troops in the Ardennes Forest, in southeast Belgium.

Lily pored over the newspapers with her fellow kitchen staff, her heart breaking at the news that 19,000 men in the US army had been killed in freezing rain, thick fog, snow drifts and record-breaking low temperatures, 47,500 wounded and 23,000 were missing. Stories spread across the city of massacred soldiers, boys dying of pneumonia, trench foot and frostbite, and everyone was sobered by the Nazi onslaught.

It was impossible to extinguish the feeling of sadness that lingered for the millions who had loved ones off at war, or worse. Pale widows dressed in black crowded the subways. Mothers wept for their lost sons on the streets and behind closed doors. At the newspaper stands, elderly men lined up to scour the papers, afterward gathering in heated debates in the city's cafés, openly berating the world.

One frosty morning, Lily walked into the front entrance of Valentino's with her arms full of produce from the Schwab garden.

Giorgio came in with her, stamping his feet against the cold. Outside, a light blanket of freshly fallen snow covered the sidewalks.

Lily closed the restaurant's front door behind Giorgio, the enormous wreath that Sidney had placed on the brass knocker swinging in the cold breeze. She paused midway through taking off her gloves. The phone was pealing behind the reception desk, and the maître d' rushed across the black-and-white tiled floor.

"Valentino's." The maître d' jotted down some notes and placed his hand over the receiver, calling out to the room in general. "Humphrey Bogart is coming for dinner at eight o'clock!"

Lily stopped unwinding her woolen scarf.

"Humphrey Bogart?" Giorgio strode toward the desk. His eyes lit up and he rubbed his hands together. He stopped next to Lily. "Well then. That is something."

Lily smiled, her cheeks flushing in the warmth of the restaurant. "Well, we certainly need some good news, Giorgio. I'll go downstairs and see what treats we can prepare for him. What an honor."

But Giorgio laid a hand on her arm. "You remember, the newspapermen will try everything: the back door, the windows looking down in the kitchens. You close blinds and you don't breathe a word of this to anyone outside Valentino's."

Lily nodded. "Of course, Giorgio."

He looked thoughtful. "If you want to prepare a special dessert, now that wouldn't go amiss."

"I'll see what I can come up with. Let's hope he has a sense of humor though."

Giorgio patted her on the shoulder, and Lily distracted herself with frantic thoughts about recipes that would be suitable for a film star.

That afternoon, Ellen and Julius stayed back after luncheon service to source ideas. The three of them sat around Lily's desk with notepads filled with ingredients and recipes, and at four o'clock, Lily looked up from her notes. "I've got it," she said. "As a special treat for Mr. Bogart, let's make him a wartime Valentino's Christmas cake."

Julius raised a brow. "But can we do it in time, Lily?"

"We have some stores of dried fruit," Lily said. "And if we grate up a carrot and use golden syrup for sweetening, then we'll only need sugar, margarine, bicarbonate of soda and vanilla essence, almond essence of course, along with cinnamon, and we'll have quite the pièce de résistance. It's our best bet."

Julius chuckled. "You tell me, lovely, but I'm thinking we've not got enough kick in your cake at this point."

Lily tapped the table triumphantly. "Well, then, we put a cup of warm coffee and a splash of precious rum into it."

Julius sat back in his seat and laughed out loud. He lowered his voice. "You, Lily Rose, are a genius, and don't ever let anyone tell you any differently."

"Oh, I won't," Lily said, sitting back. "I've been trying to convince everyone of that for years."

Julius' eyes twinkled at her.

Ellen looked up from writing out her own notes. "Before we serve Mr. Bogart the cake, we could delight him with this wartime pudding I've just adapted from one of Gabriel's books. Look at this."

Lily ran her finger down the ingredients that Ellen had written out on a scrap of paper. "Custard sauce, milk, custard powder, sugar, fine breadcrumbs, jam and vanilla essence, with a mock-cream topping made of margarine, caster sugar, dried milk powder and a tablespoon of milk." Lily looked up at Ellen. "A soft pudding with a mock-cream top? You can serve it in individual ramekins."

Ellen was pink with delight, tapping her pen on Lily's desk.

"I think Mr. Bogart would be mighty proud to enjoy *both* those recipes," Julius said. "Let's spoil him with two desserts. He can have the cake with his coffee after the pudding is served."

Lily reached forward and squeezed Ellen's hand. "Let's get cooking."

The rest of the afternoon passed by in a flurry in the warm kitchen downstairs, while, outside, snow fell in soft white folds onto the sidewalks. By the time the rest of the staff arrived, Lily had a beautiful Christmas cake ready for Humphrey Bogart and Ellen had a row of puddings set up on the bench, the creamy, custard underneath topped with mock cream and chocolate swirls.

"I'm excited," Ellen said. "I've a good feeling in my bones."

Lily hugged her. "I adore working with you. I have since the moment you walked into the kitchen."

After dinner, Giorgio came downstairs and clapped his hands. "Humphrey Bogart sends his compliments to the chef who's in charge of the Valentino's kitchen, my dears!"

Everyone paused from cleaning up their stations.

"Well, that's grand news," Jimmy said. "We are glad to hear it, Giorgio."

"Lily, he'd like to meet you." Giorgio rubbed his hands together, his face lit up in a way Lily had not seen for a long time.

Lily stopped wiping down a bench. "Oh, no, Giorgio?"

"Why ever not?" Ellen smiled from her station. She placed her hands on her hips. "Chefs who feed famous folk should be recognized, not hidden away. I say it's marvelous he wants to meet you."

Giorgio held out a hand. "Come on, Lily."

"You want me in the main *restaurant,* in my cooking outfit?" She stared down at her old black trousers.

"I've said so."

Lily adjusted her chef's hat, threw a glance around her team and took Giorgio's arm, her insides a basket of nerves when they clapped her as she walked out of the kitchen to go upstairs.

The restaurant turned silent when Lily entered, still on Giorgio's arm. The string quartet stopped playing, putting their hands together to clap Lily, along with every other guest in the room.

In a private booth up back, Lily gasped at the sight of the famous actor. Alongside him sat a beautiful redheaded woman in a stunning velvet dress.

The drop-dead handsome man stood up, placing his napkin on the table, and he reached out to shake Lily's hand.

"Well, I'll be," he murmured. "When Giorgio said he'd bring the head chef, I was not expecting to see a woman."

Lily blushed. She couldn't help it, but she took his hand.

Mr. Bogart's eyes lit up in that way the whole country knew. "Here's looking at you, Chef!"

Snow piled up on the sidewalks on Christmas morning. Outside Lily's bedroom window, drifts swirled in the quiet streets. Lily traced her finger across the frosty glass. She turned around to the little room she'd come to think of as home. The Christmas cards she'd received from the kitchen staff and the Contis sat atop her chest of drawers, along with several elegant cards from her old school friends.

Vianne had brought her a pretty green-and-red wreath decorated with berries to hang on a hook on the wall above the fireplace and Josie had sent her a lovely warm blue cape. Her father had sent her a new bound book for recipes, a silver pen and a couple of his latest hats. But there was nothing from her mom.

Conversations with her mother had been strained and difficult. Lily had ended up telling her family she had to work at Christmas. Josie had understood, but, heartbreakingly, her father's gifts for her had arrived in the mail.

Lily washed and dressed quickly, not allowing herself to linger at the mirror, because when she looked at her reflection, she knew she'd see the truth: a girl who was worried sick about the effects of her escalating conflicts with her mother, and a girl who was terrified the man she loved would never come home.

Lily tucked her hairbrush back in her bureau drawer, pushing away the bunch of Nathaniel's letters that peeked out. He wrote her every week—robust, cheerful descriptions of the food on board the ship, his fellow officers, navy life. Because she hadn't responded to his initial declarations of affection, Nathaniel had pared his own outpourings back. And she respected him for that. Lily only hoped that, when he came home, he'd accept that they had to return to their old childhood friendship. Nothing more.

She pinned her hair up and placed her chef's hat on her head, then turned out of the room to make her way down to the kitchens.

"Lily, my dear." Giorgio stopped her halfway down the stairs. "Merry Christmas."

Lily leaned into his embrace. "Thank you," she said. "Merry Christmas, Giorgio."

He held her at arm's-length. "You know you could have had the day off. Martina could have run things for us. She is only celebrating quietly with her mom."

"And miss the chance to bake ginger cake without eggs, and gingerbread cookies with margarine?"

"Well, you have a point there." Giorgio looked thoughtful.

"Happy Christmas, dearest Giorgio." Lily felt the weight of his stare on her back as she continued downstairs.

Accompanied by the heavy snowfalls outside, the kitchen was filled with the scents and sounds of Christmas. Jimmy brought an old transistor radio into the kitchen, setting it up well away from the food, and Judy Garland's "Have Yourself a Merry Little Christmas" filled the room with nostalgia.

As usual, Lily rushed to the newspapers, her eyes desperately scanning the front page. As if somehow, magically, there would be an announcement of a missing serviceman, found, safe in Italy.

She read with at least a sense of relief for the American troops in the Battle of the Bulge. Finally, the weather conditions had cleared enough for the Allied forces to strike back at the Nazis. The ground had frozen solid, allowing tanks and air forces to maneuver and get to the boys who had been blocked off. With her heart sinking, Lily read how American soldiers were only glad to see the sun come up. It meant that they were alive for one more day.

Nevertheless, she felt a tiny flicker of hope that the newspapers were finally talking about breaking the Nazi war machine.

Giorgio and Lily had managed to procure a good selection of turkeys and the ovens sizzled as they baked golden, filling the air with warmth and deliciousness. Leo basted them and Rosa busied herself making green bean casseroles, sweet potato casseroles and mashed potatoes, while Lily herself made hot chocolates decorated with marshmallows.

She lined up several more of her special Humphrey Bogart Christmas cakes, which, along with every other recipe she and her team had conjured up, was now featured in her wartime recipe book, and the scent of gingerbread and ginger cake filled the air from Julius's station once the turkeys had all gone out.

After all the feasting was done in the restaurant, Giorgio came downstairs.

Lily rested her chapped hands on the kitchen counter.

Giorgio called them all to attention. "My dears. The restaurant is closed tonight, and while most folks are still working across the country this Christmastime, my staff will enjoy a magnificent dinner. Please, come celebrate with us in the restaurant!" Giorgio waved them all upstairs.

Lily paused. She sent up a small prayer for Tom. *May he be safe and warm this Christmas. He'd want to be here.*

And, in her heart, he always would be with her.

*

That night, once the staff dinner was done, and everyone was putting on their scarves to try to make their way home in the snow, Giorgio drew Lily aside.

"Lily, we have another tradition at Valentino's," he said. "Come with me."

At the front bar, sitting up enjoying eggnog made by the barmen, were a row of homeless men. They turned to Giorgio and raised their glasses to him.

"Oh, Giorgio," Lily whispered. Behind them, a giant fir tree decorated with golden and red baubles glittered under the lights. "Would you like me to go downstairs and bring up some of the leftover turkey and vegetable casseroles for them?"

Giorgio's expression softened. "Thank you. That was what I hoped you'd say."

Lily laid a hand on his arm a moment, before returning downstairs to her empty, silent kitchen, the place where she felt more at home these days than anywhere else.

Later, Lily was helping the waiters tidy the empty bar area, when the front doors swung open, frozen air billowing into the foyer. Lily stopped what she was doing, holding a couple of plates in her hands. Her mouth fell open, and for a moment she stood stuck on the spot. But after a few, stunned seconds, she handed her plates to the nearest waiter and flew into the arms of Josie, standing inside the entrance to Valentino's.

Lily breathed in the scent of Josie's perfume, her hair.

"Dearest," Josie whispered.

"My *darling* gram…" Finally, Lily drew back. Her eyes locked with Giorgio's, standing right behind her grandmother, rubbing his gloved hands.

Josie clasped her hands together. "Well, oh, my," she breathed.

"Oh, Giorgio, thank you dearly for bringing my dear gram here," Lily said. "I'm so appreciative, I could hug you as well. Did you go to the Village in this weather to pick her up?"

Josie held Lily at arm's-length. Her red cashmere gloves were wondrously soft. "I called the restaurant to say happy Christmas. Giorgio told me to sit tight and he'd be right on his way to pick me up so I could see you. How about that?"

"How about that?" Lily said, her voice softening. She held out a hand to Giorgio. "And you braved the snow."

"It was no trouble at all. Dears, Vianne has gone upstairs to rest now. I've had the staff keep the fire going in one of the back private rooms. Lily? Would you like to take your grandmother in there for coffee and Christmas cake?"

Lily tucked her arm in her grandmother's. "I presume you're talking about my wartime Christmas cake. I sure won't tell Josie what's in it, but it was good enough for Humphrey Bogart, so I'm hoping it will do the job!"

Josie's eyebrows raised in a pair of perfect arcs. "Sounds like we have some catching up to do," she said. She unwound her scarf and tucked her lustrous gray hair behind one ear.

Giorgio ushered them down the warm, paneled hallway.

"Thank you, Giorgio," Lily said.

Giorgio bowed his head and closed the door behind them.

Lily breathed in the scent of orange-and-cinnamon candles that were dotted around the private room for Christmas. Pine cones burned in the open fire. She settled down with Josie on a soft leather sofa and a waiter brought in a tray with coffee in a silver pot, miniature Humphrey's Christmas cakes and cookies from the kitchen stores.

"Shall I pour?" Lily asked.

"Of course, dear."

Josie was quiet while Lily poured coffee and served the cake and cookies.

"You know how proud I am of you," Josie said. "Giorgio tells me you are indispensable to him." She took a sip of her coffee and placed the cup back down on the saucer. "Darling, there is something I want to talk to you about, though."

Lily folded her hands in her lap.

Josie sighed. "Lily, it is your parents' silver wedding anniversary on New Year's Eve. Please come home and see them, darling."

Lily turned away. The flames danced around the burning pine cones, licking at them until they dissolved. Lily brought a shaky hand to her forehead. "I don't think Mom will ever give up. Nor will she forgive me for not falling at Nathaniel's feet with gratitude for his interest in me."

Josie reached out and stroked a tendril of Lily's hair. "But could you find it within you to give her a chance to redeem herself, darling?"

"Well," Lily whispered, "I don't want to lose my family to marry the man I love. If he comes home." She lowered her head.

Josie's hand fluttered toward Lily, before, shakily, she drew it back. "You are putting on a brave face, I know that."

Lily moved closer to her gram, and she leaned her head on Josie's shoulder. "I just want him back."

Josie stilled. "I know."

Lily dug for a tissue in her pocket.

Josie stroked her head with her soft fingertips as the fire crackled behind them.

Chapter Thirty-Five

In the early hours of New Year's Day, 1945, Lily closed the apartment door behind the last of her parents' silver anniversary guests. Remnants of the party lingered in the sitting room: champagne glasses, trays of half-finished canapés, even the notes from the speech her father had made about his adored wife lay on a side table. He'd spoken with such sincere admiration for the intelligent, clever woman he'd married, and about the daughter of whom he was superbly proud. Lily knew he'd never give up hope that she and her mother would someday see eye to eye.

Josie pulled on her gloves next to her, wrapping herself up in her old navy cape, while Jacob prepared to drive her home to the Village. Josie reached up to kiss Lily on the cheek, enfolding her in a hug, before holding her at arm's-length.

"Darling, tell your mom you're engaged to Tom. Please. For all our sakes." She shot a glance at Lily's dad, standing across the room out of earshot, straight and tall.

He moved toward them, held out his arm to his mother, and with a wave of her hand, Josie left the party with her only son.

Lily sighed. She turned back into the empty sitting room, her mother's maid tidying up the last of the glasses, picking up the plates of leftovers in the room where, just a few moments ago, Lily had sat with old friends, pretending that everything was peachy. Pretending she had not a personal care in the world outside the war.

"Mother?" Her voice was high, tremulous, but Lily curled her hands into two strong fists.

Her mother looked up from where she sat on a sofa. The maid scuttled out.

Lily settled down on a chair opposite Victoria, and in spite of the late hour, her mother regarded her with clear eyes. "Mom," she said, her voice soft, "There's something I want to talk to you about." She cleared her throat. "I've been writing to one of my fellow chefs from the restaurant. We've become very close, and—"

But Victoria held up a hand. "Please, spare me. I've known about that for an age."

Lily started. "How?"

"Oh, Sidney told me there was some boy ages ago." She waved her hand in the air as if batting away a fly.

Sidney? "When?"

"Please don't be slow. It was that morning I was there setting up for the lunch for dear Katherine. The day Nathaniel had gone to war. I decided whatever Sidney was talking about was an aberration. There's no need to remind me of it. I know it's done."

"*You* decided it was an aberration?" Lily felt her voice rising. She checked herself. Closed her eyes. Remembered Josie, her father. "You decided it was done?" she whispered.

Her mother dropped her voice. "Let me give you a piece of wise advice. There will be plenty of unworthy men keen to fall in love with you, just don't fall in love back, especially if it's only to spite me."

Lily closed her eyes. "You overestimate your hold on me. I would never treat a man with such contempt, nor would I play such games."

Her mother let out a snort. "And you underestimate me!"

"Mom. It's not over. And it's not an aberration. I love Tom. He loves me back. If he comes home..." she took in a ragged breath. "When he comes home, I'm going to marry him. And I would like your blessing." She looked up, held her mother's gaze.

Victoria's eyes gleamed. "You silly girl," she said. "Over my dead body will I give you my blessing for any such thing. How could you ask?"

"Think of Dad, think of Gram."

Victoria flipped her hair back. "And why should I do that? When has Josie ever thought of me?"

And with that, Victoria swept out of the room, and Lily stared at the indent on the cushion where her mother had just sat.

Slowly, Lily stood up. Stretching, she moved to her mother's writing desk. She'd write her mom a letter. Give herself a chance to explain Tom to her properly. Conversations were going to be useless, but she would convince Victoria, would have her love Tom, in the end.

Lily slipped her shoes off and reached for a piece of her mother's scented notepaper, breathing in the familiar smell. But as she did, an envelope fluttered from the desk down onto the ground. Frowning, Lily reached for it, frowned again at the sight of the handwriting, and pulled out the note inside. And as she read, her whole body started shaking as if she were rattling on some old train, and the room turned icy cold.

Chapter Thirty-Six

Lily

May, 1945

Spring flowers decorated every table in Valentino's, along with the twinkle of candlelight. Every face in the room was turned toward Giorgio—kitchen staff, waiters and guests in diamonds and pearls. He stood on a podium by the gleaming grand piano and turned on the giant microphone.

Next to him, Vianne beamed at the crowds. She'd pinned a green brooch to the front of her slim-fitting orange dress, and around her neck she wore a green-and-white striped silk scarf.

"Friends of Valentino's," Giorgio said. "It is with great pleasure that we share the most…" He gathered himself a moment and cleared his voice. "The most momentous celebrations. The last ten days have been wonderful, incredible. Since Mussolini was finally captured and executed, since Hitler's suicide, we cannot tell you how delighted we were to see the surrender of the German forces in Italy." He reached for Vianne's hand, holding it way above both their heads, before leaning toward her and hugging her, enfolding her in his arms.

Cheers went up. Feet thundered on the floor. But at a corner booth, Lily spotted a young woman crying into her handkerchief. Lily forced herself to tear her eyes away.

Today, she'd read in the newspapers about the vast changes that would result from war, changes that would last for decades. But in her desperation for news of Tom, Lily was drawn to darker stories, her heart reaching out to those who suffered as she did, because in realizing she was not alone in her waiting and worrying, she found at least a tiny shred of comfort. For so many, the heart-wrenching fear of the potential loss of loved ones, sons, brothers, sweethearts and friends had to be held deep within themselves amidst the exultation of VE day.

Lily knew it wasn't good for her, but she couldn't help but read of the ongoing devastation, how the United States had lost almost 408,000 troops in both Europe and the Pacific, that even though Hitler had been defeated, the Japanese empire still fought on. Nathaniel was out there, somewhere in the Pacific, and her feelings of guilt and worry about her old friend, who had proclaimed he loved her, haunted her in the middle of the night, as she tossed and turned, devastated by nightmares about Tom.

Giorgio raised his glass. "Tonight, we celebrate the fact that the Germans surrendered to all the Western Allies, and victory in Europe is finally ours!"

The roar was deafening. People clambered out of their seats, hugging strangers, swilling champagne.

Lily was swept into the crowds. A middle-aged man lifted her into his arms and champagne corks popped and the room was a blur of shrieks and hugs and cheers. She was caught in the crush, shoved from person to person until Giorgio clapped his hands into the microphone.

The room hushed. The odd champagne bottle popped, but every face turned to the podium.

"For all my wonderful guests, for my staff, all of you. I would like to give you a free bottle of French champagne from my collection. Waiters!" Giorgio snapped his fingers and the pianist took up a striking version of the Italian national anthem.

Lily felt the soft tug of a hand on her arm.

Martina was next to her, pulling her into a hug. She held tight to the young woman who had stood by and cooked her heart out under Lily's direction, slaving day in and day out in the basement during this terrible war. If she'd felt like Valentino's was a family back in '42, now she felt like she was part of a tight-knit circle in the kitchen whose bonds could never be severed.

When Jimmy whisked Martina away, his arm openly around her shoulder, her eyes dancing as she looked up at him, Lily watched them, a flutter settling in her chest at the sight of their obvious happiness. *Send me a miracle.* As each day ground on, the idea of hearing that Tom was alive was becoming more and more like an impossible occurrence.

Lily moved through the crowds toward the rest of her team, who were gathered on one side of the restaurant under the blazing lights. Ellen and Meg were enfolded in each other's arms. Agnes, Leo and Julius's faces were alight with joy. Leo in particular was grinning. His missing son had been found alive, albeit a prisoner of war. Lily jammed her hands into her pockets. She was deeply happy for him.

At the bar, men threw their arms around each other, laughing, wiping tears. Hats were thrown in the air. The sounds of cheers thundered throughout the building. Outside in the street, horns honked and people blew whistles and whooped with joy.

Unexpectedly, Vianne was in front of her. Giorgio's wife popped opened a bottle of champagne and poured out two glasses, handing one to Lily.

"*Cin cin!*" she said. "You heard what Giorgio said." She cast her eyes toward the kitchen chefs. "*Chérie,* you must have champagne to celebrate properly with us!"

Lily softened at the delight in Vianne's eyes.

"So. What is next for you, *chérie?*" Vianne's eyes were alight, and she shouted into Lily's ear.

Tom will come home. "I'll continue with my job…" Lily managed.

Vianne's expression clouded a moment. She leaned in closer. "And, now that the war is done, *chérie,* make room in your life for falling in love. I know I am French, but you deserve to love and be loved!"

The stem of Lily's champagne glass felt cold, but she raised it and managed a brave smile, and Vianne was whipped away into the crowds.

Needing a moment to herself, Lily wove her way to one of the large windows overlooking Park Avenue, putting the champagne glass down and leaning heavily on the windowsill. While she fought an unbearable ache over Tom, she still had another cold battle raging in her heart.

Ever since that sickening, dreadful moment when she'd read her mother's correspondence on New Year's Eve, Lily had cut herself off from her mom and dad completely. While her dad had tried to call, every time the maître d' announced Jacob wanted Lily, Lily recoiled, avoiding the inevitable conversation she would have to have. Did her dad know what her mother had done?

On the occasions that she'd visited Josie, she'd seen the bewilderment in her dear gram's eyes at the state of things, and she refused to even utter to Josie what she'd found on New Year's Eve, because, quite simply, she could not believe it.

The secret she held was so unspeakable that she had not been able to tell a soul. She could not conceive of it herself. Instead, she'd buried it somewhere deep inside, her state of inaction growing into a festering, internal civil war.

Outside, a man hoisted another man up on his shoulders, and Lily was face to face with him. He blew her a kiss before tumbling down to the ground.

The room seemed to sway. She gathered herself, and she held her head up and made her way back downstairs. As she moved through the wine room, Lily felt her tense shoulders relax just a little. More than ever, the Valentino's kitchen felt like home. These days, Lily hardly left the building on Park Avenue. Her work was her salvation. It was the only thing she had.

Chapter Thirty-Seven

Victoria

Summer, 1945

On August 14, Victoria was at the breakfast table before Jacob had stirred. Wide awake, she reached for the *New York Times*, an article catching her attention.

"*Ha!*" she muttered out loud to the quiet dining room, portraits of unknowns gazing down at her, the grandfather clock in the corner ticking the seconds by. Restaurant and hotel owners couldn't *wait* until the soldiers returned so that they would no longer have to hire unqualified people. She collected her scissors from her bureau and cut the article out in clean, straight lines.

She had been right all along.

That night, the last place Victoria wanted to be standing was in the middle of Times Square. She wanted to be home, making plans for when Lily came running back in tears. But Jacob had insisted. Crowds swirled around them, and Victoria stood alongside her husband, not sure whether to roll her eyes while he goggled at the Times Tower's zipper sign, or resign herself to looking upward. He'd told her how New York would emerge as the power and glory of the world's stage in the aftermath of war.

At precisely 7.03 p.m., 15,000 light bulbs on the sign spelt out five words, and the crowds erupted into a roar. "Official: Truman announces Japanese surrender."

Jacob pulled her to him, her face pressing into his shoulder. "It is over," he murmured into her ear. "My darling." His lips brushed the top of her head. "It is completely done."

The following morning at breakfast, Jacob was up earlier than ever. The headlines shouted "Whole City Goes Wild!" The outpouring of relief at the formal signing of the surrender filled every street, every house, every New Yorker's heart.

"Years of scarcity, years of sacrifice," Jacob said. "London bombed, Paris humiliated, and now Rome, Berlin and Tokyo occupied by foreign troops. My dear, don't you see?" he clutched Victoria's hands over the breakfast table. "This is the dawn of a new age; our boys will be home. The prospects are huge! A whole new workforce will be back."

"I had considered that." Victoria raised a brow. *Just not in the way you had imagined.*

"And the Carters will buy the factory, and you can retire," Victoria reminded him. She placed her coffee cup down in her saucer.

But Jacob leaned forward in his chair. "Well now, I don't know that I will retire after all. Given things are not proceeding as you'd thought with—"

"Lily." Victoria slapped down her napkin.

"Not only because of that," Jacob said.

Honestly. That girl would ruin the entire family quite happily, as long as she could be in a kitchen.

She folded her arms. "I *tried*," she said, drawing out the second word as if it pained her to pronounce it. "I *assumed* Lily would care about Rose Millinery. Turns out, I was utterly mistaken."

Jacob set his own coffee cup down. He eyed her over the rims of his half-moon glasses. His once dark hair was now completely gray, lines feathered out from his brown eyes, and a new frown line ran from his forehead to his nose. "Vicky, I've driven Rose

Millinery through a Depression and a World War. New York is awash with possibility now. I've decided not to retire, dearest." He leaned forward, his voice laced with an enthusiasm Victoria had not heard since the '20s. "Last night, it felt as if the city were alive again. There were no strangers amongst us. You mark my words; our returning veterans are going to be lured to New York by the promise of a better life. I think we'll see mass migration from Europe, South America, and also from the American South. I see opportunities to expand out to the suburbs. I'm not retiring now. Not one bit of it."

Victoria sent him an arched look. "The *suburbs?*"

"But, of course. Life in the city is becoming congested for families. Since 1940, folks have been moving out. I've been keeping my eye on it. I think we'll see a middle-class exodus out to the suburbs and an influx of single folk into the city. You know, my darling, folks out in the suburbs will want hats. I think they will be some of my most significant new customers. They'll want to keep the old ways going. I can feel it."

Victoria smoothed down her dress. "And what of our plans to spend more time together?" She fidgeted with her pearls. "I don't understand, Jacob."

Gently, he cupped her chin in his hand. "The ducks aren't lined up as we thought they'd be, and I don't think we're going to have the recession that everyone feared would result after the war. I've gotten us through the last ten years, and now, I want to expand. I'm not made of cash, darling, things have been tough, but now New York is going to be the center of the world. The other major capitals all have to rebuild."

Victoria pulled away from him. She cranked her chair across the floor. "I'd always thought that one way you could afford to retire was if Josie would sell that old self-portrait of her father's. Peter Quigley's becoming even more famous, and she only owns one of his paintings, so why not capitalize? Sitting on that basement wall! But, of course, I would never say anything. I just stare at the thing every time I go there and think the man should be on display in the Met."

Jacob pressed his lips together. "Vicky," he said, his voice low. "My mother will never see my grandfather's portrait as anything but a treasure. It's not a commodity to her. She doesn't think like you."

Victoria opened her mouth, but Jacob's eyes swiveled to the kitchen door, where the sounds of the maid's singing filtered through. "Lily is not a commodity either, Vicky. I want you to stop viewing her that way."

Victoria reached out and gripped the table. "What are you implying?"

Jacob stayed still. "I'm saying I'm not putting up with not seeing my daughter any longer."

Victoria's nostrils flared. "She could come home if she wished. She knows where we are."

"Vicky, millions of young people have been obliterated. Thousands of American families are mourning their children. Our daughter is alive and well in Manhattan. You need to repair things before it's too late. Victoria, I mean it."

She started at his use of her full name. "Lily is fine. She always runs off. And she always runs back home again. She's been doing so since she started going to your mother's by herself when she was a girl."

Jacob was silent.

Victoria let out a high-pitched laugh. "She has not confronted me on anything. I don't see why she doesn't just come home!"

Jacob dropped his voice further. "She's withdrawn from your constant manipulation. She's not going to argue. She's ignoring you. You have to heal things. Not her."

Victoria stared at him, her eyes wide.

Jacob's voice was soft. "I want you to do what she asked you to do in that note she left you."

"What?"

"I saw you reading it." Jacob stood up. He moved toward the door, and then, quietly, he turned around. "And because it was from my daughter, I read it myself. The damage you have done could be irreparable. Please fix it. Otherwise, I want you to move out, and not come back. The choice is yours. Either you make things right or I will go and see Lily and ensure she is accepted and included in this family for the rest of her life. I will leave you to make your choice."

Victoria raised her shaking, jittering hand to her mouth.

But Jacob turned, walked out the door and closed it with a click behind him.

That afternoon, Victoria sat in the sunshine on a bench in Gramercy Park for two hours, her white-gloved hands folded in her lap. In her handbag was the letter that Lily had written her on the night of their silver wedding anniversary.

Dear Mother,

I am unable to speak to you, for there are no words. I am enclosing the dreadful missive that I have just discovered amongst the items on your desk in the contents of this note, as I find myself totally unable to trust myself to speak to you about it. If you had any care for me, any regard for my feelings, for my dreams, for the fact that I am a woman, not merely a daughter, you could never have undertaken to do what you have done.

To discover that my own mother utilized her contacts to engineer Tom's immediate and early dispatch to war, after one hint of rumor that I might have feelings for him! He is the man I love, a good man, a man who is so adored by his own mother that she is almost driven into the ground with worry about his missing status. As am I.

What you have done is something so reprehensible that I cannot be in the same room as you.

In the morning, I will be gone.

Go and see Tom Morelli's mother. See how she is coping with your own eyes. And tell her what you have done. Until then, I will be working, and waiting for the man I love—Tom Morelli.

Lily

Jacob had left for the milliner's early. Victoria had heard him moving around in the apartment before dawn. Of course she had! She'd not slept a wink since his dreadful outburst.

Victoria had dressed with her usual care, sat in front of the mirror, applied powder and dabbed rouge from her pot to her wan cheeks, and yet, she had been distracted, hardly noticing until her maid pointed it out that her buttons were all done up incorrectly down the front of her shirt-waisted dress. She'd stood up and marched back into her empty bedroom. The perfect excuse to leave the breakfast she could not manage untouched. Her maid would have seen clearly that Jacob had slept in the spare room last night.

Now, she pressed her fingers into the wooden bench, staring at the building she'd called home for thirty years. She brought a hand to her mouth. Why couldn't Lily be reasonable? Stupid, silly girl. She had her head in the clouds. And that had ruined the family, and any chance of real success they'd ever had.

Nevertheless, it was clear that someone had to make a sacrifice. Lily wasn't going to, nor was Jacob, and, certainly, Josie was not a woman Victoria could confide in. So it was clear that the person who was going to have to compromise would be herself. As usual.

*

Half an hour later, Victoria raised her gloved hand to the door knocker of a most uninspiring tenement house in the Village. She paused a moment. Was she really going to sink so far?

But then, she had no choice. Moving like an automaton, she knocked on the old door three times. And waited.

Soon, light treads could be heard on the stairs.

Victoria took in a breath and held it. A young woman of about Lily's age appeared at the door. She had long black hair, was wearing a polka-dotted dress, and the most ridiculous false eyelashes, which she batted at Victoria. *Why couldn't Tom Morelli fall for her?*

Victoria clutched her handbag. "Do you know if a Mrs. Morelli is at home?"

The girl shrugged. "Go see for yourself. Second floor, first door on the right."

Victoria placed one polished shoe in the doorway. The girl made a great show of stepping aside. Victoria sighed deeply and wound her way up the impossibly narrow flight of old, wooden stairs.

After what seemed an age in the old row house's stuffy atmosphere, she found herself face to face with a closed, white painted door. The paint, at least, looked fresh. Victoria reached to knock, only to have the door swing wide open, and she was face to face with a striking woman about her own age.

Victoria primed her lips, stunned to be confronted with such an attractive woman. She was dressed in a deep blue floral-print dress, her long brown legs bare, her wavy hair cascading around her shoulder's like a girl's. How old did the woman think she was? She reminded Victoria of Josie.

Her dark eyes flashed. "Victoria Rose," she murmured.

"How did you possibly know?"

"Random guess." The woman stepped aside and waved her in. "Gia Morelli," she said, her voice deep and soft, as Victoria swept on by. If she were not mistaken, a glint of humor seemed to pass over the woman's face.

Victoria followed her down a narrow sort of corridor that gave out into a tiny kitchen, complete with a twee round wooden table, and bunches of herbs in pots on the windowsill. The windowpanes were polished, sparkling clean. In fact, the whole place was spotless.

Victoria went over to the window and looked downwards, trying to avoid having to stare at other rooftops.

"Why, you have a vegetable garden," she said, peering out at the unexpected orderly garden beds. "How charming." The tenement garden that Lily had been so keen to replicate.

"I've noticed," the woman said. "Is there anything I can do for you, Mrs. Rose?"

Victoria turned around to face her. "I imagine you know why I am here."

The woman stayed still, her brown eyes remaining clear, her expression open. "Why don't you sit down and I'll make coffee," she said.

Ten minutes later, Victoria was seated at Gia's table. She'd accepted the woman's offer of an iced coffee, and reluctantly admitted, only to herself, that it was delicious, cooling and invigorating all at once. A *little* like that smoked salmon bagel that she'd endured with Jacob at Russ and Daughters, an aberration, and only that.

Victoria drew in a breath. This had to stop. "I want Lily to make a marriage that will be of advantage to her. I'm sure you understand."

But Gia simply stood there, her expression unchanged. "No," she said. "I really don't. Perhaps you would care to explain it to me?"

Victoria spoke slowly. "A boy that we are very fond of, an old family friend, is in love with her. For the sake of our families, the marriage must go ahead."

"And what does Lily want, Victoria?"

The woman was *still* not at all intimidated. Victoria bristled at the way the Morelli woman called her by her first name. She opened her mouth to correct her, only to close it. She had to play this smart, stick to the point. "Lily is young," she said. "She does not know her own mind as yet..." Her voice trailed off. And, sitting here opposite the lovely, healthy-looking woman who seemed so content in her own home, Victoria began to wonder what to say next.

Gia snorted. "I don't for one minute imagine that I have anything to prove to you, nor should I have to explain or justify Tom's feelings, but I will tell you this. Tom will never let your daughter down. I am certain of it. He loves Lily. And she loves my son." Gia bit on her lip. She stared out the window, and a single bird flew by, silhouetted against the cloudless blue sky. "He may never come home. I may never see him again. He's been missing far too long..."

Victoria sat back, overwhelmed with everything. She felt, quite simply, emotionally drained. Here was a woman who, for all intents and purposes, had nothing. Except her children. And she was likely to have lost her beloved son.

Victoria shifted in her chair, swallowed hard, but a lump formed in her throat. She'd only acted in the best interests of her own child. *Hadn't she?* When Sidney had told her that he thought there was an *amour* developing between her Lily and some chef at Valentino's, what would any mother do? She'd gone straight to Matthew Carter, Nathaniel's father, asked him to pull a few strings, and gotten Tom drafted.

She sat up taller in her seat. "I'm sure Tom was keen to go to war."

The Morelli woman shook her head, her face blank. Silently, she reached for a photograph on a small side table nearby, the expression on her face so tender that Victoria's chin started to quiver. She gathered her hands in her lap.

"Here he is," Gia said, softly. She handed the framed photograph to Victoria and sat back down. "That was taken on a rare trip to the beach. He was twenty-one. He loved the sea. You know, I thought if he did enlist, he'd join the navy, but he was drafted into the army. So…"

Victoria stared at the photo. For some reason, she was quite unable to tear her gaze away. The boy seemed to be looking straight at her. *Gosh, he was handsome!* Crouching down on the beach, grinning at the camera, his body lean and muscled, clearly grinning at his mom. A beautiful young man.

"Yes, well, I can see the attraction," Victoria said. She placed the photo down on the table, but the boy still grinned at her. She grimaced, and bit on her lip.

"When you see him and Lily together, sparks fly," Gia said, her voice softening, "but there's also a tenderness between them, that is so charming. When she came to the station to say goodbye to him, I knew they were in love."

Victoria felt her eyes fill with tears. Lily had not confided any of this to her! She pinned her arms around her stomach. She had no idea what was going on in her daughter's life, she had been cut off.

And unless she did something right now, she'd never, ever get Lily back. And she'd lose Jacob too.

Victoria replayed her discussion with Sidney over and over in her mind, as she had for months. He'd said that Tom was just the son of an immigrant, warned her off. And she'd taken the appropriate action.

She stood up, marched back over to the window and stared down at the pretty garden, the rows of vegetables so neat, so orderly, so well-tended and colorful and luscious. Simple. Like this house. This homely kitchen. Sparkling clean. No hint of grandeur. But cared for. It was unsettling. Because it reminded her of the home her mother had created. The home she'd walked out of when she was seventeen, to run off with Jacob, never to return again.

Victoria stayed where she was. For the last few weeks, she'd woken every single night in the early hours, tossing and turning, after enduring nightmares about losing her own child, just as her mother had lost her.

Since the spring, Victoria, uncertain why she felt so unsettled, had cut herself off from her old school friends, refused invitations to their luncheons, unable to bear their constant chatter about their children's wonderful, illustrious engagements, sitting there and feeling exactly as she did when she'd first arrived at that school. As if she belonged nowhere.

When Katherine Carter called, Victoria had told the maid she wasn't in. The last thing she wanted to discuss was Nathaniel. In the end, Katherine had given up. She hadn't heard from her for several weeks.

Gradually, Victoria had isolated herself. Gradually, she'd come to hate herself more and more. And now, even Jacob had threatened her with separation. What did that mean? *Divorce?*

Victoria took in great, hitching breaths.

Gia was sitting quite still.

Deep down, Victoria knew what was keeping her awake at night, what was causing this crying in the bathroom while Jacob slept. It was the dark revelation that was unfurling inside her: All her aspirations meant nothing now Lily was gone from their lives.

After all, when Sidney had whispered in her ear, warning her of Lily's infatuation with a handsome chef in the kitchen, she thought her intentions were right, but she had caused *everything* that was happening now, and she had lost her daughter through her own blind determination that Lily would not end up living in a home like this.

It had all come full circle in some horrible, fateful way. Was she paying for her past sins? Her actions as a daughter mirroring the way she treated her own mother all those year ago?

Suddenly, Victoria swung around, the sight of the dear little room only nauseating her further. She swept back to the table, pulled out a chair, sat down and placed her head in her hands. And, to her astonishment, she heard the sound of Gia's chair scraping back on the linoleum floor, and felt the woman's hand rubbing her back, heard her soothing tone.

And that only made things worse. Tom's mother caring for her! Showing her sympathy, being treated by another woman in a way she hadn't experienced since... since she'd swept off and broken her own mother's heart, because she lived in a home with a kitchen just like this.

For the first time in over forty years, Victoria laid her head on the table and wept.

Chapter Thirty-Eight

Lily

The rest of that summer, New York rode on a wave of triumph. Valentino's boomed. The restaurant was filled to capacity every lunchtime and Lily and her team worked themselves to the bone. Her job had become more than a passion; it was a determined distraction from the *constant* ache because there was no news of Tom. Every night, she fell into bed and turned on her side to stare at the wall. The likelihood that he was dead was becoming more and more real with every day that passed.

Giorgio served three times more covers than he did before the war. Thousands of veterans returned home. Great navy ships disgorged a sea of frail, wrecked shadows onto the docks and Lily spent her Sundays at the hot dog stand, scouring the returning men for any glimpse of Tom. In her wildest imaginings, when she lay awake at night, she pictured the young recruit whom she'd given Tom's photo to, striding home off one of those ships with Tom right by his side. Perhaps the boy would be propping Tom up. Tom could have crutches, an arm in a sling.

Only in her dreams did he come safely home.

One weekday lunchtime, Lily was in the middle of supervising over one thousand covers with all the private rooms and the restaurant filled to capacity, the kitchen a pool of sweaty, stinking kitchen hands and exhausted cooks. Waiters poured in and out of the swinging doors and tempers flared.

"Excuse me, Chef," Rosa said, appearing right behind her. "There's someone at the door to the kitchen asking for you. Do you want me to tell her to go away?"

Lily looked up. Next to her, Julius continued whipping up batches of Boston cream pie.

A familiar silhouette hovered in the doorway, her damp curls clinging to her sweating face.

Gia.

Lily lay down her piping bag, undid her apron and almost floated across the boiling room. The noise and the chaos and the waiters shouting filtered into a swirl.

Lily tried to scour Gia's face for signs. *Anything.*

"Gia?"

"Is there somewhere we can talk?" Gia's voice was shaky.

Lily led Gia through the chaos, somehow making it to her office, stepping inside and closing the door. Lily focused on Marco's beloved bookcase a moment, blinking at it, the books dancing around in front of her eyes. Sweat pooled on her upper lip and every noise in the kitchen, every shout, every clang of every saucepan, caused her to jump with nerves.

Slowly she turned around and interlaced her fingers on the back of her desk chair for support. There was nothing kind about war. It was not selective in its victims. She was prepared.

Gia sank down into the leather chair opposite the desk.

"He is back," she said. "He is home." And stared at Lily, her eyes huge.

Lily let out a sharp scream, hands rushing toward her mouth, her breathing seemed to halt for one split second, before she rushed into Gia's arms.

As she buried her head in Gia's shoulder, she heard Gia's quiet sobs of relief. The cries of just one mother out of millions whose sons had been torn from their homes to fight for a freedom which had obliterated an entire generation of innocent boys.

"I am blessed," Gia managed.

Lily closed her eyes. "We both are."

"Oh, darling girl. We are all so lucky, so fortunate he is back." But right then, Gia pulled away, her expression serious. "Lily. You should know. He is changed."

"But that is to be expected," Lily whispered. "How could he not experience what he has, and not be affected by it?"

But Gia's expression was serious. "Can you come now?"

"Of course." Hardly knowing what she was doing, Lily rushed out to the kitchen, Gia trailing behind her. She spoke to Martina, who pulled her into a hug, wiping her own eyes with relief for Tom, and telling her to go. The kitchen would be fine. Ellen and Meg were both on duty. Tom was home. It was all that mattered.

Heart hammering, Lily grabbed her handbag from the office, rushed downstairs to the changing room, threw on a dress and stared at herself in the mirror, flapping her hands about wildly.

But still Gia's warning rang in her ears. *Changed?* He was her Tom and he was alive. As long as he still loved her, there would be nothing that could stand in their way.

Not a thing.

Lily stood on the subway next to Gia, unable to speak, unable to cry, move, slow down her pounding heart or carry her bag without her hands shaking and her legs wanting to buckle into a heap. Gia stood steadfast beside her, her face the color of a white dove. The sweltering train rocked them from side to side.

In a soft, low voice, Gia began to speak. "The fact that he was wounded saved him. I will never be able to thank the Italian family enough for looking after him." Gia wiped a stray tear from her cheek. "After he was shot."

Lily gasped. "Shot?" she echoed.

Opposite them, a young man dressed in military uniform lifted his head.

The train thundered forward.

"I wish that he'd stayed with the kind folks who rescued him and sat out the war, but that's not my Tom. Is it?"

"No, it's not."

Gia ran a jerky hand through her hair. "I worry about what he experienced afterward. What he has told me worries me."

Lily nodded, too scared that Gia would lose the thread of her story if she interrupted her. There was so much she needed to know before she saw him. She needed to understand everything he'd been through.

Gia spoke in a low, rough voice, her words barely distinguishable over the constant rattle of the train. "Fighting with the partisans in rough bands in the hills and mountains, he made decisions on his own terms. He became a renegade after he could not find his unit. He has had to explain that to the authorities."

Dark worries nipped at Lily's mind. She stayed quiet, listening to Gia's words.

"Italy was in the worst possible firestorm. When the partisans freed cities before the Allies arrived, they were often greeted with red flags. Some places even became republics under the partisans before the Allies turned up. Tom was working with radicals, with revolutionaries."

The train came to a standstill. Folks formed queues to get out the doors.

Lily gripped the windowsill with a trembling hand.

"Lily, what you have to understand is that he followed his own path." Gia moved forward and they left the train. "He has come back a different man."

Lily took in a sharp breath. Silently, she nodded. It had been three long years. How different would he be?

Before she knew it, they were up the stairs and in the small foyer outside Gia's apartment. Lily smoothed her fingers over her hair, ran her hands down the simple blue dress. What if he didn't love her anymore?

Slowly, Gia pushed the door open. "Tom?" she called, poking her head inside.

Lily's hands shook by her sides, her feet rooted to the ground. She took in deep breaths to stop her whole body from shuddering. She forced herself to prepare for what she might see.

Gia halted at the open door to the living room. In a chair with wooden handles, sat an emaciated, shrunken man. He was unrecognizable.

Lily drank Tom in, roaming his features. He'd always been slim, languid and elegant in the blue jeans Giorgio let him wear, his lips curling into rueful smiles, but now he was like a stick. Dark bruises bloomed beneath his eyes and his cheeks were hollowed and gray.

He visibly tensed at the sight of her and tightened his grip on the wooden arm of his easy chair, his fingers pressing into the upholstery.

She would have passed him in the street and not known him.

The room seemed to sway. Nausea spread up through her, her head was swimming. Lily gripped the sides of the doorway for support.

Her eyes locked with Tom's, and she managed, finally, to nod at him.

He tried to pull himself out of the chair, only to sink down again. "Hey there." His voice was soft, halting. He reached up to his throat and his breaths seemed to catch.

"*Tom*," she whispered. A bark of laughter escaped from her lips.

This time, he managed to push himself up and out of the chair. With agonizingly slow steps, he moved toward her. His blue jeans dropped from his hips, and his arms stuck out from his rolled-up shirtsleeves like a pair of twigs.

In a swift movement, Gia turned and went to the kitchen.

Tom tilted his head at her, his expression clouding as if he were asking her a question.

Her hand lifted toward him, then lowered. "Oh, Tom." Her voice was choked with tears.

And then, he came toward her in halting, uneven steps, his stick-like body moving in strange little steps, and then he pulled her into his arms. She leaned her head gently against his thin, dear shoulder.

"*Cara mia*," he murmured into her hair, his voice deeper, unrecognizable from the boy who had left for war.

Lily felt the sting of tears coursing down her cheeks, and she sagged with relief.

He stepped back, running a hand over her hair, drawing it back from her face. His expression softened and tears rolled down his cheeks, and she went to him again, losing herself in his shirt, running her fingers softly over the contours of his bony, achingly thin body. He traced the back of his thumb over her lips. And then, he leaned down, hesitating as if asking for her approval.

She let out a sob and suddenly he was kissing her. She wound her arms around his neck.

"*Cara mia*," he whispered, drawing her into his frail embrace.

Chapter Thirty-Nine

Lily

Giorgio came into Lily's head chef's office early the next morning before the rest of the staff had arrived, his hands folded behind his back. Lily looked up from her weekly menus, rubbing a hand across her tired eyes. She'd hardly slept a wink all night, instead, sitting up on her bed, hugging her knees, trying to reconcile the weak, half-starved man who could hardly talk with the man she fell in love with.

But everything would be all right. Just as they'd planned. Wouldn't it?

Giorgio stood opposite her desk. He cleared his throat before he spoke.

"Lily, you know how much I appreciate you. What you have done for Valentino's during the war."

Lily nodded. "Of course, Giorgio. And I'm looking forward to doing so much more in the coming months. I have such plans, you can't imagine, now the war is finally done!" She sent him a brave smile.

Giorgio ran a hand over his gray hair. He sighed and sat down, rubbed his palms down his trousers. "You see, dear, part of running a business is making tough decisions, and I've had to make a decision that I really did not want to make."

Lily frowned at him, fear curling through her insides. What was this? Surely nothing was wrong? Valentino's seemed to be going from strength to strength. They were booming. She'd never worked so hard or had so much to do in her life. New York was booming. What could possibly be wrong? "I trust you are happy with the kitchen, Giorgio?" she said.

He nodded, up and down. "Oh, of course, dear. Of course." His expression clouded, and he frowned. "But, Lily, now Tom is back, you can have a well-deserved rest from running the kitchen. You will be relieved that he is back home, just as we all are. He will be taking over as my new head chef."

Lily sank back into her chair in disbelief. She did a double take at Giorgio. At the man who had given her every opportunity in the world. Who had championed her, despite the fact that she was a woman.

"Hang on, Giorgio," Lily said, stupefied. "You are *firing* me?"

He sighed, staring down at the floor, clearly unable to look her in the face.

"*Giorgio?*" Her voice rose and pitched. She clenched the sides of her chair, overwhelmed with dizziness.

Giorgio whispered the words. "I'm afraid that now the men are back, we just don't have positions available for women anymore. It is happening everywhere, Lily, dearest. Our men have fought for the country. They need work. They deserve work. I am so sorry, dear. I hate this as much as you do."

"Well, I doubt that." Lily frowned, still unable to reconcile what he was telling her. *Fired? Truly, fired? No more Valentino's?* "But this is my life, Giorgio. And, I don't believe you are capable of this." Her voice shook, but she ground out the words.

But Giorgio's brows tightened. "I have not slept, dear. I tossed and turned all night worrying myself. And, Lily, believe me, I hate it, but I have enough male kitchen staff returning and they have the right to get their jobs back. I have no choice."

Lily stared at him. Evidence of her hard work, her commitment surrounded them. Her recipe books, menu plans, her careful rosters of staff. What about the female cooks whom she'd cultivated, mentored, taught, promoted, danced with, laughed with, and, most importantly, who had sweated alongside her, working far longer and far harder than anyone expected them to, and for all their loyalty to Valentino's, they were to be fired?

A coldness spread through Lily's insides. "Meg and Ellen, Martina, Rosa, Agnes?" she glared at Giorgio now. She couldn't help it. This was reprehensible. "We are to be fired because we are *women?*"

The maid stood outside the office with her duster in the air. Catching Lily's eye, she quickly returned to her work.

"We will be forever grateful." Giorgio ran a hand across his tired eyes.

"Julius, Leo, Jimmy. *They* will keep their jobs. Won't they?" Lily clenched her hands now, sitting up in her seat, facing him head-on.

"The government has advised that we must employ our men—"

"The *government* says women are to be put out of work?"

Giorgio sighed. "The war was a state of emergency. Women were needed to keep the home front going until the men returned."

Lily's lip curled.

"Lily, you are not the only one. There were other women acting as head chefs of restaurants while the men were gone."

"And they too have lost their jobs." Her tone was carefully controlled. She narrowed her eyes, pressed her hands into her desk. She rose out of her seat. "Wait." She leaned on the desk, looking down at him. "You knew, all along, that you would fire us when the war was done?" She stared at the top of his head, incredulous.

Giorgio stared at the ground like a child. "Not at all. Please, Lily, this is hard for me."

"Vianne—" Lily started. "Surely she would not let you do this to us? And surely you of all people understand a woman's desire to have a career."

He mumbled the words: "The fashion industry is different. It is populated by women, because they are seamstresses, like Vianne once was. It is an entirely different industry. I am so sorry, dear."

Lily's jaw dropped. And then something dawned on her, so very clear that she almost laughed, horribly, out loud. "I do not for one moment believe Tom would accept your offer, Giorgio. He won't take my job."

But Giorgio's eyes raised to her. "Lily, he already has. I called him last night."

"*What?*" Lily's voice shook. She could hear the sound of her own noisy breath, in, out, in, out. "How *dare* you, Giorgio."

He lifted his head, eyes pleading with her. "I am sorry," he whispered. "This has not been easy for me." He pushed back his chair.

Slowly, Lily sank back down in hers. Tom had taken her role? "*Impossible*," she breathed. He would never, ever do such a thing.

"Lily, I have thought about you being hostess. Front of house—"

Silently, she held up her hand and shook her head.

Outside Lily's open office door, the maid looked up from her sweeping. In an imperceptible movement, Lily caught her mirrored gaze.

And Lily recognized the woman's expression of resignation.

After luncheon service the following day, Giorgio called Rosa, Ellen, Martina, Agnes and Meg into his office.

One by one, they all went in.

One by one, they all came out.

Martina stood, wooden and pale at the *chef de cuisine*'s station, leaning her shaking hands against the bench where she'd cooked faithfully for three years, where she'd created the exquisite dishes that the Valentino's clientele expected, lending her exceptional talents toward keeping the famous restaurant going throughout the war.

Jimmy, a dishcloth strewn over his shoulder, face equally pale, went and stood behind her, silently rubbing her back.

Neal and Julius worked quietly with their heads down, hands moving deftly as they had for more than twenty years under

Giorgio's watch. Lily knew they'd seen staff come and go countless times before. But so many all at once?

She started at an unexpected tap on her shoulder. Swiveling around, she came face to face with Leo.

The man was puce.

She held a hand up. The last thing she needed was a lecture. Around her, Ellen and Meg, Rosa and Agnes stood in shocked silence, their faces pinched.

"You listen here," Leo said.

Lily sighed.

"At first," he went on, heaving in a great breath. "At first, I did not think that employing women as cooks down here in this… atmosphere," he waved a meaty hand around the kitchen, "would come to any good."

Lily raised her head.

"But in the last three years, despite my reservations…" he coughed.

Lily's eyes rounded. She doubted he'd ever made such a long speech in his life.

"In the last three years, despite the fact that I never thought I'd see the day when I would have a woman for a boss, you girls have proven yourself to be exceptional. And to that end, this morning, I went and told Giorgio myself. I told him he was making a mistake."

A collective murmur stirred amongst the women chefs. Martina raised her head, and Jimmy's hand stilled on her back.

"I told him he was a fool to let go of the best team we've ever had."

Lily's voice came out in a whisper. "Thank you, Leo." She was impossibly moved by his outburst. Never in a million years had she expected this. From him.

Leo folded his arms and looked over Lily's head. "All I can say is that this is a very sad day for Valentino's, and I, for one, will be sorry to see you go."

Slowly, the women came forward, first, Ellen, pulling Leo into a hug, until all of them stood, huddled together, victims of circumstance, victims not of war, but of its aftermath. An aftermath that would leave everything they'd worked so hard for in doubt.

Once Leo had shuffled back to his station, Lily gathered Martina, Ellen, Meg, Rosa and Agnes into her office and closed the door. They all stared helplessly at her, their tired, pale faces blanched with shock.

"Very well, ladies," Lily said, her voice low. "I think we should get out of here. Go someplace else and talk."

Rosa, Agnes and Meg stood in silence. Meg's face was dangerously pale. Tears traced their way down her cheeks.

"Come on," Lily said. She reached for her coat. "I'll meet you out the side entrance. Go get changed."

Once they were all gathered on the sidewalk, a sorry, bedraggled little group, Lily turned toward the train station. "Follow me," she said.

"Where are you taking us?" Ellen asked, trying to keep pace.

Lily strode along, swinging her umbrella like an old-fashioned cane.

"The Village. Where else?"

The train was full. The girls had to stand, and every one of them stared out the window in silence. Back out in the fresh air, Lily made a beeline through Washington Square Park to Josie's house. She knocked on the basement door, and Emmeline let them in, her eyes widening at the sight of Lily and her entourage.

Emmeline stood aside. "I'll go and get Mrs. Rose," she mumbled, face reddening. "Oh, my heart."

Lily stood with her hands on her hips. "Oh, do, Emmeline. Come in everyone!"

Passing by her great-grandfather's portrait, Lily waved her loyal team in.

Emmeline rushed up to the first floor. In ten seconds flat, the sound of Josie's measured footsteps sounded on the wooden stairs, and there she was, towering over Lily's team in a kaftan the color of sapphires and emeralds, and a pair of loose navy trousers peeking out below. Everyone stilled at the sight of the formidable, beautiful Josie.

"Darling," she said. "What's going on here?"

Emmeline bustled around preparing coffee. "Mrs. Rose? Shall I put out those cookies I baked?"

"Of course, dear." She eyed Lily. "Emmeline made those wartime biscuits you made on the day you told me you were training for head chef."

Lily sent a grateful smile to Emmeline. "Well, things have progressed in a downward spiral today." Lily took off her gloves and pulled out a chair. "Do sit down, girls. Make yourselves at home." She introduced everyone, and in a state of awed silence, the women all settled themselves at Josie's table.

Lily filled Josie in on Giorgio's firing them all.

"What on earth is Giorgio thinking?" Josie said, her eyes crinkling in concern, and lingering on Lily.

Lily pulled out a chair, sat up straight and folded her hands. "I'm horrified. But I'm not taking this lying down."

Agnes tapped her finger against the tabletop. "It's a man's world. Why would things be any different now they're back from war?"

"They went away, women ran everything. Now they're back, we have to step aside," Martina said.

Ellen's blue eyes were huge. "I guess I'll have to find work in a coffee shop baking cakes or something."

"Well, what are you going to do about it?" Josie sat up to her full height in her seat.

Everyone turned and stared at Lily's grandmother.

Lily swiveled her gaze around the group. She spoke with a new urgency in her voice. "You, Meg, are a sous-chef. Rosa, you have a fine talent and could work your way up to sous-chef yourself. Agnes, you have a wonderful way with entrées and could be a *chef de cuisine* one day. And, Martina, you have been the best *chef de cuisine* I could have asked for. You could run a restaurant, or cook at the very highest level anywhere you wanted to."

There was a silence. Lily waited a beat.

"Giorgio's offered me a job as the hostess at Valentino's. And my fiancé has been offered my job."

Josie gasped and sent Lily an incredulous stare.

Lily drew in her breath. "I want to assure you all that I don't view my engagement as a retirement plan. And I do not for one minute believe that my fiancé would ever accept the role I have been doing for three years while he was at war."

"Oh, my darling," Josie whispered. "I agree. It cannot be true."

Lily pressed her lips together. "I do not believe it either. Tom is not capable of such a thing."

"So, what *are* we going to do? Your grandmother is right. I am at a loss right now," Martina asked, her tone as dark as one of her rich chocolate cakes.

"I will *not* be working as the hostess, for a start." Lily lowered her voice. "And I will not be abandoning you."

"But is there anything you can do about it, Lily?" Agnes said. "I have kids to feed. I'll have to get another job. Doing I don't know what."

"First of all," Lily said, "Tom will fight for us. He is not one to let women down."

She sent Josie a determined smile.

"Secondly, I will think and I will plan and I will try to sort out something for all of us. Just you wait. Give me and Tom a chance to sort this out together. Because that is our best bet."

"Oh, darling," Josie said. "I'm sure you and Tom will be able to do something. He will help you." Josie settled back in her chair and smiled at the group of worried women. She patted Lily's arm. "Don't worry. All of you. I'm sure Giorgio will come around."

*

The following afternoon, Lily perched on a bench in Washington Square Park next to Tom. She chewed on her nails and focused on a group of boys playing ball on the grass.

Tom's stare was vacant next to her. He coughed violently.

"Please, go see a doctor, darling," she said, squeezing his bony hand. "I will go with you."

"I've been. I have penicillin."

"Good." Lily folded her hands in her lap. "Tom..."

"*Cara*." Lightly, he stroked her forearm, his voice husky.

Lily heaved out a sigh. "This is the last conversation I wanted to have with you right now, but the truth is, we have a dreadful problem, and I need your help. Giorgio's sacked me, along with all my female staff. None of them deserve to be thrown out."

He pulled away and sat back again, folding his arms in front of him. "No..." his voice sounded faraway, as if he'd barely registered what she'd said.

A slight shiver spread up the back of Lily's neck. She stared at a pigeon picking crumbs out of the dirt. "I don't want to tire you out," she said, choosing her words. "But these women have been working for Giorgio for three years. I can't stand by and let them lose their jobs. And I can't lose mine."

"Cara..." he began, but he was overtaken with another bout of coughing.

Lily glanced at him quickly. "Tom?"

His forehead wrinkled, and he eased himself out of the seat. "Cara, I think I should go home now."

Lily stared at him. She stood up, and he leaned heavily on her arm, a pale, shadowy version of the man Lily thought she'd known, as he took slow steps toward home.

*

When she was preparing to leave the kitchen for the afternoon, the phone rang in her office. Her father was on the line. In a few short words, he asked Lily to come home to talk. He begged her to do so.

Having scrambled together a quick meal for herself, Lily found herself perched on the edge of the sofa in the living room of her parents' apartment later that evening. Her father stood in front of the fireplace. Her mom ran her hands through the pearls around her neck as if they were rosary beads.

Lily stared at Victoria. Her mother looked pale and tired, her hair was in disarray. Her father's expression was grim.

"Mother, Dad?" Lily said. She sent her mother a worried glance.

Victoria held up a hand. "Lily." She lifted her chin. "I went to see Gia."

Lily's brow wrinkled. "What did you say?"

Her mom's gilt clock chimed eight times on the mantelpiece. Victoria waited, and then she spoke in a soft, almost unrecognizable voice. "I met her. We talked, and I…" She took in a shuddering breath. "I accept that your Tom sounds like a charming young man, and I hope you will both be happy together."

Lily's eyes swiveled from her mother to her father and back. "What?"

But Jacob sagged back in his seat. "Vicky…" he whispered. "I'm proud of you."

Victoria held up a hand. "I realize that what I did was interfering, and unacceptable. Lily, I ask your forgiveness, and hope that my blessing of your engagement will be my way of making things right. Gia is a lovely woman. I would welcome such a fine person into our family."

Lily opened her mouth in shock. *What to say to this?* "But what about Katherine? Nathaniel?"

Victoria waved her hand in the air. "Oh, Nathaniel will fall in love with another girl. He is sailing home as we speak. There are about one hundred young women lined up waiting for him to notice them. And, Katherine," Victoria looked at Lily archly, the hint of her usual self shining through. "Katherine is a survivor. She always was. Ever since I first knew her." Victoria lowered her voice. "I realized this is about you, not me, and not the Carters."

Lily gaped. She turned to her father, and saw the way he was letting out a huge breath.

"Well, that is something. Thank you." Lily realized she sounded uncertain, but she plowed on. "Mother, Dad, I'm afraid I've bad news. Giorgio Conti has fired me, along with all of my female staff, on the grounds that the men are back." She lowered her voice. "On the grounds that Tom is back."

Victoria gripped at her pearls.

Lily chose her words carefully. "Giorgio's offered Tom my job."

Her dad's eyes flickered. He stood up and came to sit next to her. Silently, Lily leaned her head on his shoulder.

"I want to help the women who have all lost their jobs at Valentino's," she murmured into his warm, familiar chest.

Victoria stood up and went over to the mantelpiece.

Lily stared downward at her dad's diamond-patterned socks. "I talked to Tom this afternoon, but I think he's too tired after the war right now to think clearly."

Her father stroked his chin.

When Lily spoke, her voice was soft. "What if I started up my own restaurant?" She sensed her mother stirring. "Dad, what if I started up my own restaurant and employed all the women Giorgio sacked?"

"Oh, my goodness me," Victoria whispered.

Lily sat up, turned to her dad. "Will you loan me the money, Dad? I've run a kitchen that catered for a thousand covers a day for three years. Please. You know that I can do this." Lily reached in her skirt pocket for the notebook she'd been writing in all afternoon. "Look. I've done some figures."

But Jacob sighed. "Sweetheart, opening your own restaurant would be quite different from running a kitchen under an experienced entrepreneur like Giorgio Conti."

Lily leaned forward. She folded her hands in her lap. "I know how to budget. I'm in regular contact with all the best suppliers. I know how to plan menus and how to innovate with food. I know how to manage staff. I know how to hire and to fire and I've coordinated everything from debutante balls to ladies' lunches to house parties to weekends away."

He stayed quiet. Her mother was silent.

"I want to find a space of my own and do what Giorgio did. I know what I'm doing. I just need you to have faith in me too." She paused. "What do you think of that?"

Her dad rubbed the back of his neck. "I hear you, but, darling, I just don't have the funds to give you a loan. And the responsibility of it—"

"Lily could do it."

Lily's head shot up at the sound of her mother's voice.

But Jacob stood up and straightened his trousers. "I'm sorry. I'm sorry for what has happened, but it's happening everywhere, Lily. Restaurateurs have been saying for weeks that they can't wait to get their real staff back. And, unfortunately, that means many women will lose their jobs. I wish I could help, but it's impossible right now. Now, if you'll excuse me. I don't want to get into arguments, darling." He sighed, sent Lily a sad look and made his way out the door.

Her mother reached out to her, laid a hand on her shoulder. "I believe in you, Lily," she whispered. "I think that was the problem. Deep down, I always knew you were right."

Incredulously, Lily nodded at her mom. She brought her hand up to her shoulder, resting her fingers lightly atop her mother's.

Chapter Forty

Lily

Everyone in New York City was in the mood, but all Lily could do was cling onto each day until she'd have to leave Valentino's. Tom was unreachable. Several times, she'd raised her concerns with him when she'd visited MacDougal Street in the evenings, only to have him stare blankly at her. Gia, worry for her son etched on her features, offered to talk to Lino, the owner of Albertina's in Greenwich Village, so that Lily could at least get some shifts there. She warned Lily that Tom was fragile, hardly knew what was going on.

On the first free morning she had, Lily took the train to Josie's house. Lily leaned against the window, her breath misting against the glass. But once she'd trudged through the Village, instead of feeling consolation at the sight of Josie's red-brick house, Lily came to a standstill halfway up Bank Street.

Her father stood outside Josie's front door, with his head bowed, clutching his felt hat against his trouser leg. Golden leaves spiraled down from the trees all around him.

Before Lily could take a step forward, Emmeline rushed out the front door. She stood on the front steps, her face buried in her hands.

"Ooh, Mr. Rose, I cannot go back in there. I can't!"

Lily jerked forward, her nerves quivering. "*Daddy?*"

Her father and Emmeline swiveled in her direction, but it was Emmeline who ran toward her, apron flying, her hands waving around in the air. "*Oh,* Miss Lily!"

All at once, Emmeline threw herself into Lily's arms, sobbing on her shoulder clasping onto the collar of Lily's dress.

"*Father?*" she called over Emmeline's heaving shoulder.

Lily reeled in horror as her dad's mouth contorted, falling into a grimace.

"Oh, Miss Lily. She's gone. This morning. She died peacefully in her sleep."

Lily turned rigid. Her dad opened his mouth, as if trying to stammer something, but nothing came and his eyes widened helplessly. Lily brought her hand to her mouth, her knees buckled.

And everything turned black.

For days, she sat, listless, staring out her window, unable to utter a word or to eat or to cry. Every emotion hit her in relentless cycles: guilt that she had not spent enough time with Josie, regret that she would never have the chance to do so again, and most of all, a deep sadness at the loss of her beloved gram. The thought that she would never see her again seemed impossible. The pain of losing her grandmother threatened to split her in two when she tried to sleep.

Tom came to visit a couple of times. Gia brought him on the train, only leaving him for an hour at a time. They walked together through Gramercy Park. Tom seemed as lost as she was numb. As she became more and more overwhelmed with the loss of Josie, Lily put the loss of her job into context, and did not push Tom further for answers she knew he couldn't give. Not for one minute did she think the old Tom would be capable of taking her job away, but this man, he was a different human being from the one who had left three years ago.

When her mother announced she had taken a job at Macy's, managing a womenswear department, Lily simply nodded, resigned to the fact that nothing was going to be the same again.

Nathaniel returned from the war. He called one day, and Lily made her quiet, resigned peace with him. He was charming, accepting, of course he was.

With the end of the war had come the end of everything Lily had known. But the sinking feeling that nothing was as she'd hoped or expected lingered over her, and it was all Lily could do to cling onto the tiniest of hopes that, somehow, she'd come out of the fog she'd found herself in. A fog that was different, distinct from Tom's. It was as if she'd lost her childhood at the same time as her dreams.

The sun shone warmly on the day of Josie's funeral, and Lily stood surrounded by her family at the Trinity Church Cemetery. Josie was laid to rest surrounded by a rose garden, where only the rarest and most special species of roses were grown. Lily was the first to place a single, white bloom on Josie's coffin. No more would Josie's basement kitchen ring with the joyous sounds of her voice, her wonderful house was silent now, but as Lily stared out over the Hudson river beyond the beautiful garden, she knew that her memories would always live on in her heart, and she would be forever grateful for every day she had spent with her gram.

After her father helped bring home Lily's suitcases from the studio at Valentino's, she walked out the front door and kept going. Hardly knowing what she was doing, she wound up outside Josie's house.

Lily stood still a moment, the sound of birds going about their business seeming strange and unfamiliar now. After a while, she trudged up the front steps. Emmeline opened the door, her face stained with tears.

"Lily?"

Lily ignored protocol and pulled the girl into a hug as fierce and strong as that they'd shared last time they stood out in the street. "Do you have a job to go to, dear? I'm so sorry. I've been entirely caught up in my own grief and I should have asked."

Emmeline smiled sadly. "Oh, your mother has offered me work at your house. As…" Emmeline reddened. "Your maid."

Lily stiffened. "Emmy, do you mind if I come inside?'

"Sure, Lily," the girl said.

Lily took a step inside the familiar, empty rooms of Josie's house, the floors and the walls seeming to echo with loss.

"Your father's been clearing out some of her things."

Lily stared at the boxes in the parlor. All Josie's photographs had been taken down from atop her grand piano. Lily reached up and traced a hand over her teary eyes.

Emmeline opened her mouth to say something, only to change feet and start again. "I know how much your grandmother meant to you." Emmeline's eyes teared up. "I don't think it would be out of line if I showed you something."

Lily scoured her face.

"Come upstairs with me a moment."

Listlessly, Lily made her way up the staircase behind the maid. Quietly, Emmeline opened the door into Josie's bedroom.

Lily brought her hand up to her mouth at the sight of all Josie's personal belongings laid out. Everything from her grandmother's shawls to her beautiful velvet kaftans, to her favorite navy-blue cape, to the books she'd been reading, right down to a half-full bottle of perfume were spread across the room.

"Your father and I found this the other day. It's for you."

Emmeline handed her a buff-colored large envelope. On it, in Josie's dear hand, there were three words: *For my Lily.*

Emmeline slipped out the door into the hallway. Lily stared at the envelope, breathing in its scent. Lily felt the shadow of her grandmother's presence in the stillness amongst her beloved things.

Hands shaking, Lily tugged at the opening. Two items slipped out and landed on the bed. One was a name badge, and the other was a photo.

Lily's gaze ran over the old photograph. And the face staring back at her was so close to her own it made her gasp. But the girl in the photo was not Lily, it was Josie. Her long dark hair was swept back in a smooth bun. Lily stared at it. Because Josie stood behind a counter. Unmistakably, behind her were rows and rows of coats—fur coats, cashmere coats, and hats and umbrellas too. On the counter in front of Josie, there sat a vase filled with spring flowers and a wooden plaque reading "Coat check." Lily could picture it all: it was the coat check at Valentino's.

Lily held the pearly photo up to the light. With her free hand, she reached for the brass piece that had fallen out of the envelope and picked it up from the bed. It read "*Josephine.*"

Slowly, Lily sank down into the easy chair under Josie's window. Outside, cherry branches brushed against the glass. "You never told me," she whispered into the clear dark air. "You never said."

Lily sat there a long time, thinking about the opportunities that Josie never had. Outside, the afternoon faded and the old-fashioned streetlamps outside Josie's house flickered to life. Lily sat in the stillness until, finally, her thoughts were as gentle as the hands that had once taught her to cook, that had once taught her to dream, the person whom she never, ever wanted to forget. The woman who had not only given up her own dreams, but who had covered up her past. She'd been a working woman. Not the daughter of a wealthy artist, as Victoria had always insisted.

Josie told Lily she'd given up her passion, lost her independence, married a man she didn't love.

And now, Josie was gone forever.

But could Lily take up the sword Josie had, for whatever reason, had to lay down? Fight for not only herself, but the memory of the woman she'd loved more than anyone in the world? Did Lily have any hope of rectifying for herself what Josie had lost?

*

Three weeks later, Lily took off her gloves and placed them on her father's desk in his study. The apartment was quiet. Her mother had gone uptown visiting.

"Lily," he said.

Lily perched on the chair opposite him. "I can't stay here. Not in New York."

"What are you saying, dear? What are you planning to do?"

"I'll do what I've always wanted to do, Papa," she whispered. "Cook." She stared out at the trees. "Paris is rebuilding. I will get a job there."

Slowly, her father raised his eyes to meet hers.

"I need a new start. I couldn't save all the other women's jobs. I can't face staying in New York, Dad."

He regarded her.

"I need to get away for a while, at least. Everything has changed too much."

"Darling. No."

"I have my savings. The Contis didn't charge me rent all the time I lived there and I hardly spent a cent. I should be able to survive for six months without work. I saved nearly everything I earned for the duration, and I will find work, but I can't stay here and watch."

Her father rubbed his chin. "And Tom Morelli?"

Lily pressed her lips together. "Please, Papa." She stared past him. "Tom has returned very different to how he was before. He has accepted my job, and I am dealing with that as best as I can. In fact, there is nothing to be done. I just have to go away and sort this out on my own." Her chin wobbled, but she held herself with dignity. Tom was still entirely closed off to her and in his own world. She visited him regularly, but every time she did so, he seemed more and more distant, and less like the man she'd long known and loved.

Her father rubbed his hands over the gray stubble on his chin.

Lily leaned down, her stomach turning. She kissed her papa on the top of his head.

Lily knocked on the tradesmen's entrance at Valentino's. A new, unfamiliar bellboy stuck his head out to answer.

"Good afternoon," she said. "My name is Lily Rose. I used to be Valentino's head chef."

His eyes ran the length of her navy suit, raking up to her hat.

"Oh, never mind," she said. "I would like to go speak with Giorgio."

"*You* used to work here?"

"Are you going to let me in?"

Finally, he opened the door for her.

Lily followed him up the familiar corridor, drinking in the memories when the sound of laughter and music rang out from the restaurant.

The bellboy stopped outside Giorgio's office.

"Mr. Conti?"

The boy turned to her, his question plain to see.

"Lily Rose," she reminded him.

"Lily Rose is here to see you," he told Giorgio.

"Send her in," Giorgio said. "Lily!" His hands fumbled around on the desk, finally settling on a paperweight that he clung to. "We need to talk about training you for your new role."

Lily clasped her handbag to her chest. "I won't be accepting the role of hostess. We both knew that. I wanted to inform you in person."

His hands stilled.

"It would be impossible." She slid an envelope across the table to him. "I am asking you to accept my resignation."

Giorgio cleared his throat. "Lily, please."

Lily leaned forward. She held eye contact with him and folded her hands on his desk. "I wanted to save my staff, Giorgio. When I learned there wasn't any way I could do that and stay here in New York, well, I decided it's best I leave. I can't face working here while they have nothing. It would be a slap in the face to them. And surely you must know how much I want to cook."

"I had no choice but to make Tom head chef, Lily. He was higher than you in the *brigade de cuisine* when he left."

"And for three years, I was head chef. I ran your kitchen at the highest level, and brought it through one of the most difficult times this century has seen so far." She fought the anger that wanted to hurl out of her, the anger that wanted to insult the man she thought she could trust. She would not lower herself. She would be professional. But her shoulders shook and she fought her own boiling rage. Lily held out a hand. "Goodbye, Giorgio. Thank you for everything. I will never forget my time here."

He buried his face in his hands.

She took back her hand, nodded at him, then turned around and walked out of his office, pulling the door closed behind her.

Ignoring the stares of the waiters who stopped in the corridors, and walking right under Sidney's upturned nose, Lily strode purposefully through the halls of Valentino's and down the basement stairs to the kitchen. She barreled straight to her old office, only to crash headlong into Tom outside the familiar door.

"Hello," he said. He leaned down as if he was about to hug her, only to step back and open the office door.

She forced herself not to inhale his warm, familiar scent.

"I'm going away. Leaving New York." She risked a glance around the kitchen. "Somewhere I can start again." The all-male team sent her covert looks from under their hats. Jimmy laid down his knife and Julius wiped his hands on a cloth and frowned at her. Leo stopped working altogether and crossed his arms.

Lily stepped into the head chef's office. Her old office. She took in a ragged breath, forced her eyes away from the bookshelf and raised her chin.

"Come with me, Tom. Let's make a new start together."

Tom scratched the back of his head. Dark shadows bruised the skin under his eyes. "I want things to go back to how they were. It is what we fought for…"

"But things haven't been how they were since you were called to war," Lily sighed.

He looked at the floor. His voice was still strange, this new, shadowy version of himself masking the man Lily had once known and loved so very much. She would always love him, she knew that. But the war had taken away her Tom, not as she'd worried it would, but in a way she'd never imagined could be possible.

The man she'd loved was gone.

And she didn't want to fight with him, didn't want to hurt him as she'd been hurt by his actions, by Giorgio's actions. If he didn't want to start afresh with her, and move away from this impossible situation, then that, she knew, was it.

"Maybe we have both changed too much. If that's what you want, I won't hold you back. But I can't go with you," he said, his voice filled with sadness.

She bit her lip, silently nodded her head.

So, that was it.

Gently, she sent him a sad, long gaze, opened the door and walked out. Somehow, Lily made it through the kitchen. Chefs working the line raised their heads and downed their utensils at the sight of her striding by. Lily held her chin up, determined not to show a soul how utterly bereft she was. She averted her eyes from the new *chef de cuisine*, who'd replaced Martina, the two male sous-chefs, who had been hired so fast, ousting Meg and Ellen, and she stalked past the army of young male dishwashers, prep cooks, apprentice chefs, all freshly back from the war.

The new sous-chef barked instructions at them, shouting about the state of the chefs' line stations, muttering under his breath about late supplies and fiddly menus and waiters who would not know what shoe polish was if he held it under their noses.

Once she was out of the kitchen, Lily didn't even bother swiping at the tears streaming freely down her cheeks.

She pounded up the stairs in silence and went straight toward the door. As she stepped out into the New York afternoon, she caught a glimpse of a dashing figure, an unmistakable, elegant person rushing down Park Avenue ahead of her. She was well dressed, in an exquisitely tailored suit, the slightly lowered heels she wore out of respect to the ongoing war restrictions clipping against the pavement, and a telltale line drawn up the back of her calves.

Vianne. A successful, determined businesswoman who had held her own, built up everything herself, and stayed married to the man she loved.

In spite of everything, in spite of the heaviness that lingered like a rock in her chest, Lily couldn't help but follow the woman down Park Avenue. When Vianne turned into her boutique a few blocks down on Park Avenue, Lily marched right after her and swung into the chic first-floor salon. A few female attendants were helping customers, women in impossibly beautiful outfits that had all been designed by Vianne.

But it was Vianne she could not lose sight of. She was clipping up a staircase at the back of her boutique. Ignoring the protestations of the staff, Lily marched right on up after her, only stopping to catch her breath at the top of the stairs. She stood in a large gallery, where even more stunning creations were on display. Mannequins were draped in evening gowns of the most exquisite designs Lily had seen in her life.

"Vianne," she said. Her voice a full stop, not a question. She had to speak to this woman. Had to know that someone thought firing six women chefs was wrong.

The older woman turned, her features puckering into a frown. "*Lily?* What on earth are you doing here, dear? Come in. Come into my office."

Her heart beating wilder than she thought it ever had before, Lily followed Vianne into her office, with its picture window looking down over the length of Park Avenue. There it was, all spread out before them. Vianne had made it. Why couldn't she?

"Will you sit down, please, Lily?" Vianne said, her blue eyes scouring Lily's.

Lily settled herself opposite Vianne's walnut desk. Across it were scattered designs. Lily closed her eyes and reminded herself of all the recipes she had yet to make. Of the fact that her gram had not ever had this chance. And of the fact that she, Lily, had what it took.

"Vianne." She held the woman's eye and it was as if Josie was talking to her. It was as if Josie was spurring her on. She could see her, resplendent in a kaftan, saying, "*Well, you're here now. What are you going to do about it?*" Lily sat up tall in her chair, the idea that had formed in her mind while she walked up the street falling into a complete picture. "I want to do what you are doing." She told Vianne. "I want a business of my own, so that I can make my own decisions, hire and fire my own staff, run things on my own. I'm ready. I know that, and I want to run my own restaurant, but I cannot get a bank loan to do so. My father will not lend me money. Can you tell me where I can get backing? Can you tell me what to do to achieve my dream?"

Vianne folded her arms a moment and regarded her.

Lily pressed her lips together and waited.

"You are certain?"

Lily nodded. "Oh, yes."

Vianne sighed, for a moment a few expressions passed across her features, and then she folded her hands on her desk. "I see so much fight in you, Lily. So much of my younger self. It was no easier for me, you know."

"And yet you made it. And I want to as well."

Vianne reached out and laid a hand over Lily's.

Lily raked her eyes over the beautiful woman's face.

But, a few moments later, Vianne raised a finger. She stood up and pushed on a panel in the wall and pulled out a metal box.

Lily sat up. She pushed her chair in closer toward Vianne's desk.

"I cannot think of a better outcome for this," Vianne whispered.

Lily frowned at the box.

Vianne sat back. "When I first came to New York, I had nothing. And yet, I worked hard and saved every penny I could, for the first ten years of my business. And this is where I kept it." She chuckled. "Giorgio supported me, and so I kept a nest egg. Just in case." She stared off to the side a moment. "I'm sorry about Tom taking your job. I am sure you will understand that I did not think Giorgio was right. No matter how upset he was over this decision, he said he had to take, I told him I did not agree with it." She shook her head and tutted.

Lily managed to nod. She couldn't trust herself to speak.

Vianne looked at her. "I am a businesswoman. And you, Lily, are a talented chef. We both know you could run a restaurant with your eyes closed. But it won't be easy, dear."

Lily folded her hands together in her lap and squeezed them tight.

Vianne pulled a chain out from her décolletage. She produced a key and held it. "Aha!" she said. With great reverence, Vianne turned the key in the lock and lifted the lid. Inside, lay piles and piles of crisp dollar notes.

"Oh, my," Lily breathed.

Vianne spoke in clear, enunciated words. "Lily," she said. "With this money, you will be able to set up something to rival Valentino's." She regarded Lily with her clear eyes. "And a bit of competition? That won't do my husband and… that Tom of yours any harm. In fact, I'd say they've earned it."

Lily covered her mouth with her hand. "You are sure?"

Vianne shrugged. "You're the hardest-working, smartest girl I know. You can run a restaurant, Lily. Be your own head chef."

"I don't know how to thank you." Lily couldn't trust herself to move an inch. She was so overcome with *every* emotion. She just sat there with her hands clasped in her lap. And at the same time, something dawned on her. She *had* finally done something entirely on her own, on her own terms. And that, she realized, was all that mattered. That was what she needed. Her belief in herself was what would get her through.

"I'm going to give you this money, and you can start looking for premises," Vianne said.

Lily pressed her hands into the table. "Vianne, I can't thank you enough."

"You can do it," Vianne said.

Lily tilted her head to one side. "I will get them back. All of them. Martina, Ellen, Meg, Rosa and Agnes."

Vianne's face lit up in a gorgeous smile.

Lily reached out and held Vianne's hand. "I'd given up. I thought I was totally on my own. Now, I realize I'm not."

Vianne leaned forward and she lowered her voice. "Lily? Let me tell you one thing. From one woman to another. You never, *ever* give up."

Epilogue

Lily

Three months later

Lily led her team through her brand-new restaurant, candles glinting on tables, and a bevy of newly hired waitstaff buzzing about. Everyone stilled at the sight of Lily, Martina, Rosa, Meg, Ellen and Agnes walking out toward the front door. And alongside them, laughing as if she'd known the other women all her life, strode Josie's erstwhile maid, Emmeline. She was reveling in the opportunity Lily had given her to work her way up the *brigade de cuisine*.

Lily held the glass door open for her loyal team of women, smiling at every one of them as they went out into the spring sunshine.

A crowd was gathered behind the red ribbon that stretched across the sidewalk. Vianne Conti stood with a pair of oversized scissors.

Eager first-day restaurant guests and folks who were passing by turned quiet when Vianne raised a hand.

"Ladies and gentlemen," she said.

Lily scanned the crowd. She caught a glimpse of Nathaniel standing with a pretty girl in a pink dress, and he winked at her, bringing the girl's fingers up to his lips. She shook her head and smiled back at him.

Vianne cleared her throat and stepped toward the microphone. "It is with great pleasure that I welcome you all to the opening of this new restaurant, that will be run by Lily Rose, a woman who is not only an extraordinary chef, who not only has a full understanding of how to run a restaurant and who has fought hard to do so in a world run by men, but who has exceptional loyalty and a big heart that saw my husband's restaurant, Valentino's, thrive right throughout the war, bringing it out booming and stronger than ever before."

The crowds sent up a cheer and Lily's cheeks burned.

"Ladies and gentlemen. I welcome you to *Josephine's*."

The crowd roared their appreciation, and with a flourish that was worthy of Katherine Carter herself, Vianne snipped the red ribbon in two, allowing it to fly free in the wind.

Lily tucked her hand into the crook of Vianne's elbow.

Vianne leaned in to whisper in Lily's ear. "Let me tell you something else."

Lily raised a brow. "What more could there be?"

"I have gotten you a position as an Officer of the National Restaurant Association. We want you to work toward making things better for women to obtain capital for restaurants."

Lily wiped a tear from her cheek. Out of the corner of her eye, she saw her dad standing in the front row along with the crowds. She smiled at him, and he blew her a kiss back.

"I am hugely proud of her. Enormously so." Lily heard the distinct sound of Victoria's voice ringing above the chit-chat.

Lily raised her eyebrows to the sky.

"What is that, *chérie?*" Vianne pointed at the small framed photograph that Lily held in her hand of Josie working in the 1890s. Slowly, she turned it face up to show Vianne. "Oh, *chérie*," she said. "Is that you?"

Lily ran a finger over the silver frame. "It's not me, it's my grandmother. She used to work as a coat checker at Valentino's, but I never knew. And she's going right in the foyer of the new restaurant," she said.

And each night, Lily would be going home to Josie's house, which was Lily's home now. Her grandmother had left Lily everything in her will. Lily had moved into the very dearest home she'd known all her life, while setting up the restaurant, and she'd promised herself she'd look after it just as Josie had, and she'd fill it with as much laughter and happiness as she could.

Vianne pushed the solid front door of *Josephine's* open underneath the curving sign and held the door wide. "Welcome," she said to Lily.

Lily pulled Vianne close to her and drew her into a hug, until they were both swept away into the crowds of folks pouring inside. Lily's new waitstaff directed diners with opening-day reservations to tables, while her *maître d'* took bookings. Already, they were full for the next two months.

Lily stood aside a moment, folding her arms around her waist, until an untold sadness overcame her. She slipped into her office. Once she was inside, she sat down at her desk, gathering herself together with a reminder to be thankful for everything she had.

"Hey."

Lily looked up. She pushed back her chair and moved across the room to the woman who stood there.

"Hello there," Gia whispered. "I saw you disappear in here on your own. Are you all right?"

Lily pulled her dear friend into her arms. "I don't know," she said, pulling back and tapping a loose fist against her chest. "I'm happy, I guess."

Gia's brown eyes crinkled with warmth. "Lily, Natalia and I are both thrilled for you. She came with me today to see your opening, and I know she wouldn't have missed it for the world, now she's safely back from the war. And… someone else insisted on being in your adoring crowd too. I'm going to let that someone into your office. I'm going to shut the door, and I want you to hear him out."

Lily opened and closed her mouth, but before she could say anything, Gia had disappeared. The door shut with a soft click and Tom stood right in front of her.

"Lily," he said, his hat held nervously in his hands, his eyes raking over hers.

Lily took a step backward. "Look at you..." she whispered, dazed at the sight of the handsome, well-built man who towered in her office. He was nothing like the thin replica she'd encountered last time she'd laid eyes on him several months back. His face was tanned and his green eyes were deliciously alight. His hair had been cut and his shoulders were broader than she remembered.

And he wore a pair of new blue jeans.

He leaned his hands on her desk, drinking her in. And then his expression softened. "I want to say some things."

Lily turned away. "Tom..."

But his voice was low and determined behind her. "I want you to get back out to your celebrations. Goodness knows, they are well deserved. But I couldn't let today pass by without telling you how sorry I am for what happened after the war."

"Please. Not now.'"

"Will you hear me out?"

There was a new energy in his voice, and Lily gripped the back of her chair.

"I've quit the head chef job at Valentino's."

She took in a breath.

"I only stayed to help find and train the new executive chef."

Lily turned away from him.

"After the war, I wasn't thinking straight. I'm sorry. I wanted to return to normality, but I didn't acknowledge that was at the expense of your own dreams. Giorgio never really wanted to fire you. He just thought he had no choice. But as soon as I was well again, I told him he did have a choice, that he could have acted on his own terms, not followed the crowd, not doing what other restaurateurs were doing. He sees that now, and I know he regrets his actions. In time, he'll tell you so."

Lily stared at the floor.

Tom's voice was firm. "And, there's something else. I learned how important it was to make my own choices too."

Lily's pulse quickened.

"*Cara*," he went on. "I've bought Albertina's. It's a chance for me to cook the Sicilian food I love. Lino is opening another deli. And he's sold me the whole building on Bleecker Street as well. I've taken out a loan from him, and I'm going to pay it off as quickly as I can with the profits from the business."

Lily's forehead wrinkled.

"I'm hoping those buildings in the Village might be worth something someday."

Lily swung around to face him.

He took in a shuddering breath. "Perhaps I can bring something that is *good* from my Sicilian heritage back to New York. It seemed like an important thing to do. To bring folks and traditions together after that war. What better way to do that than with food? Something everyone loves."

She drew in a shaking breath. Lily pressed her lips together. Her heart was cantering and she reached up to grab at an old necklace of Josie's that she wore around her neck. "I waited all through the war for you, and I never stopped believing in you. Not once."

"Oh, *cara mia*," he murmured. "What I'm saying, very badly, is that I'm in love with you. I always was. I want you to follow every dream in your heart. I'm so so sorry I let you down. I was not myself after the war," he whispered. "God forbid the world ever has to go through anything like that ever again. I'm sorry, darling."

Lily heaved out a breath, tears pricking her eyelids. She battled to still her heart. "I love you too, Tom, you know that. And you know I always wanted something real, with you." Her lip quivered. Was there hope she could have the love she'd waited for as well as her own restaurant?

He took a step closer to her, and suddenly, his eyes caught on the photo of Josie, sitting upturned on Lily's desk. "She was an incredible woman," he said. "She knew what was what all along."

"She did." Lily smiled. "Oh, dearest Josie. This is all for her." Lily glanced down at Josie's photograph, tears really pricking her eyes now. Now, she picked it up, carefully, and propped it on her desk, so that the young, beautiful Josie smiled straight and clear out into the room. "All of it."

She swore that Josie's smiling face would greet every guest who stepped foot in the door of the restaurant.

With Tom standing close behind her, stroking her hair, his lips touching the top of her head, Lily turned around and reached up to stroke his cheek. He leaned down, brushing her lips with his.

"Welcome, Tom," Lily whispered, "to *Josephine's.*"

A Letter from Ella Carey

Dear reader,

I want to say a huge thank you for choosing to read *A New York Secret*. If you did enjoy it, and want to keep up to date with all my latest releases, just sign up at the following link. Your email address will never be shared and you can unsubscribe at any time.

www.bookouture.com/ella-carey

I adored writing this book. For me, bringing Lily, Josie, Victoria and all the other characters to life was a complete joy, especially after visiting New York to research the novel. I stayed in Greenwich Village, not far from where Josie's house would have been, and spent many hours wandering around that charming old part of New York, getting to know the food, going on foodie tours—this book was so great to research!

I had so much fun recreating some of the recipes in the book. Lily is such a sassy, intriguing character, and she jumped into my head with her little car and her can-do attitude.

As for Josie, I adore her, and I hope you loved her too. I wanted to give her a fitting tribute, and acknowledge everything she did to bring joy into Lily's life.

I hope you loved *A New York Secret* and if you did I would be very grateful if you could write a review. I'd love to hear what you think, and it makes such a difference helping new readers to discover one of my books for the first time.

I love hearing from my readers—you can get in touch on my Facebook page, through Twitter, Goodreads or my website.

Thanks,
Ella

 ellacareyauthor

@Ella_Carey

www.ellacarey.com

Acknowledgments

My thanks to my editor, Maisie Lawrence, for embracing Lily's story and for your expertise in helping bring this book to fruition. I can't thank you enough. To my agent, Giles Milburn, my dearest thanks for believing in this novel from the outset. Your support means the world to me. Huge thanks to Liane Louise Smith, Sophie Pellisier and Georgina Simmonds for securing so many wonderful foreign rights deals for this book, and my thanks to everyone at The Madeleine Milburn Literary Agency.

My sincere thanks to everyone at Bookouture. You truly are an incredible team of people. Especial thanks to Kim Nash, Sarah Hardy, Noelle Holton, Alexandra Holmes, Peta Nightingale, and Alex Crow. Thanks to everyone else at Bookouture who has worked on this book.

Thank you to the talented cover designer, Sarah Whittaker. My deepest thanks to copyeditor Jade Craddock and proofreader Anne O'Brien for your careful work.

Thanks to Max Tucci, grandson of Oscar Tucci, the former owner of Delmonico's restaurant in Manhattan. Max, thank you for sharing your insights into the running of a restaurant during the 1940s. Thanks to the current owners of Delmonico's and thanks to head chef Billy Oliva for sharing his knowledge of the running of a New York restaurant.

My thanks to my readers for your enthusiasm and excitement about this story. Many of you have been with me since the publication of my very first novel, and I appreciate every one of you no end.

Dearest thanks to Geoff and huge thanks to my son Ben, for your endearing support of my books. My sincere thanks to my daughter, Sophie, for traveling to New York with me to research this book. This one is for you: may you always have every opportunity possible to follow your dreams.

Made in the USA
Las Vegas, NV
05 March 2024

86718217R00193